STORMY WEATHER

Created by: Thomas Astruc
Comics adaptation by: Nicole D'Andria
Written by: FRED LENOIR
ranged by: Cheryl Black
revision: Cindy Morrow
tered by Justin Birch

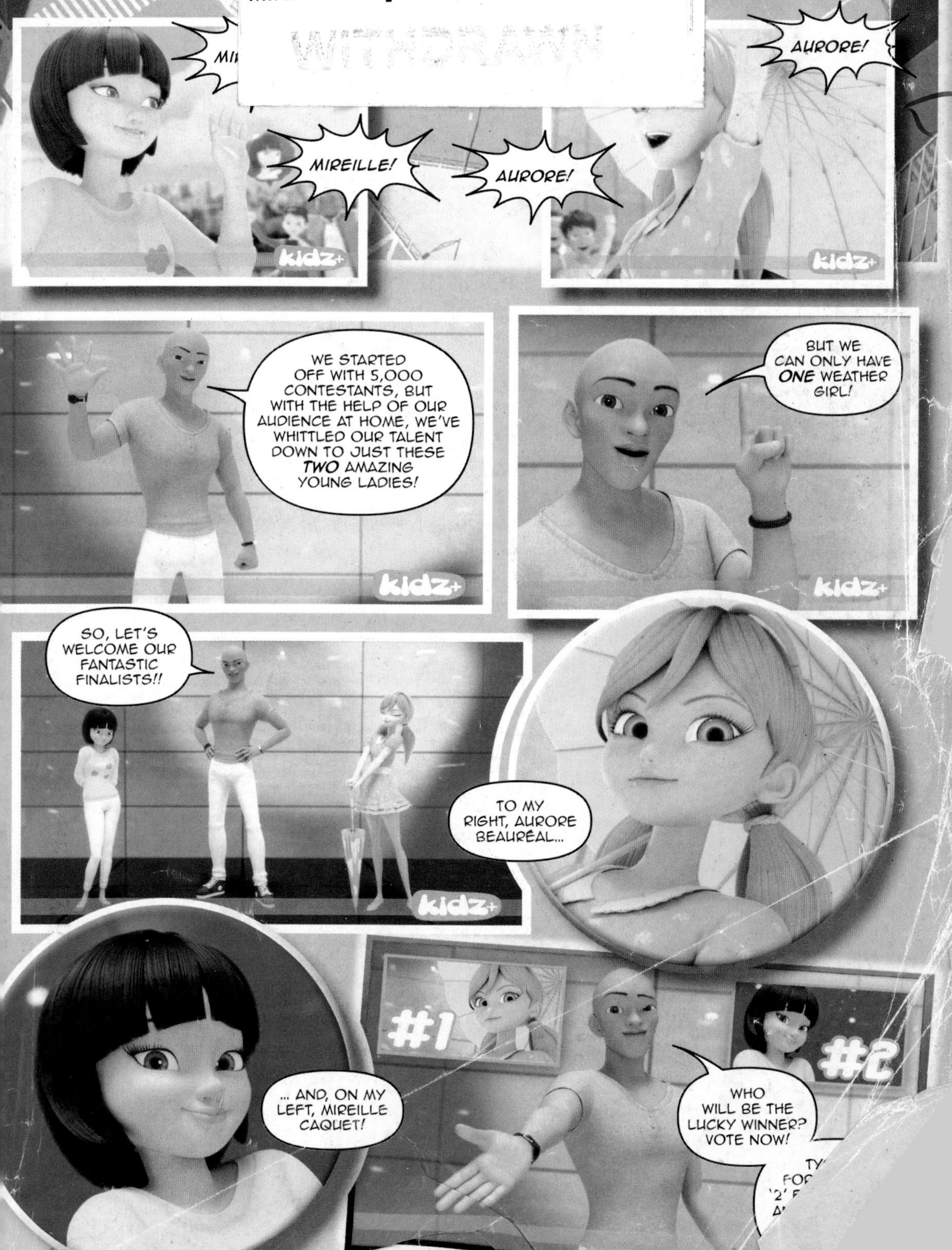
WELCOME TO THE KIDS PLUS WEATHERGIRL FINALS!
AURORE!
MIREILLE!
AURORE!
kidz+
kidz+
WE STARTED OFF WITH 5,000 CONTESTANTS, BUT WITH THE HELP OF OUR AUDIENCE AT HOME, WE'VE WHITTLED OUR TALENT DOWN TO JUST THESE *TWO* AMAZING YOUNG LADIES!
kidz+
BUT WE CAN ONLY HAVE *ONE* WEATHER GIRL!
kidz+
SO, LET'S WELCOME OUR FANTASTIC FINALISTS!!
kidz+
TO MY RIGHT, AURORE BEAUREAL...
... AND, ON MY LEFT, MIREILLE CAQUET!
#1
#2
WHO WILL BE THE LUCKY WINNER? VOTE NOW!

MIRACULOUS #1, JULY 2016. Published by Action Lab Entertainment. No part of this publication may be reproduced or transmitted without pe
Printed in Canada. First Printing.

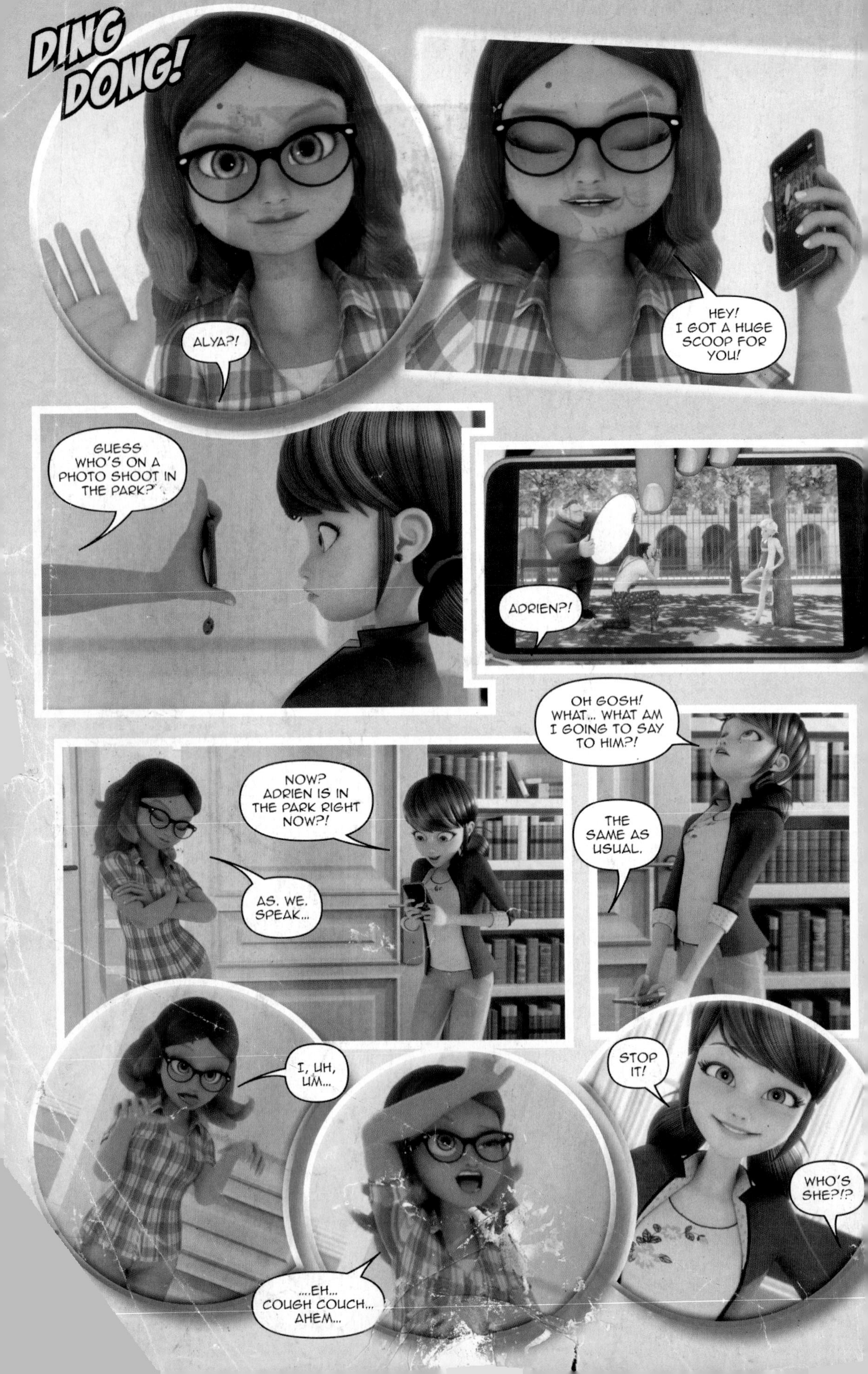
DING DONG!
ALYA?!
HEY! I GOT A HUGE SCOOP FOR YOU!
GUESS WHO'S ON A PHOTO SHOOT IN THE PARK?
ADRIEN?!
NOW? ADRIEN IS IN THE PARK RIGHT NOW?!
AS. WE. SPEAK...
OH GOSH! WHAT... WHAT AM I GOING TO SAY TO HIM?!
THE SAME AS USUAL.
I, UH, UM...
...EH... COUGH COUCH... AHEM...
STOP IT!
WHO'S SHE?!?

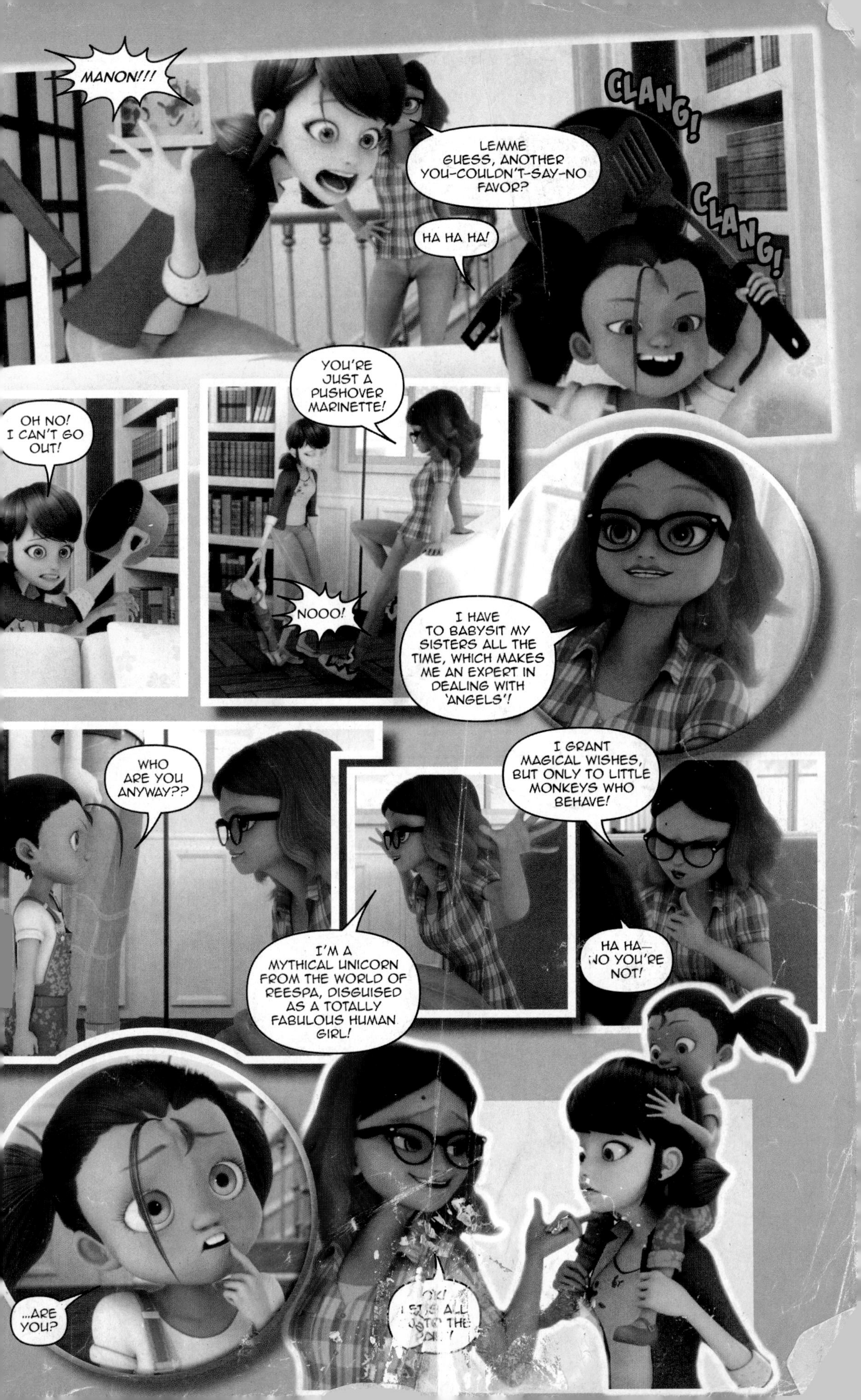
MANON!!!
LEMME GUESS, ANOTHER YOU-COULDN'T-SAY-NO FAVOR?
HA HA HA!
CLANG!
CLANG!
OH NO! I CAN'T GO OUT!
YOU'RE JUST A PUSHOVER MARINETTE!
NOOO!
I HAVE TO BABYSIT MY SISTERS ALL THE TIME, WHICH MAKES ME AN EXPERT IN DEALING WITH 'ANGELS'!
WHO ARE YOU ANYWAY??
I'M A MYTHICAL UNICORN FROM THE WORLD OF REESPA, DISGUISED AS A TOTALLY FABULOUS HUMAN GIRL!
I GRANT MAGICAL WISHES, BUT ONLY TO LITTLE MONKEYS WHO BEHAVE!
HA HA— NO YOU'RE NOT!
...ARE YOU?

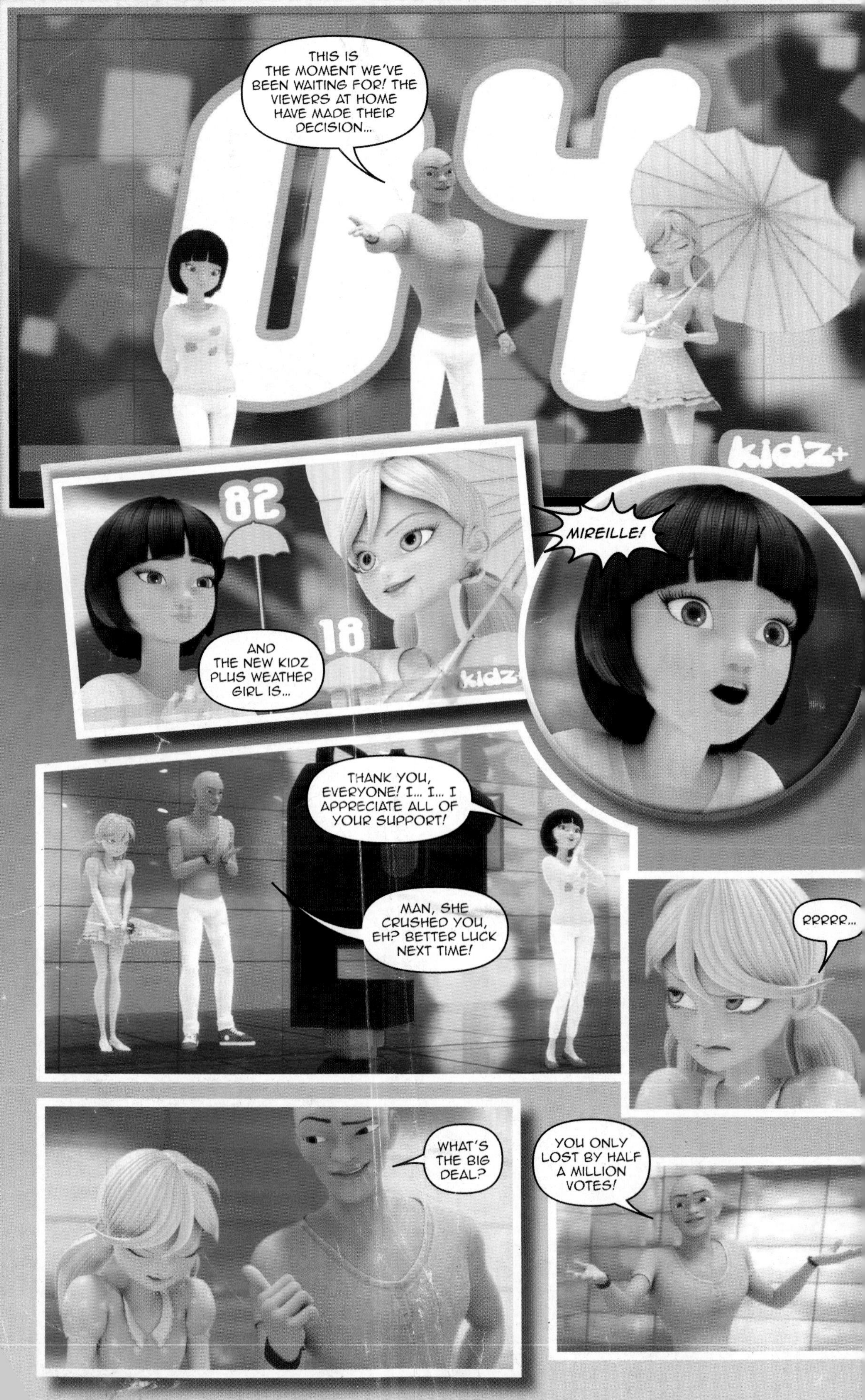
THIS IS THE MOMENT WE'VE BEEN WAITING FOR! THE VIEWERS AT HOME HAVE MADE THEIR DECISION...
kidz+
82
18
kidz+
AND THE NEW KIDZ PLUS WEATHER GIRL IS...
MIREILLE!
THANK YOU, EVERYONE! I... I... I APPRECIATE ALL OF YOUR SUPPORT!
MAN, SHE CRUSHED YOU, EH? BETTER LUCK NEXT TIME!
RRRRR...
WHAT'S THE BIG DEAL?
YOU ONLY LOST BY HALF A MILLION VOTES!

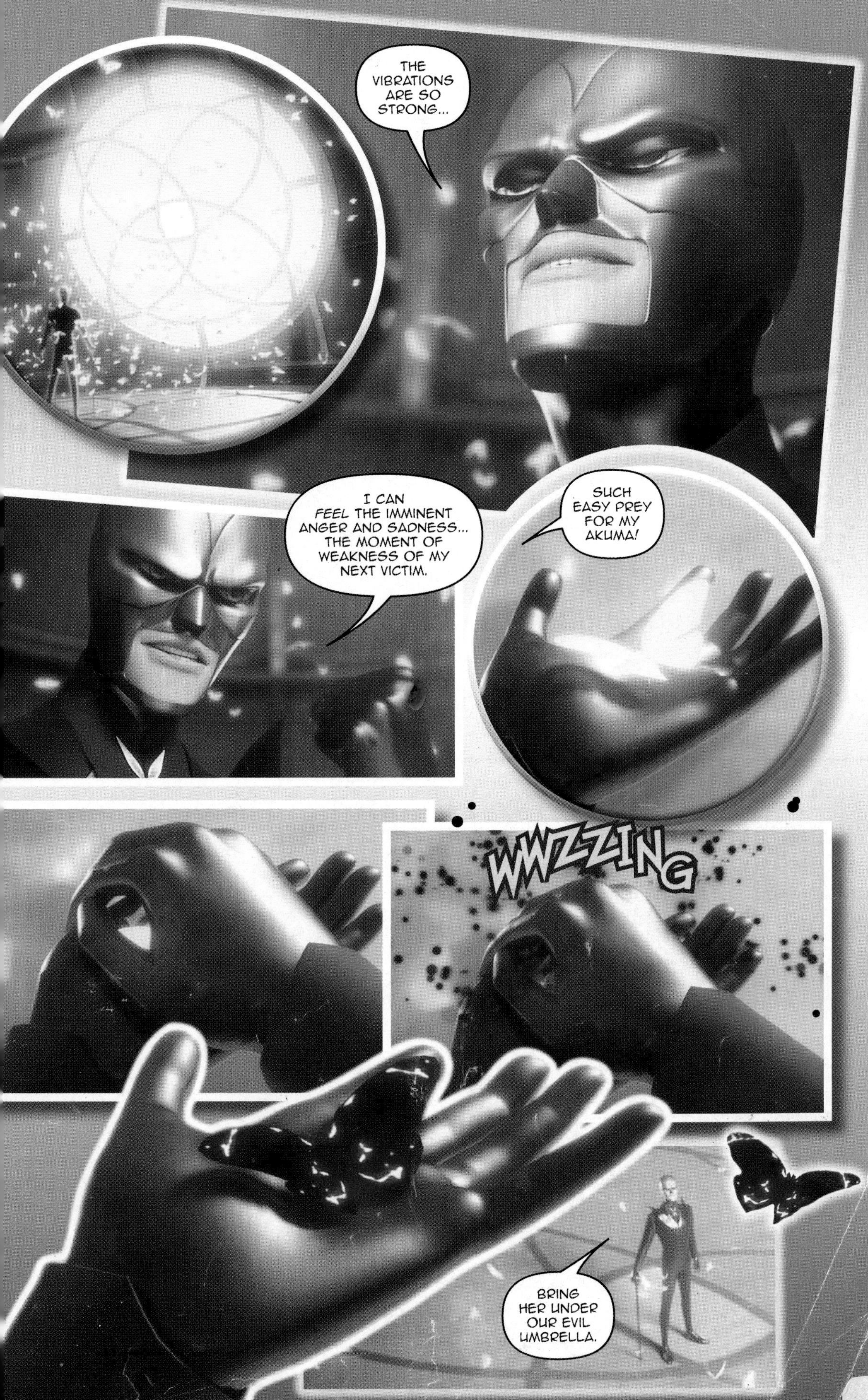
THE VIBRATIONS ARE SO STRONG...
I CAN *FEEL* THE IMMINENT ANGER AND SADNESS... THE MOMENT OF WEAKNESS OF MY NEXT VICTIM.
SUCH EASY PREY FOR MY AKUMA!
WWZZING
BRING HER UNDER OUR EVIL UMBRELLA.

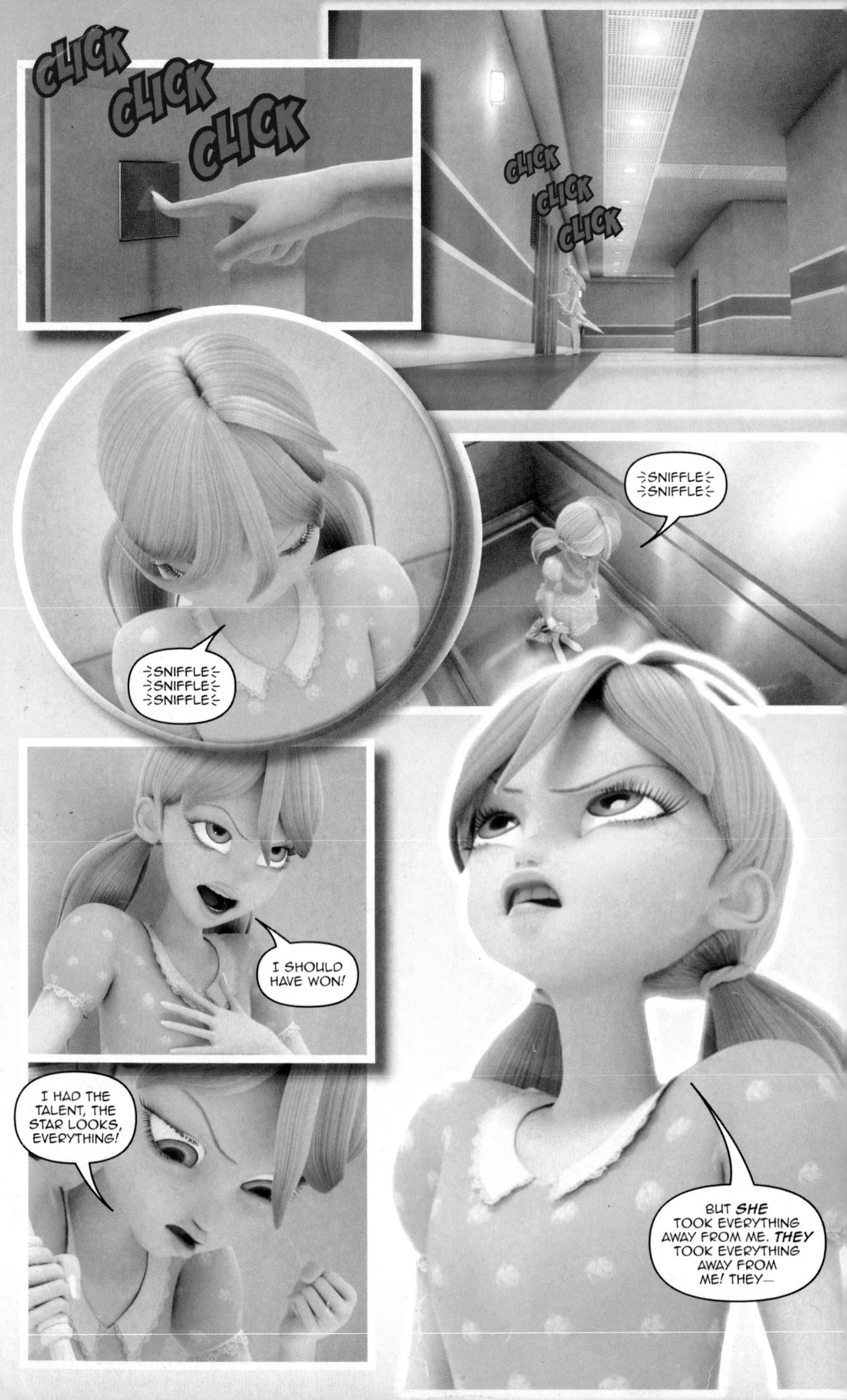

CLICK CLICK CLICK
CLICK CLICK CLICK
SNIFFLE SNIFFLE SNIFFLE
SNIFFLE SNIFFLE
I SHOULD HAVE WON!
I HAD THE TALENT, THE STAR LOOKS, EVERYTHING!
BUT *SHE* TOOK EVERYTHING AWAY FROM ME. *THEY* TOOK EVERYTHING AWAY FROM ME! THEY—

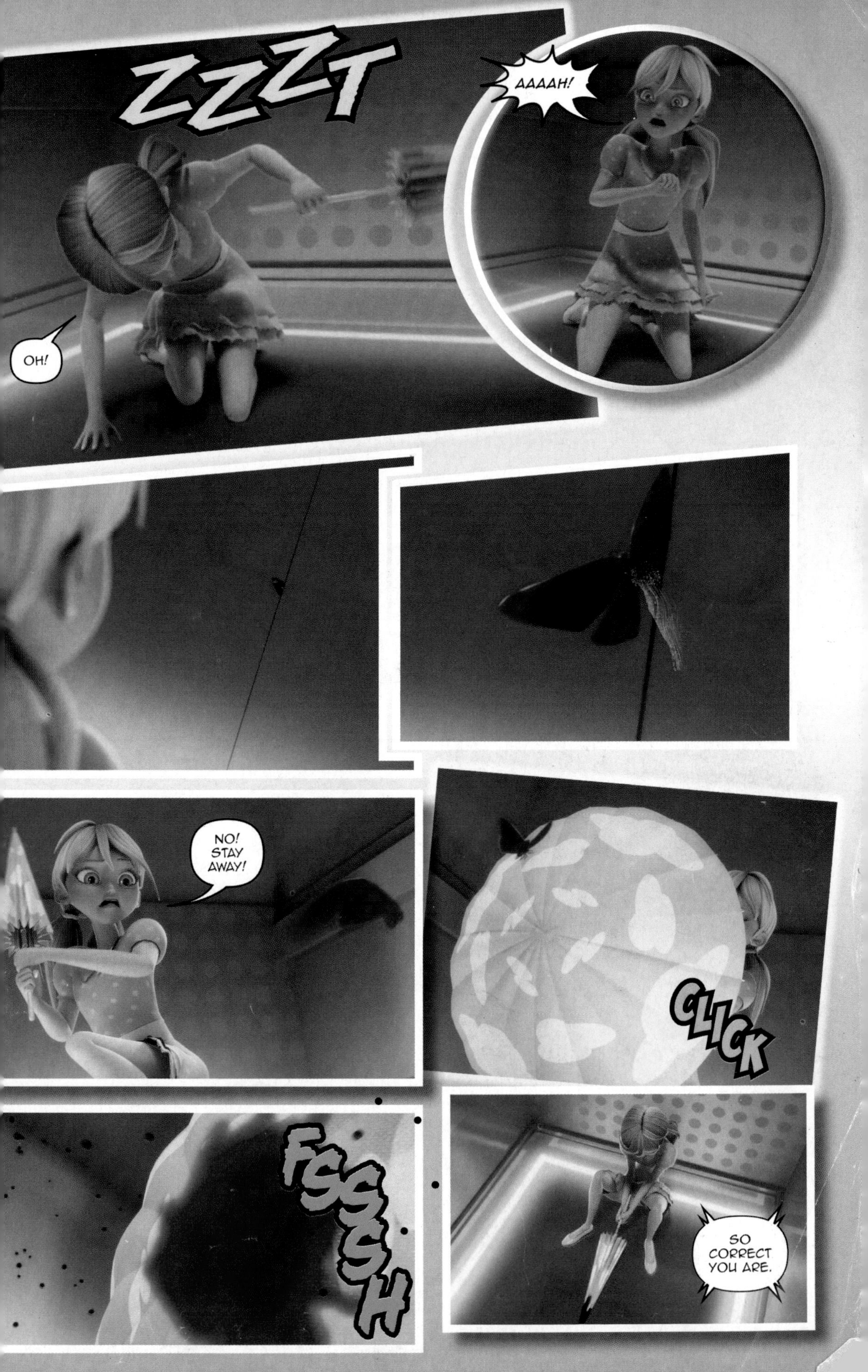
ZZZZT
AAAAH!
OH!
NO! STAY AWAY!
CLICK
FSSSH
SO CORRECT YOU ARE.

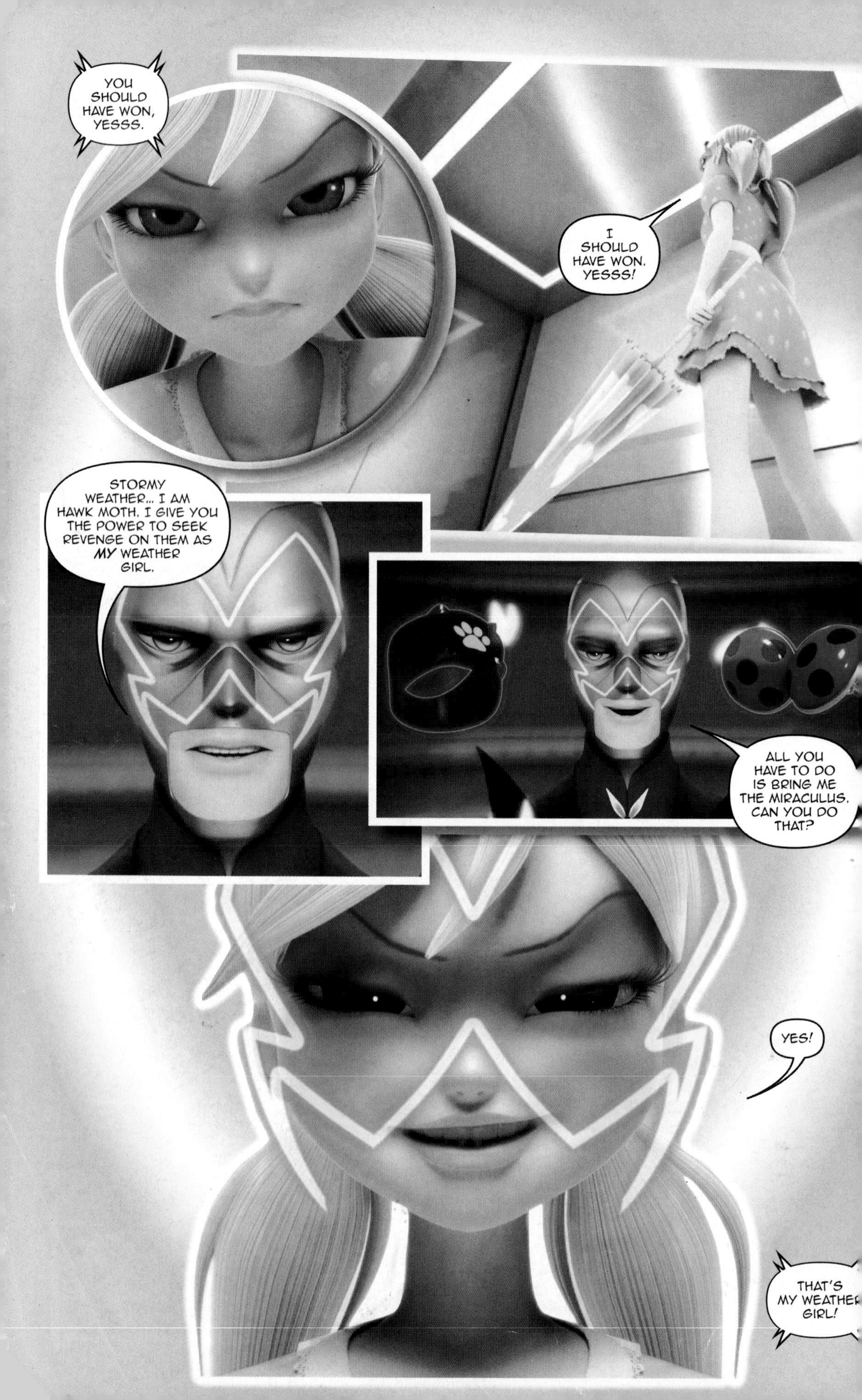
YOU SHOULD HAVE WON, YESSS.
I SHOULD HAVE WON. YESSS!
STORMY WEATHER... I AM HAWK MOTH. I GIVE YOU THE POWER TO SEEK REVENGE ON THEM AS *MY* WEATHER GIRL.
ALL YOU HAVE TO DO IS BRING ME THE MIRACULUS. CAN YOU DO THAT?
YES!
THAT'S MY WEATHER GIRL!

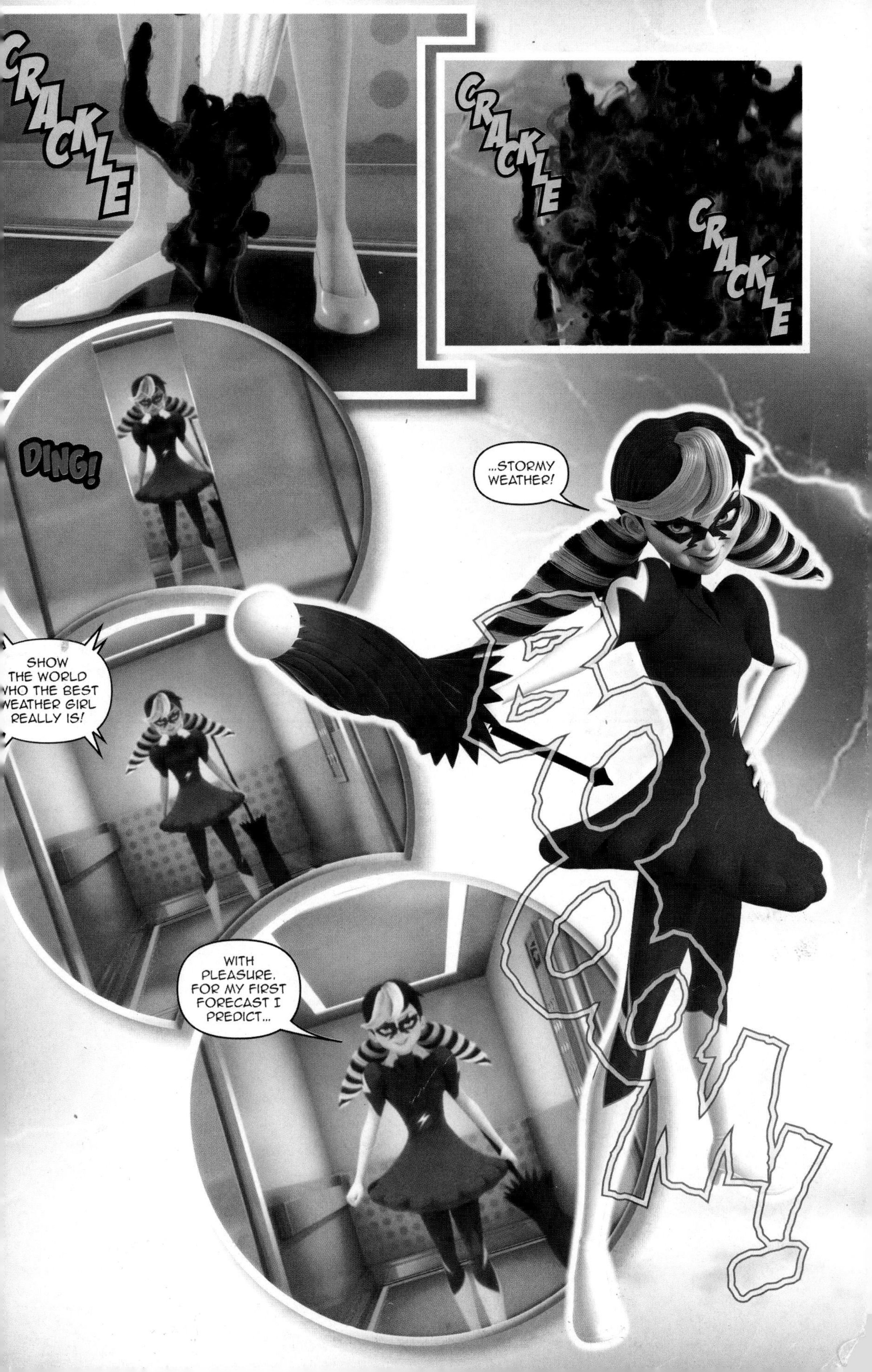
CRACKLE
CRACKLE
CRACKLE
DING!
SHOW THE WORLD WHO THE BEST WEATHER GIRL REALLY IS!
WITH PLEASURE. FOR MY FIRST FORECAST I PREDICT...
...STORMY WEATHER!

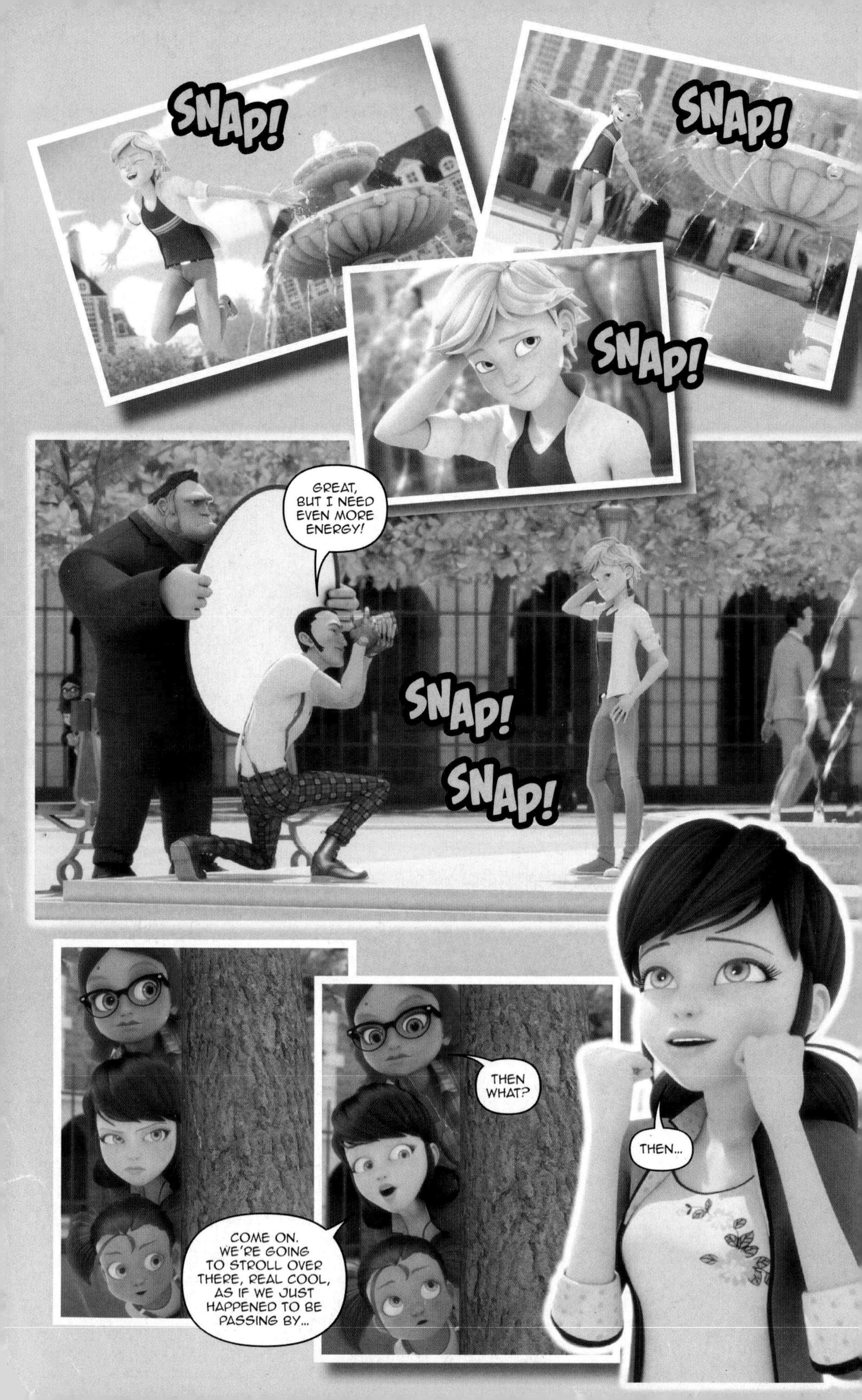
SNAP!
SNAP!
SNAP!
GREAT, BUT I NEED EVEN MORE ENERGY!
SNAP!
SNAP!
COME ON. WE'RE GOING TO STROLL OVER THERE, REAL COOL, AS IF WE JUST HAPPENED TO BE PASSING BY...
THEN WHAT?
THEN...

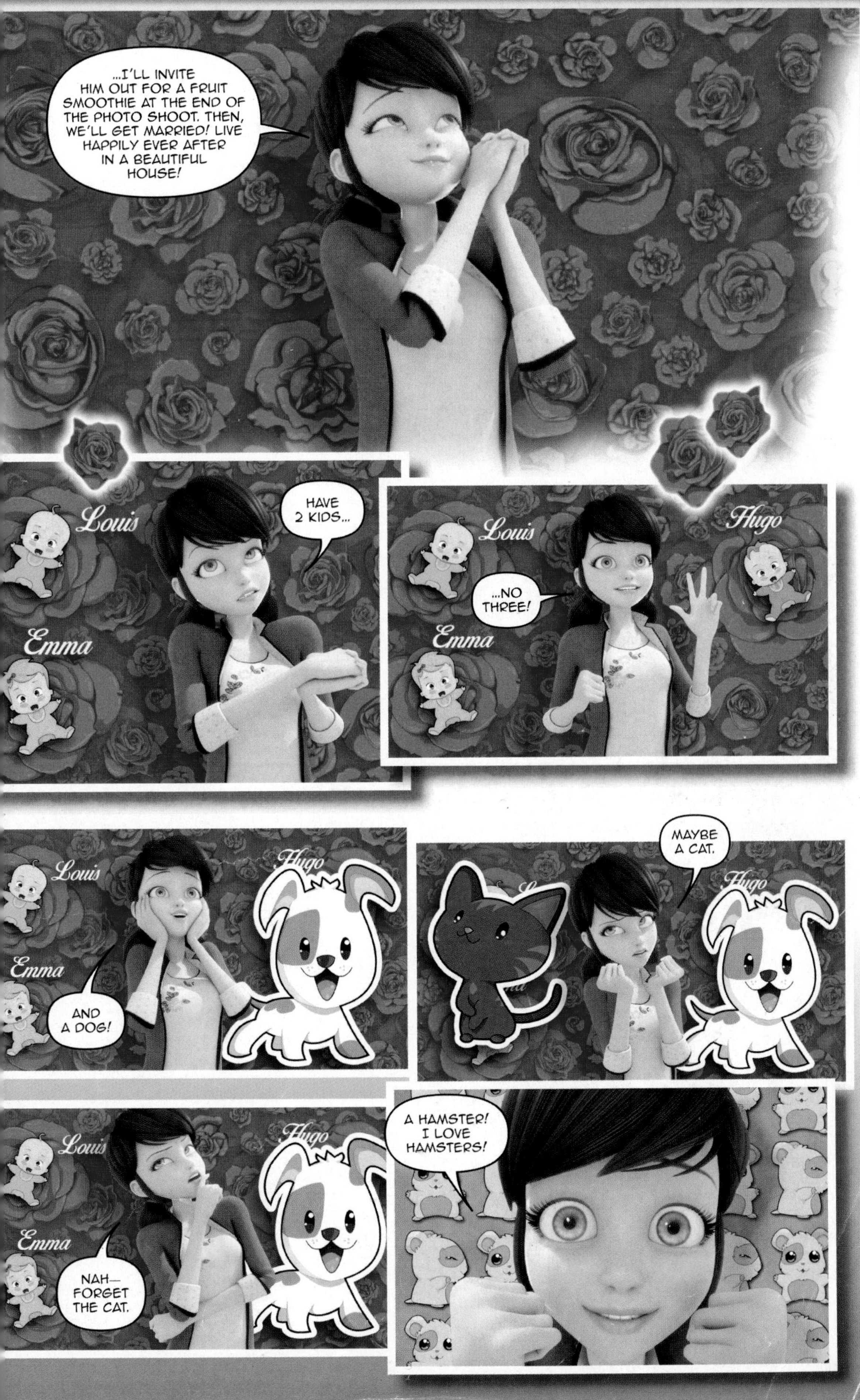
...I'LL INVITE HIM OUT FOR A FRUIT SMOOTHIE AT THE END OF THE PHOTO SHOOT. THEN, WE'LL GET MARRIED! LIVE HAPPILY EVER AFTER IN A BEAUTIFUL HOUSE!
Louis
Emma
HAVE 2 KIDS...
Louis
Hugo
Emma
...NO THREE!
Louis
Hugo
Emma
AND A DOG!
MAYBE A CAT.
Hugo
Louis
Hugo
Emma
NAH— FORGET THE CAT.
A HAMSTER! I LOVE HAMSTERS!

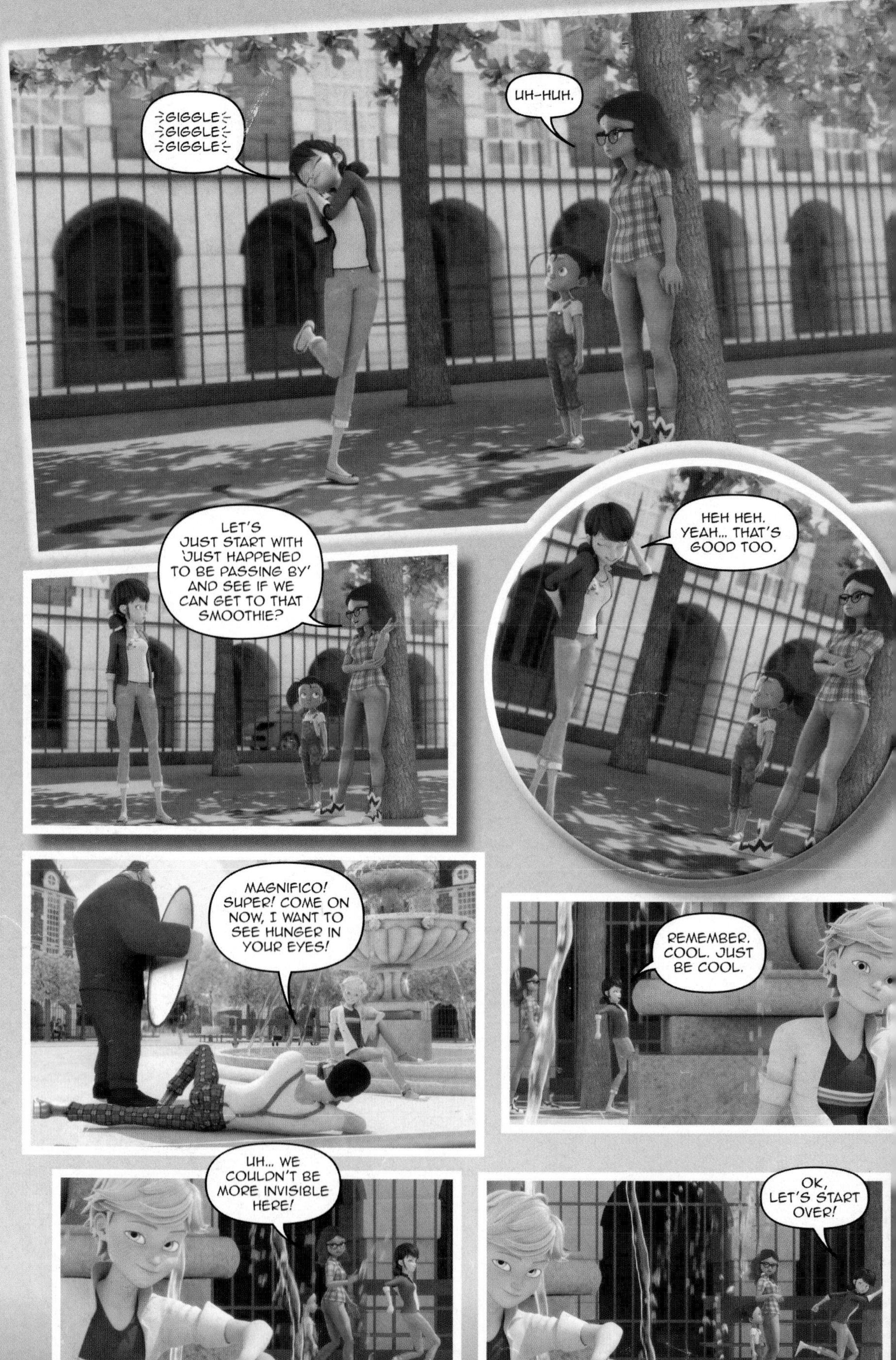
GIGGLE GIGGLE GIGGLE
UH-HUH.
LET'S JUST START WITH 'JUST HAPPENED TO BE PASSING BY' AND SEE IF WE CAN GET TO THAT SMOOTHIE?
HEH HEH. YEAH... THAT'S GOOD TOO.
MAGNIFICO! SUPER! COME ON NOW, I WANT TO SEE HUNGER IN YOUR EYES!
REMEMBER. COOL. JUST BE COOL.
UH... WE COULDN'T BE MORE INVISIBLE HERE!
OK, LET'S START OVER!

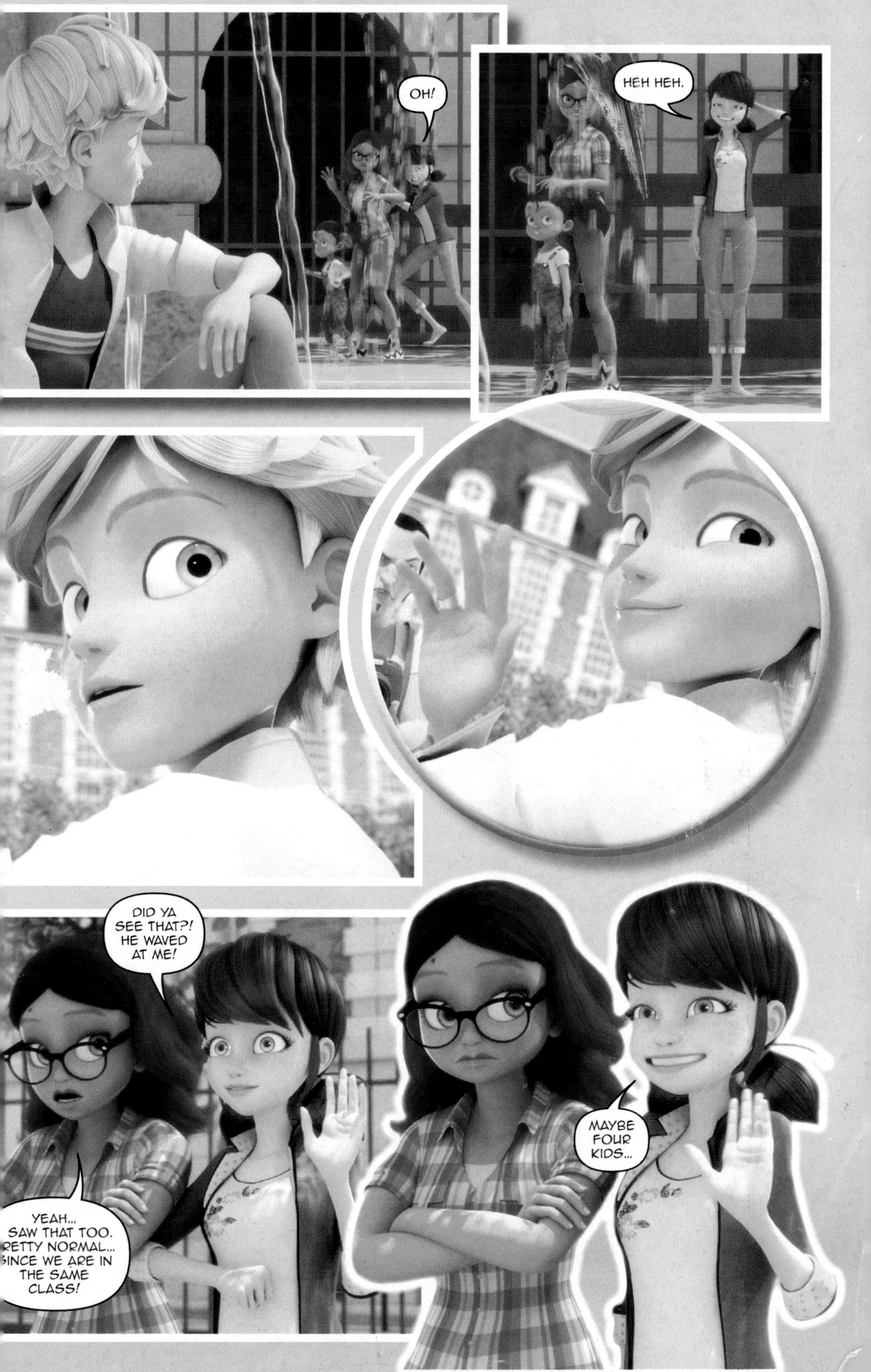
OH!
HEH HEH.
DID YA SEE THAT?! HE WAVED AT ME!
YEAH... SAW THAT TOO. RETTY NORMAL... SINCE WE ARE IN THE SAME CLASS!
MAYBE FOUR KIDS...

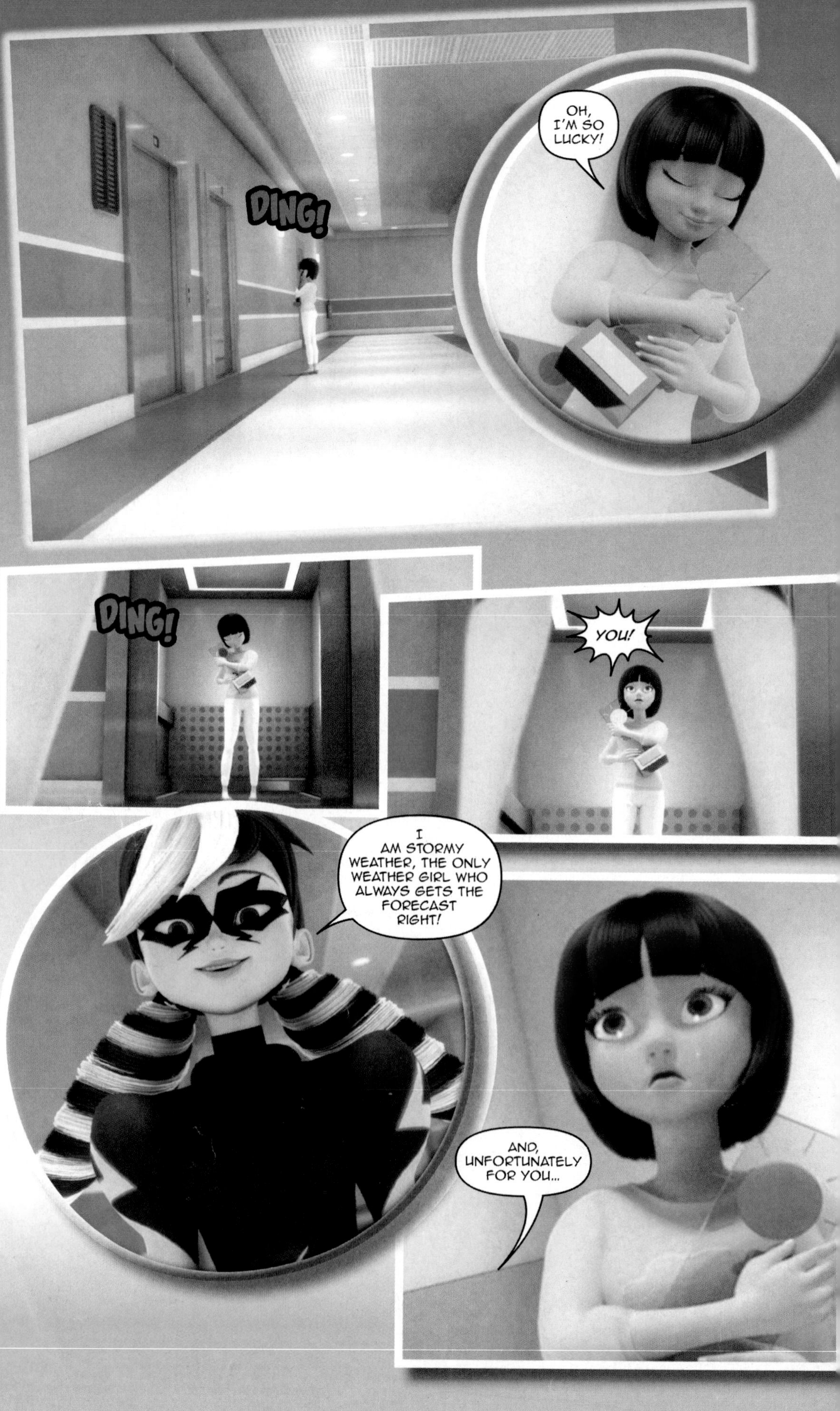
DING!
OH, I'M SO LUCKY!
DING!
YOU!
I AM STORMY WEATHER, THE ONLY WEATHER GIRL WHO ALWAYS GETS THE FORECAST RIGHT!
AND, UNFORTUNATELY FOR YOU...

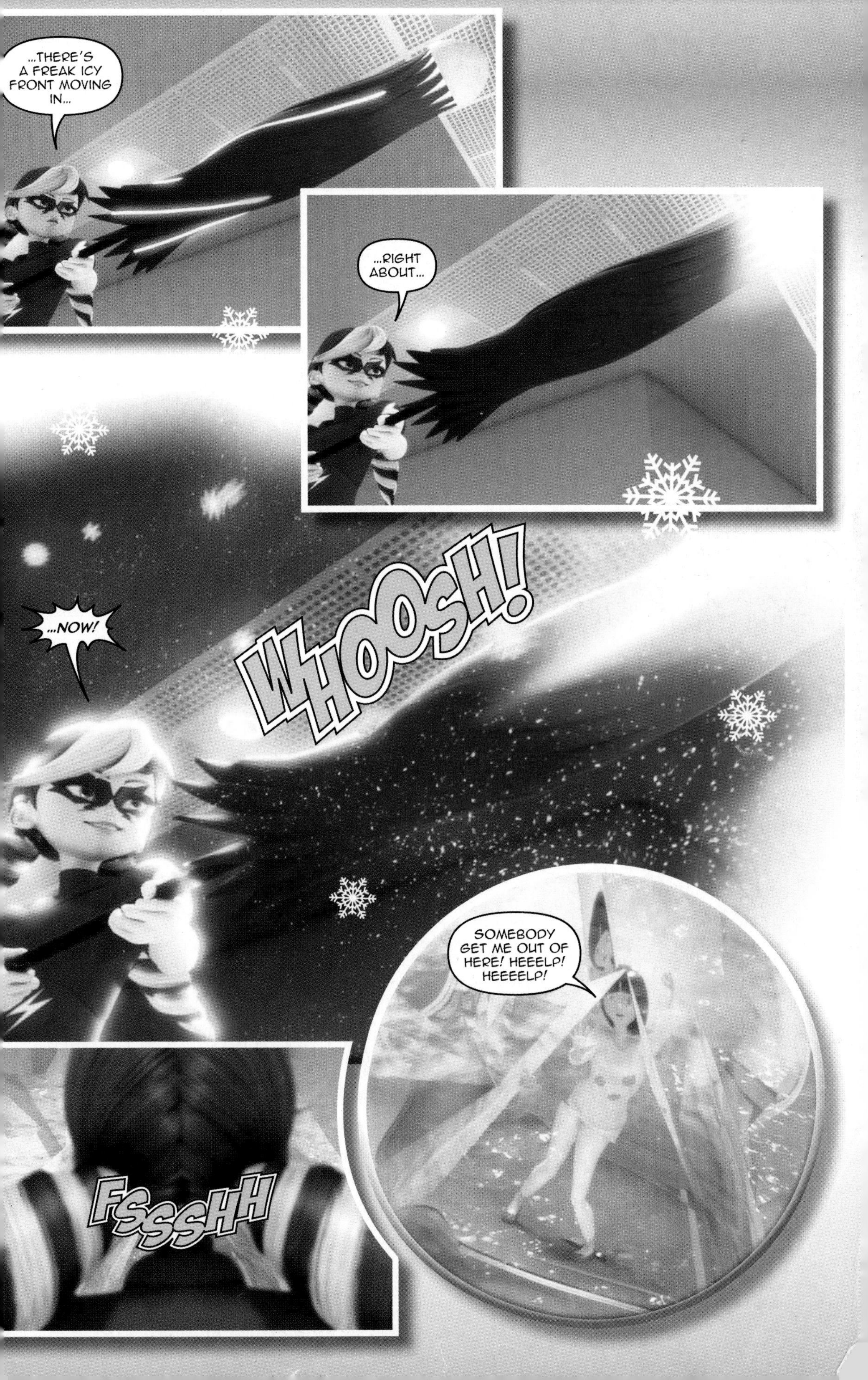
...THERE'S A FREAK ICY FRONT MOVING IN...
...RIGHT ABOUT...
...NOW!
WHOOSH!
SOMEBODY GET ME OUT OF HERE! HEEELP! HEEEELP!
FSSSHH

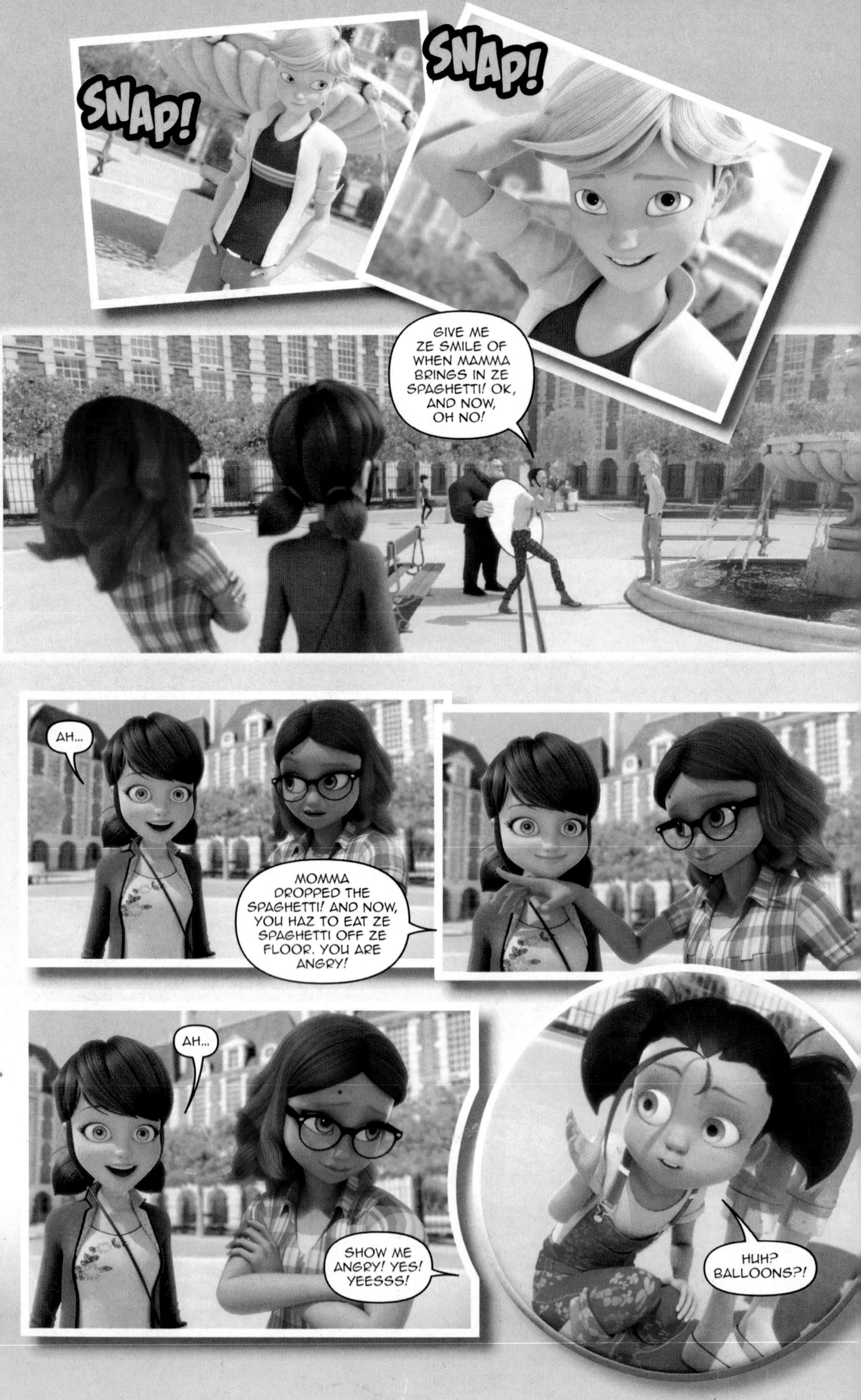
SNAP!
SNAP!
GIVE ME ZE SMILE OF WHEN MAMMA BRINGS IN ZE SPAGHETTI! OK, AND NOW, OH NO!
AH...
MOMMA DROPPED THE SPAGHETTI! AND NOW, YOU HAZ TO EAT ZE SPAGHETTI OFF ZE FLOOR. YOU ARE ANGRY!
AH...
SHOW ME ANGRY! YES! YEESSS!
HUH? BALLOONS?!

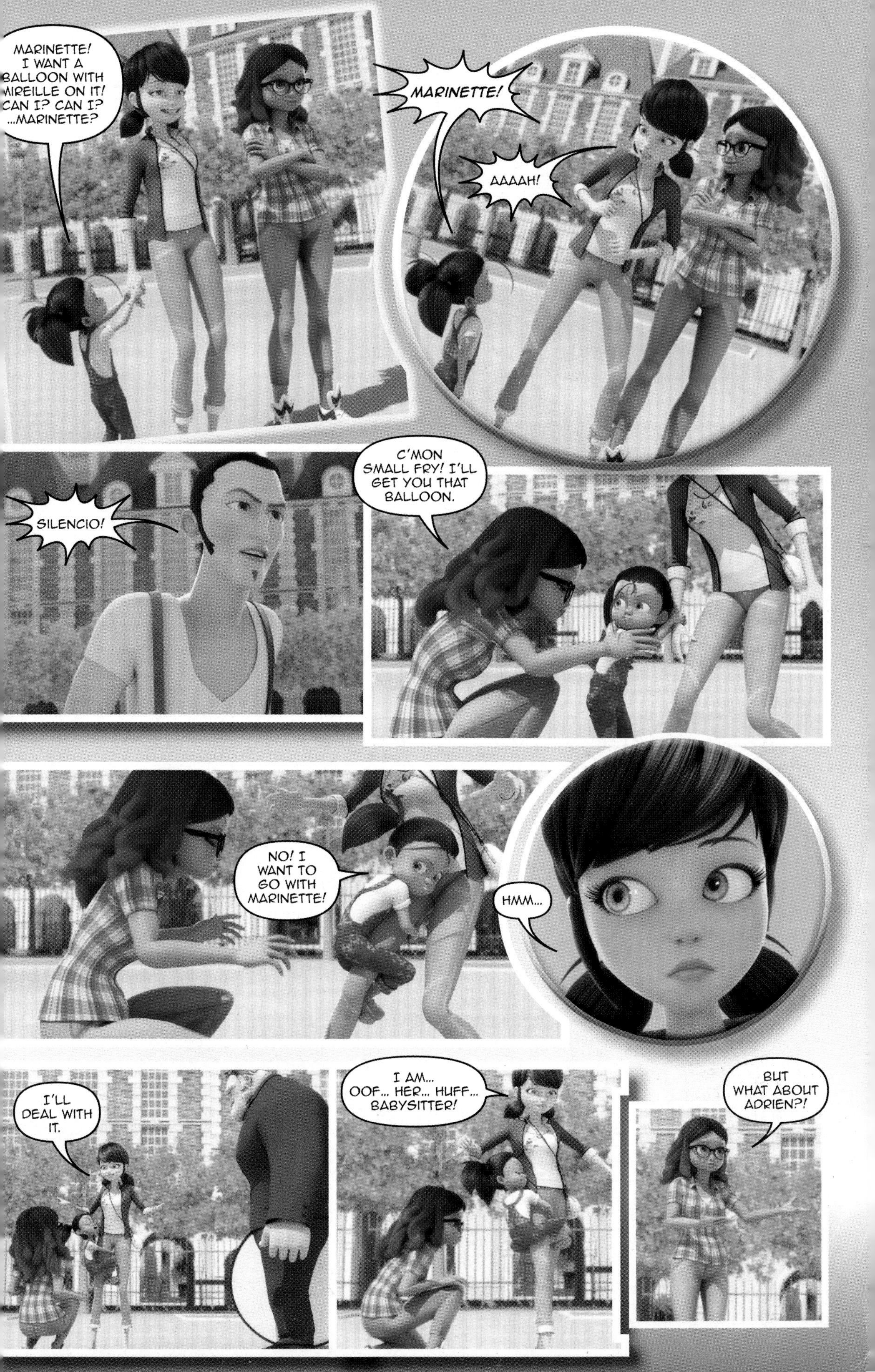
MARINETTE! I WANT A BALLOON WITH MIREILLE ON IT! CAN I? CAN I? ...MARINETTE?
MARINETTE!
AAAAH!
SILENCIO!
C'MON SMALL FRY! I'LL GET YOU THAT BALLOON.
NO! I WANT TO GO WITH MARINETTE!
HMM...
I'LL DEAL WITH IT.
I AM... OOF... HER... HUFF... BABYSITTER!
BUT WHAT ABOUT ADRIEN?!

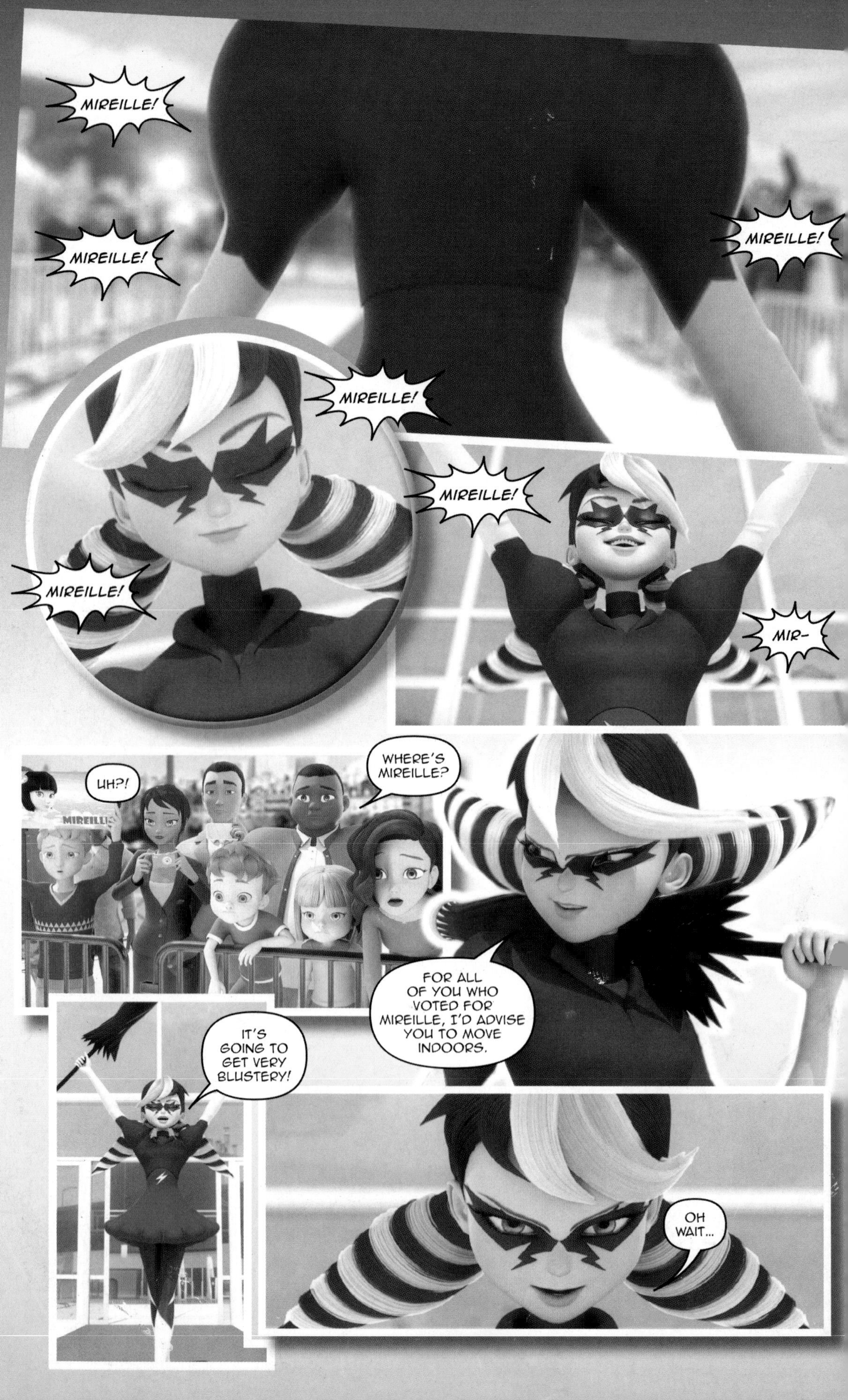

MIREILLE!
MIREILLE!
MIREILLE!
MIREILLE!
MIREILLE!
MIREILLE!
MIR-
UH?!
MIREILLE
WHERE'S MIREILLE?
FOR ALL OF YOU WHO VOTED FOR MIREILLE, I'D ADVISE YOU TO MOVE INDOORS.
IT'S GOING TO GET VERY BLUSTERY!
OH WAIT...

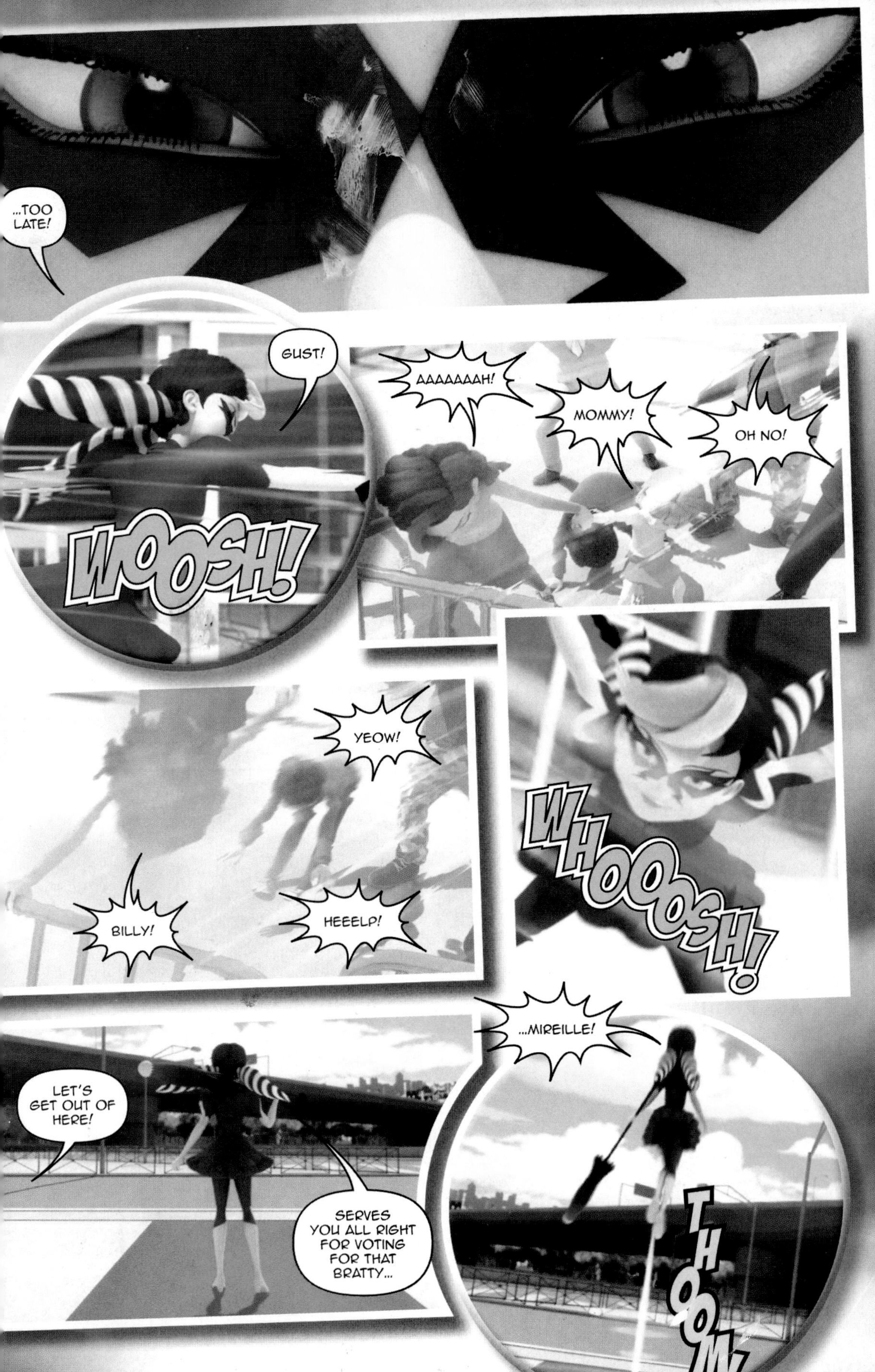
...TOO LATE!
GUST!
WOOSH!
AAAAAAAH!
MOMMY!
OH NO!
YEOW!
BILLY!
HEEELP!
WHOOOOSH!
LET'S GET OUT OF HERE!
SERVES YOU ALL RIGHT FOR VOTING FOR THAT BRATTY...
...MIREILLE!
THOOOM!

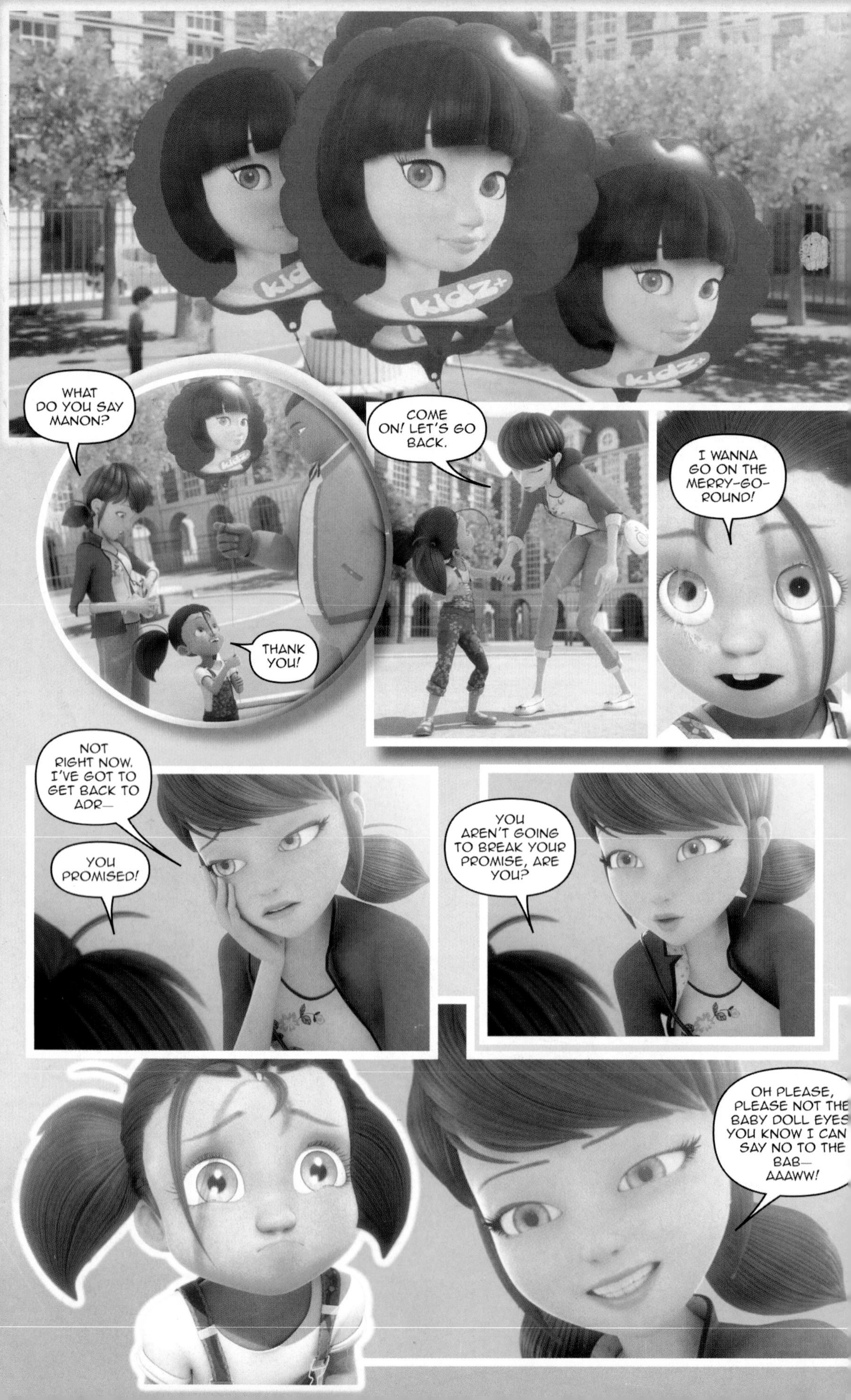
kidz+
WHAT DO YOU SAY MANON?
THANK YOU!
COME ON! LET'S GO BACK.
I WANNA GO ON THE MERRY-GO-ROUND!
NOT RIGHT NOW. I'VE GOT TO GET BACK TO ADR—
YOU PROMISED!
YOU AREN'T GOING TO BREAK YOUR PROMISE, ARE YOU?
OH PLEASE, PLEASE NOT THE BABY DOLL EYES YOU KNOW I CAN SAY NO TO THE BAB— AAAWW!

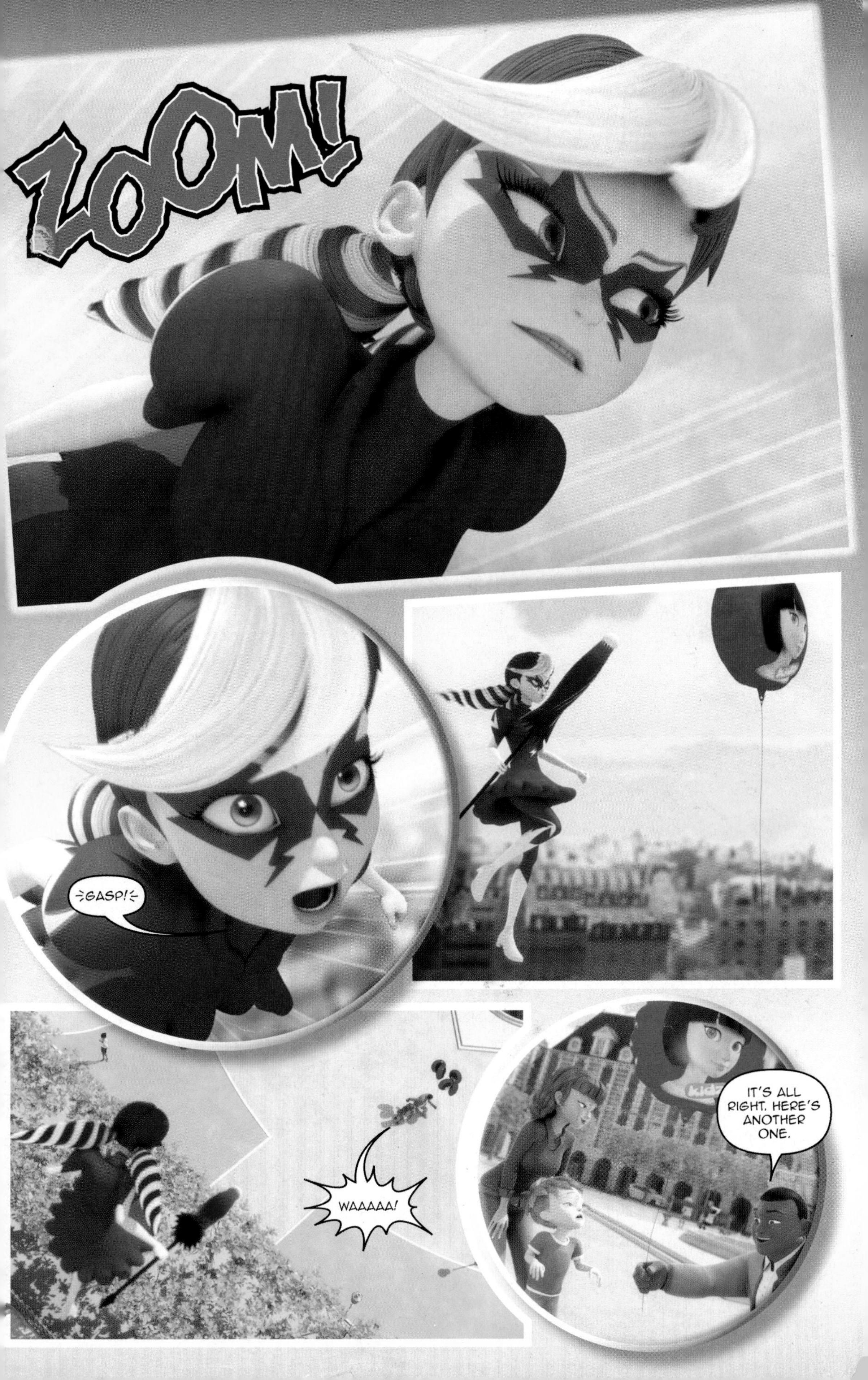
ZOOM!
GASP!
WAAAAA!
IT'S ALL RIGHT. HERE'S ANOTHER ONE.

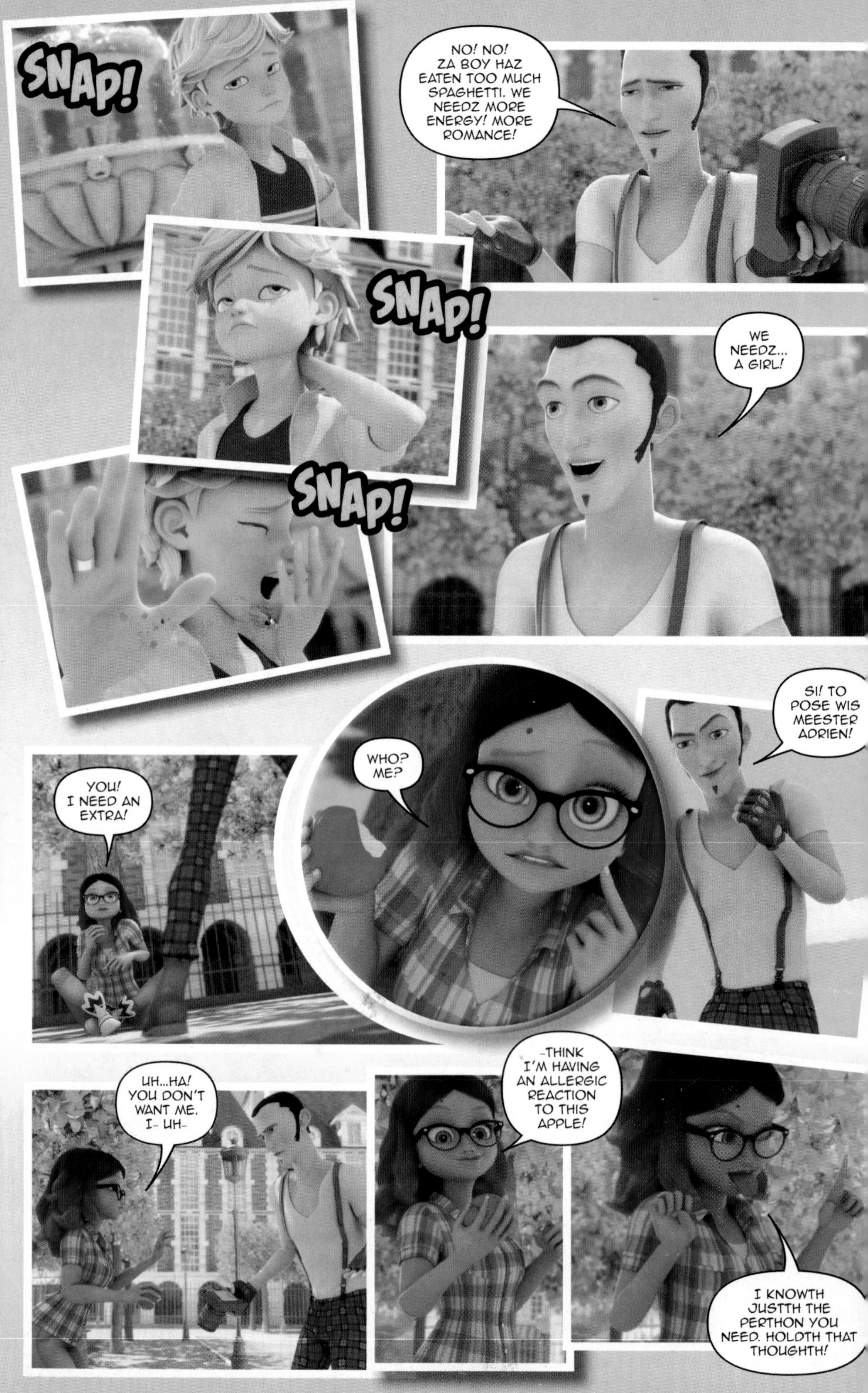
SNAP!
NO! NO! ZA BOY HAZ EATEN TOO MUCH SPAGHETTI. WE NEEDZ MORE ENERGY! MORE ROMANCE!
SNAP!
SNAP!
WE NEEDZ... A GIRL!
YOU! I NEED AN EXTRA!
WHO? ME?
SI! TO POSE WIS MEESTER ADRIEN!
UH...HA! YOU DON'T WANT ME. I- UH-
-THINK I'M HAVING AN ALLERGIC REACTION TO THIS APPLE!
I KNOWTH JUSTTH THE PERTHON YOU NEED. HOLDTH THAT THOUGHTH!

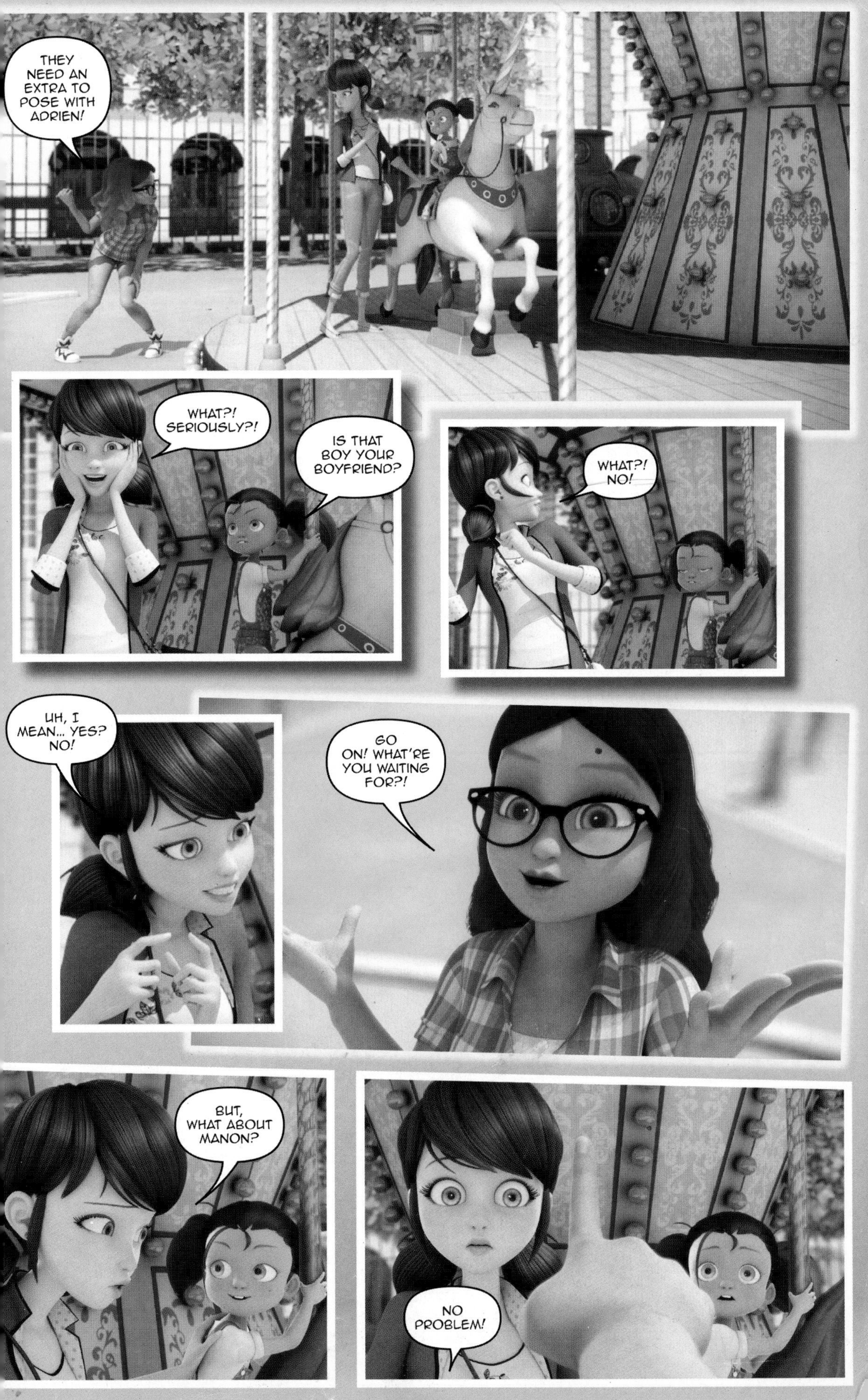
THEY NEED AN EXTRA TO POSE WITH ADRIEN!
WHAT?! SERIOUSLY?!
IS THAT BOY YOUR BOYFRIEND?
WHAT?! NO!
UH, I MEAN... YES? NO!
GO ON! WHAT'RE YOU WAITING FOR?!
BUT, WHAT ABOUT MANON?
NO PROBLEM!

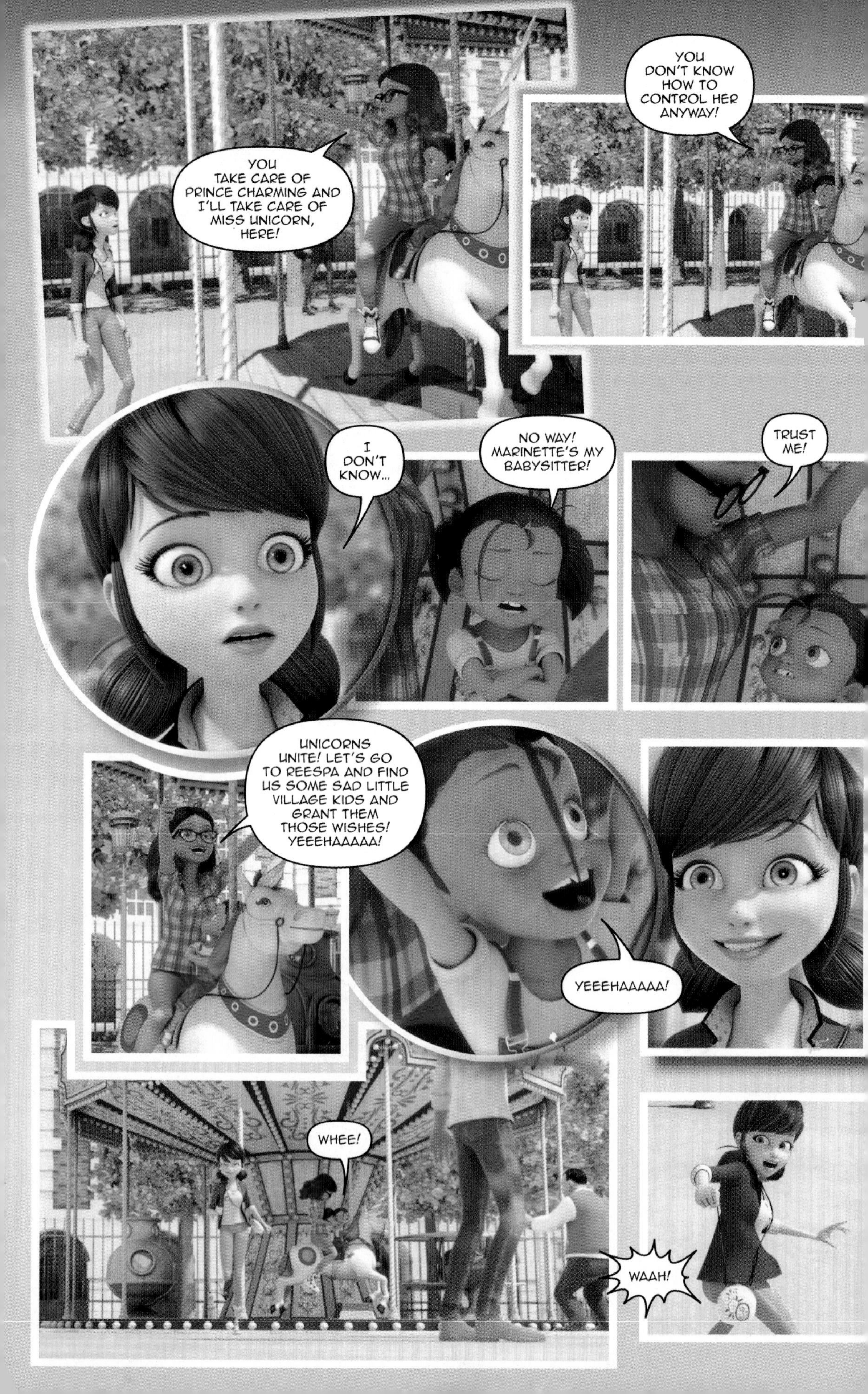

YOU TAKE CARE OF PRINCE CHARMING AND I'LL TAKE CARE OF MISS UNICORN, HERE!
YOU DON'T KNOW HOW TO CONTROL HER ANYWAY!
I DON'T KNOW...
NO WAY! MARINETTE'S MY BABYSITTER!
TRUST ME!
UNICORNS UNITE! LET'S GO TO REESPA AND FIND US SOME SAD LITTLE VILLAGE KIDS AND GRANT THEM THOSE WISHES! YEEEHAAAAA!
YEEEHAAAAA!
WHEE!
WAAH!

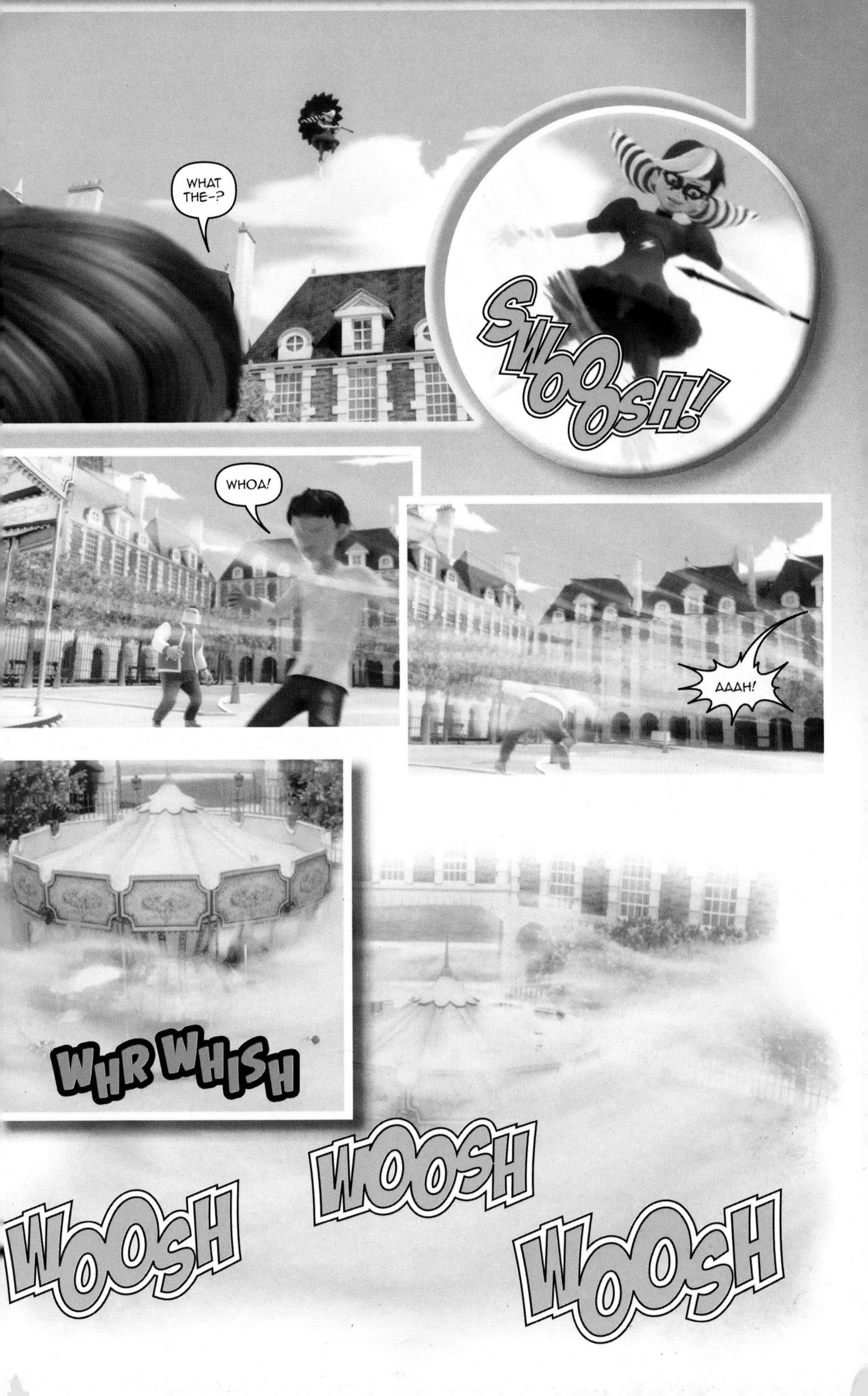
WHAT THE–?
SWOOOSH!
WHOA!
AAAH!
WHR WHISH
WOOSH
WOOSH
WOOSH

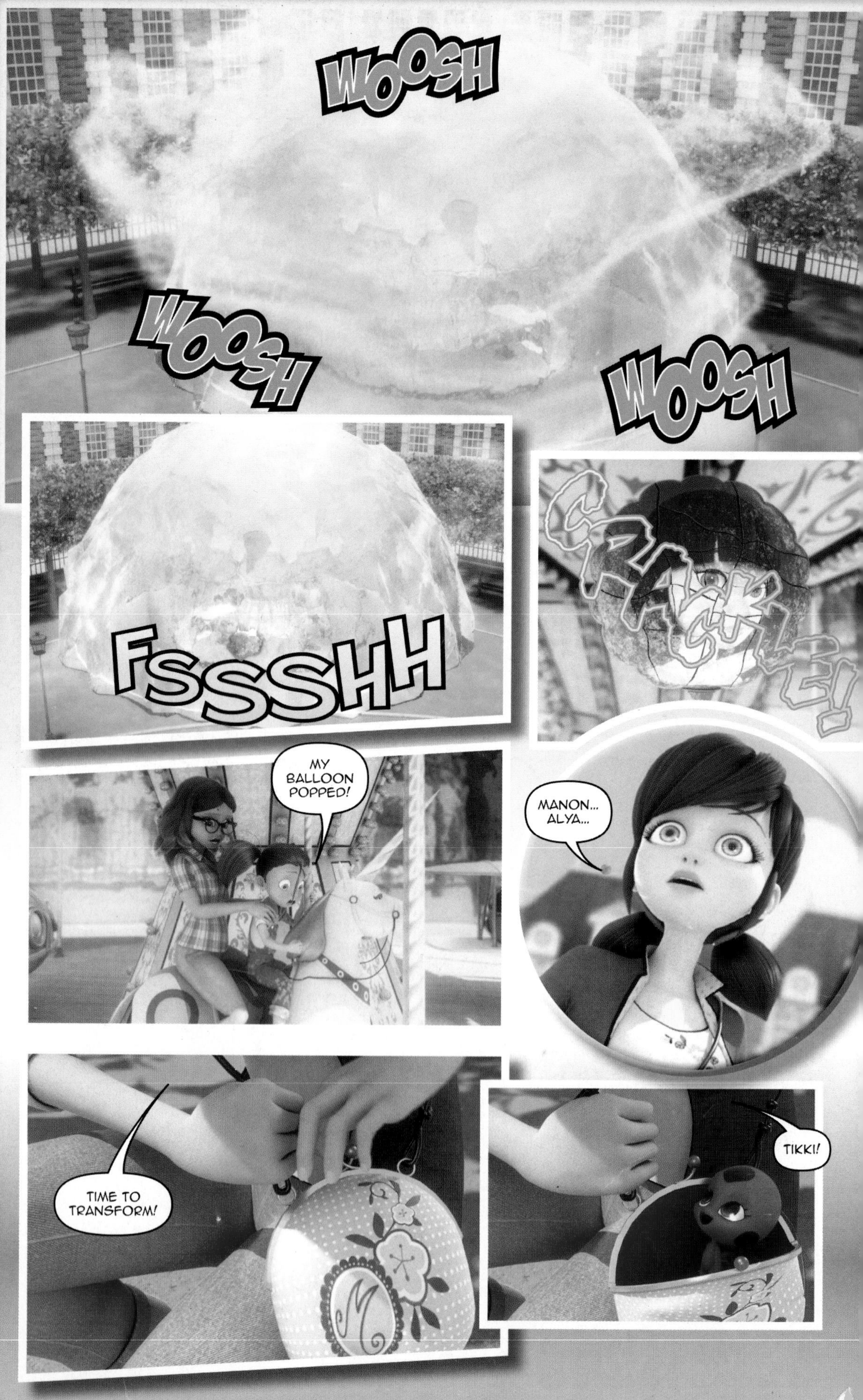
WOOSH
WOOSH
WOOSH
FSSSHH
CRACKLE!
MY BALLOON POPPED!
MANON... ALYA...
TIME TO TRANSFORM!
TIKKI!

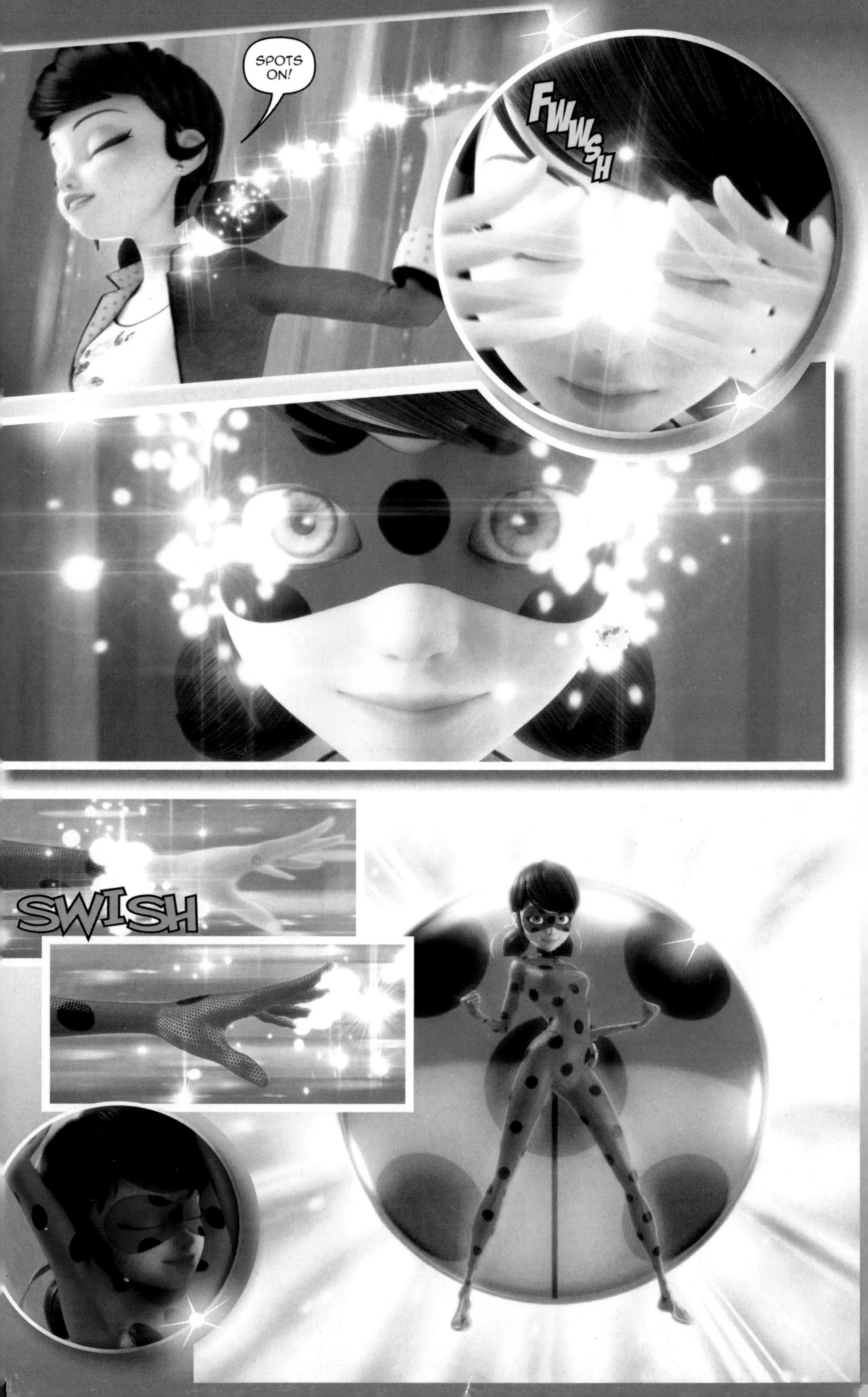
SPOTS ON!
FWWSH
SWISH

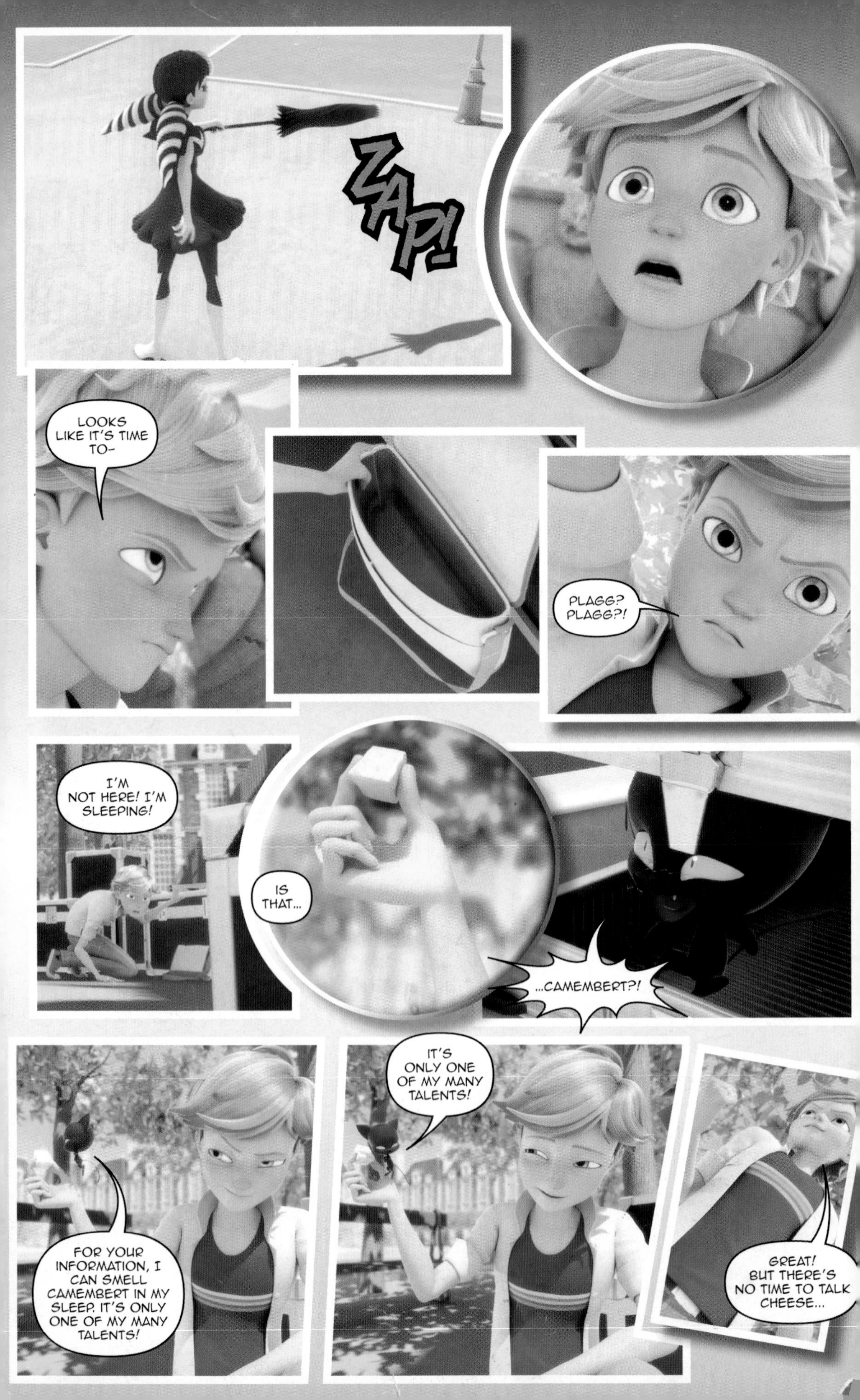
ZAP!
LOOKS LIKE IT'S TIME TO-
PLAGG? PLAGG?!
I'M NOT HERE! I'M SLEEPING!
IS THAT...
...CAMEMBERT?!
FOR YOUR INFORMATION, I CAN SMELL CAMEMBERT IN MY SLEEP. IT'S ONLY ONE OF MY MANY TALENTS!
IT'S ONLY ONE OF MY MANY TALENTS!
GREAT! BUT THERE'S NO TIME TO TALK CHEESE...

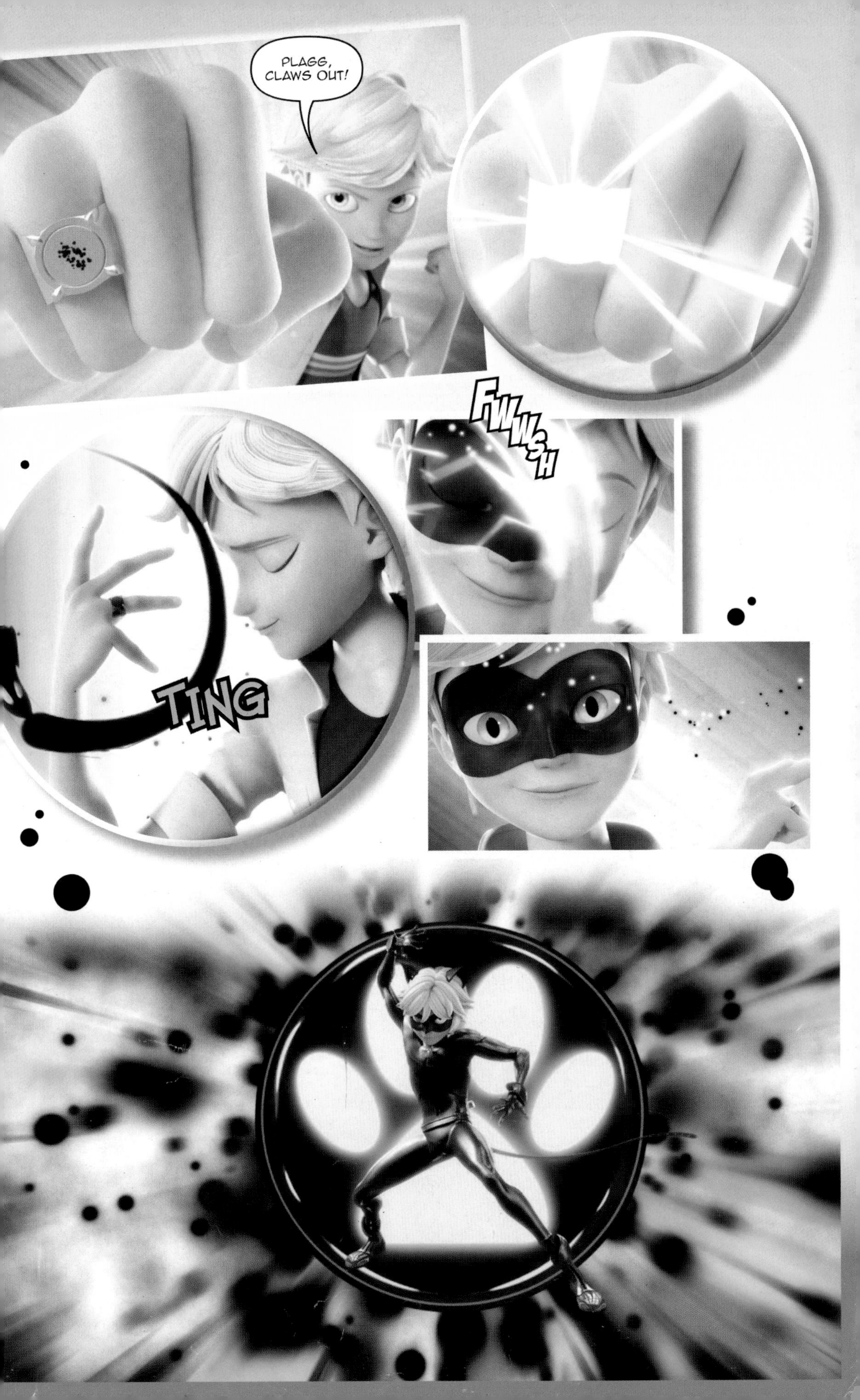
PLAGG, CLAWS OUT!
FWWSH
TING

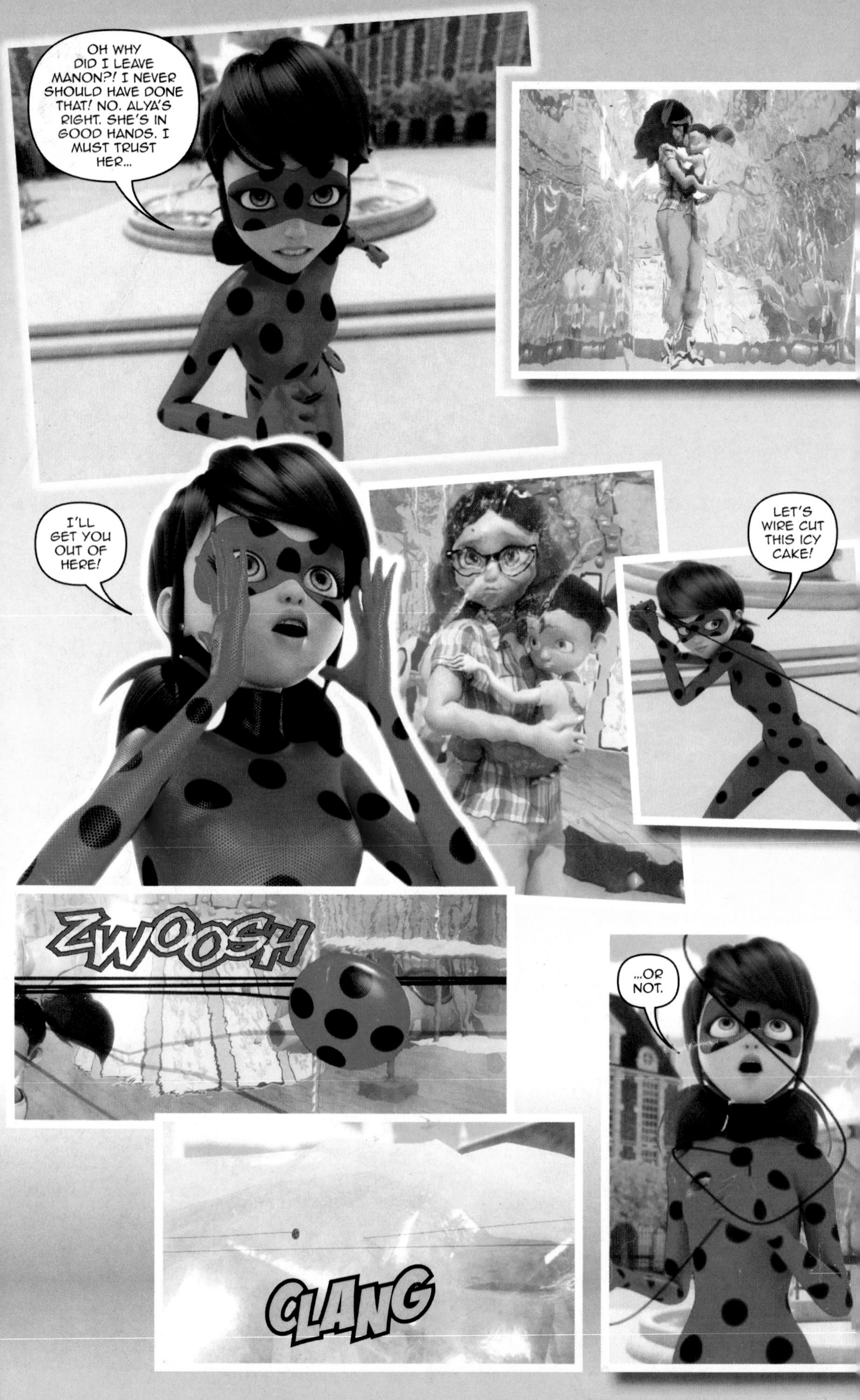
OH WHY DID I LEAVE MANON?! I NEVER SHOULD HAVE DONE THAT! NO. ALYA'S RIGHT. SHE'S IN GOOD HANDS. I MUST TRUST HER...
I'LL GET YOU OUT OF HERE!
LET'S WIRE CUT THIS ICY CAKE!
ZWOOSH
CLANG
...OR NOT.

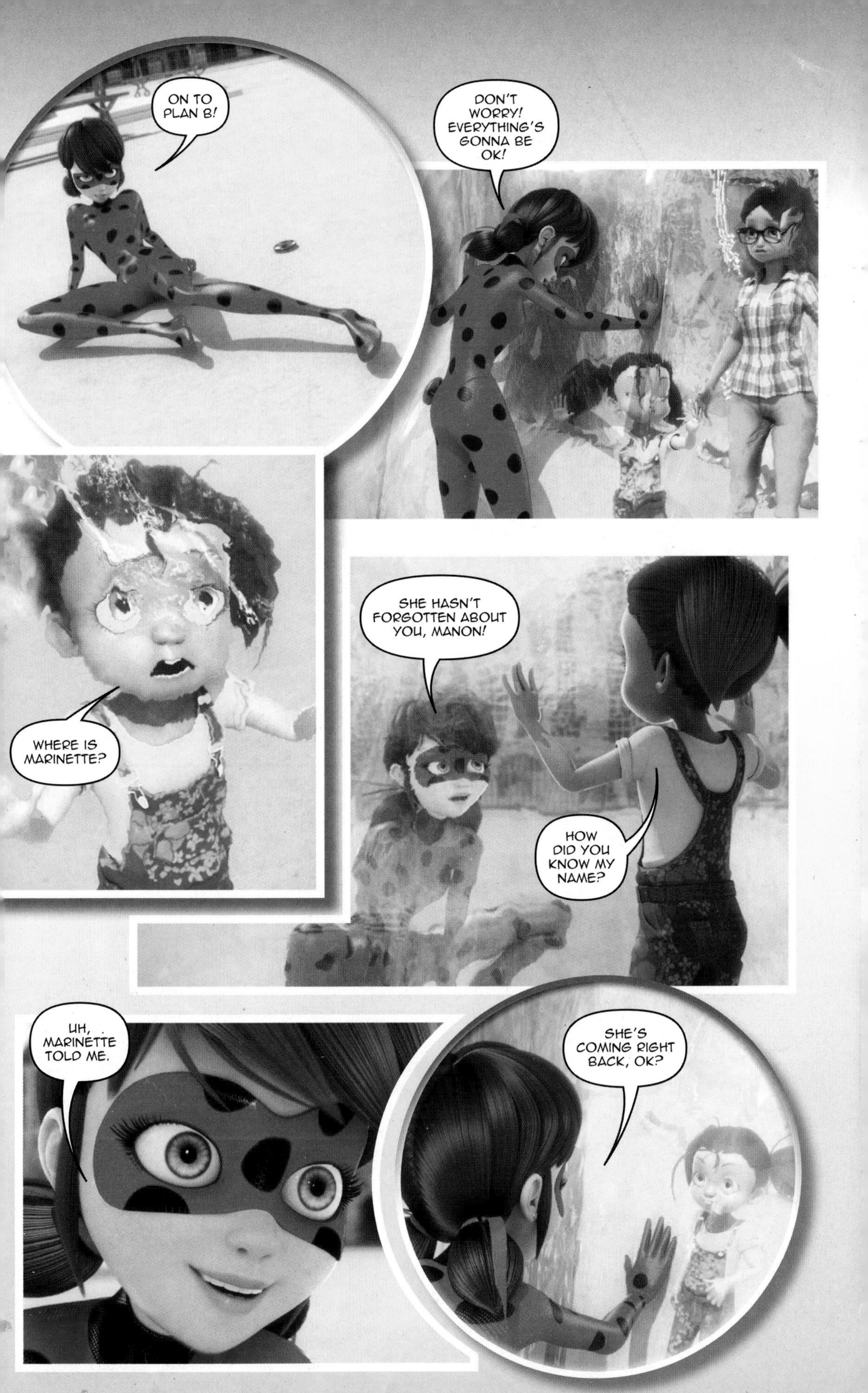
ON TO PLAN B!
DON'T WORRY! EVERYTHING'S GONNA BE OK!
WHERE IS MARINETTE?
SHE HASN'T FORGOTTEN ABOUT YOU, MANON!
HOW DID YOU KNOW MY NAME?
UH, MARINETTE TOLD ME.
SHE'S COMING RIGHT BACK, OK?

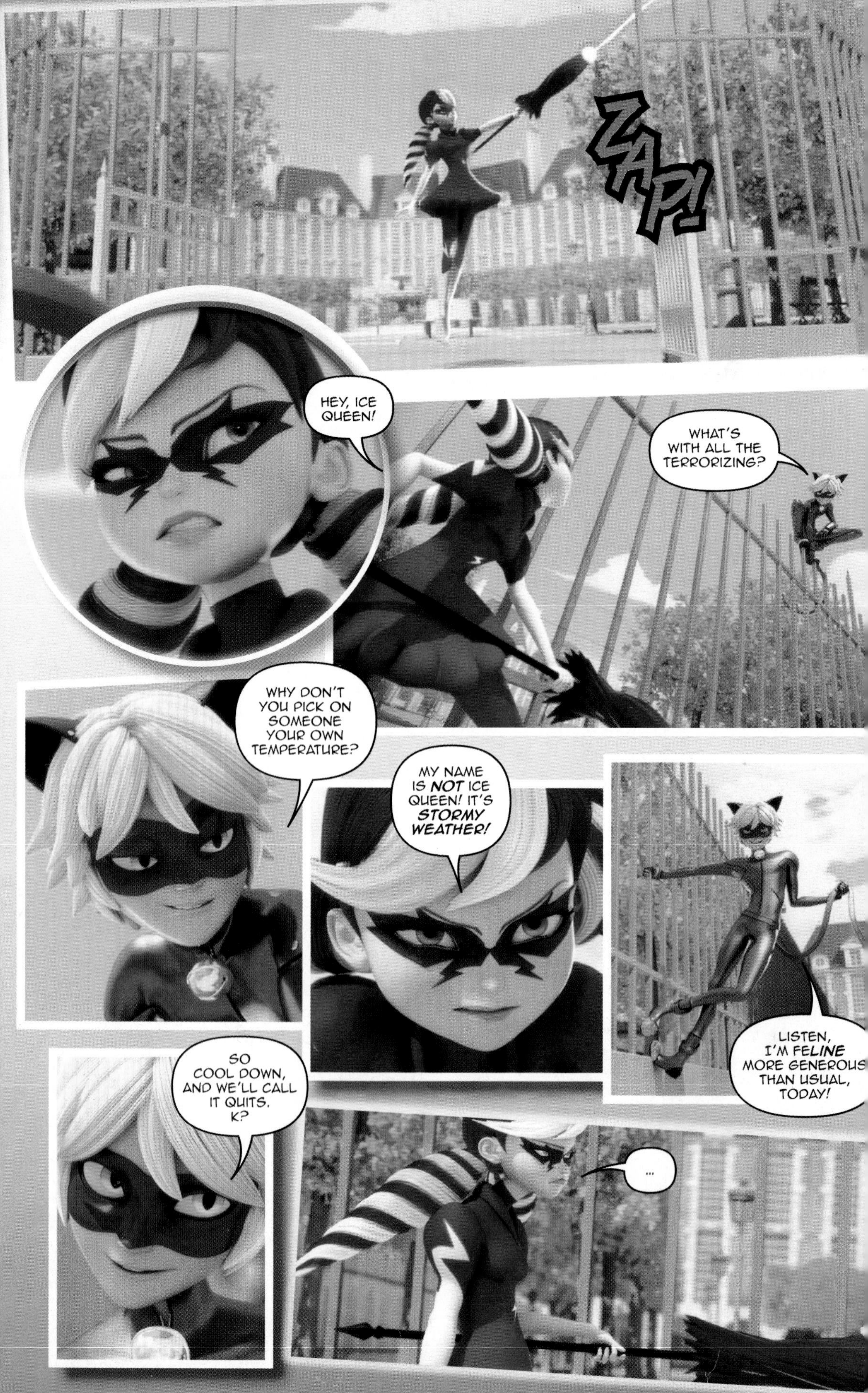
ZAP!
HEY, ICE QUEEN!
WHAT'S WITH ALL THE TERRORIZING?
WHY DON'T YOU PICK ON SOMEONE YOUR OWN TEMPERATURE?
MY NAME IS NOT ICE QUEEN! IT'S STORMY WEATHER!
LISTEN, I'M FELINE MORE GENEROUS THAN USUAL, TODAY!
SO COOL DOWN, AND WE'LL CALL IT QUITS. K?
...

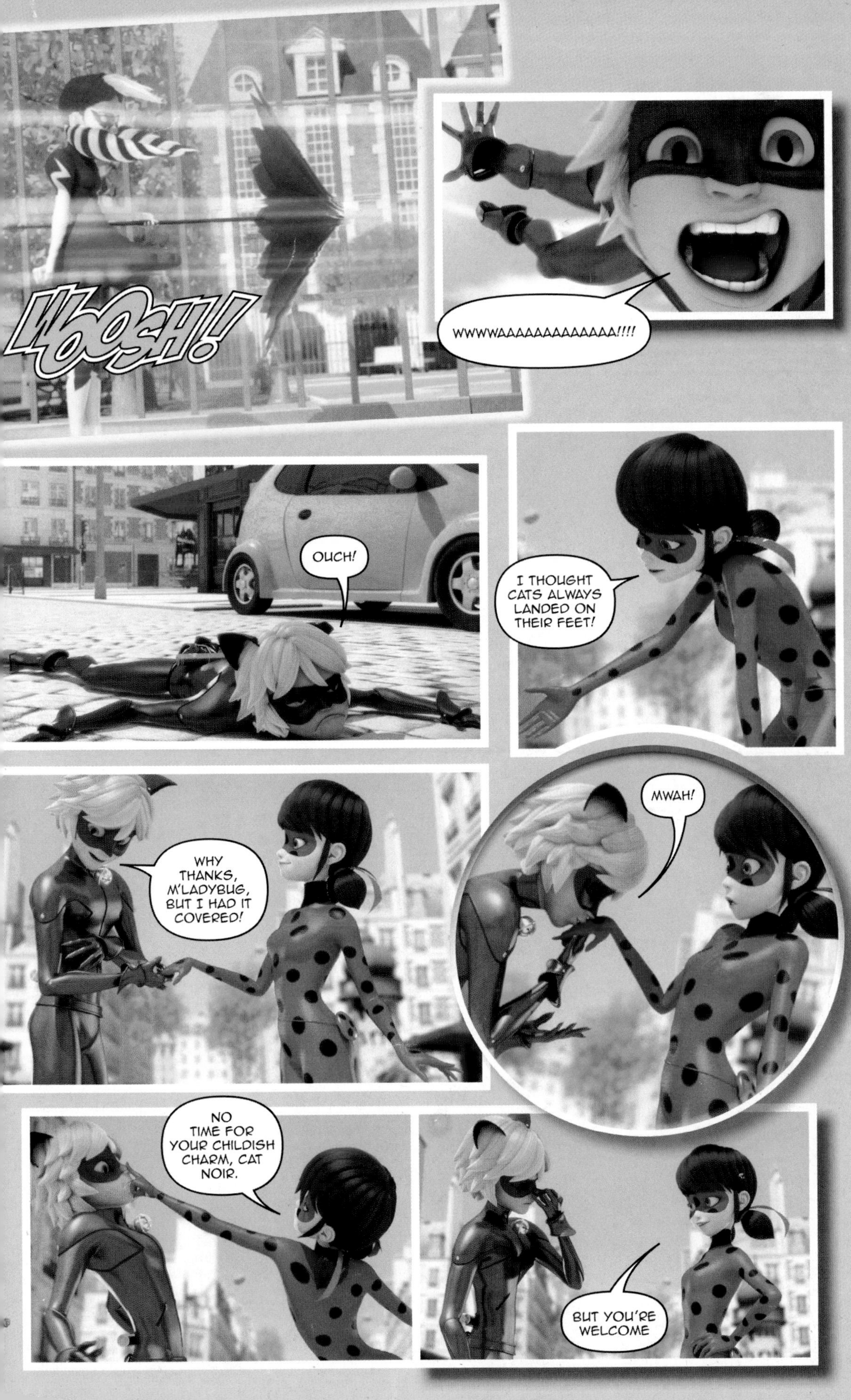
WOOSH!
WWWWAAAAAAAAAAAAAA!!!!
OUCH!
I THOUGHT CATS ALWAYS LANDED ON THEIR FEET!
WHY THANKS, M'LADYBUG, BUT I HAD IT COVERED!
MWAH!
NO TIME FOR YOUR CHILDISH CHARM, CAT NOIR.
BUT YOU'RE WELCOME

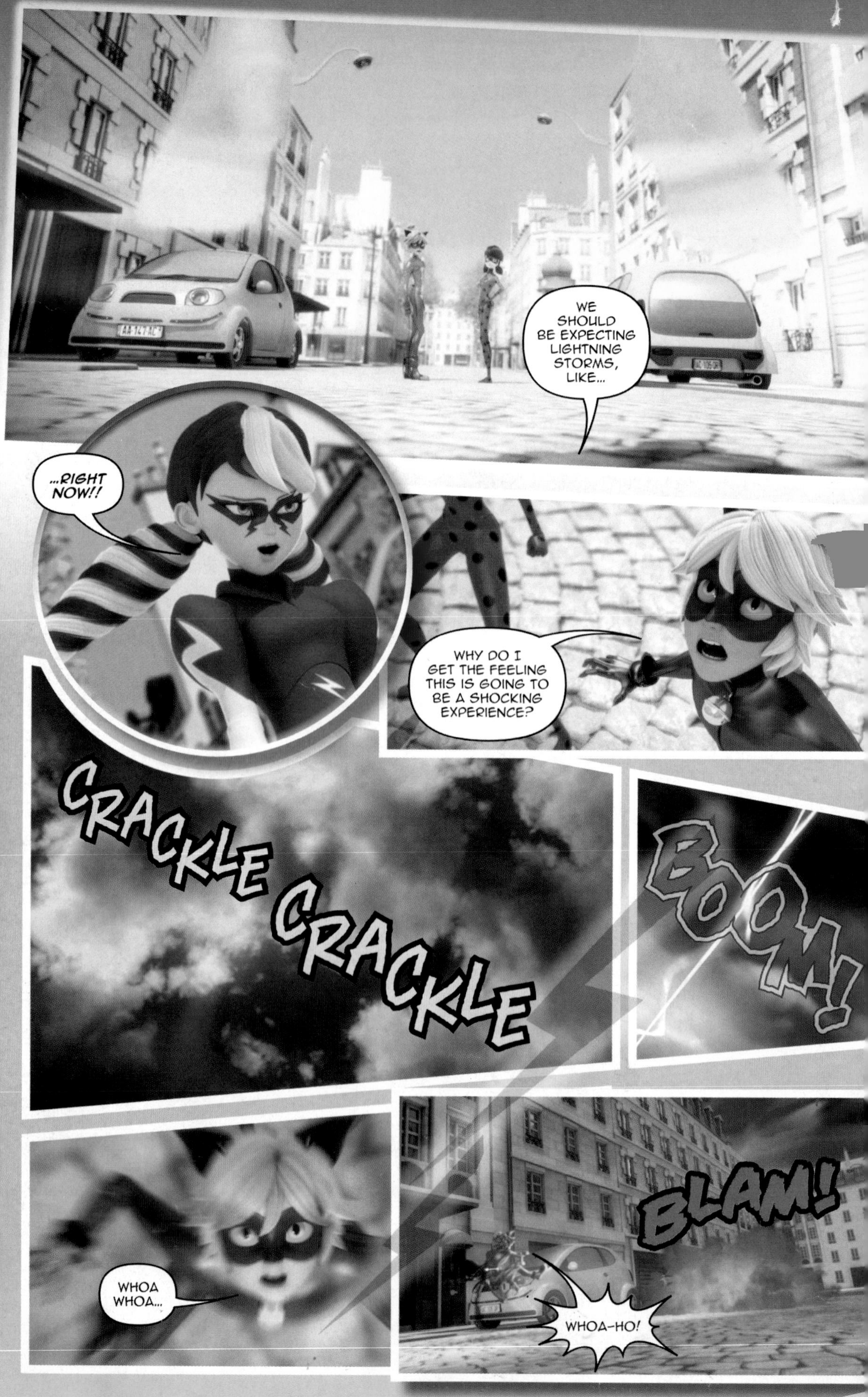
WE SHOULD BE EXPECTING LIGHTNING STORMS, LIKE...
...RIGHT NOW!!
WHY DO I GET THE FEELING THIS IS GOING TO BE A SHOCKING EXPERIENCE?
CRACKLE CRACKLE
BOOM!
WHOA WHOA...
BLAM!
WHOA-HO!

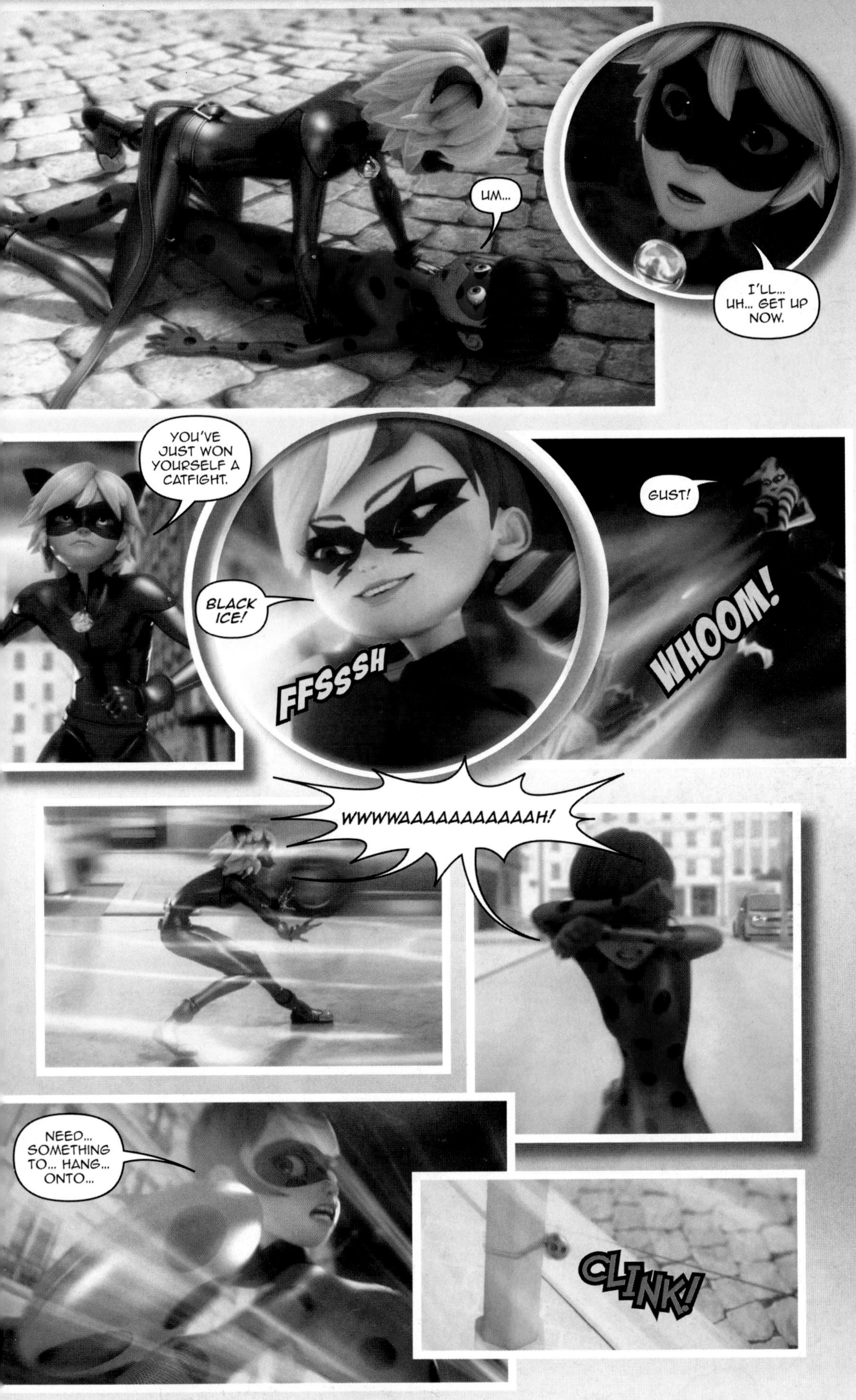
UM...
I'LL... UH... GET UP NOW.
YOU'VE JUST WON YOURSELF A CATFIGHT.
BLACK ICE!
FFSSSSH
GUST!
WHOOM!
WWWWAAAAAAAAAAAAH!
NEED... SOMETHING TO... HANG... ONTO...
CLINK!

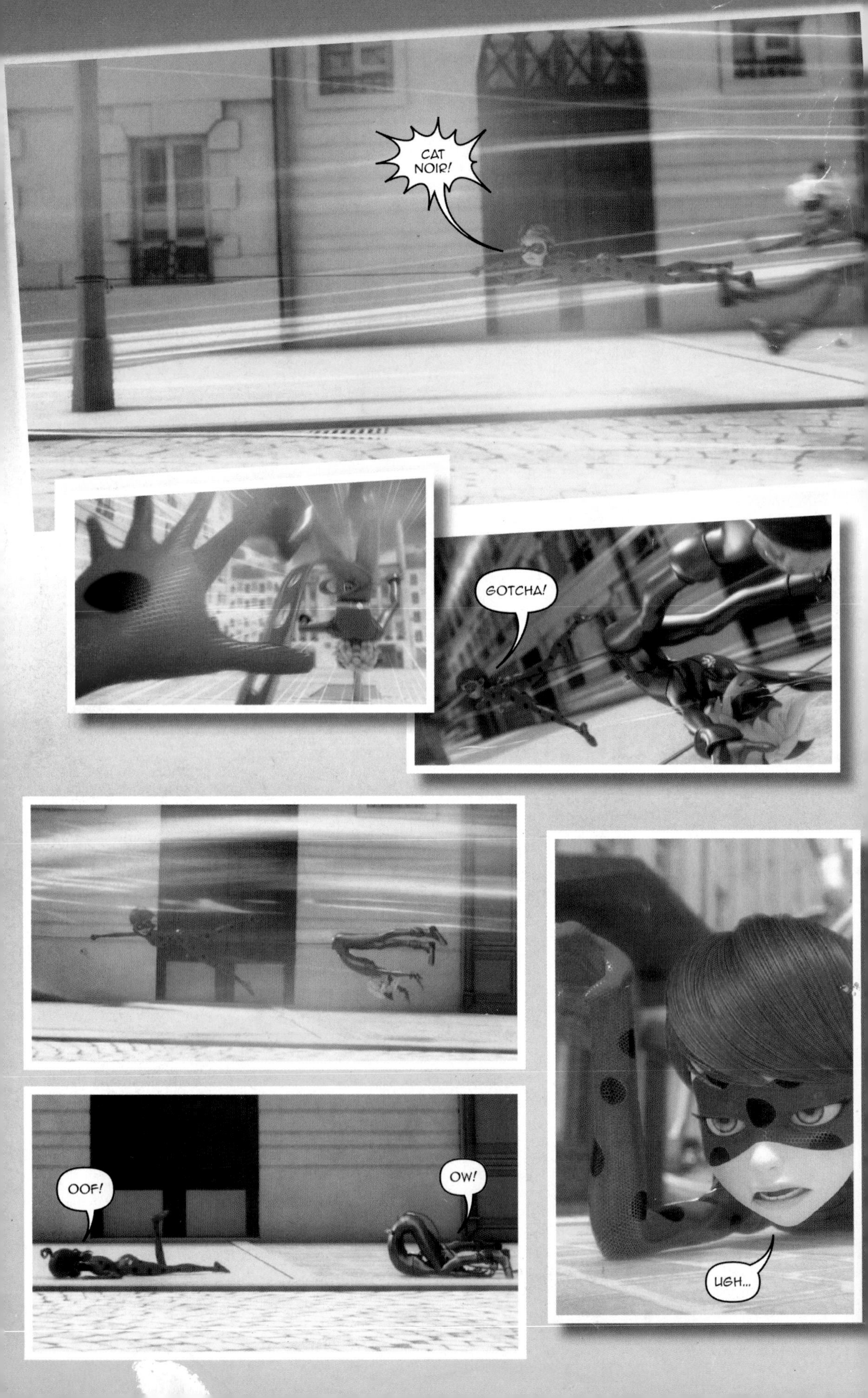
CAT NOIR!
GOTCHA!
OOF!
OW!
UGH...

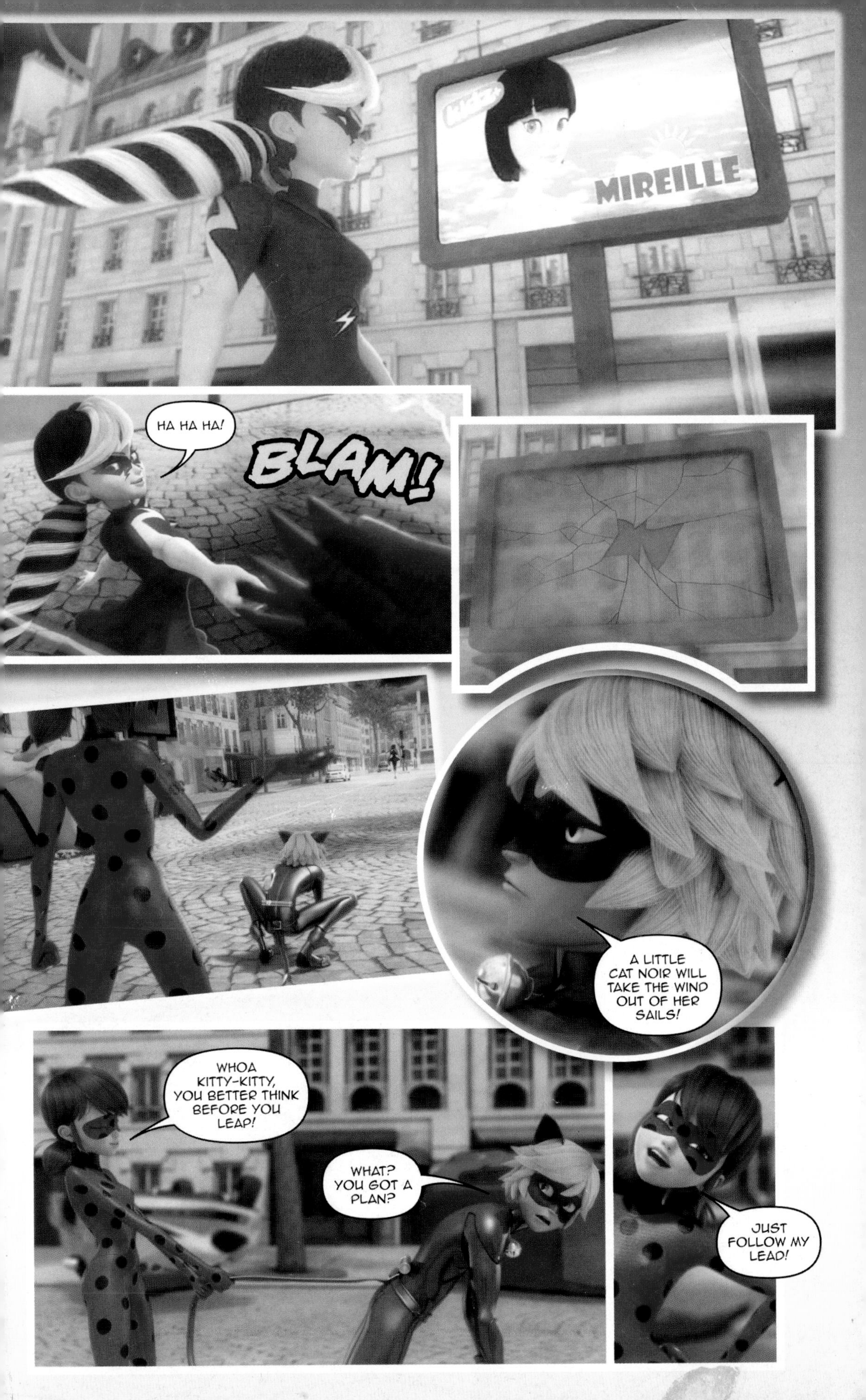
MIREILLE
HA HA HA!
BLAM!
A LITTLE CAT NOIR WILL TAKE THE WIND OUT OF HER SAILS!
WHOA KITTY-KITTY, YOU BETTER THINK BEFORE YOU LEAP!
WHAT? YOU GOT A PLAN?
JUST FOLLOW MY LEAD!

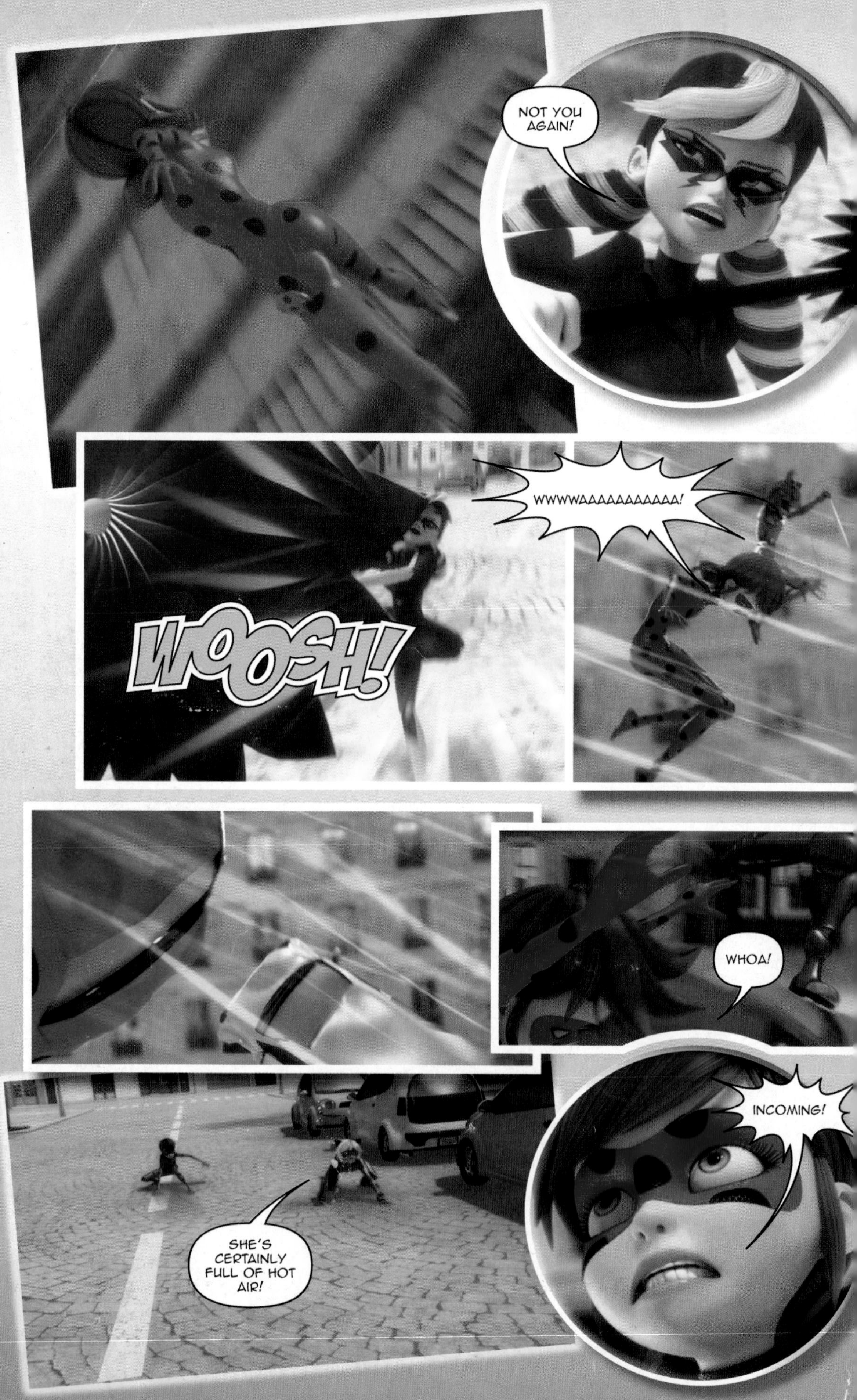
NOT YOU AGAIN!
WOOSH!
WWWWAAAAAAAAAAAA!
WHOA!
INCOMING!
SHE'S CERTAINLY FULL OF HOT AIR!

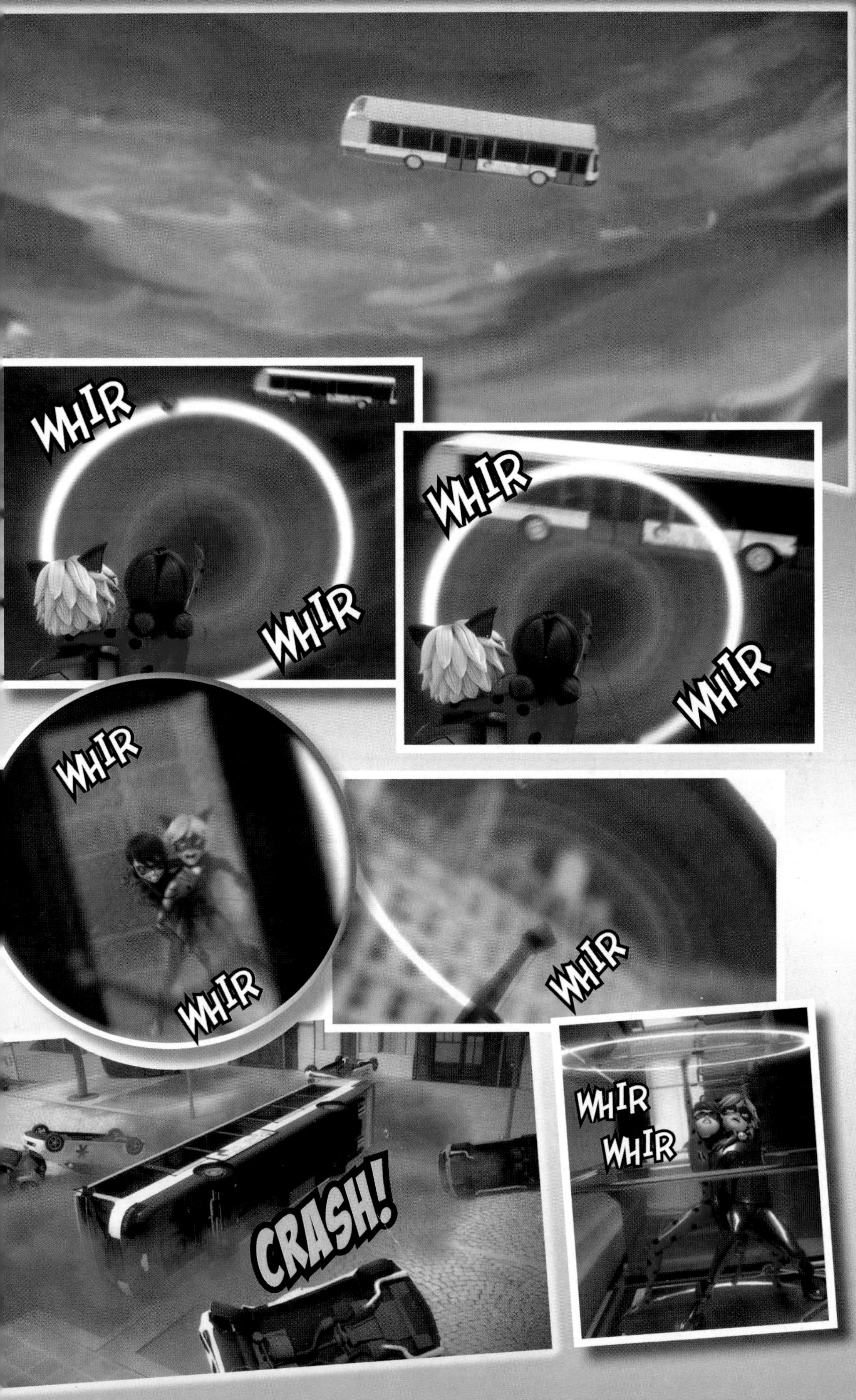
WHIR
WHIR
WHIR
WHIR
WHIR
WHIR
WHIR
CRASH!
WHIR
WHIR

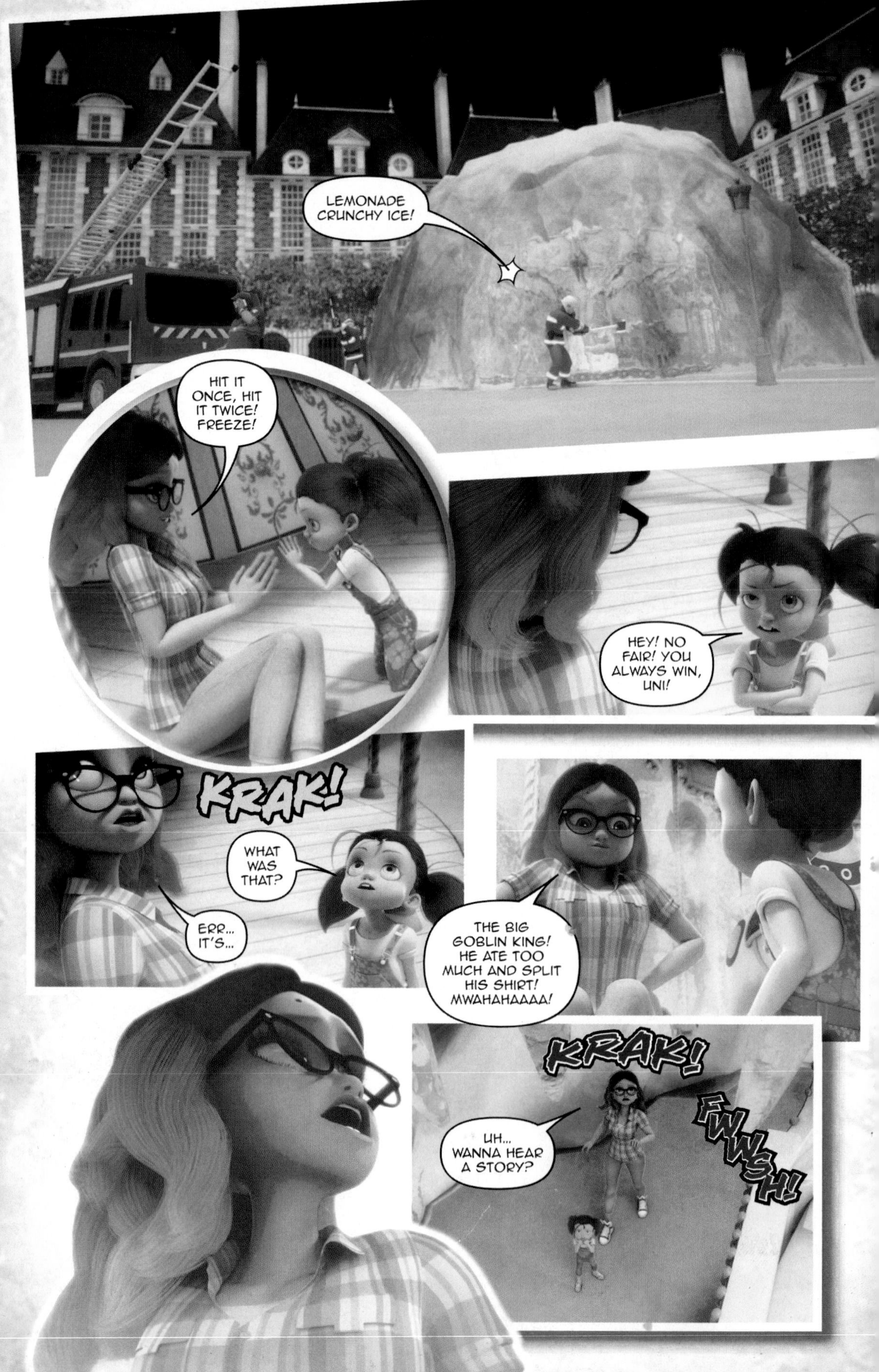
LEMONADE CRUNCHY ICE!
HIT IT ONCE, HIT IT TWICE! FREEZE!
HEY! NO FAIR! YOU ALWAYS WIN, UNI!
KRAK!
WHAT WAS THAT?
ERR... IT'S...
THE BIG GOBLIN KING! HE ATE TOO MUCH AND SPLIT HIS SHIRT! MWAHAHAAAA!
KRAK!
FWWSH!
UH... WANNA HEAR A STORY?

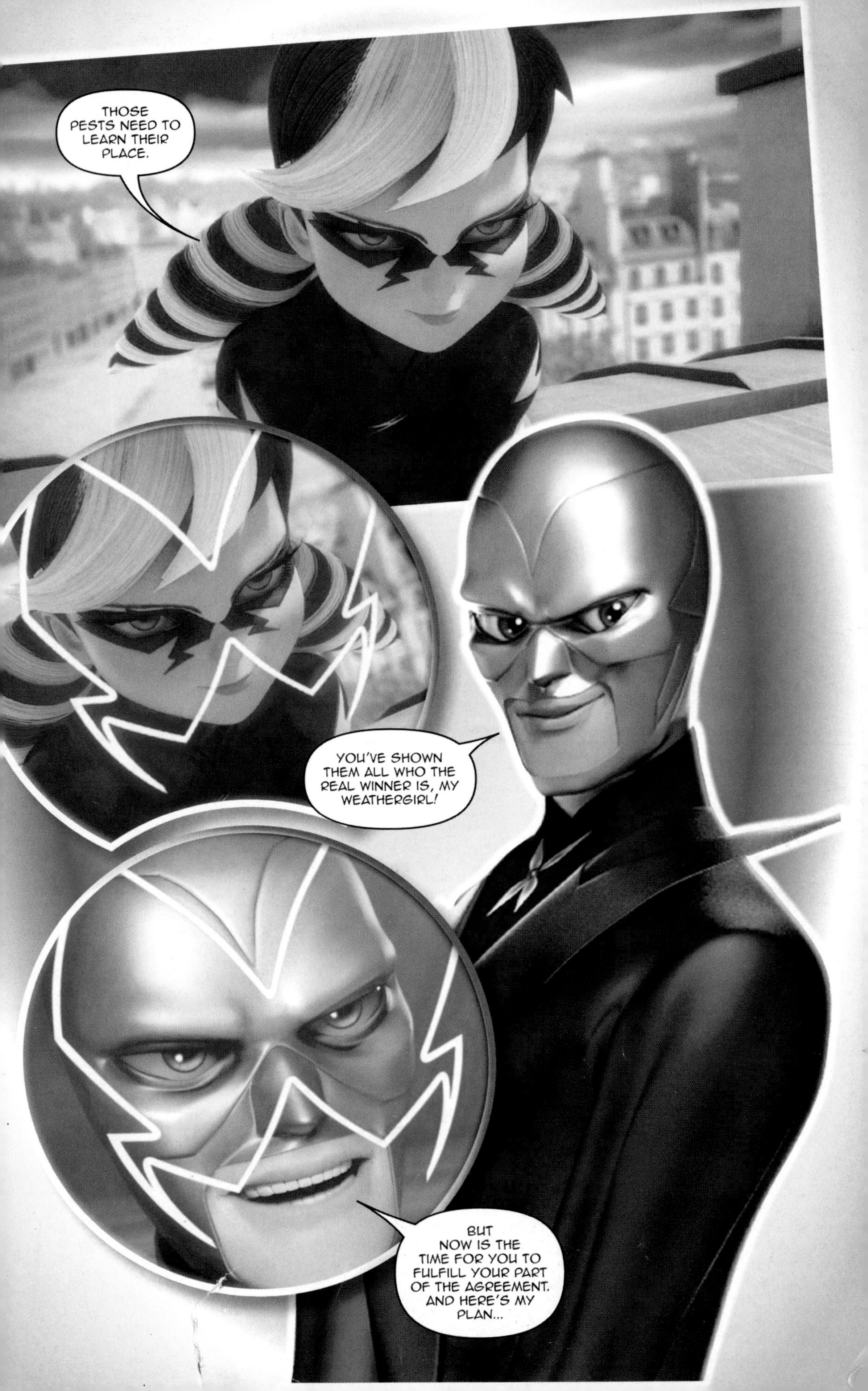
THOSE PESTS NEED TO LEARN THEIR PLACE.
YOU'VE SHOWN THEM ALL WHO THE REAL WINNER IS, MY WEATHERGIRL!
BUT NOW IS THE TIME FOR YOU TO FULFILL YOUR PART OF THE AGREEMENT. AND HERE'S MY PLAN...

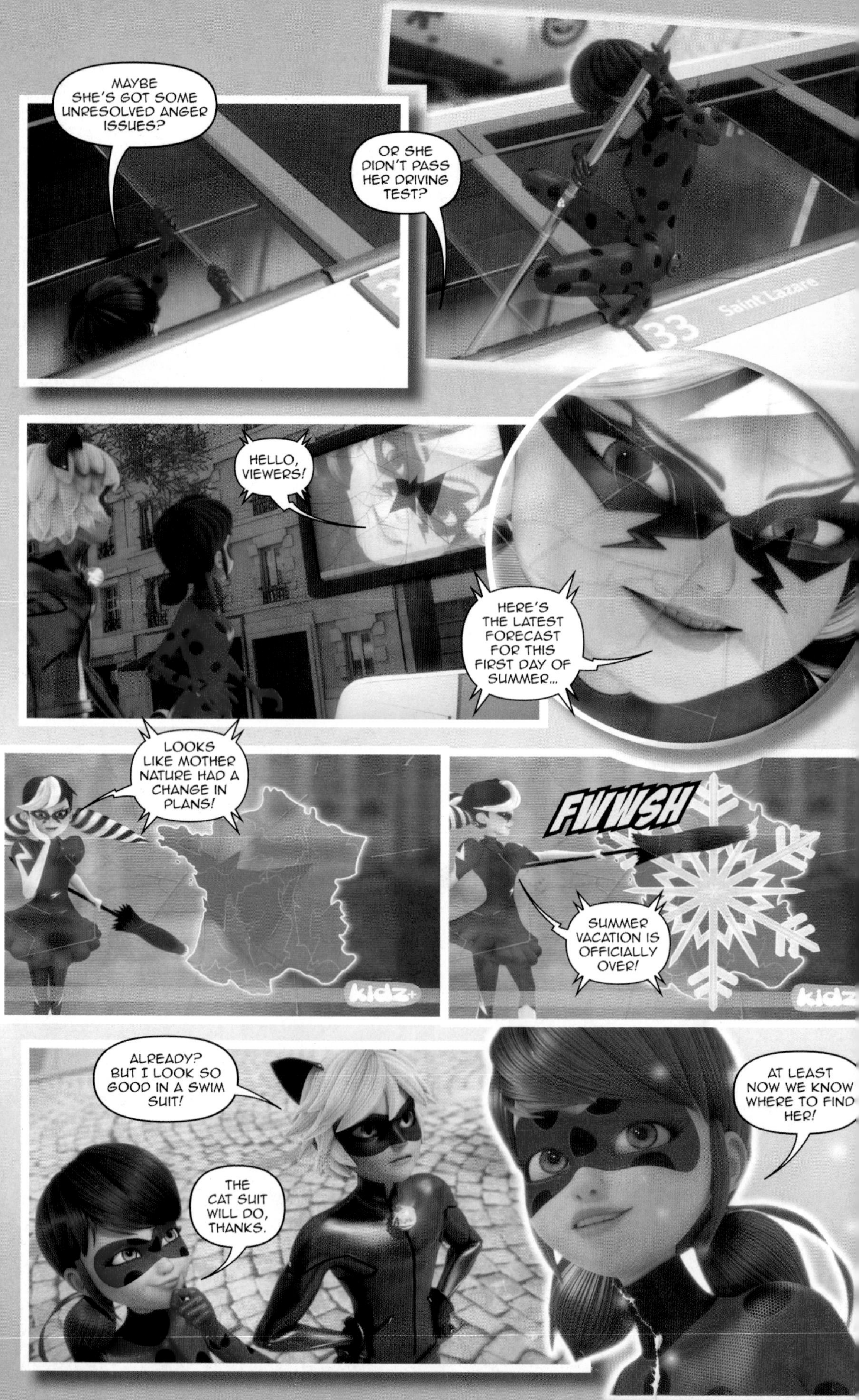
MAYBE SHE'S GOT SOME UNRESOLVED ANGER ISSUES?
OR SHE DIDN'T PASS HER DRIVING TEST?
33 Saint Lazare
HELLO, VIEWERS!
HERE'S THE LATEST FORECAST FOR THIS FIRST DAY OF SUMMER...
LOOKS LIKE MOTHER NATURE HAD A CHANGE IN PLANS!
FWWSH
SUMMER VACATION IS OFFICIALLY OVER!
ALREADY? BUT I LOOK SO GOOD IN A SWIM SUIT!
THE CAT SUIT WILL DO, THANKS.
AT LEAST NOW WE KNOW WHERE TO FIND HER!

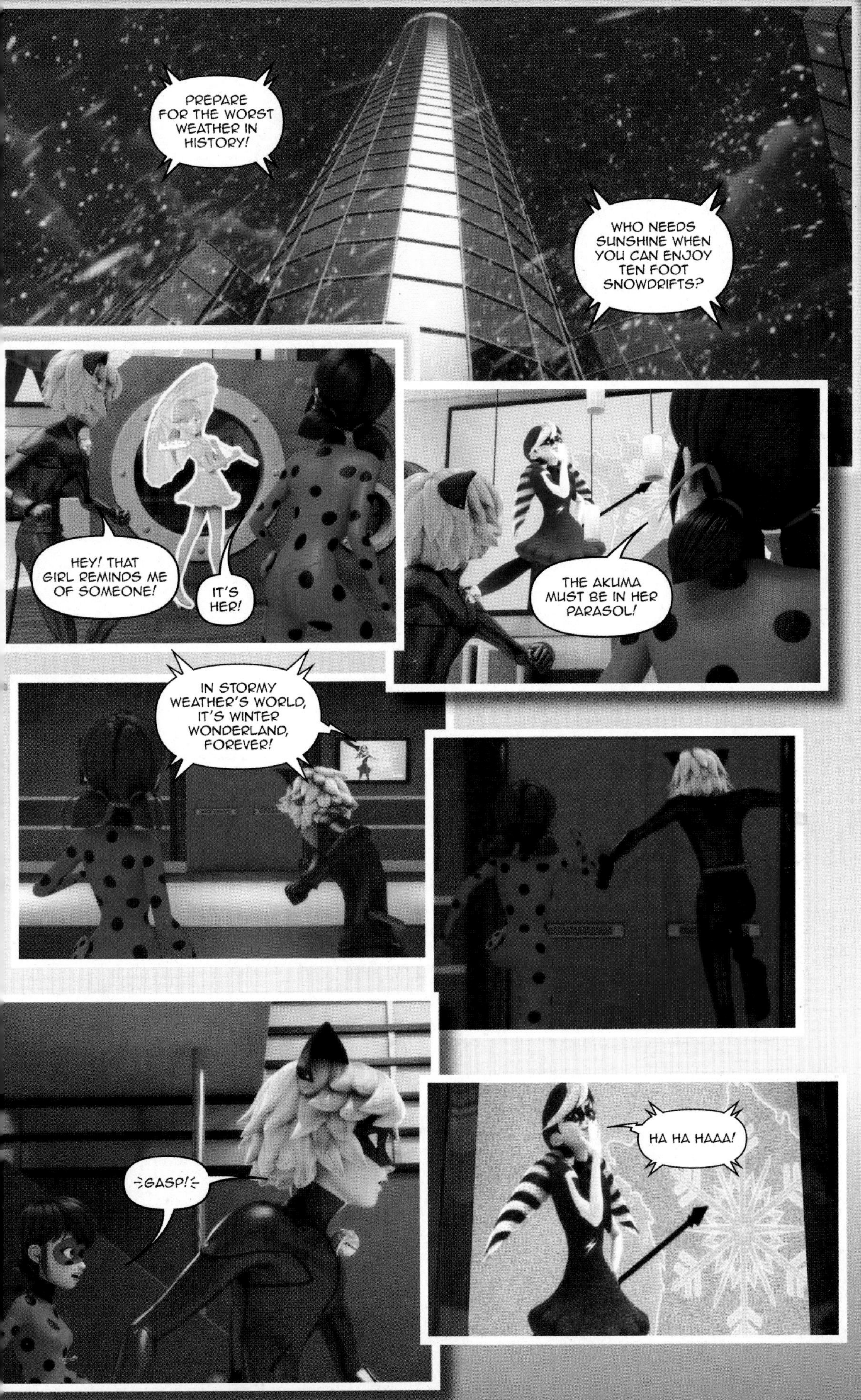
PREPARE FOR THE WORST WEATHER IN HISTORY!
WHO NEEDS SUNSHINE WHEN YOU CAN ENJOY TEN FOOT SNOWDRIFTS?
HEY! THAT GIRL REMINDS ME OF SOMEONE!
IT'S HER!
THE AKUMA MUST BE IN HER PARASOL!
IN STORMY WEATHER'S WORLD, IT'S WINTER WONDERLAND, FOREVER!
GASP!
HA HA HAAA!

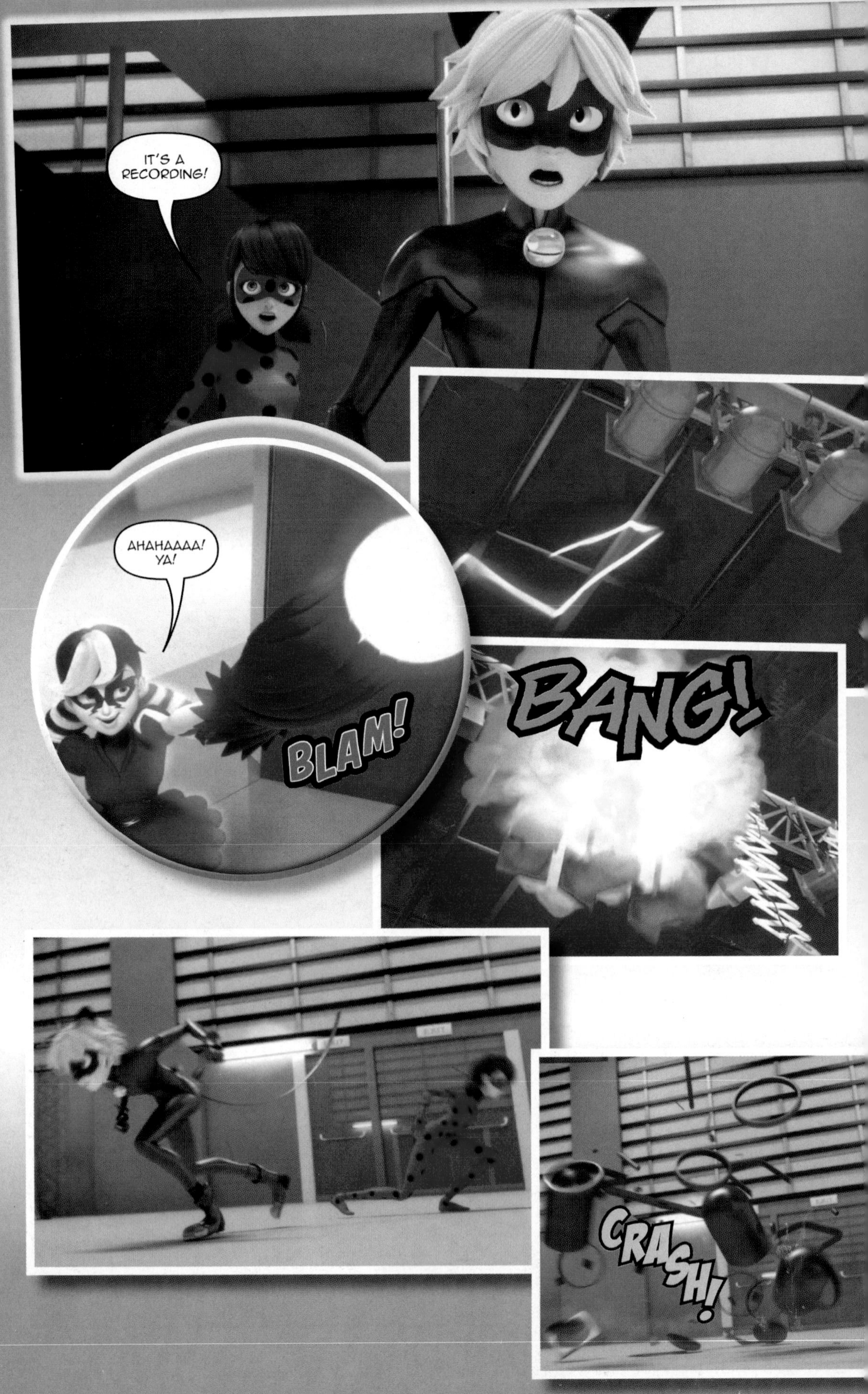
IT'S A RECORDING!
AHAHAAAA! YA!
BLAM!
BANG!
CRASH!

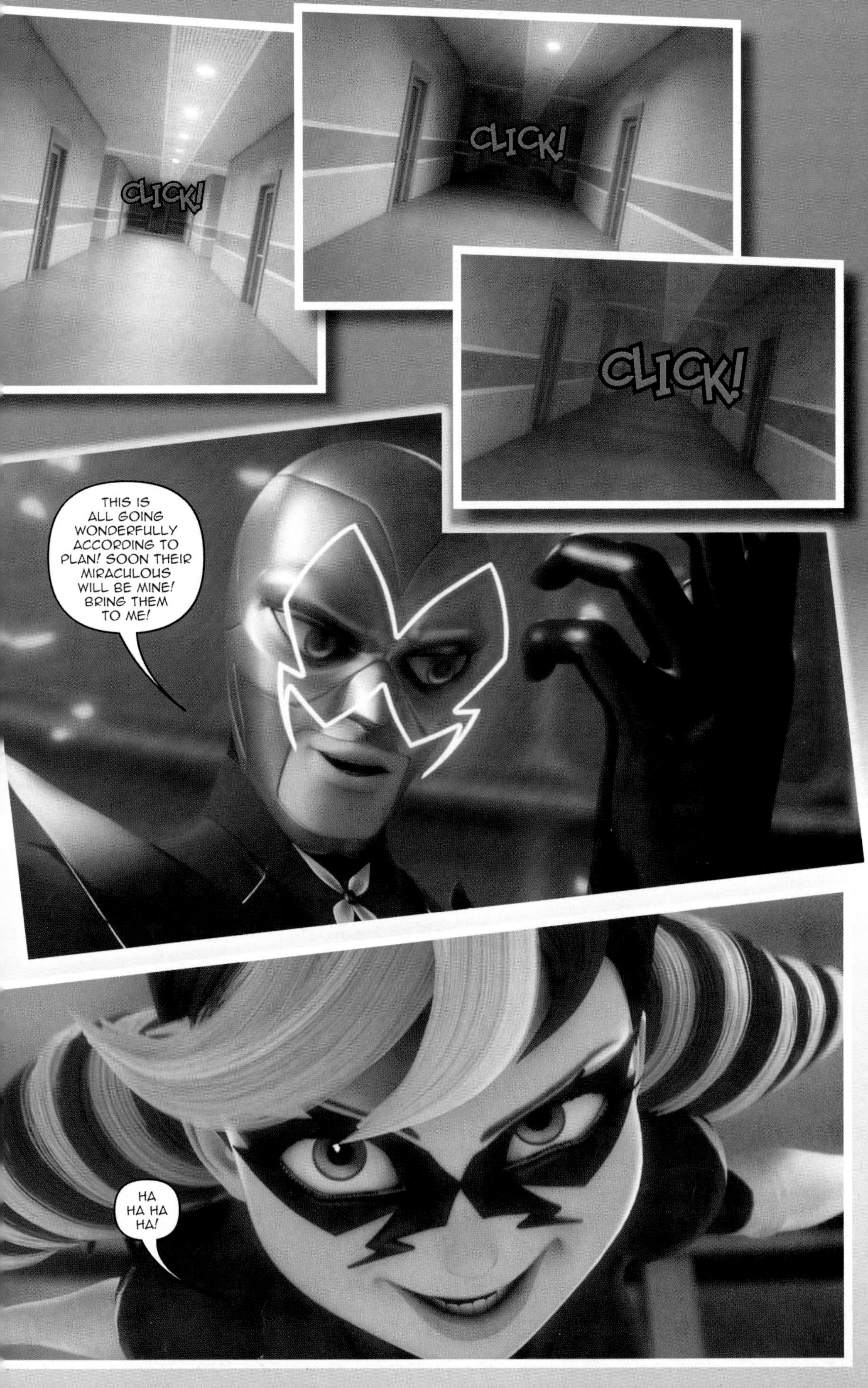
CLICK!
CLICK!
CLICK!
THIS IS ALL GOING WONDERFULLY ACCORDING TO PLAN! SOON THEIR MIRACULOUS WILL BE MINE! BRING THEM TO ME!
HA HA HA HA!

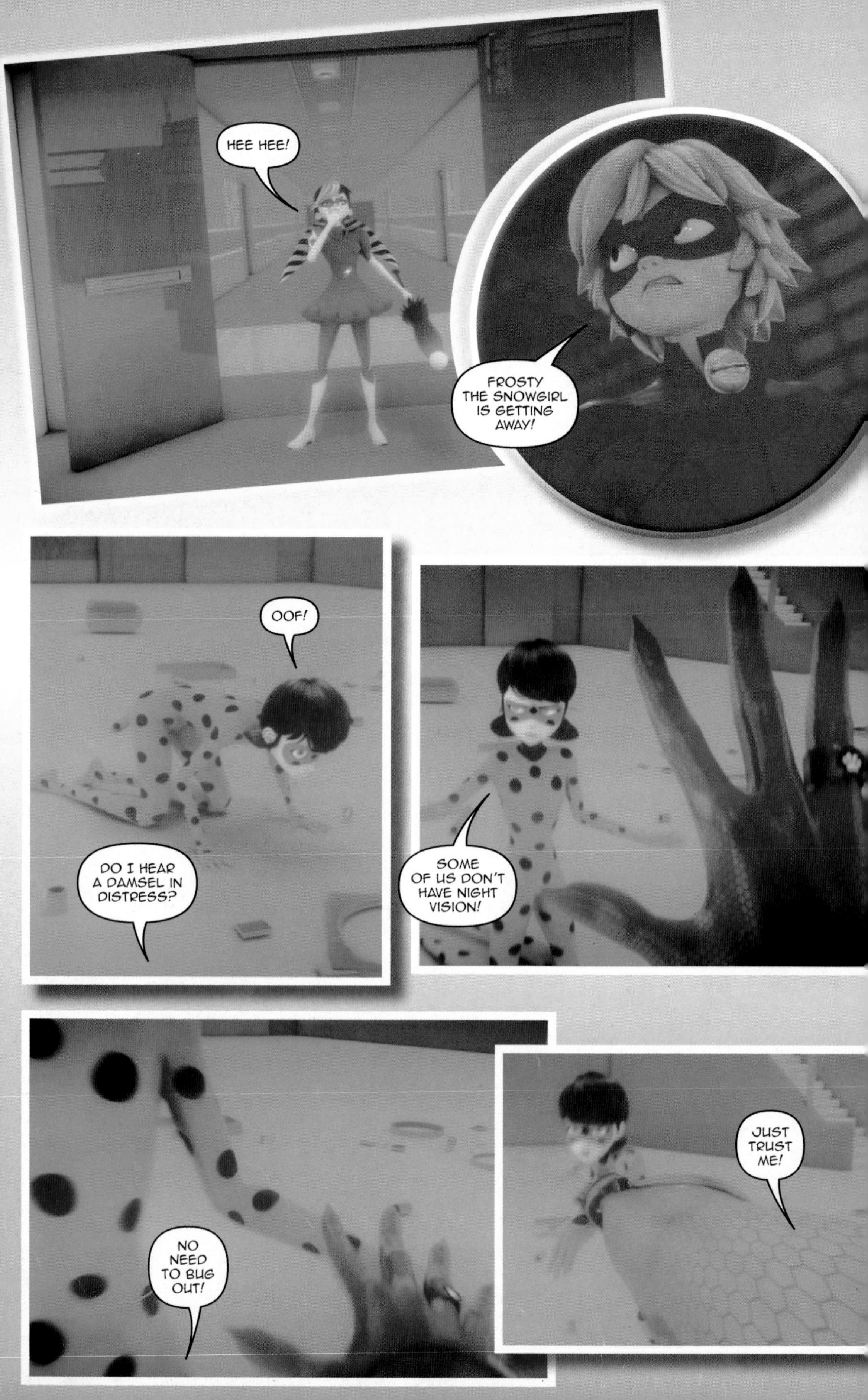
HEE HEE!
FROSTY THE SNOWGIRL IS GETTING AWAY!
OOF!
DO I HEAR A DAMSEL IN DISTRESS?
SOME OF US DON'T HAVE NIGHT VISION!
NO NEED TO BUG OUT!
JUST TRUST ME!

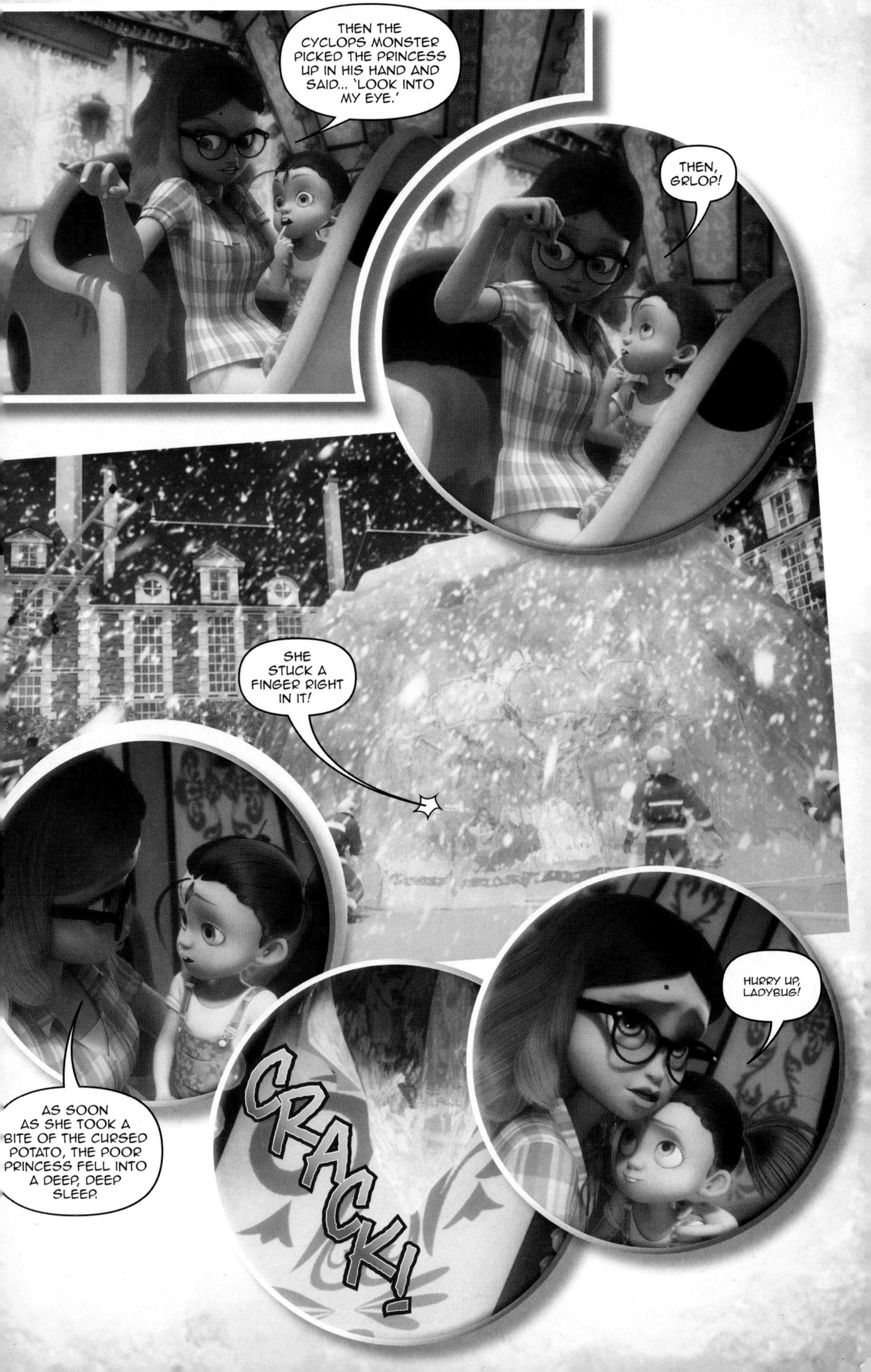
THEN THE CYCLOPS MONSTER PICKED THE PRINCESS UP IN HIS HAND AND SAID... 'LOOK INTO MY EYE.'
THEN, GRLOP!
SHE STUCK A FINGER RIGHT IN IT!
AS SOON AS SHE TOOK A BITE OF THE CURSED POTATO, THE POOR PRINCESS FELL INTO A DEEP, DEEP SLEEP.
CRACK!
HURRY UP, LADYBUG!

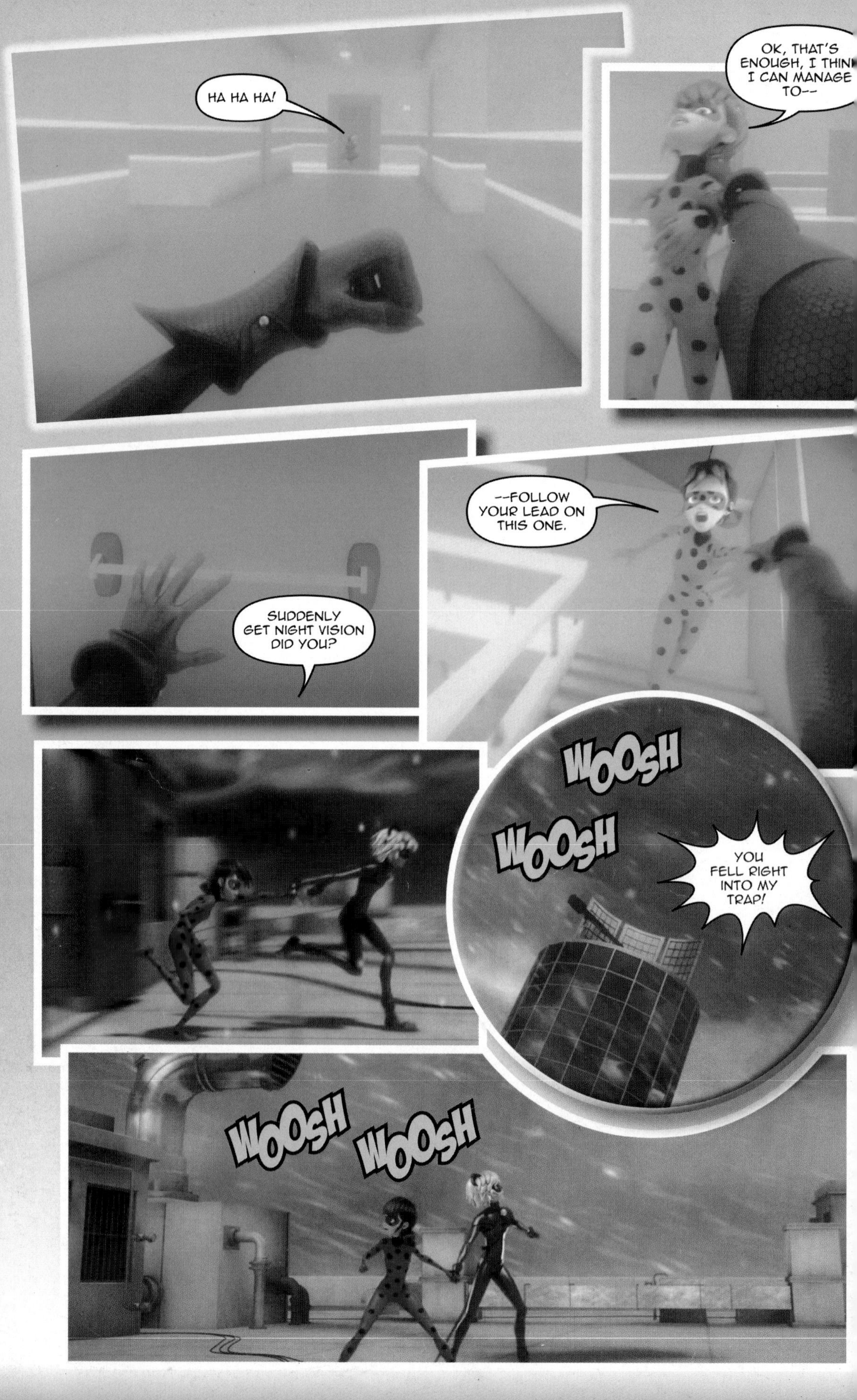
HA HA HA!
OK, THAT'S ENOUGH, I THIN I CAN MANAGE TO--
SUDDENLY GET NIGHT VISION DID YOU?
--FOLLOW YOUR LEAD ON THIS ONE.
WOOSH
WOOSH
YOU FELL RIGHT INTO MY TRAP!
WOOSH
WOOSH

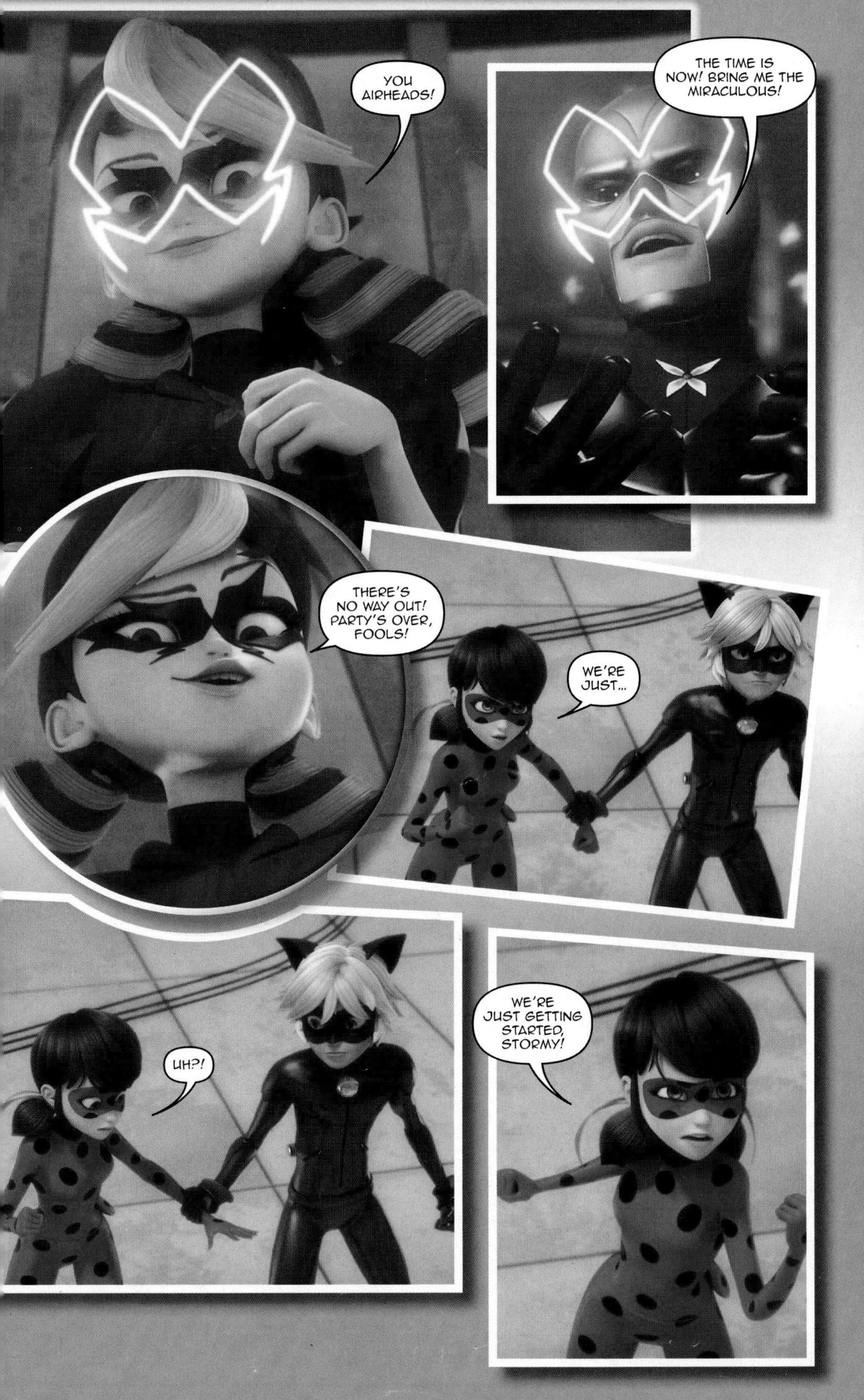
YOU AIRHEADS!
THE TIME IS NOW! BRING ME THE MIRACULOUS!
THERE'S NO WAY OUT! PARTY'S OVER, FOOLS!
WE'RE JUST...
UH?!
WE'RE JUST GETTING STARTED, STORMY!

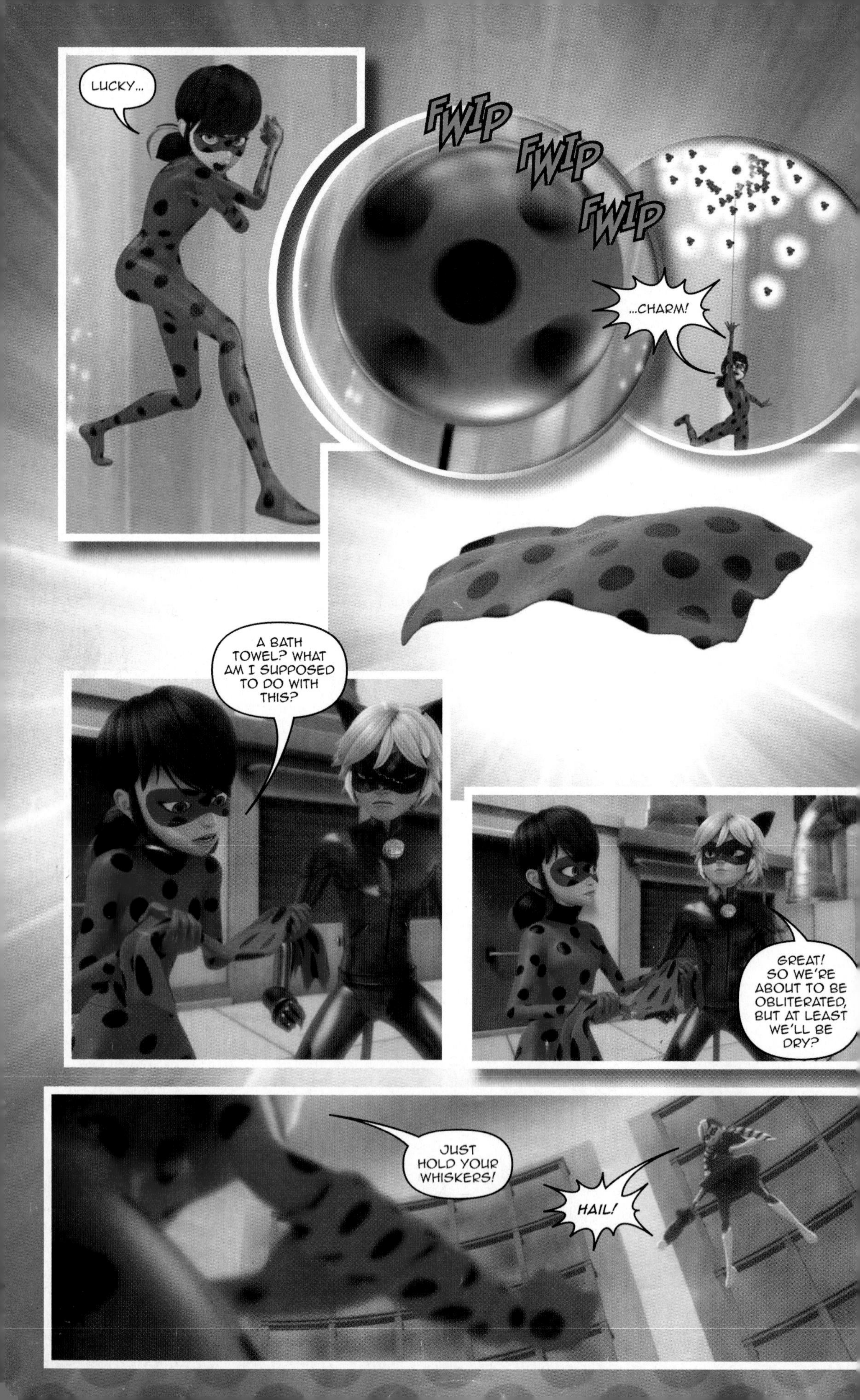
LUCKY...
FWIP
FWIP
FWIP
...CHARM!
A BATH TOWEL? WHAT AM I SUPPOSED TO DO WITH THIS?
GREAT! SO WE'RE ABOUT TO BE OBLITERATED, BUT AT LEAST WE'LL BE DRY?
JUST HOLD YOUR WHISKERS!
HAIL!

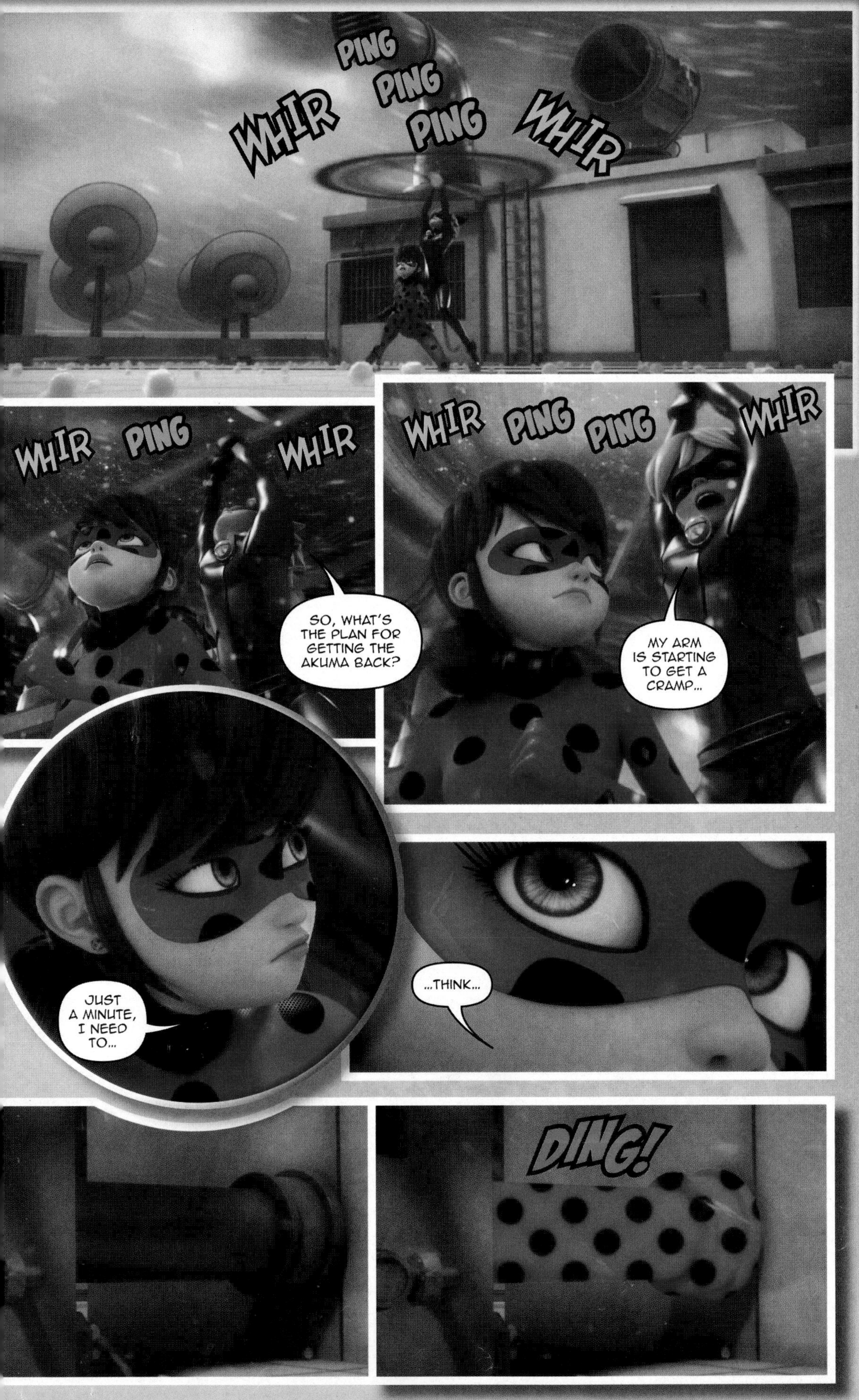
PING
WHIR
PING
PING
WHIR
WHIR
PING
WHIR
SO, WHAT'S THE PLAN FOR GETTING THE AKUMA BACK?
WHIR
PING
PING
WHIR
MY ARM IS STARTING TO GET A CRAMP...
JUST A MINUTE, I NEED TO...
...THINK...
DING!

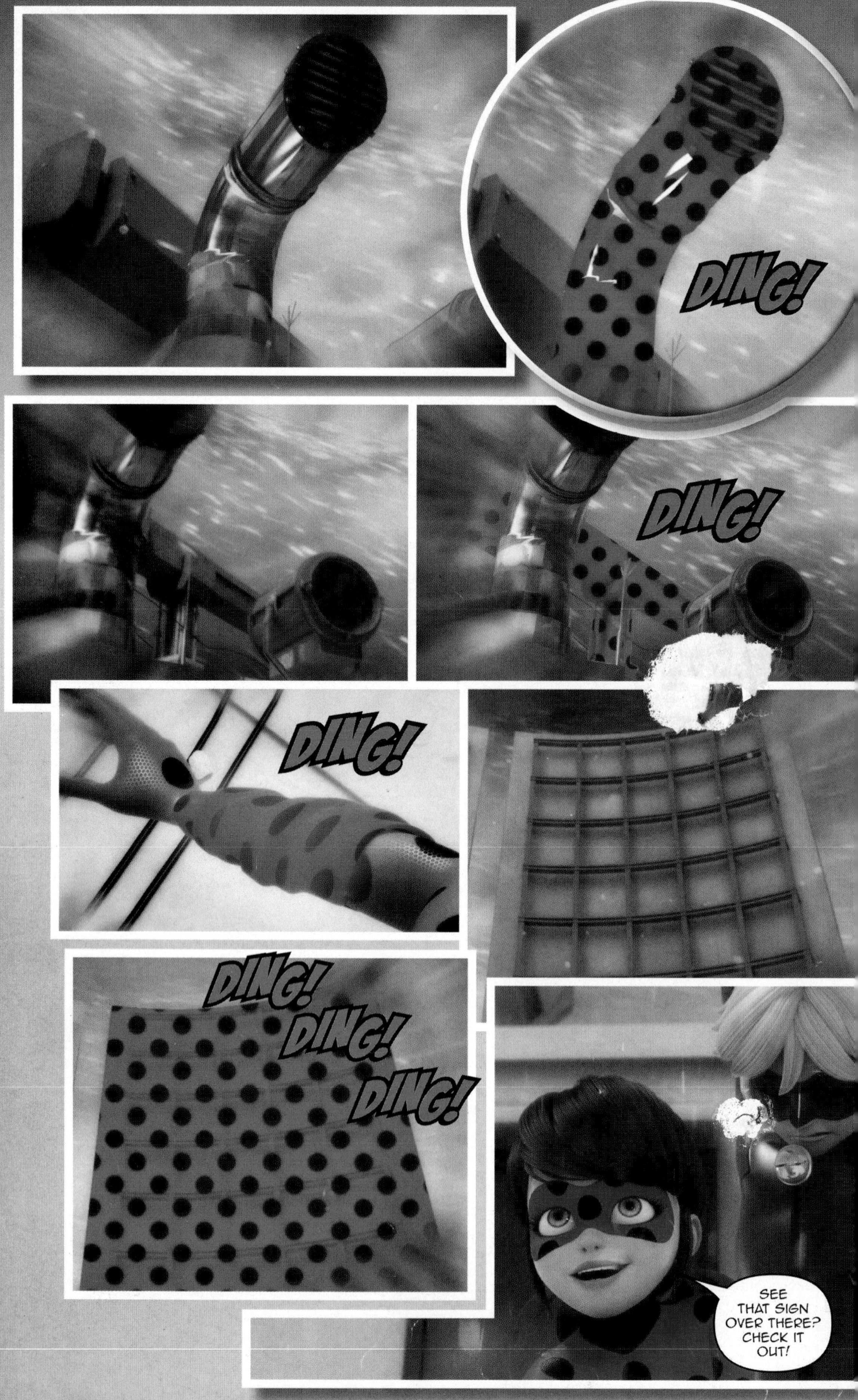
DING!
DING!
DING!
DING!
DING!
DING!
SEE THAT SIGN OVER THERE? CHECK IT OUT!

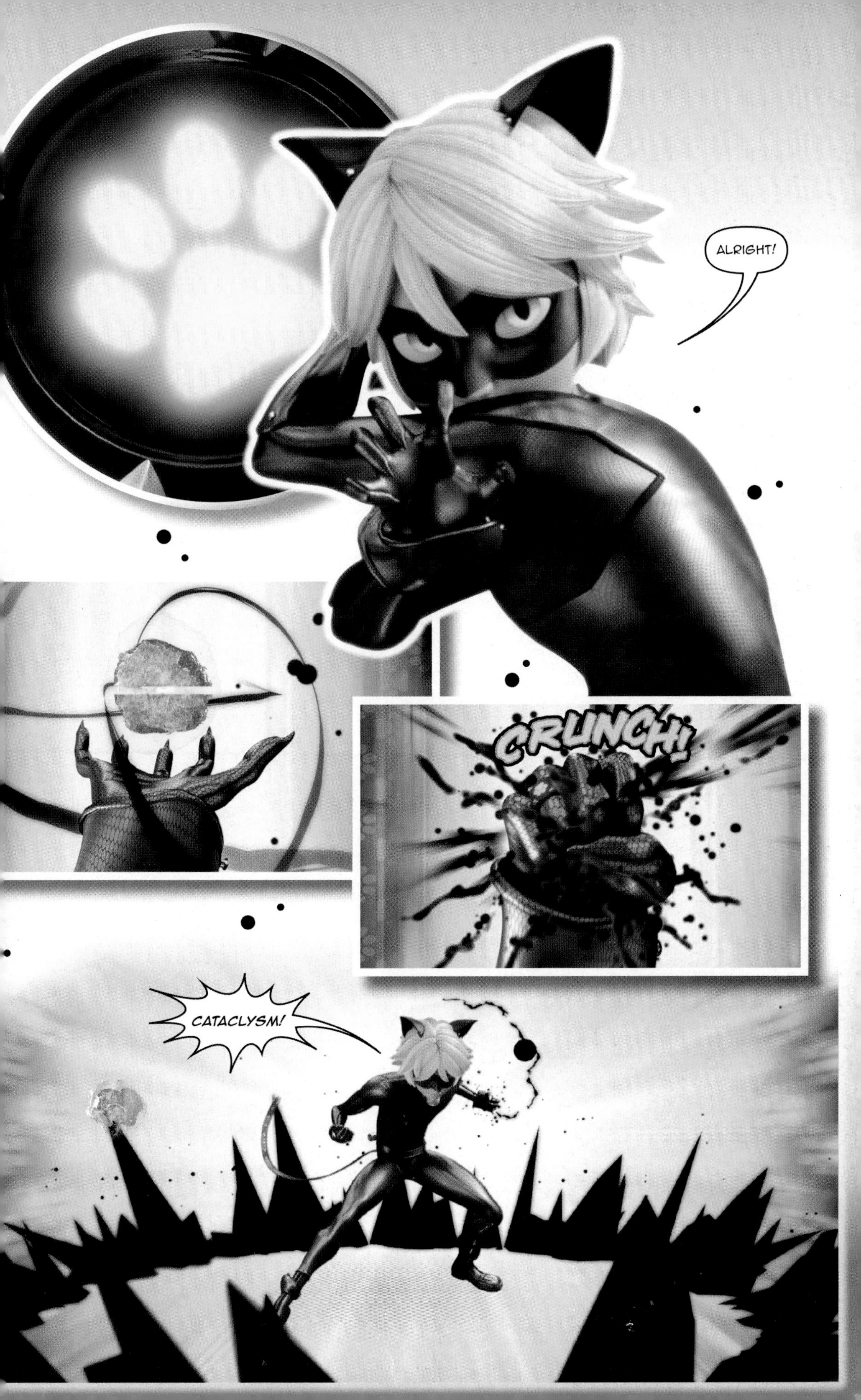
ALRIGHT!
CRUNCH!
CATACLYSM!

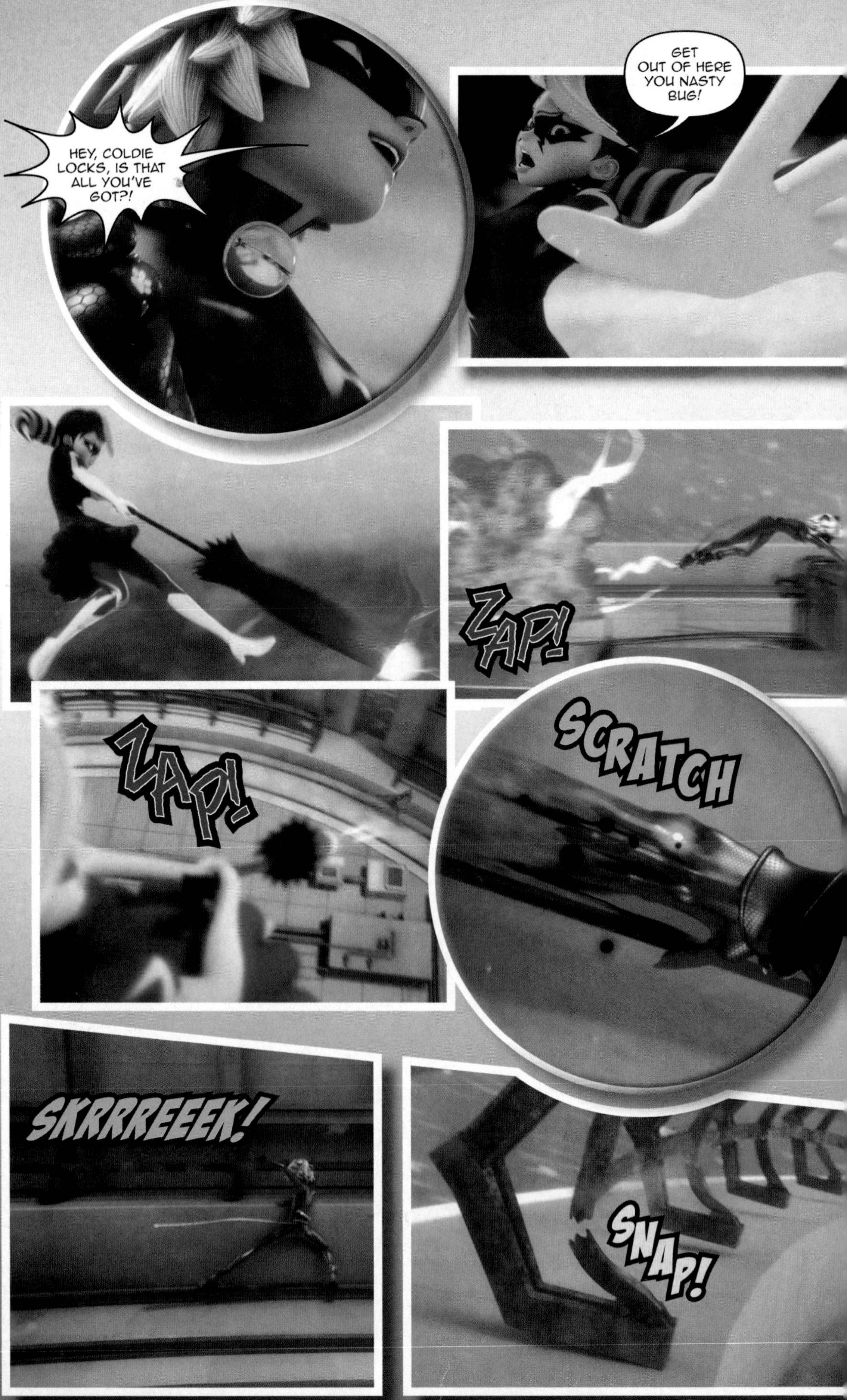
HEY, COLDIE LOCKS, IS THAT ALL YOU'VE GOT?!
GET OUT OF HERE YOU NASTY BUG!
ZAP!
ZAP!
SCRATCH
SKRRREEEK!
SNAP!

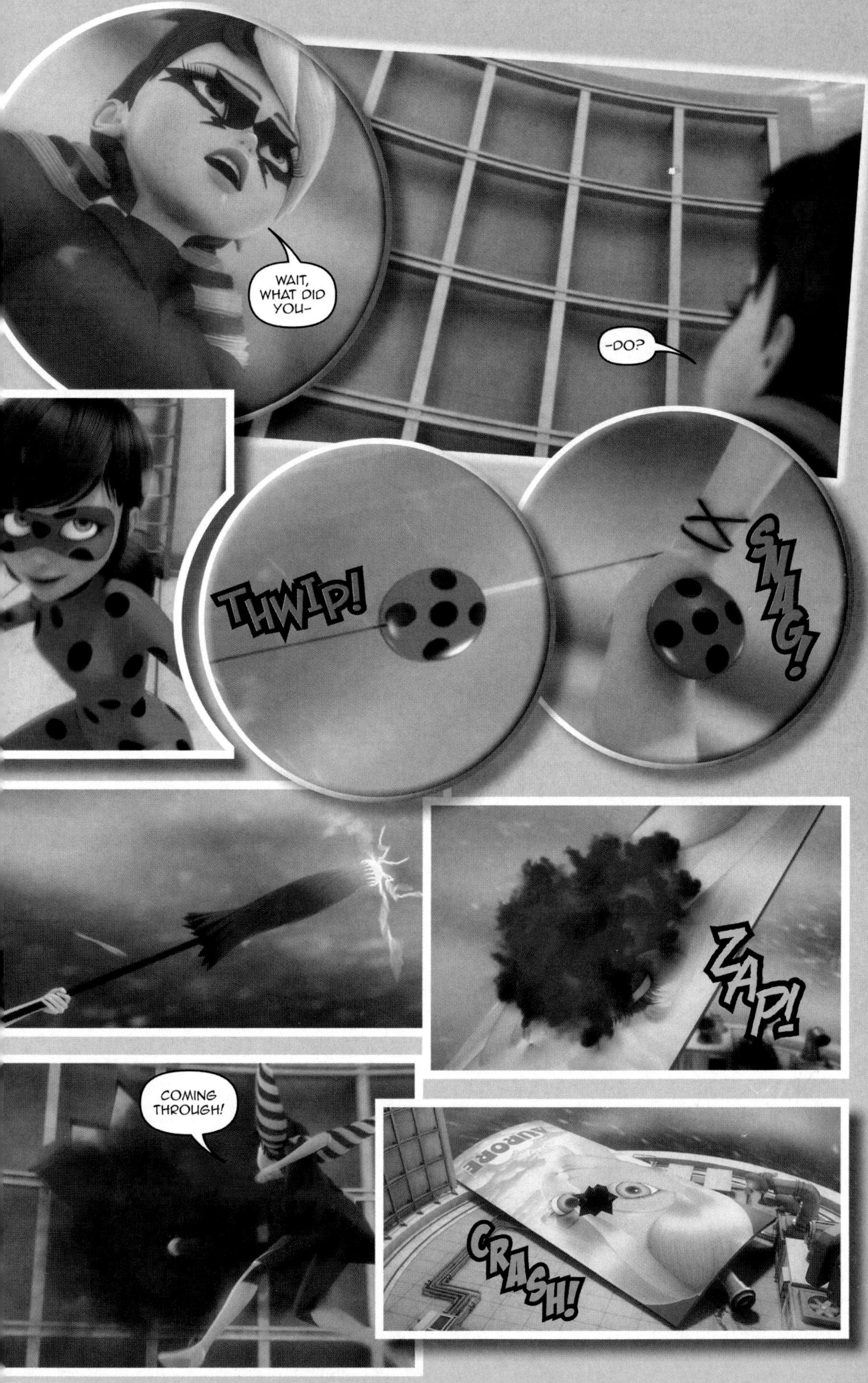
WAIT, WHAT DID YOU-
-DO?
THWIP!
SNAG!
ZAP!
COMING THROUGH!
AURORE
CRASH!

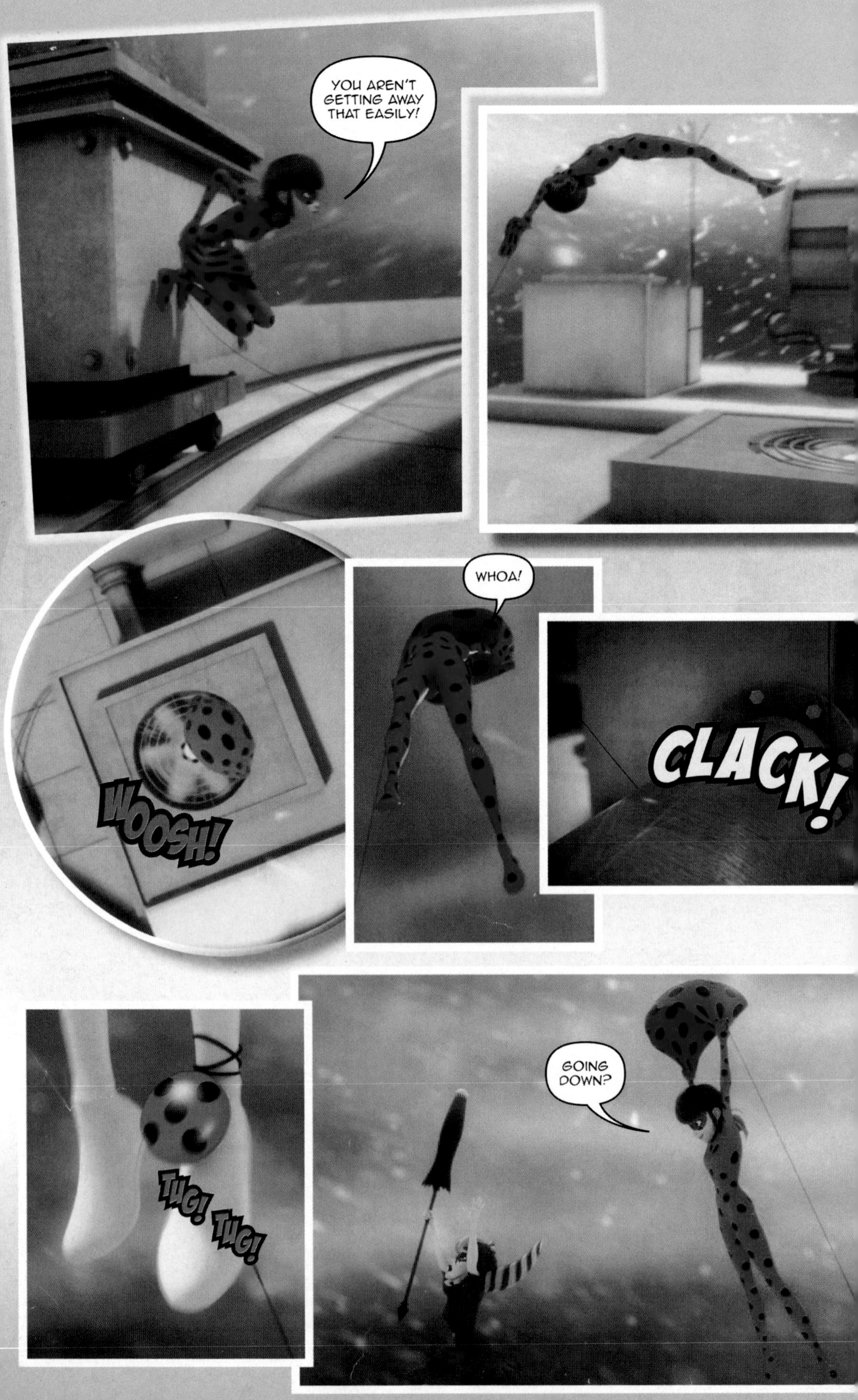
YOU AREN'T GETTING AWAY THAT EASILY!
WOOSH!
WHOA!
CLACK!
TUG! TUG!
GOING DOWN?

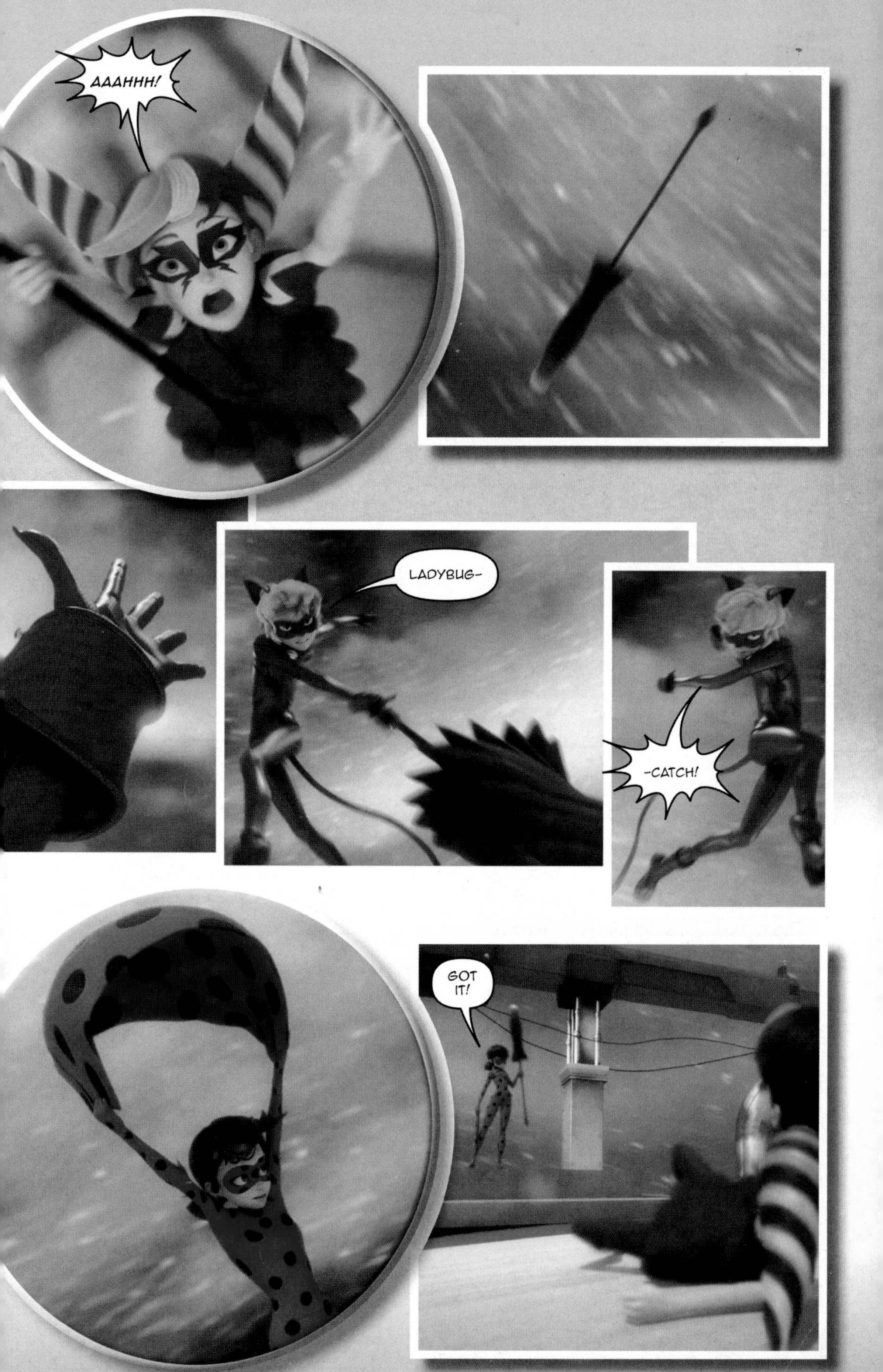
AAAHHH!
LADYBUG-
-CATCH!
GOT IT!

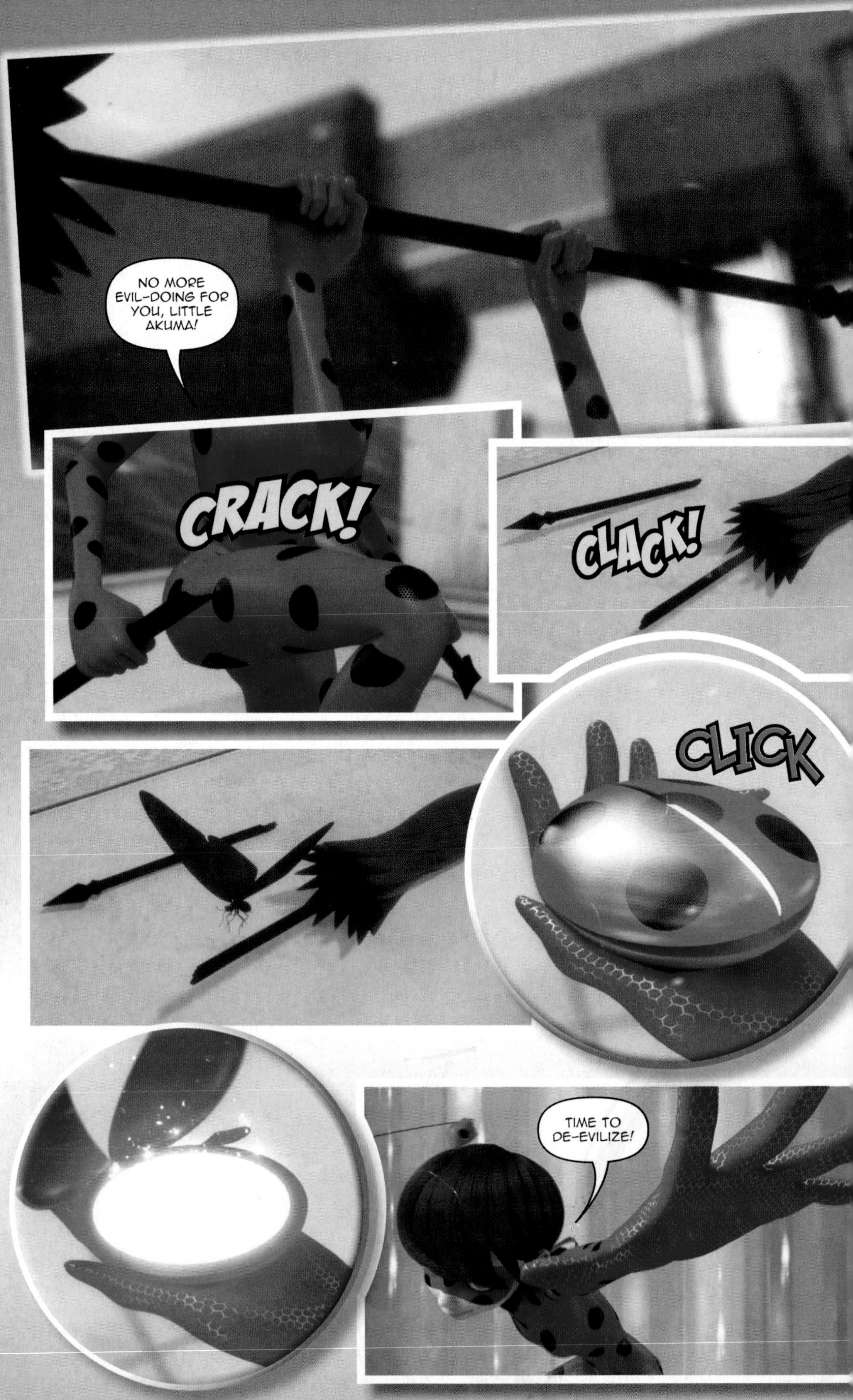
NO MORE EVIL-DOING FOR YOU, LITTLE AKUMA!
CRACK!
CLACK!
CLICK
TIME TO DE-EVILIZE!

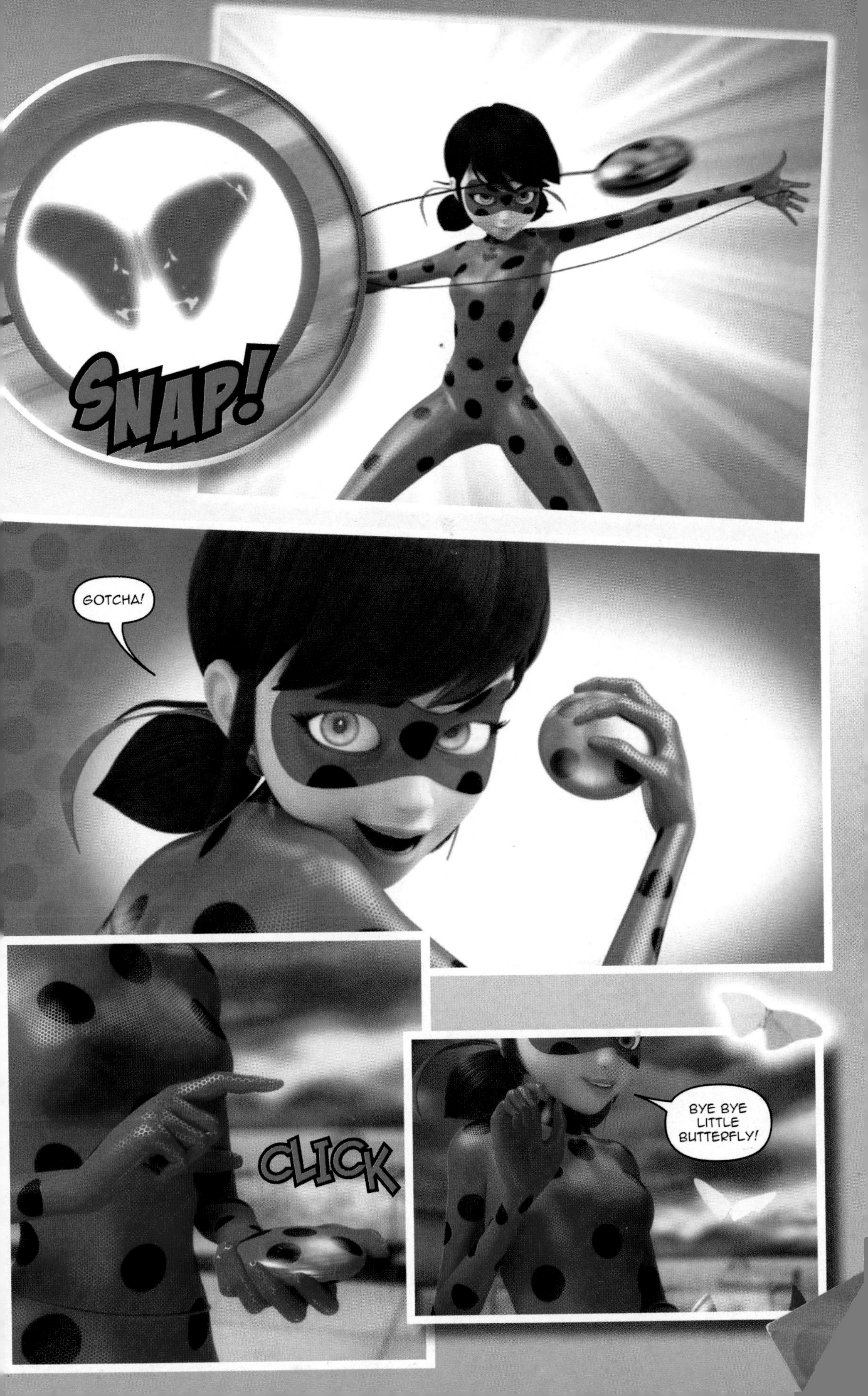
SNAP!
GOTCHA!
CLICK
BYE BYE
LITTLE
BUTTERFLY!

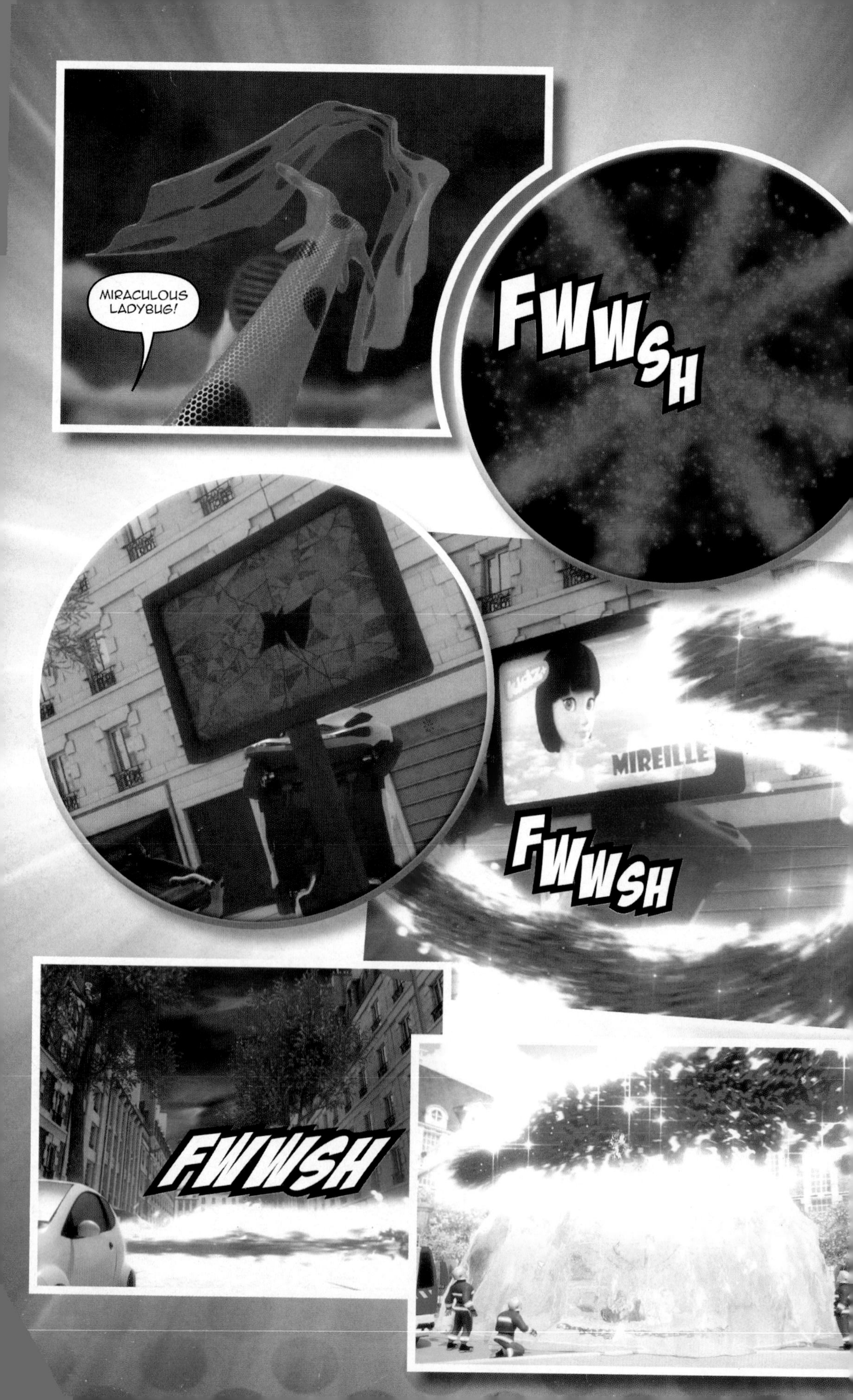
MIRACULOUS LADYBUG!
FWWSH
MIREILLE
FWWSH
FWWSH

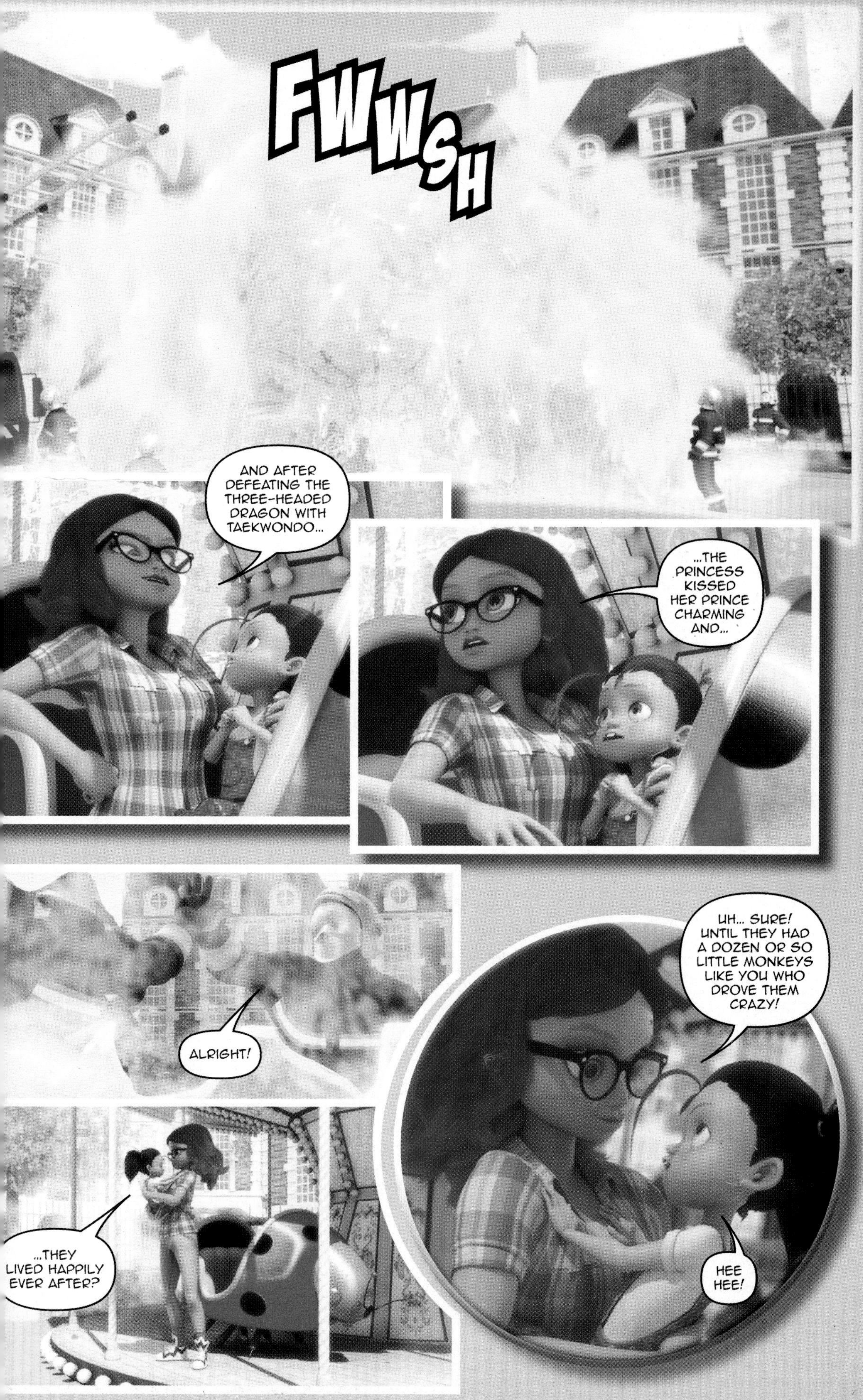
FWWSH
AND AFTER DEFEATING THE THREE-HEADED DRAGON WITH TAEKWONDO...
...THE PRINCESS KISSED HER PRINCE CHARMING AND...
ALRIGHT!
...THEY LIVED HAPPILY EVER AFTER?
UH... SURE! UNTIL THEY HAD A DOZEN OR SO LITTLE MONKEYS LIKE YOU WHO DROVE THEM CRAZY!
HEE HEE!

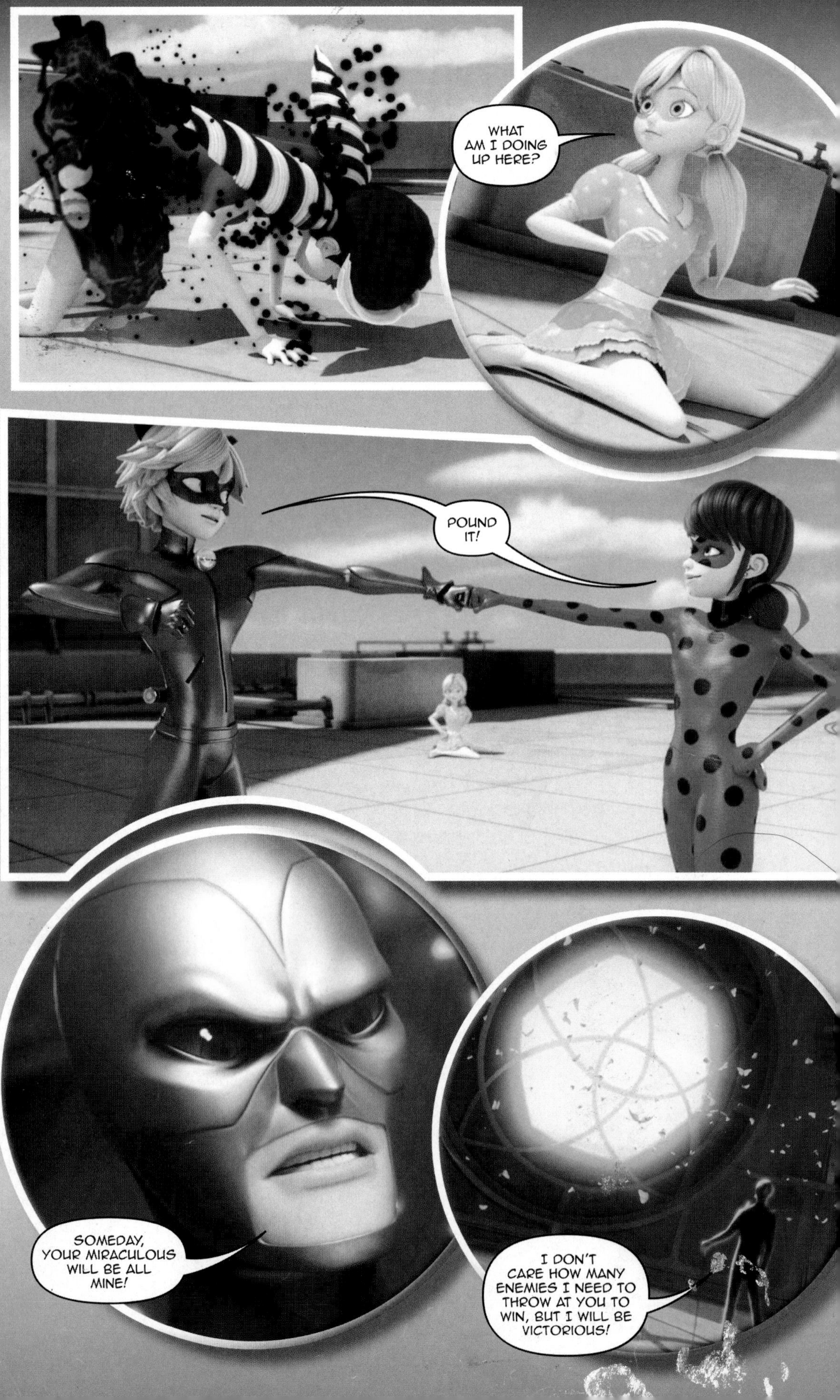
WHAT AM I DOING UP HERE?
POUND IT!
SOMEDAY, YOUR MIRACULOUS WILL BE ALL MINE!
I DON'T CARE HOW MANY ENEMIES I NEED TO THROW AT YOU TO WIN, BUT I WILL BE VICTORIOUS!

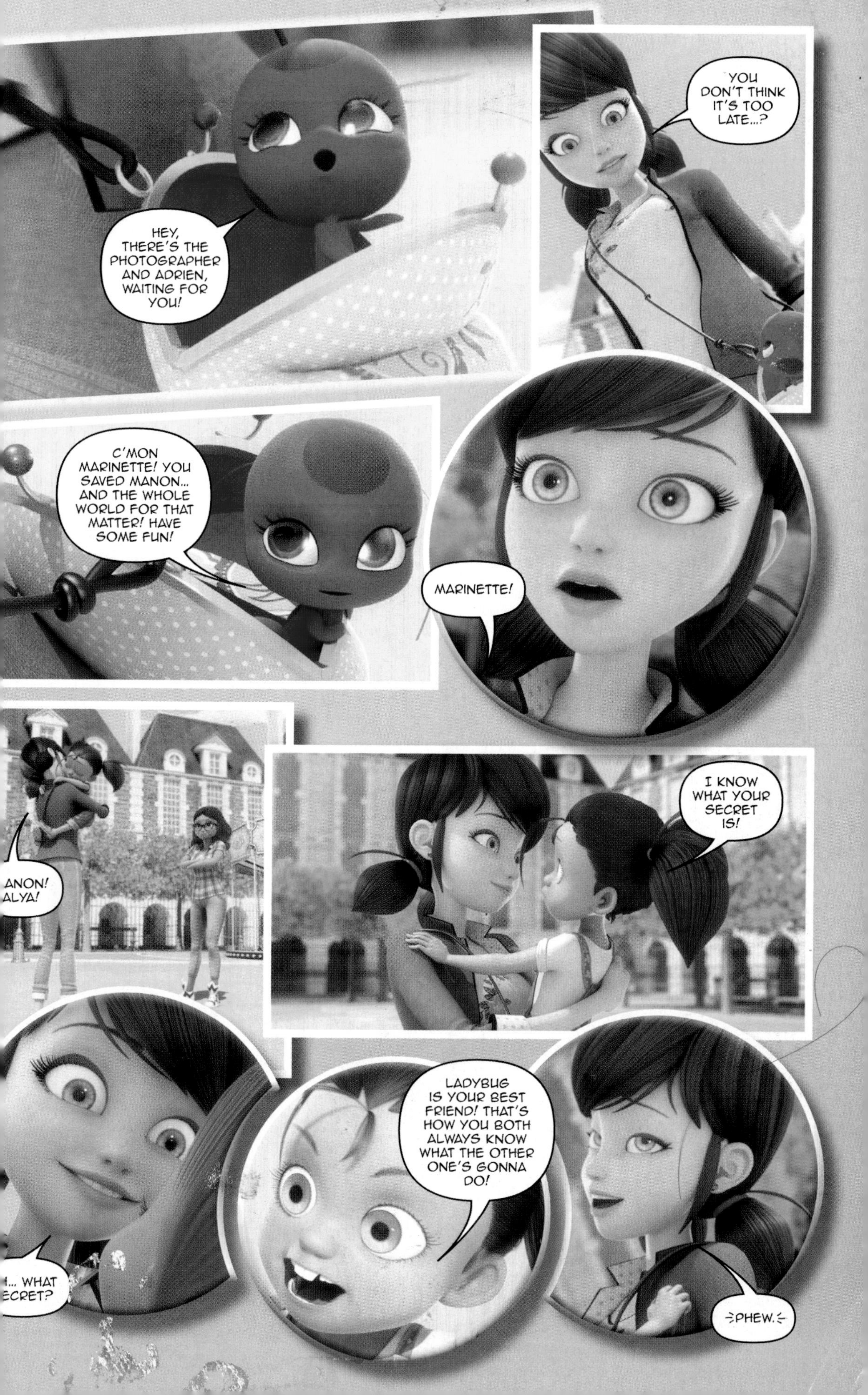
HEY, THERE'S THE PHOTOGRAPHER AND ADRIEN, WAITING FOR YOU!
YOU DON'T THINK IT'S TOO LATE...?
C'MON MARINETTE! YOU SAVED MANON... AND THE WHOLE WORLD FOR THAT MATTER! HAVE SOME FUN!
MARINETTE!
ANON! ALYA!
I KNOW WHAT YOUR SECRET IS!
...WHAT ECRET?
LADYBUG IS YOUR BEST FRIEND! THAT'S HOW YOU BOTH ALWAYS KNOW WHAT THE OTHER ONE'S GONNA DO!
PHEW.

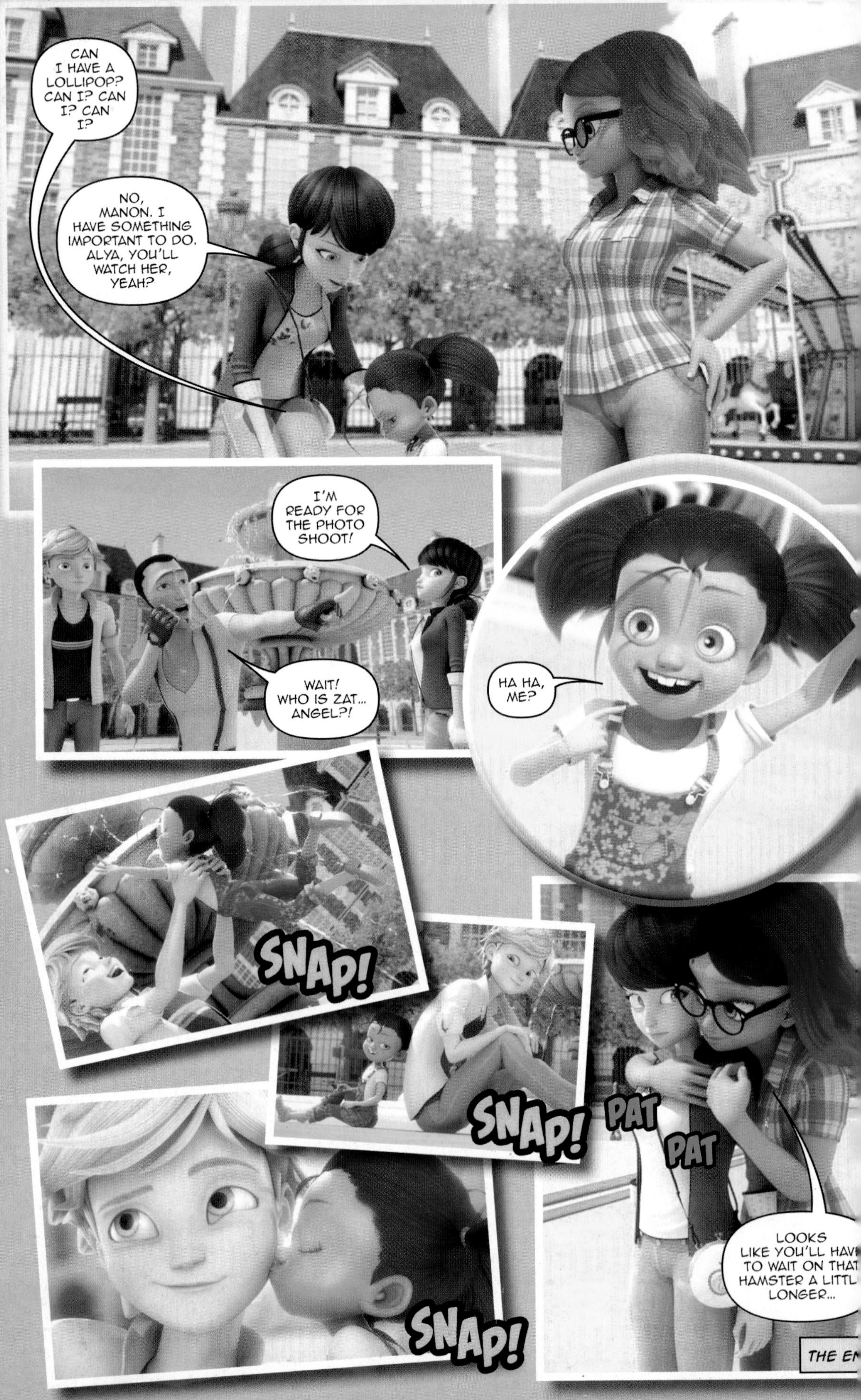
CAN I HAVE A LOLLIPOP? CAN I? CAN I? CAN I?
NO, MANON. I HAVE SOMETHING IMPORTANT TO DO. ALYA, YOU'LL WATCH HER, YEAH?
I'M READY FOR THE PHOTO SHOOT!
WAIT! WHO IS ZAT... ANGEL?!
HA HA, ME?
SNAP!
SNAP!
SNAP!
PAT
PAT
LOOKS LIKE YOU'LL HAV
TO WAIT ON THAT
HAMSTER A LITTL
LONGER...
THE EN

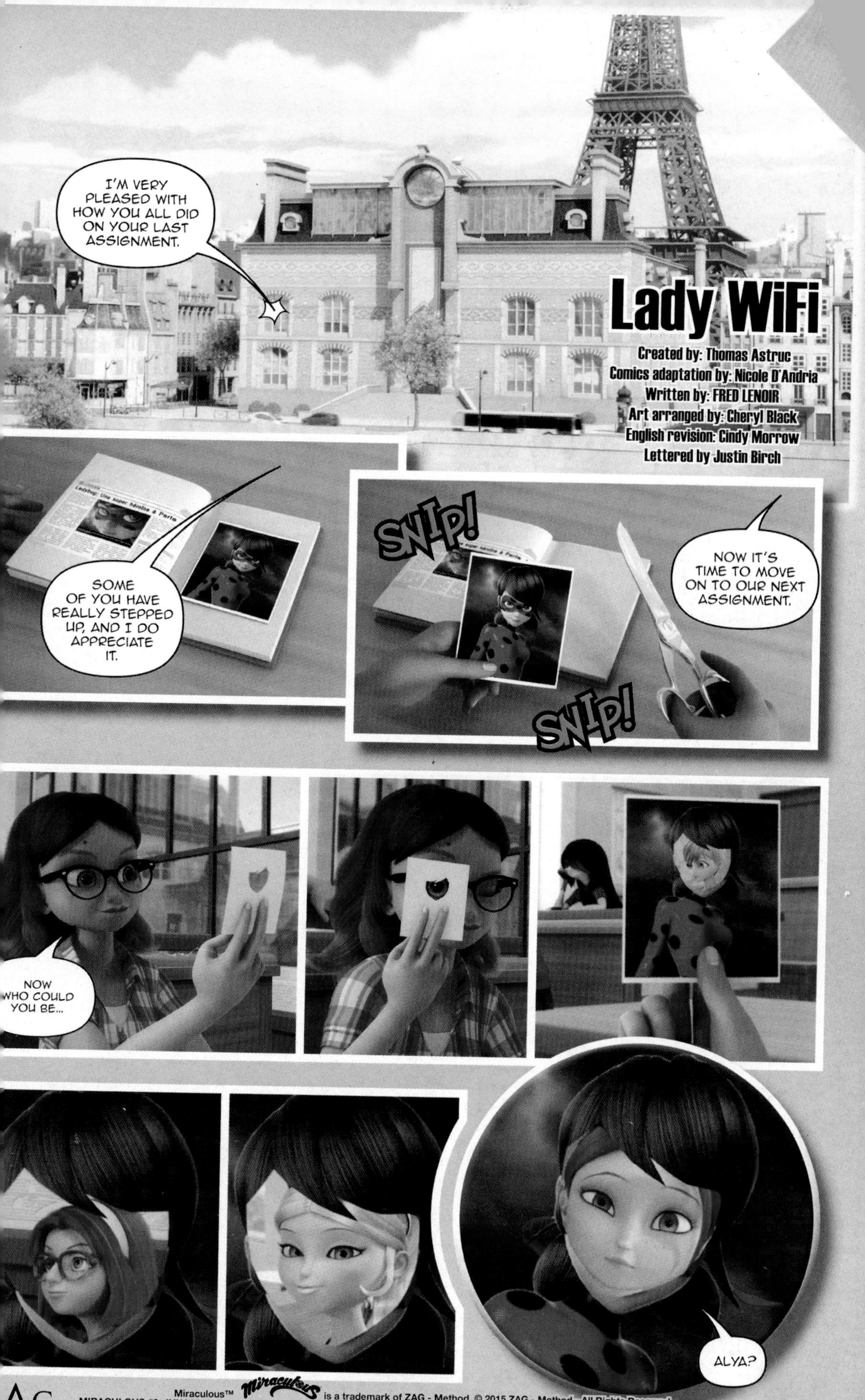
I'M VERY PLEASED WITH HOW YOU ALL DID ON YOUR LAST ASSIGNMENT.
Lady WiFi
Created by: Thomas Astruc
Comics adaptation by: Nicole D'Andria
Written by: FRED LENOIR
Art arranged by: Cheryl Black
English revision: Cindy Morrow
Lettered by Justin Birch
SOME OF YOU HAVE REALLY STEPPED UP, AND I DO APPRECIATE IT.
SNIP!
NOW IT'S TIME TO MOVE ON TO OUR NEXT ASSIGNMENT.
SNIP!
NOW WHO COULD YOU BE...
ALYA?

MIRACULOUS #2, JULY 2016. Published by Action Lab Entertainment.
Printed in Canada. First Printing.

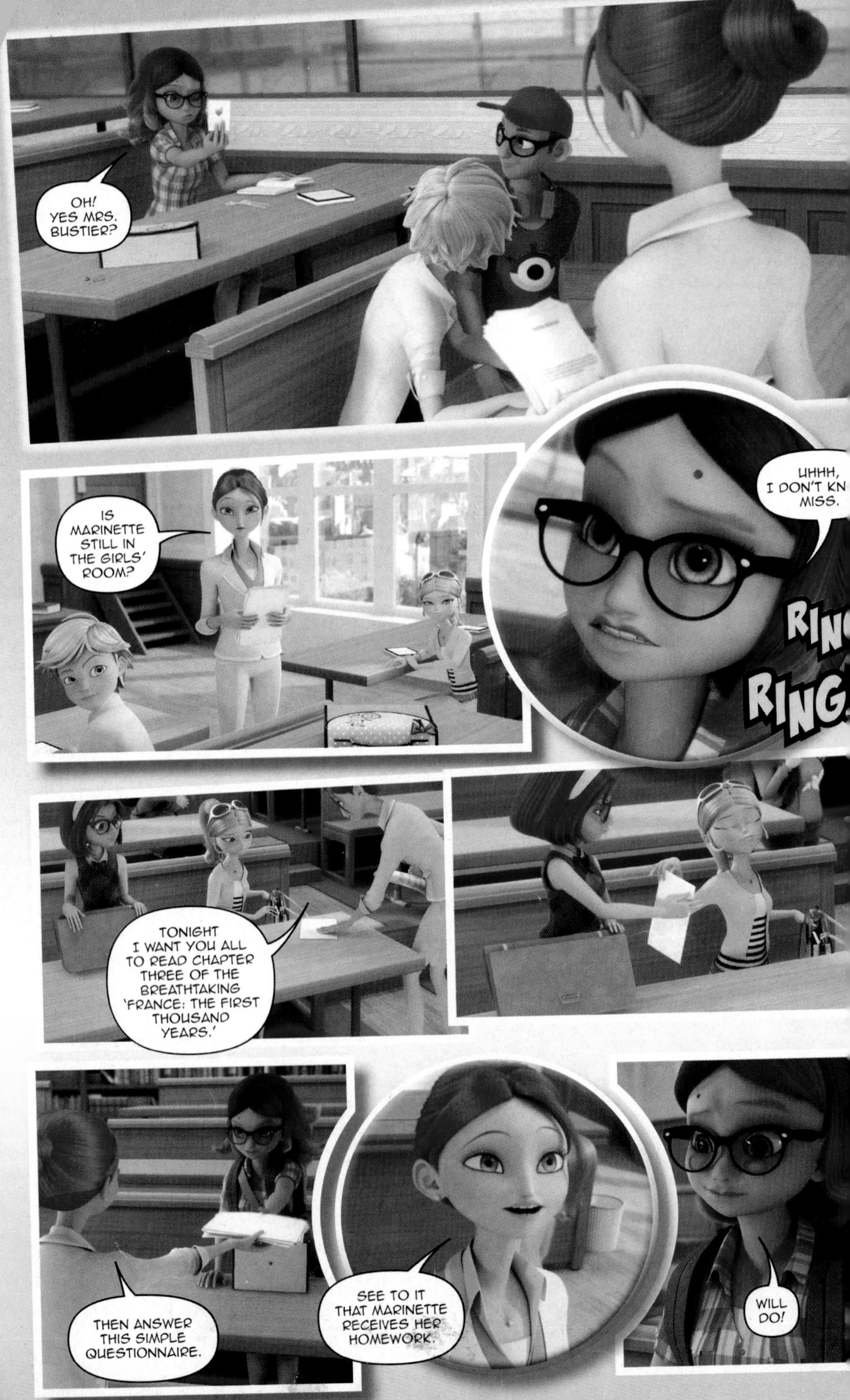
OH! YES MRS. BUSTIER?
IS MARINETTE STILL IN THE GIRLS' ROOM?
UHHH, I DON'T KN MISS.
RING RING
TONIGHT I WANT YOU ALL TO READ CHAPTER THREE OF THE BREATHTAKING 'FRANCE: THE FIRST THOUSAND YEARS.'
THEN ANSWER THIS SIMPLE QUESTIONNAIRE.
SEE TO IT THAT MARINETTE RECEIVES HER HOMEWORK.
WILL DO!

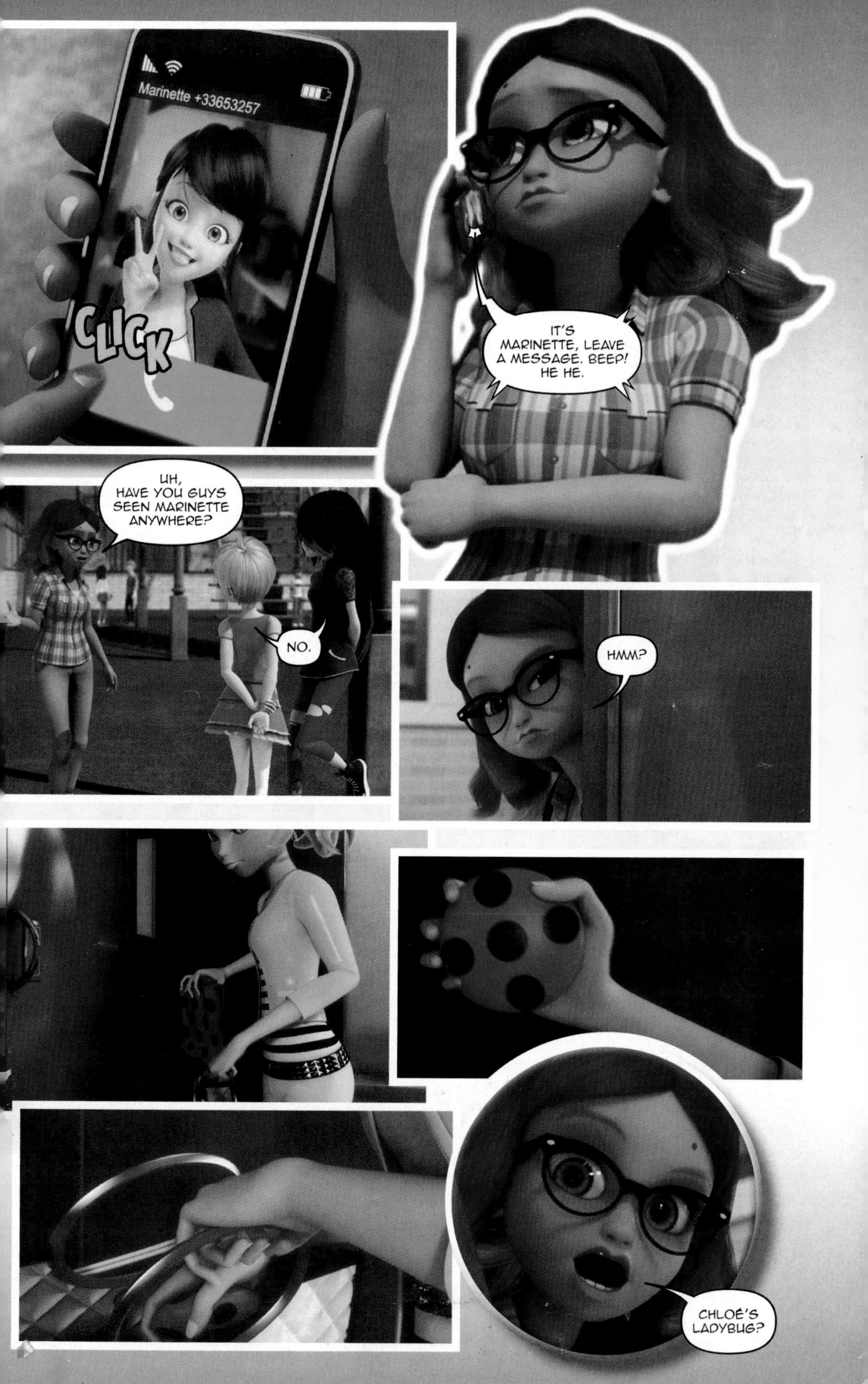
Marinette +33653257
CLICK
IT'S MARINETTE, LEAVE A MESSAGE. BEEP! HE HE.
UH, HAVE YOU GUYS SEEN MARINETTE ANYWHERE?
NO.
HMM?
CHLOÉ'S LADYBUG?

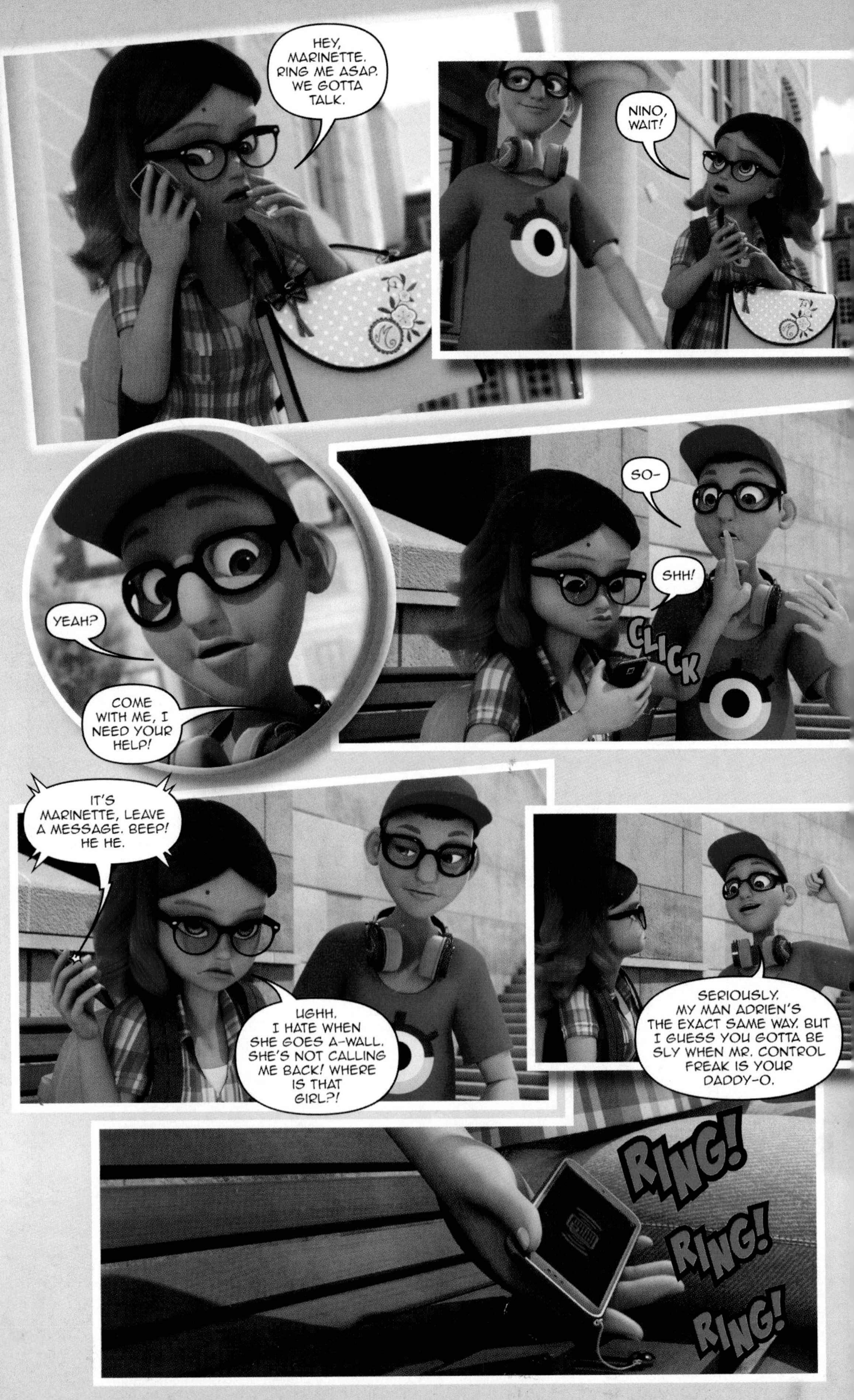
HEY, MARINETTE. RING ME ASAP. WE GOTTA TALK.
NINO, WAIT!
YEAH?
COME WITH ME, I NEED YOUR HELP!
SO-
SHH!
CLICK
IT'S MARINETTE, LEAVE A MESSAGE. BEEP! HE HE.
UGHH. I HATE WHEN SHE GOES A-WALL. SHE'S NOT CALLING ME BACK! WHERE IS THAT GIRL?!
SERIOUSLY. MY MAN ADRIEN'S THE EXACT SAME WAY. BUT I GUESS YOU GOTTA BE SLY WHEN MR. CONTROL FREAK IS YOUR DADDY-O.
RING!
RING!
RING!

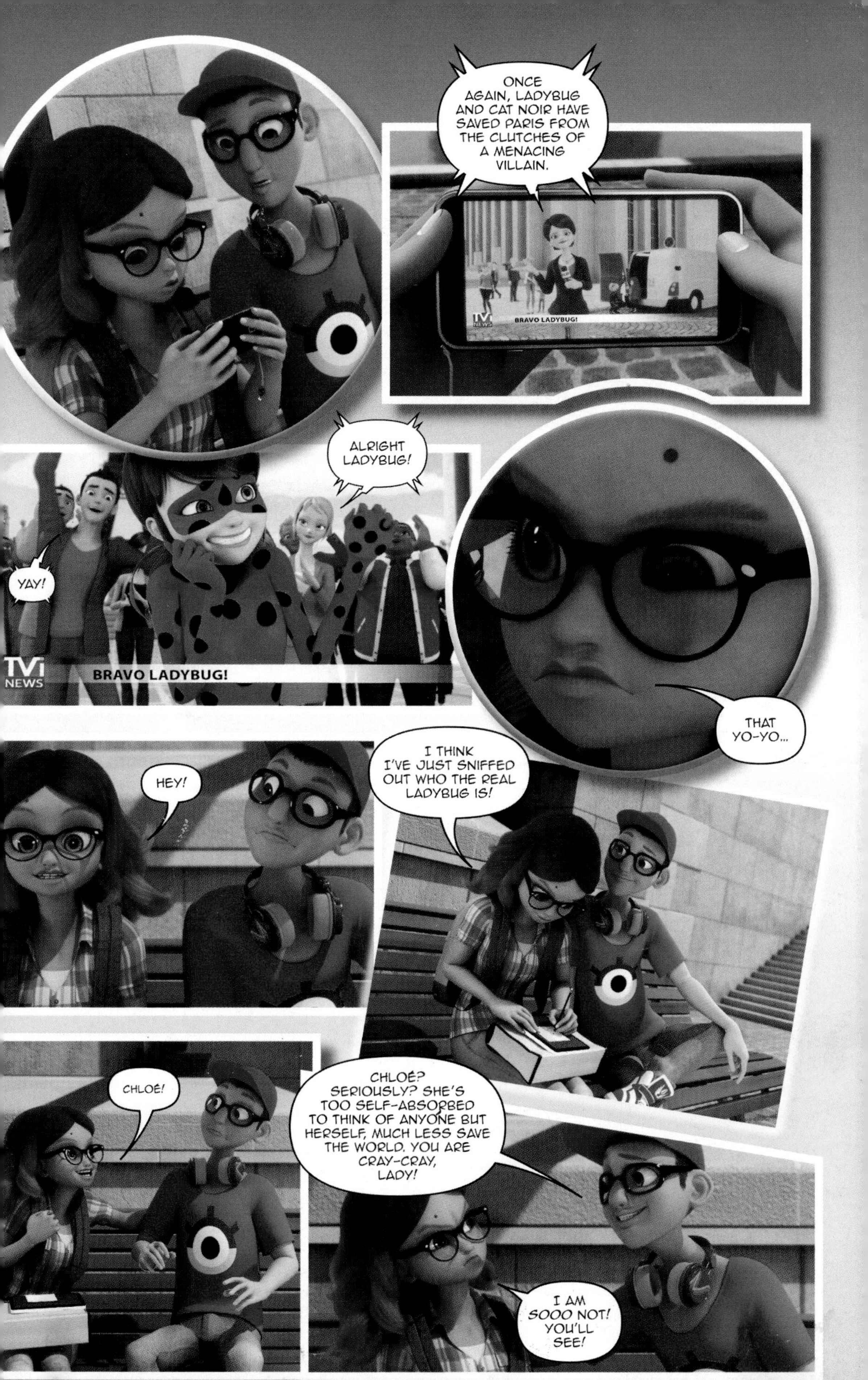
ONCE AGAIN, LADYBUG AND CAT NOIR HAVE SAVED PARIS FROM THE CLUTCHES OF A MENACING VILLAIN.
TVi NEWS
BRAVO LADYBUG!
ALRIGHT LADYBUG!
YAY!
TVi NEWS
BRAVO LADYBUG!
THAT YO-YO...
HEY!
I THINK I'VE JUST SNIFFED OUT WHO THE REAL LADYBUG IS!
CHLOÉ!
CHLOÉ? SERIOUSLY? SHE'S TOO SELF-ABSORBED TO THINK OF ANYONE BUT HERSELF, MUCH LESS SAVE THE WORLD. YOU ARE CRAY-CRAY, LADY!
I AM SOOO NOT! YOU'LL SEE!

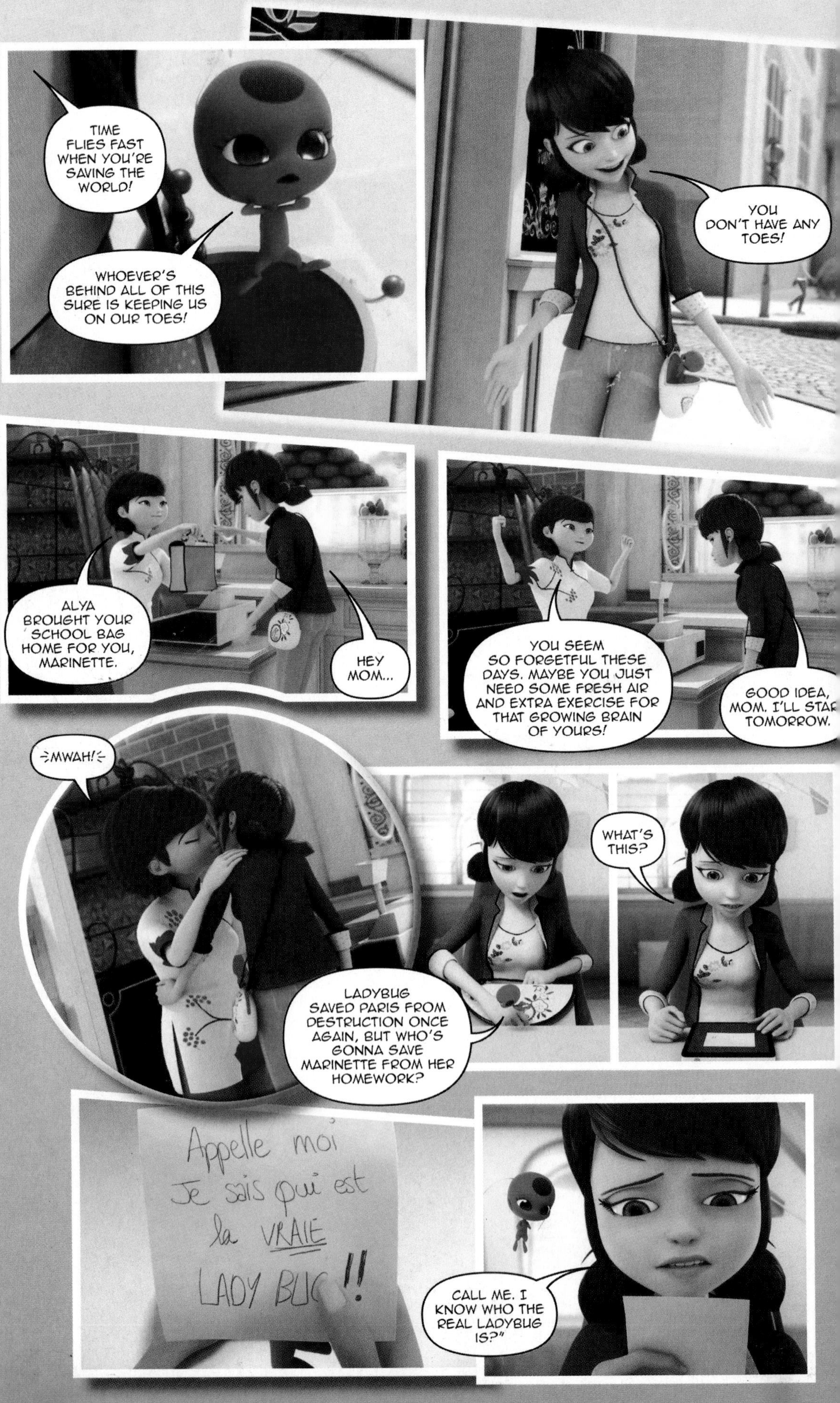
TIME FLIES FAST WHEN YOU'RE SAVING THE WORLD!
WHOEVER'S BEHIND ALL OF THIS SURE IS KEEPING US ON OUR TOES!
YOU DON'T HAVE ANY TOES!
ALYA BROUGHT YOUR SCHOOL BAG HOME FOR YOU, MARINETTE.
HEY MOM...
YOU SEEM SO FORGETFUL THESE DAYS. MAYBE YOU JUST NEED SOME FRESH AIR AND EXTRA EXERCISE FOR THAT GROWING BRAIN OF YOURS!
GOOD IDEA, MOM. I'LL STAR TOMORROW.
MWAH!
LADYBUG SAVED PARIS FROM DESTRUCTION ONCE AGAIN, BUT WHO'S GONNA SAVE MARINETTE FROM HER HOMEWORK?
WHAT'S THIS?
Appelle moi
Je sais qui est
la VRAIE
LADY BUG!!
CALL ME. I KNOW WHO THE REAL LADYBUG IS?"

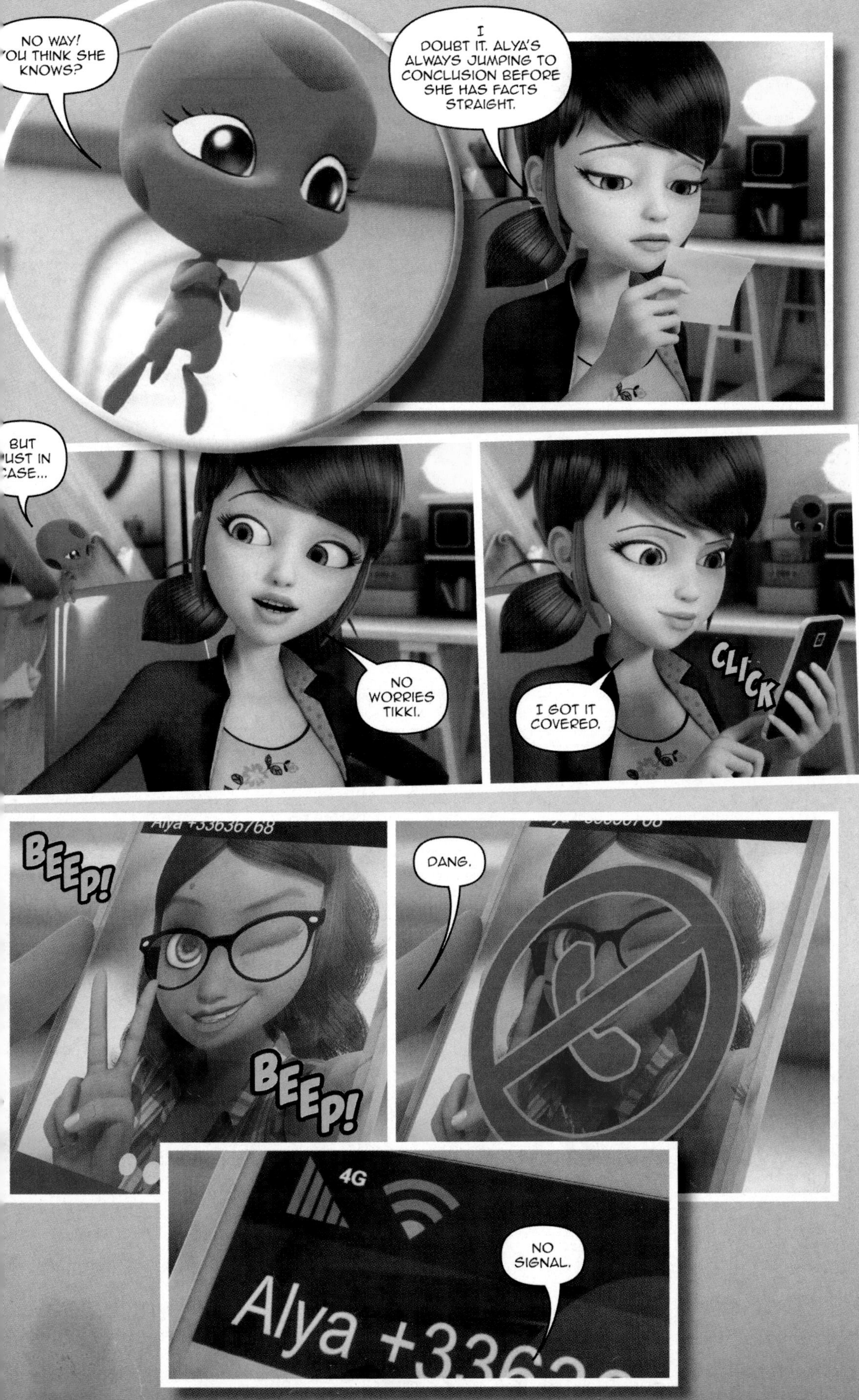
NO WAY!
'OU THINK SHE KNOWS?
I DOUBT IT. ALYA'S ALWAYS JUMPING TO CONCLUSION BEFORE SHE HAS FACTS STRAIGHT.
BUT UST IN CASE...
NO WORRIES TIKKI.
I GOT IT COVERED.
CLICK
Alya +33636768
BEEP!
BEEP!
DANG.
4G
NO SIGNAL.
Alya +3.362

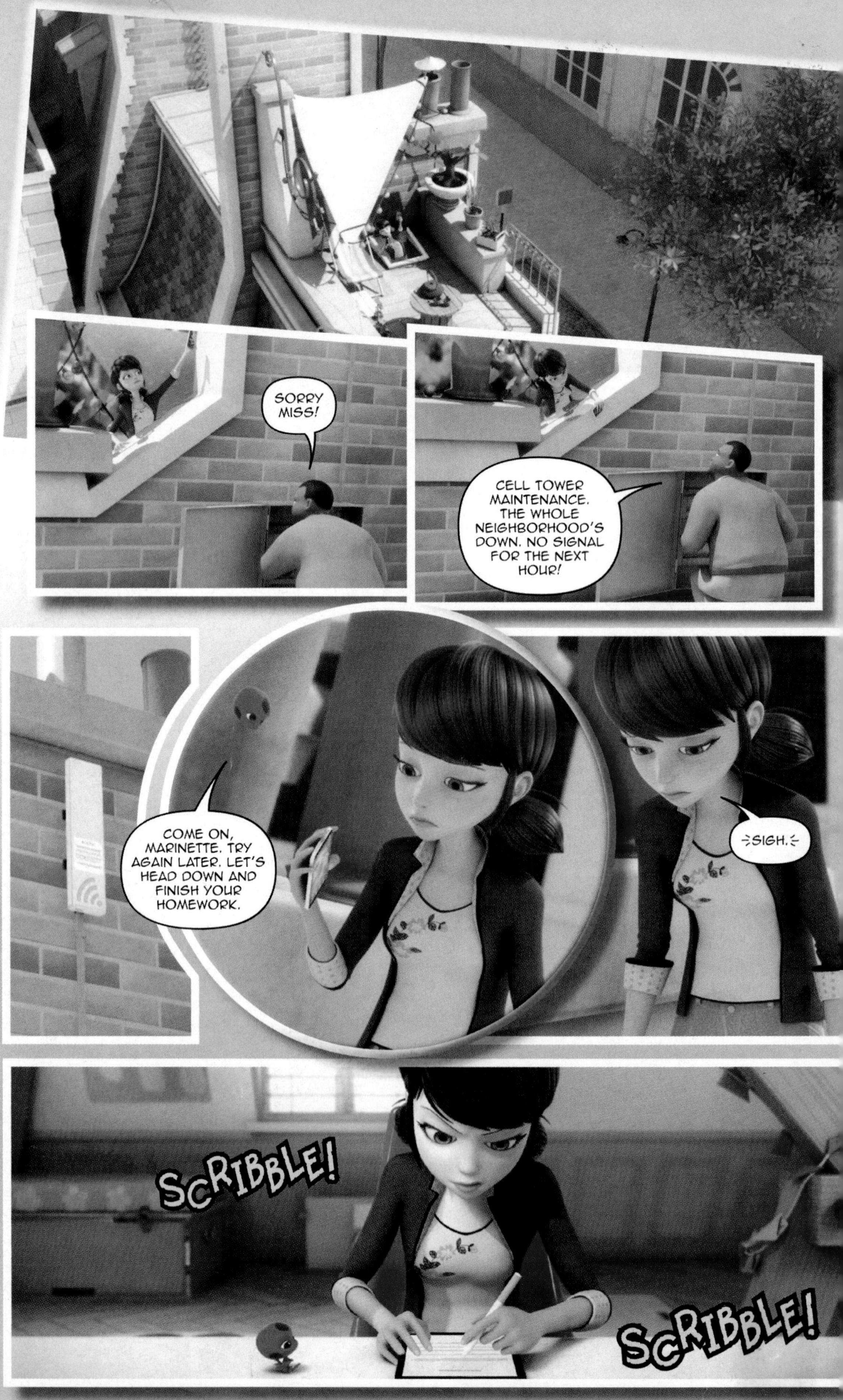
SORRY MISS!
CELL TOWER MAINTENANCE. THE WHOLE NEIGHBORHOOD'S DOWN. NO SIGNAL FOR THE NEXT HOUR!
COME ON, MARINETTE. TRY AGAIN LATER. LET'S HEAD DOWN AND FINISH YOUR HOMEWORK.
SIGH.
SCRIBBLE!
SCRIBBLE!

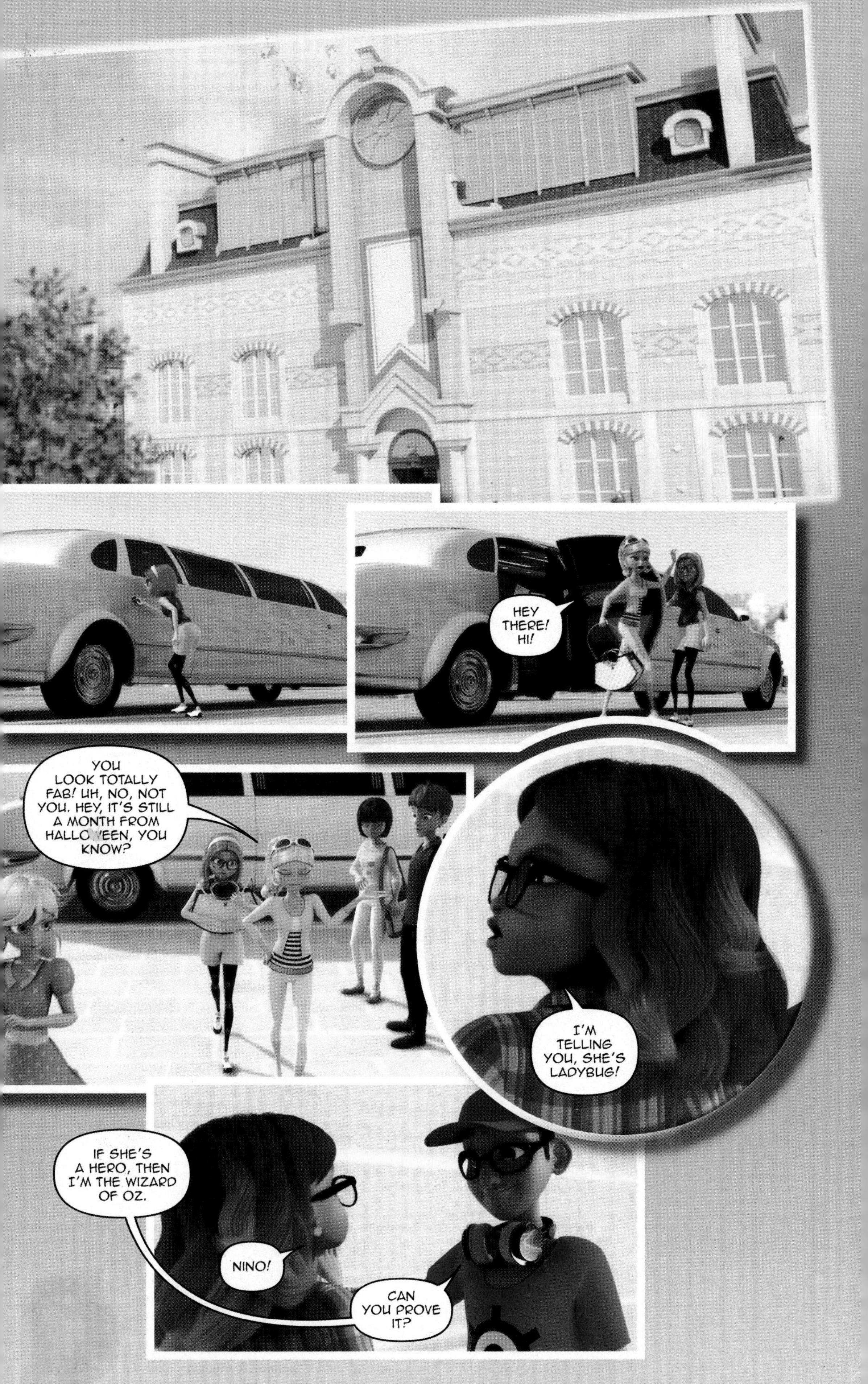
HEY THERE! HI!
YOU LOOK TOTALLY FAB! UH, NO, NOT YOU. HEY, IT'S STILL A MONTH FROM HALLOWEEN, YOU KNOW?
I'M TELLING YOU, SHE'S LADYBUG!
IF SHE'S A HERO, THEN I'M THE WIZARD OF OZ.
NINO!
CAN YOU PROVE IT?

SNORE

UH... WHAT TIME IS IT?

UHH, SCHOOL STARTS IN...

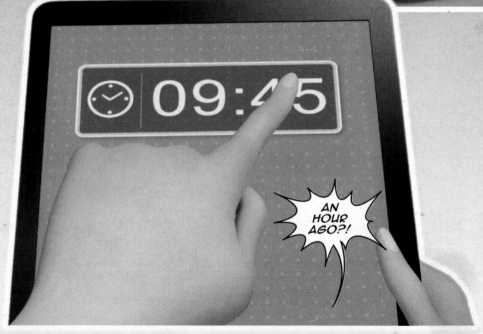

09:45

AN HOUR AGO?!

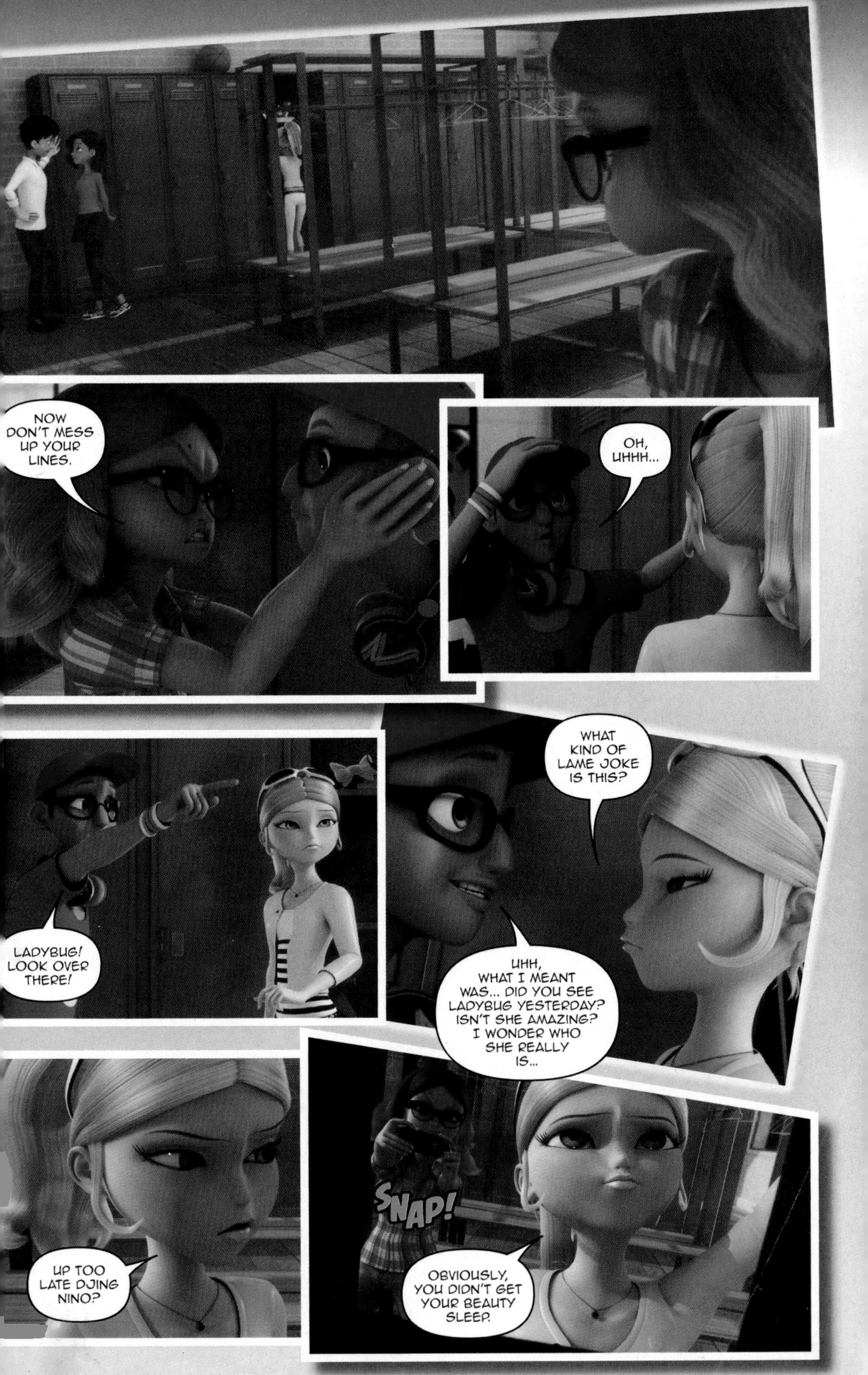
NOW DON'T MESS UP YOUR LINES.
OH, UHHH...
LADYBUG! LOOK OVER THERE!
WHAT KIND OF LAME JOKE IS THIS?
UHH, WHAT I MEANT WAS... DID YOU SEE LADYBUG YESTERDAY? ISN'T SHE AMAZING? I WONDER WHO SHE REALLY IS...
UP TOO LATE DJING NINO?
SNAP!
OBVIOUSLY, YOU DIDN'T GET YOUR BEAUTY SLEEP.

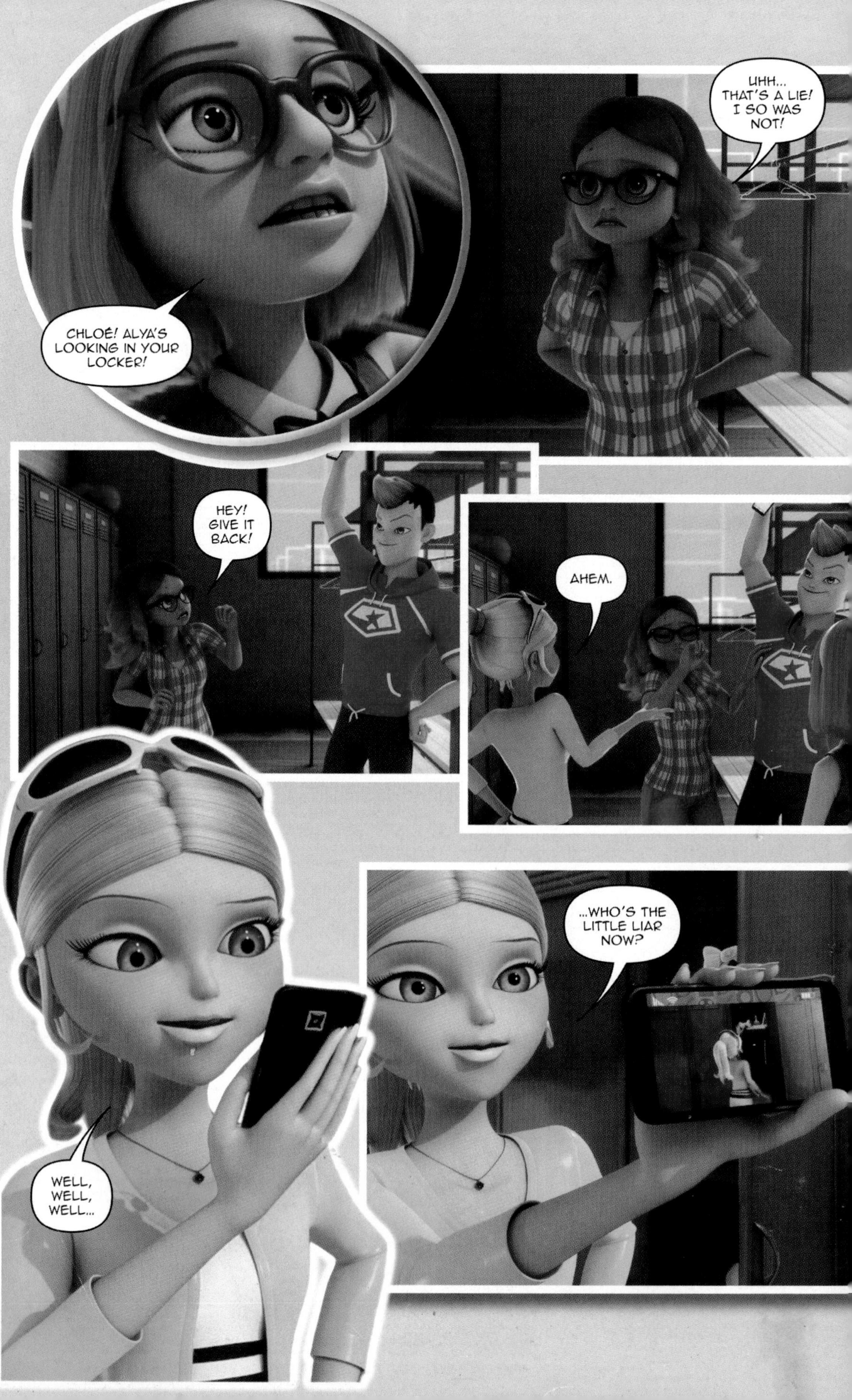
CHLOÉ! ALYA'S LOOKING IN YOUR LOCKER!
UHH... THAT'S A LIE! I SO WAS NOT!
HEY! GIVE IT BACK!
AHEM.
WELL, WELL, WELL...
...WHO'S THE LITTLE LIAR NOW?

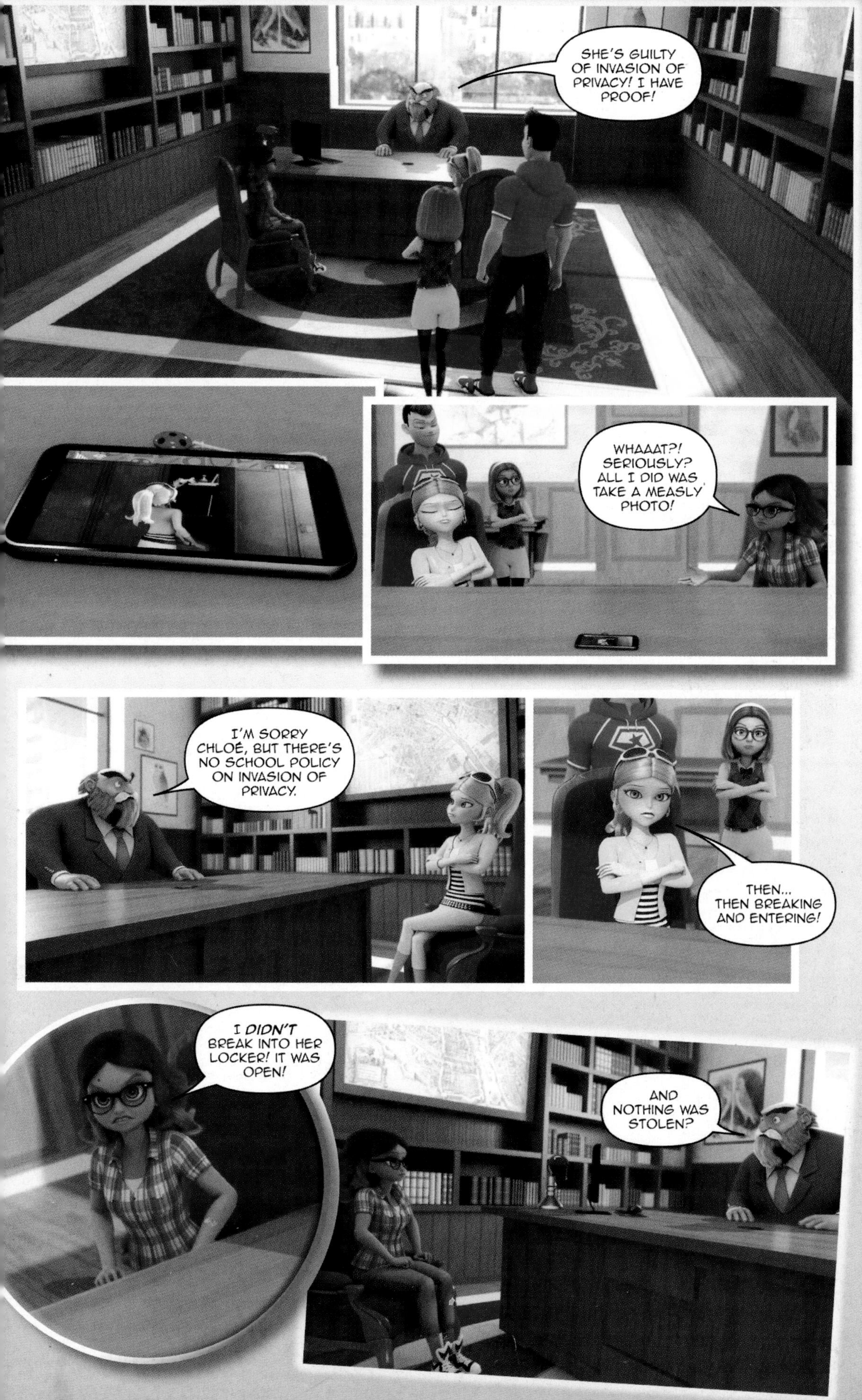
SHE'S GUILTY OF INVASION OF PRIVACY! I HAVE PROOF!
WHAAAT?! SERIOUSLY? ALL I DID WAS TAKE A MEASLY PHOTO!
I'M SORRY CHLOÉ, BUT THERE'S NO SCHOOL POLICY ON INVASION OF PRIVACY.
THEN... THEN BREAKING AND ENTERING!
I DIDN'T BREAK INTO HER LOCKER! IT WAS OPEN!
AND NOTHING WAS STOLEN?

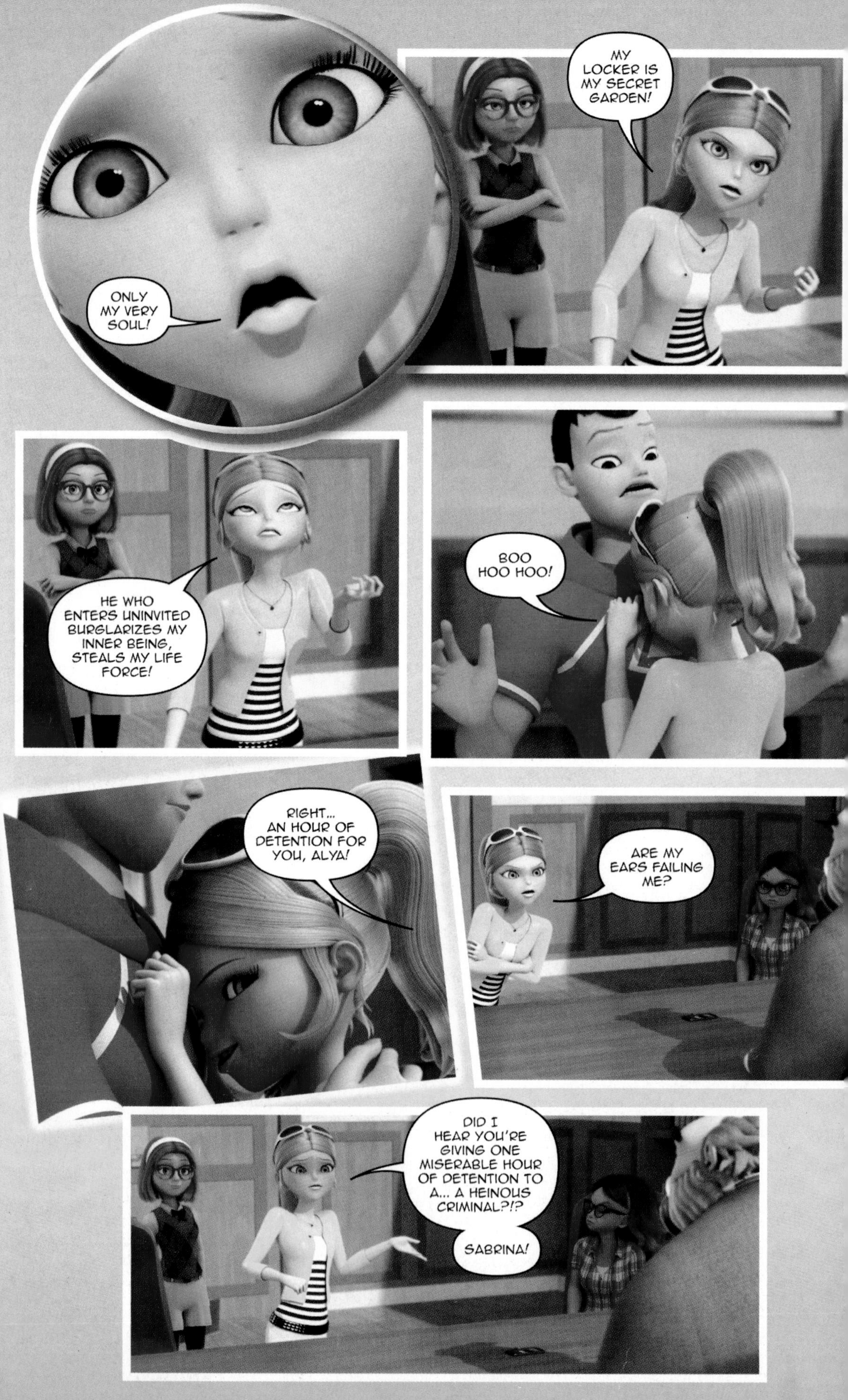
MY LOCKER IS MY SECRET GARDEN!
ONLY MY VERY SOUL!
HE WHO ENTERS UNINVITED BURGLARIZES MY INNER BEING, STEALS MY LIFE FORCE!
BOO HOO HOO!
RIGHT... AN HOUR OF DETENTION FOR YOU, ALYA!
ARE MY EARS FAILING ME?
DID I HEAR YOU'RE GIVING ONE MISERABLE HOUR OF DETENTION TO A... A HEINOUS CRIMINAL?!?
SABRINA!

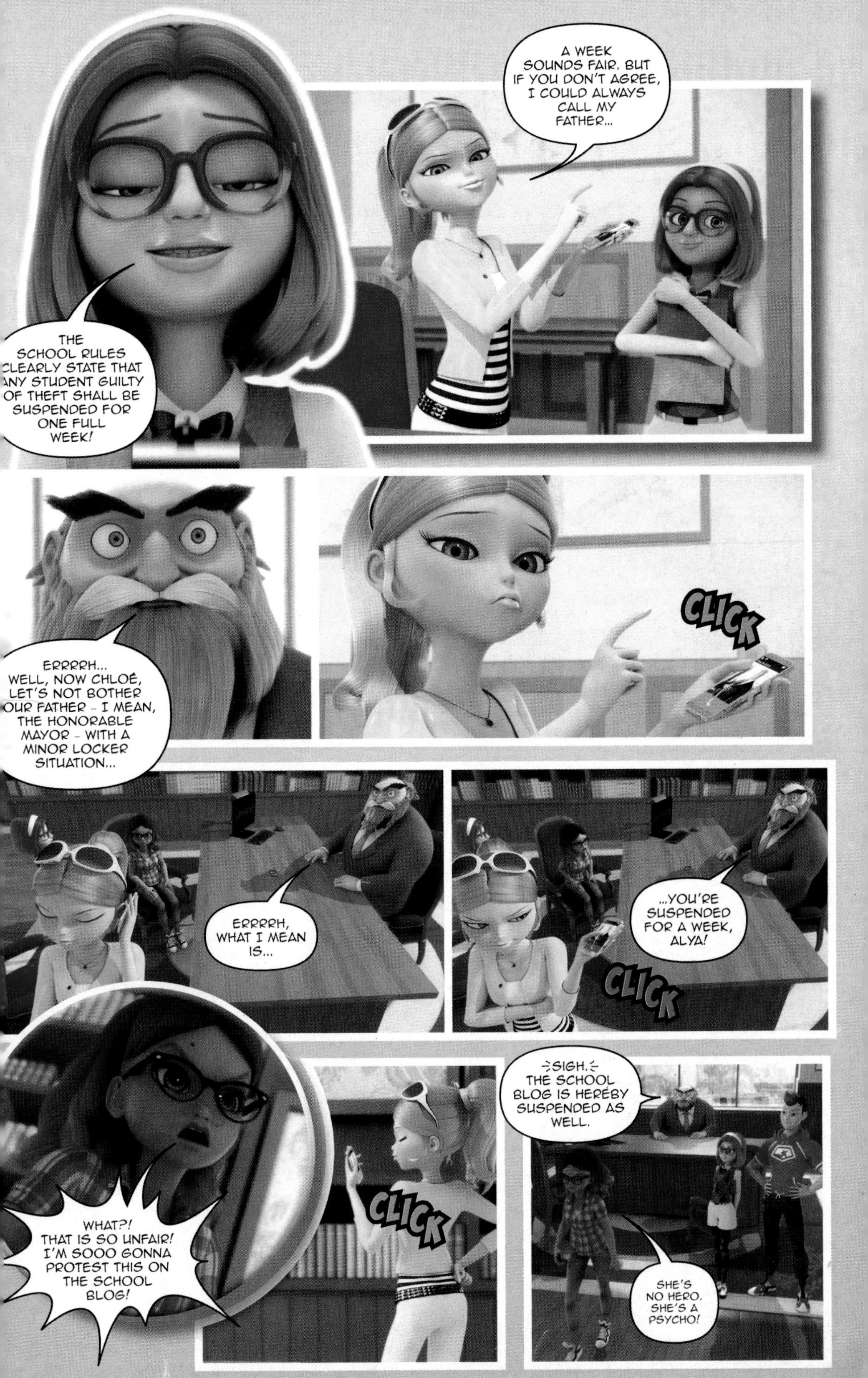
A WEEK SOUNDS FAIR. BUT IF YOU DON'T AGREE, I COULD ALWAYS CALL MY FATHER...
THE SCHOOL RULES CLEARLY STATE THAT ANY STUDENT GUILTY OF THEFT SHALL BE SUSPENDED FOR ONE FULL WEEK!
CLICK
ERRRRH... WELL, NOW CHLOÉ, LET'S NOT BOTHER OUR FATHER - I MEAN, THE HONORABLE MAYOR - WITH A MINOR LOCKER SITUATION...
ERRRRH, WHAT I MEAN IS...
...YOU'RE SUSPENDED FOR A WEEK, ALYA!
CLICK
WHAT?! THAT IS SO UNFAIR! I'M SOOO GONNA PROTEST THIS ON THE SCHOOL BLOG!
CLICK
=SIGH.= THE SCHOOL BLOG IS HEREBY SUSPENDED AS WELL.
SHE'S NO HERO. SHE'S A PSYCHO!

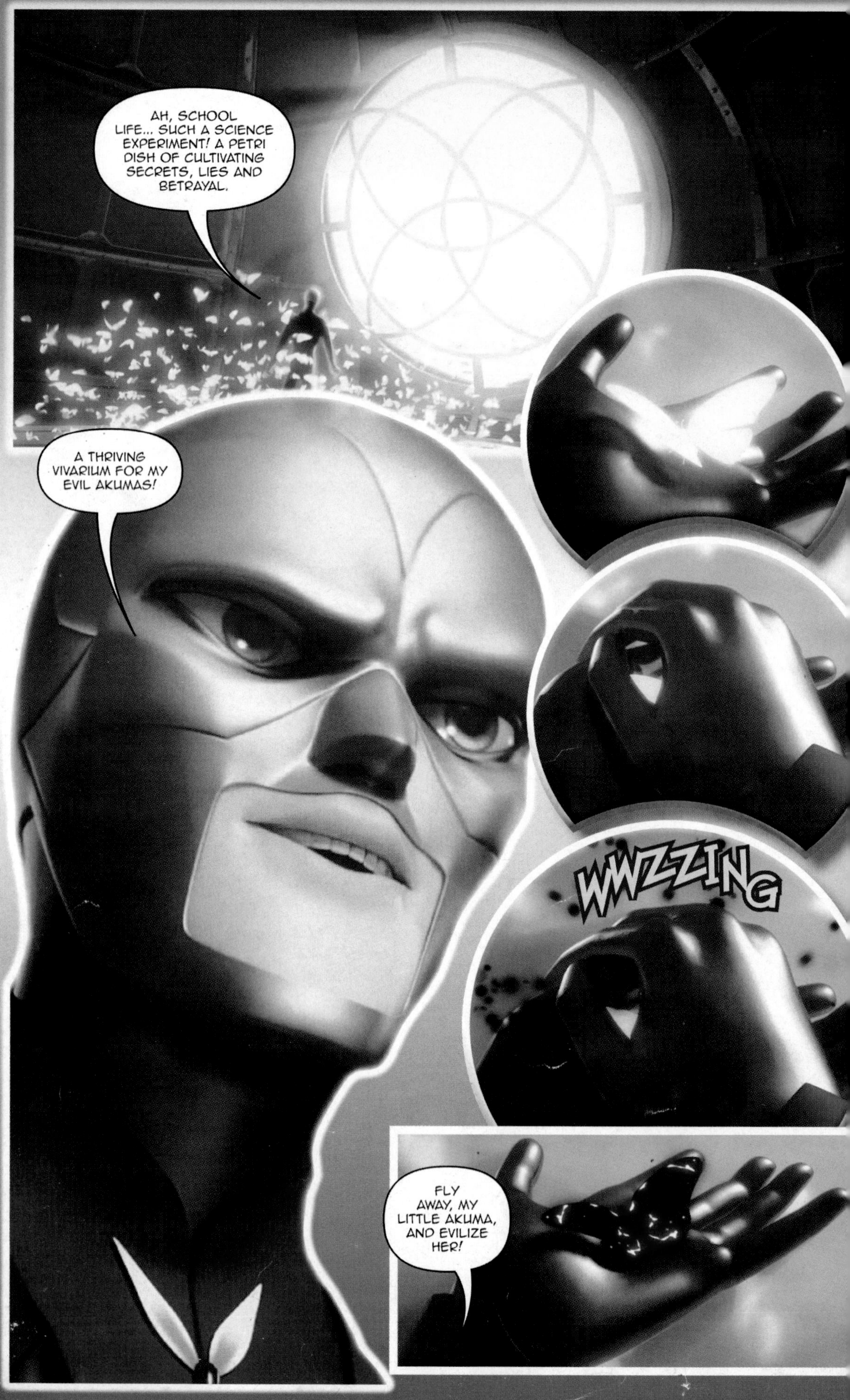
AH, SCHOOL LIFE... SUCH A SCIENCE EXPERIMENT! A PETRI DISH OF CULTIVATING SECRETS, LIES AND BETRAYAL.
A THRIVING VIVARIUM FOR MY EVIL AKUMAS!
WWZZING
FLY AWAY, MY LITTLE AKUMA, AND EVILIZE HER!

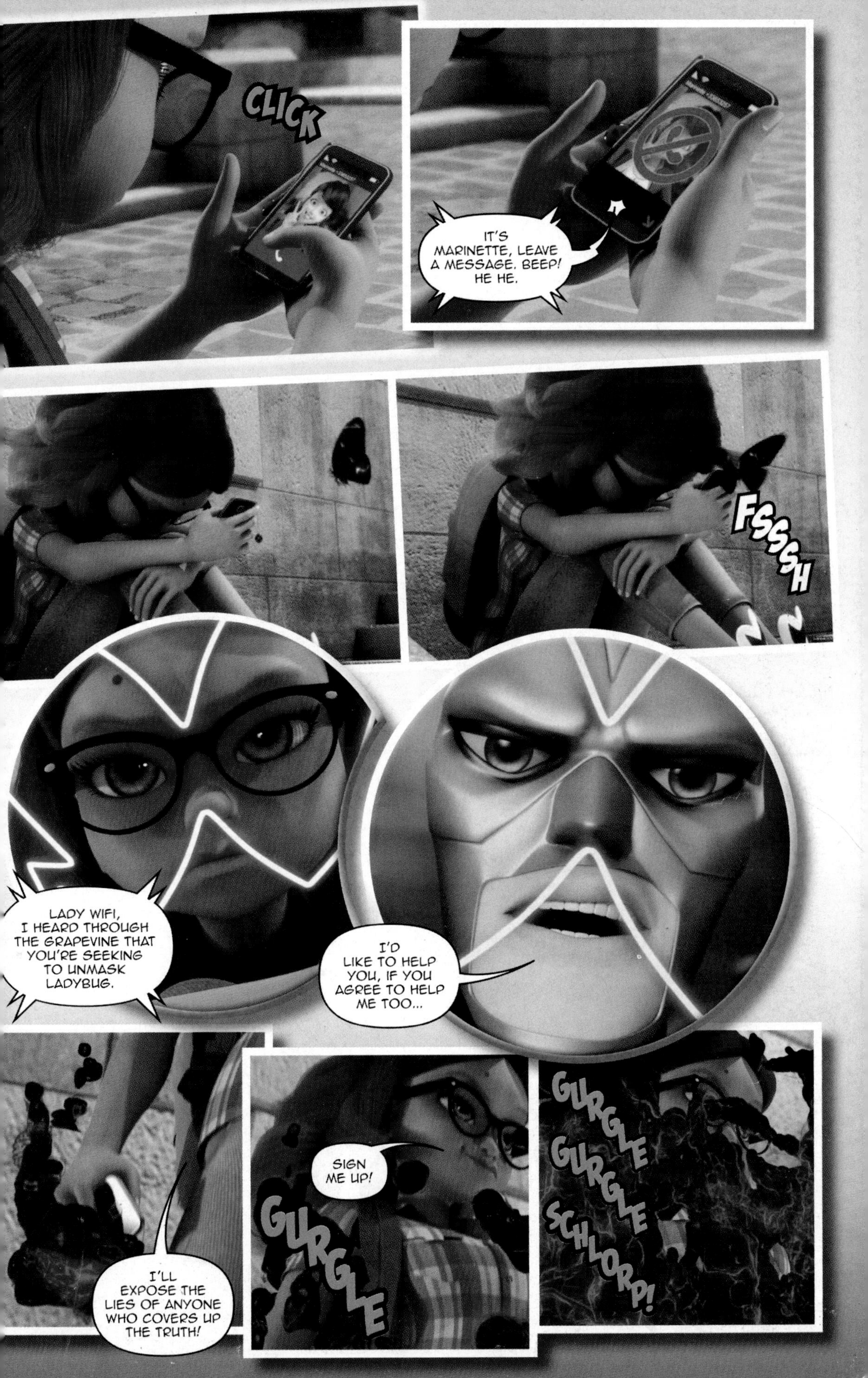
CLICK
IT'S MARINETTE, LEAVE A MESSAGE. BEEP! HE HE.
FSSSH
LADY WIFI, I HEARD THROUGH THE GRAPEVINE THAT YOU'RE SEEKING TO UNMASK LADYBUG.
I'D LIKE TO HELP YOU, IF YOU AGREE TO HELP ME TOO...
I'LL EXPOSE THE LIES OF ANYONE WHO COVERS UP THE TRUTH!
SIGN ME UP!
GURGLE
GURGLE
GURGLE
SCHLORP!

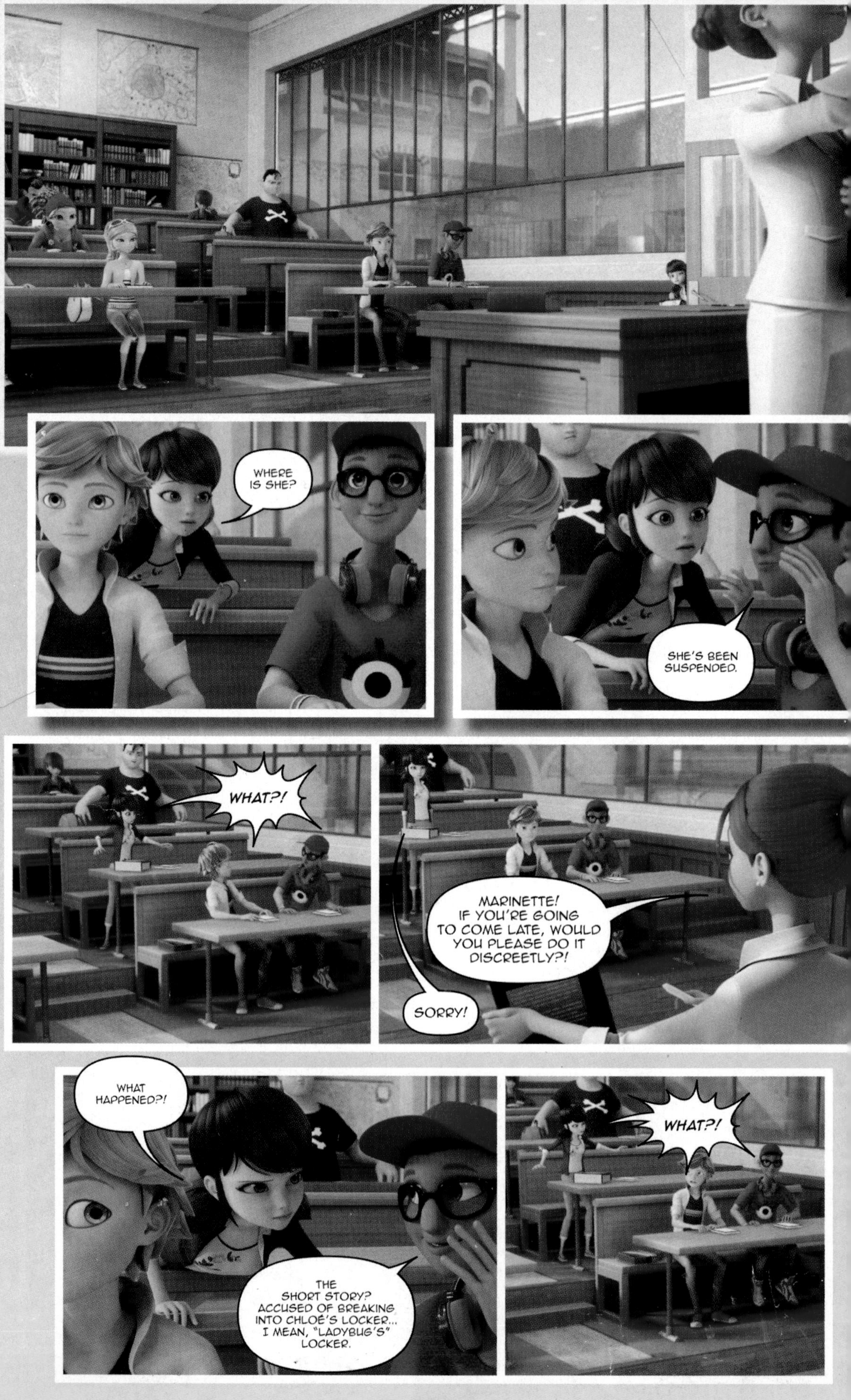
WHERE IS SHE?
SHE'S BEEN SUSPENDED.
WHAT?!
MARINETTE! IF YOU'RE GOING TO COME LATE, WOULD YOU PLEASE DO IT DISCREETLY?!
SORRY!
WHAT HAPPENED?!
THE SHORT STORY? ACCUSED OF BREAKING INTO CHLOÉ'S LOCKER... I MEAN, "LADYBUG'S" LOCKER.
WHAT?!

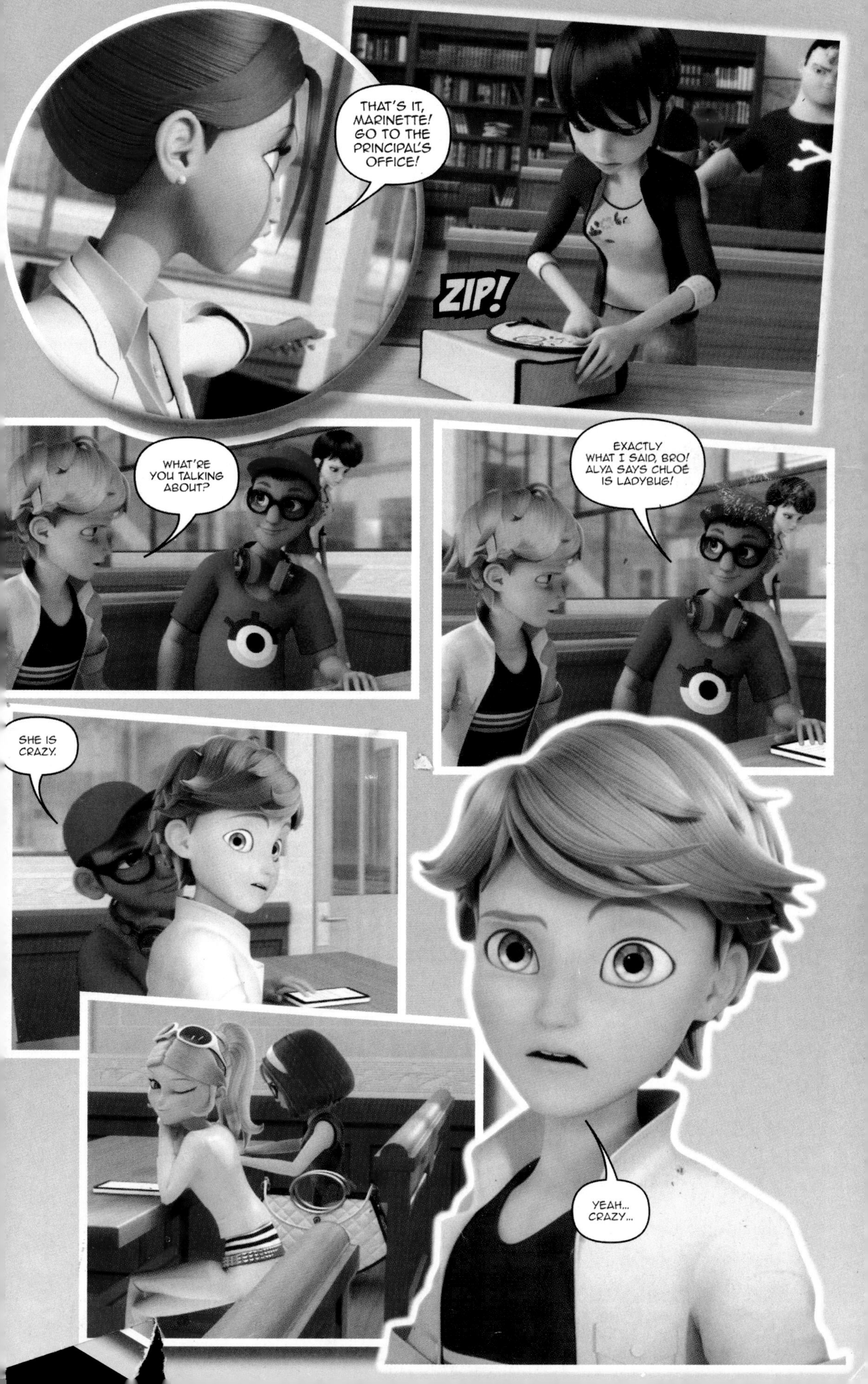
THAT'S IT, MARINETTE! GO TO THE PRINCIPAL'S OFFICE!
ZIP!
WHAT'RE YOU TALKING ABOUT?
EXACTLY WHAT I SAID, BRO! ALYA SAYS CHLOÉ IS LADYBUG!
SHE IS CRAZY.
YEAH... CRAZY...

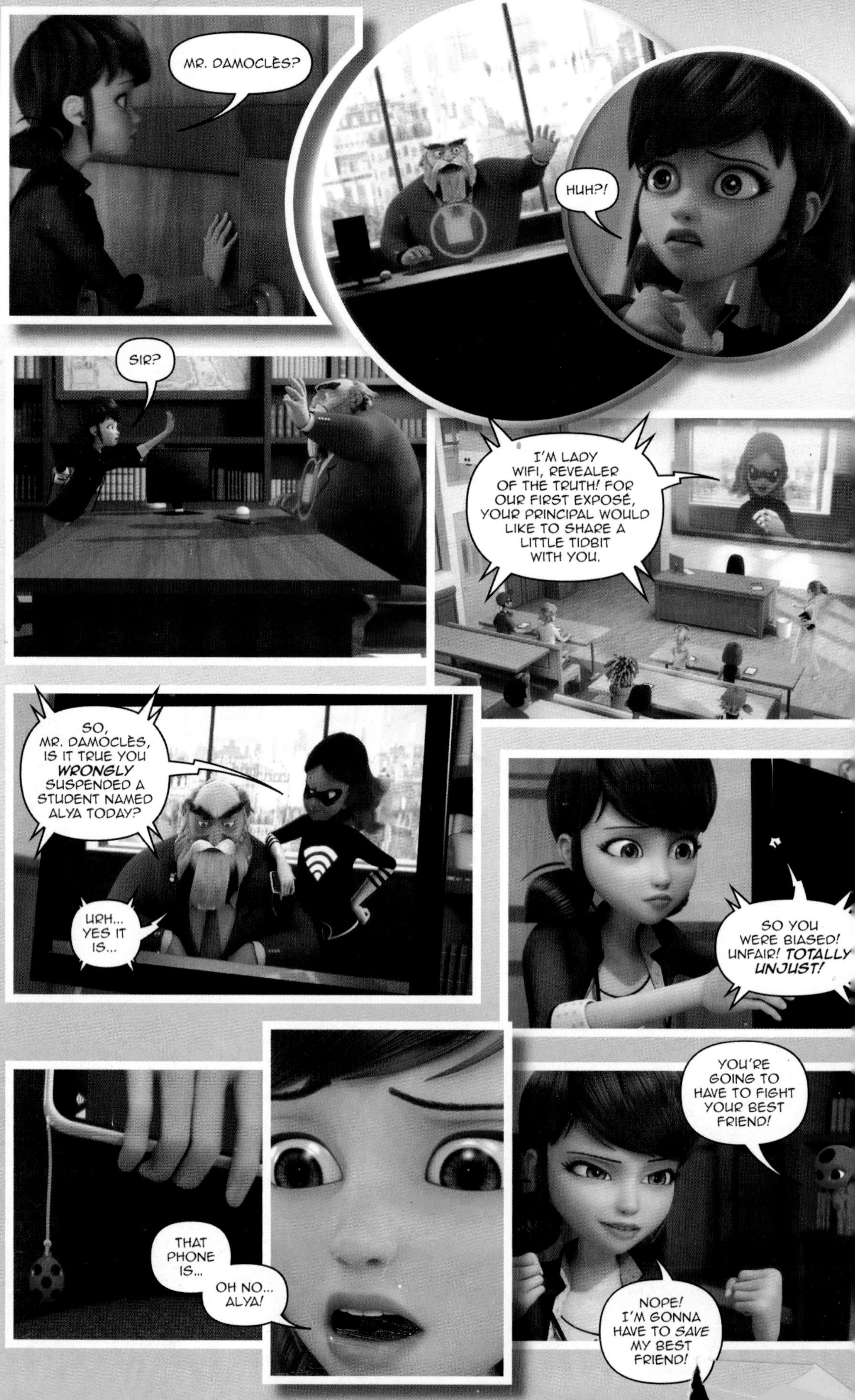
MR. DAMOCLÈS?
HUH?!
SIR?
I'M LADY WIFI, REVEALER OF THE TRUTH! FOR OUR FIRST EXPOSÉ, YOUR PRINCIPAL WOULD LIKE TO SHARE A LITTLE TIDBIT WITH YOU.
SO, MR. DAMOCLÈS, IS IT TRUE YOU *WRONGLY* SUSPENDED A STUDENT NAMED ALYA TODAY?
URH... YES IT IS...
SO YOU WERE BIASED! UNFAIR! *TOTALLY UNJUST!*
THAT PHONE IS...
OH NO... ALYA!
YOU'RE GOING TO HAVE TO FIGHT YOUR BEST FRIEND!
NOPE! I'M GONNA HAVE TO *SAVE* MY BEST FRIEND!

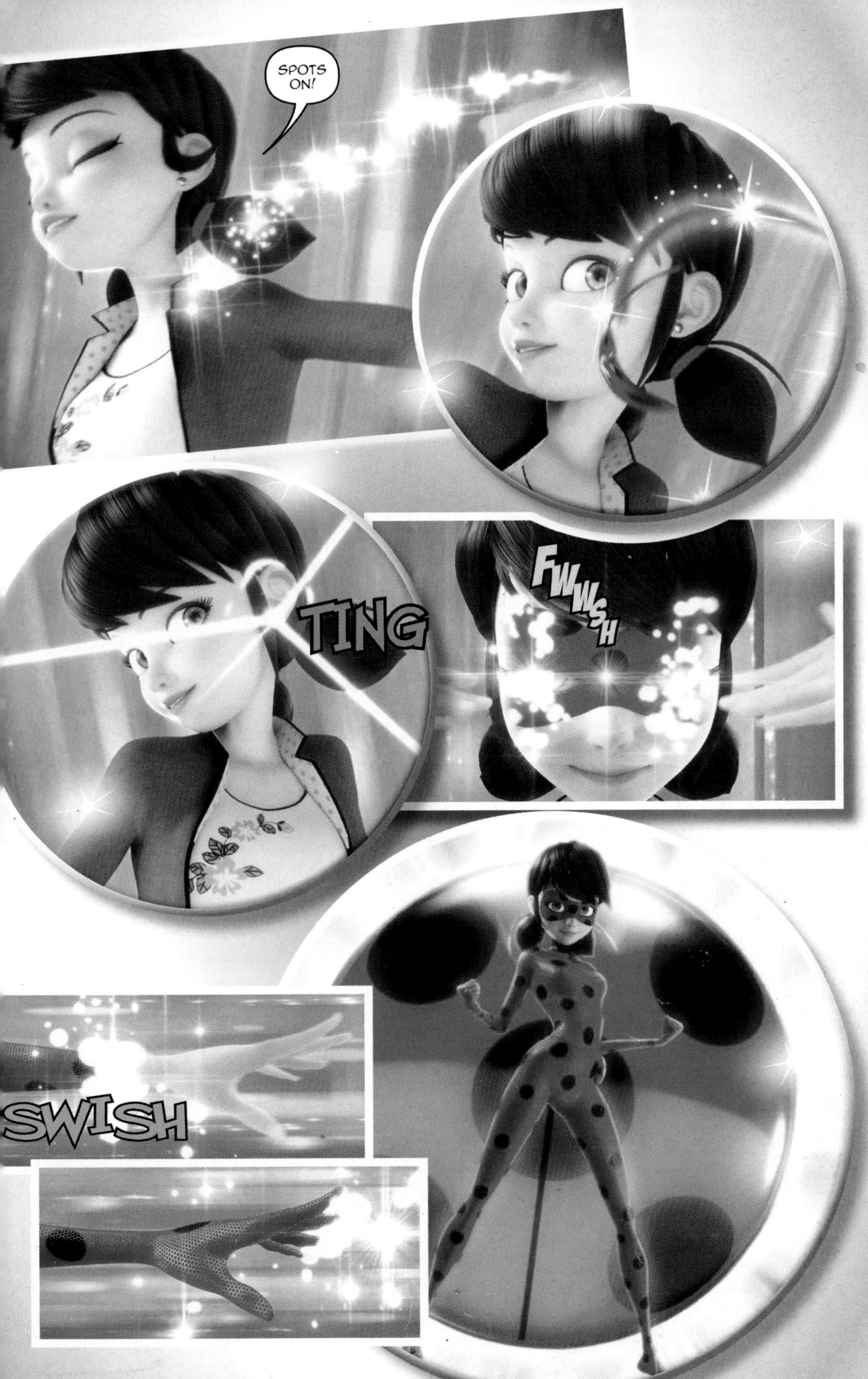
SPOTS ON!
TING
FWWSH
SWISH

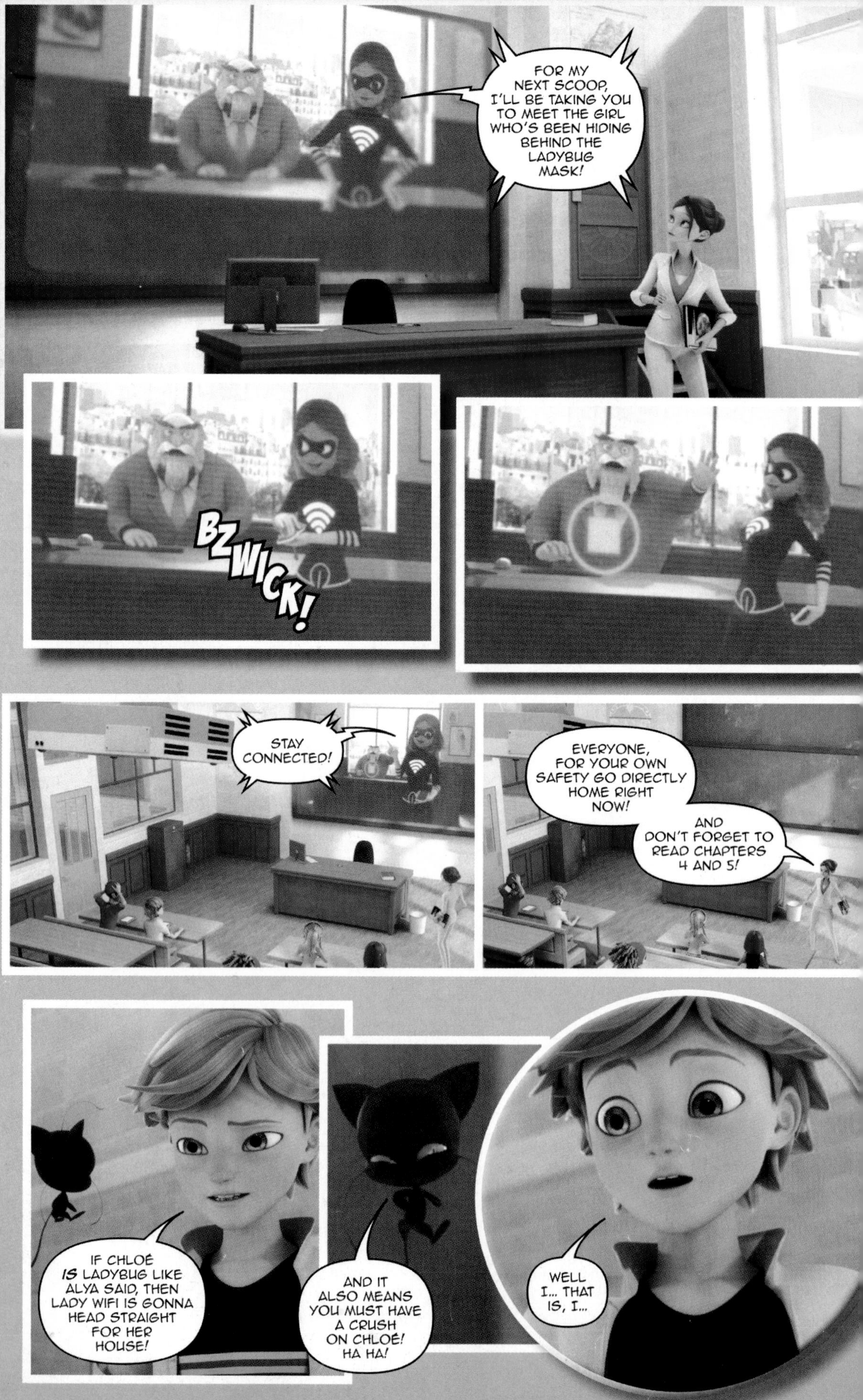
FOR MY NEXT SCOOP, I'LL BE TAKING YOU TO MEET THE GIRL WHO'S BEEN HIDING BEHIND THE LADYBUG MASK!
BZWICK!
STAY CONNECTED!
EVERYONE, FOR YOUR OWN SAFETY GO DIRECTLY HOME RIGHT NOW!
AND DON'T FORGET TO READ CHAPTERS 4 AND 5!
IF CHLOÉ *IS* LADYBUG LIKE ALYA SAID, THEN LADY WIFI IS GONNA HEAD STRAIGHT FOR HER HOUSE!
AND IT ALSO MEANS YOU MUST HAVE A CRUSH ON CHLOÉ! HA HA!
WELL I... THAT IS, I...

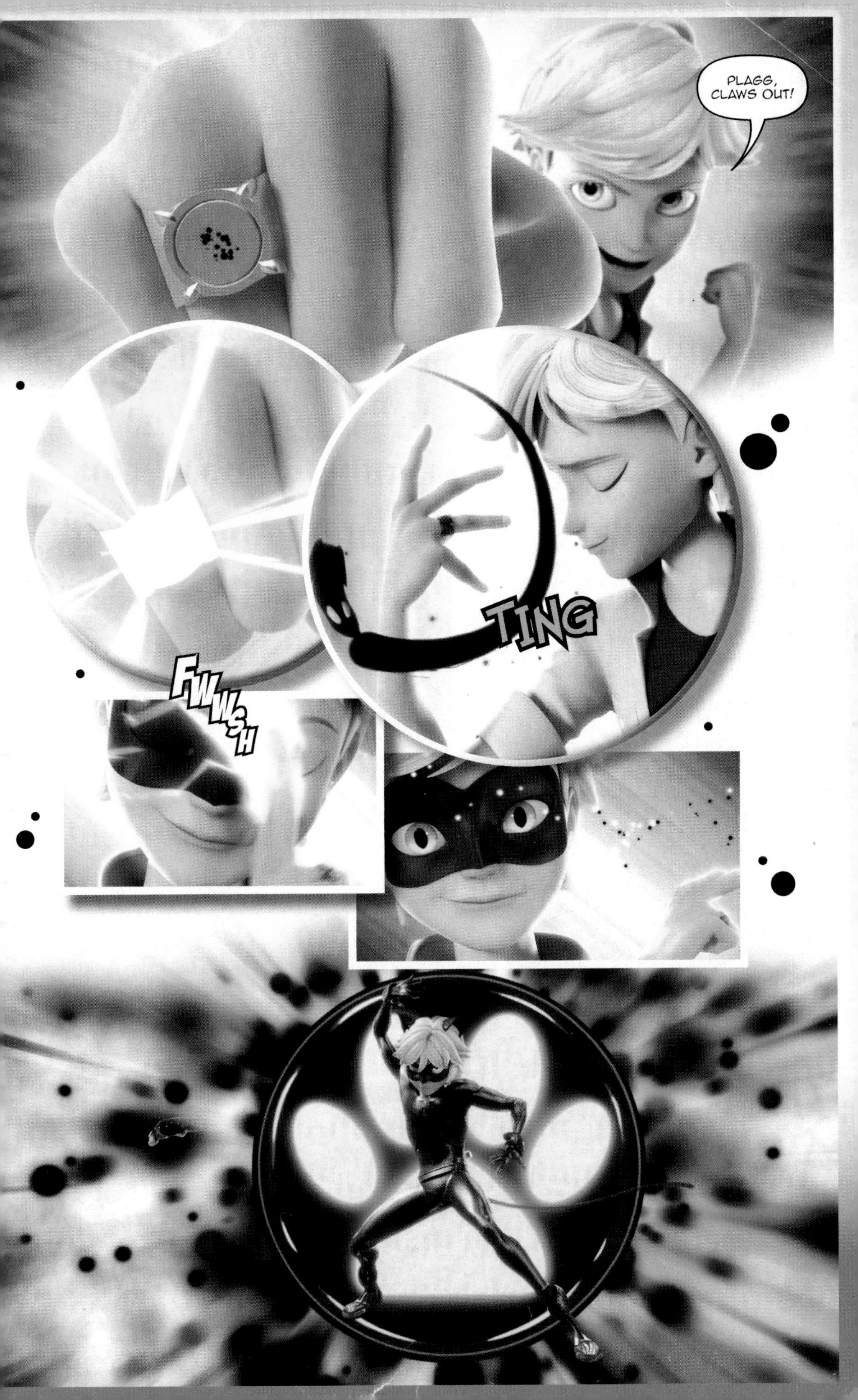
PLAGG, CLAWS OUT!
TING
FWWSH

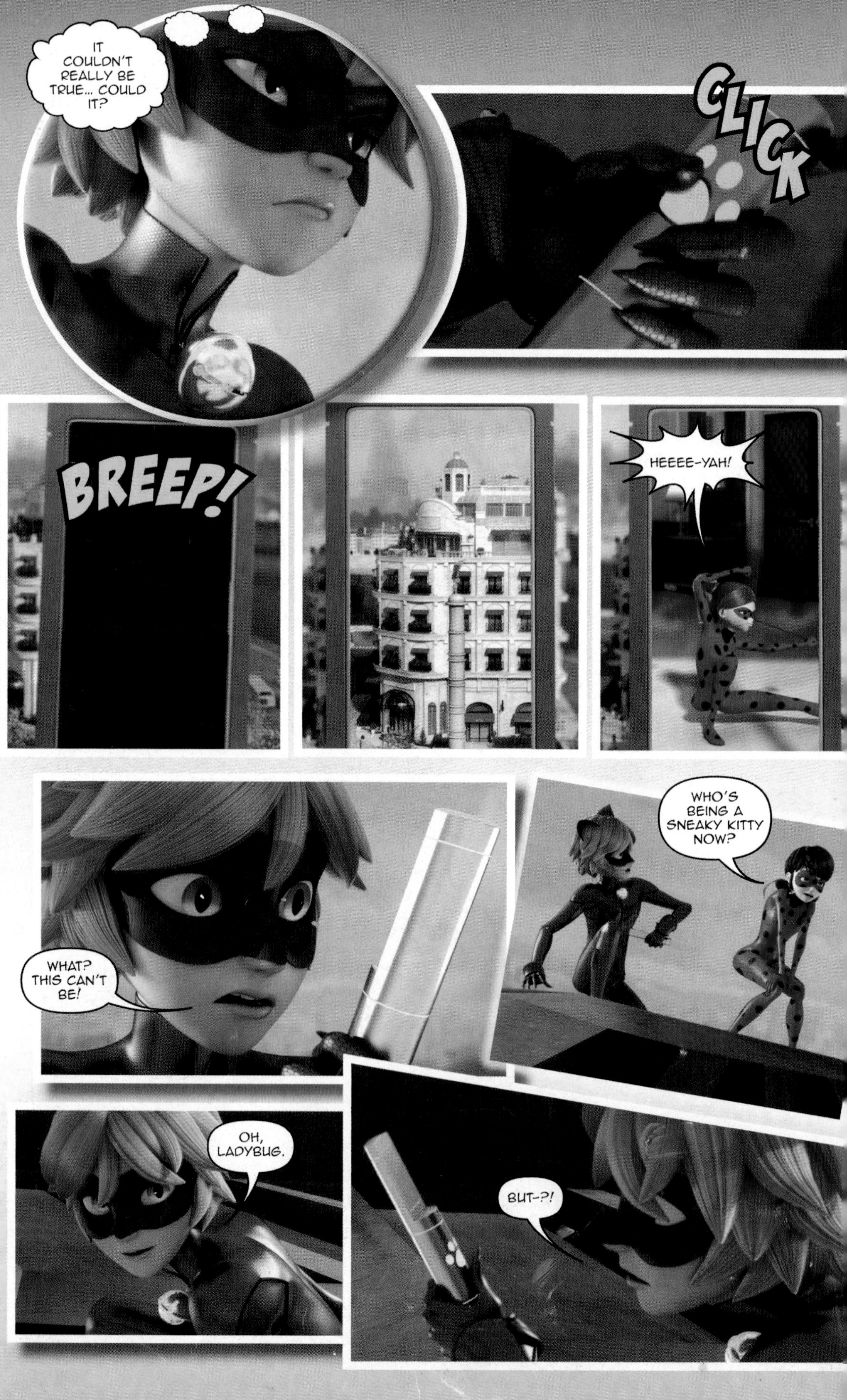
IT COULDN'T REALLY BE TRUE... COULD IT?
CLICK
BREEP!
HEEEE-YAH!
WHAT? THIS CAN'T BE!
WHO'S BEING A SNEAKY KITTY NOW?
OH, LADYBUG.
BUT-?!

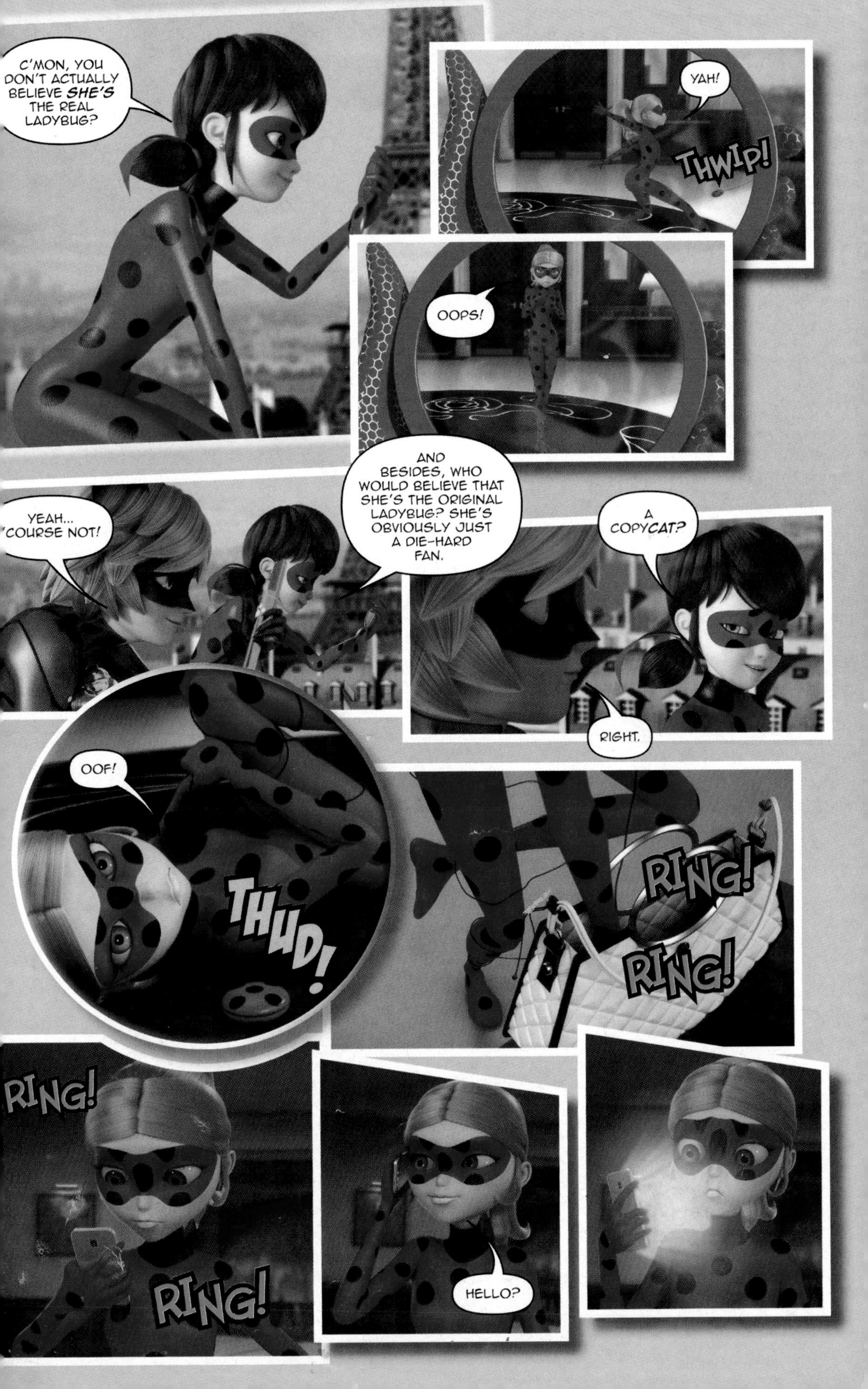
C'MON, YOU DON'T ACTUALLY BELIEVE SHE'S THE REAL LADYBUG?
YAH!
THWIP!
OOPS!
YEAH... 'COURSE NOT!
AND BESIDES, WHO WOULD BELIEVE THAT SHE'S THE ORIGINAL LADYBUG? SHE'S OBVIOUSLY JUST A DIE-HARD FAN.
A COPYCAT?
RIGHT.
OOF!
THUD!
RING!
RING!
RING!
RING!
HELLO?

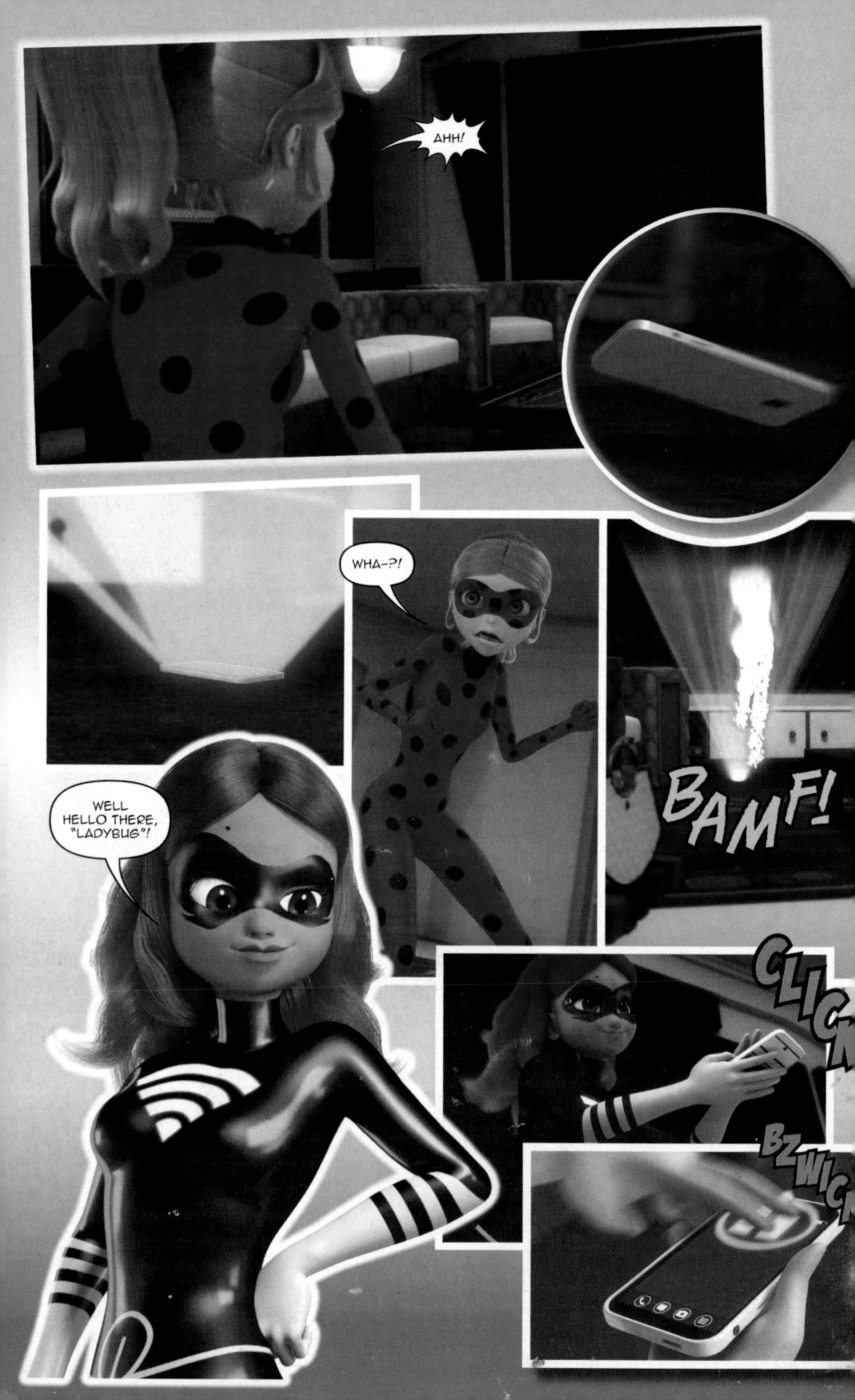
AHH!
WHA-?!
BAMF!
WELL HELLO THERE, "LADYBUG"!
CLICK
BZWICK

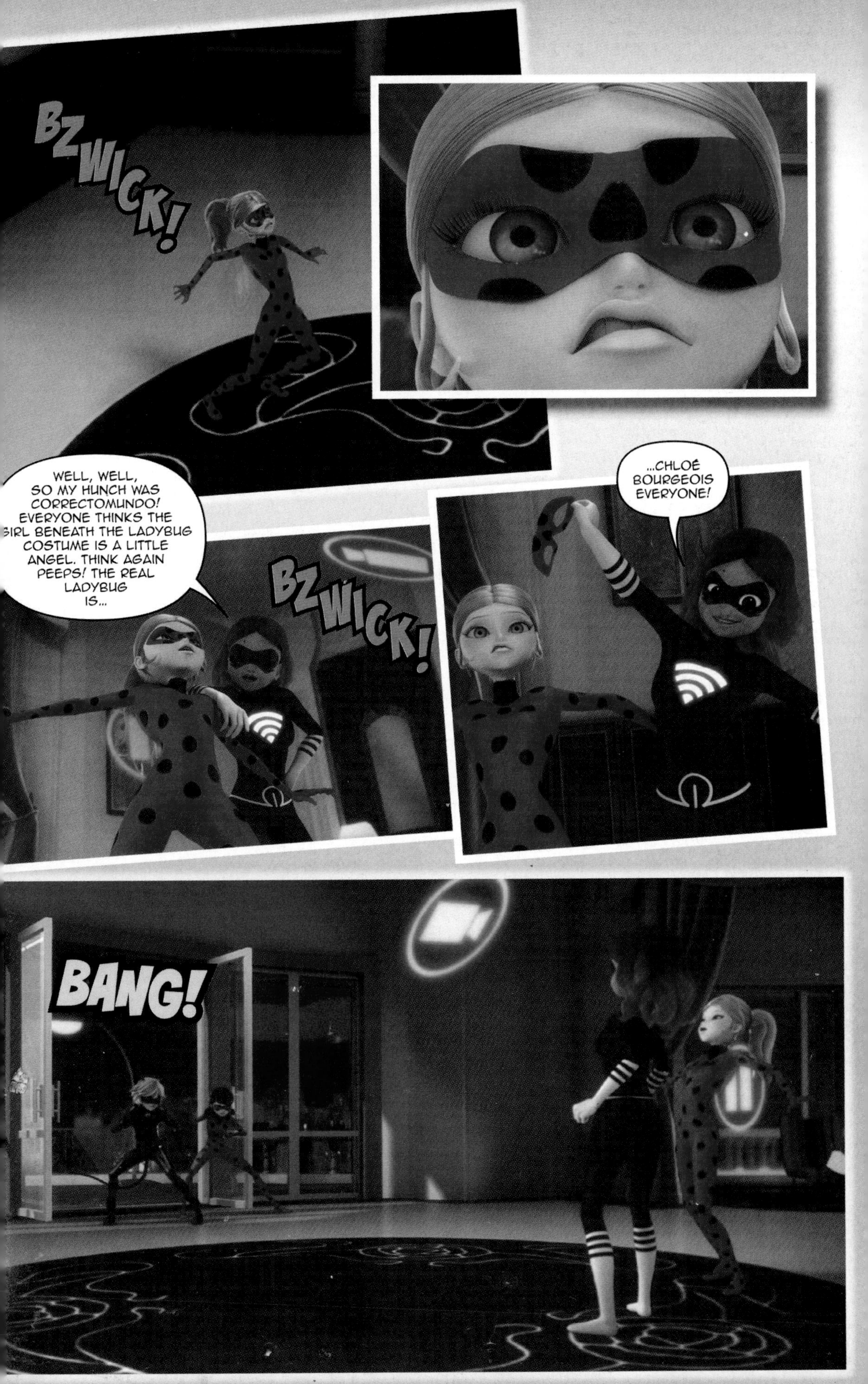
BZWICK!
WELL, WELL, SO MY HUNCH WAS CORRECTOMUNDO! EVERYONE THINKS THE GIRL BENEATH THE LADYBUG COSTUME IS A LITTLE ANGEL. THINK AGAIN PEEPS! THE REAL LADYBUG IS...
BZWICK!
...CHLOÉ BOURGEOIS EVERYONE!
BANG!

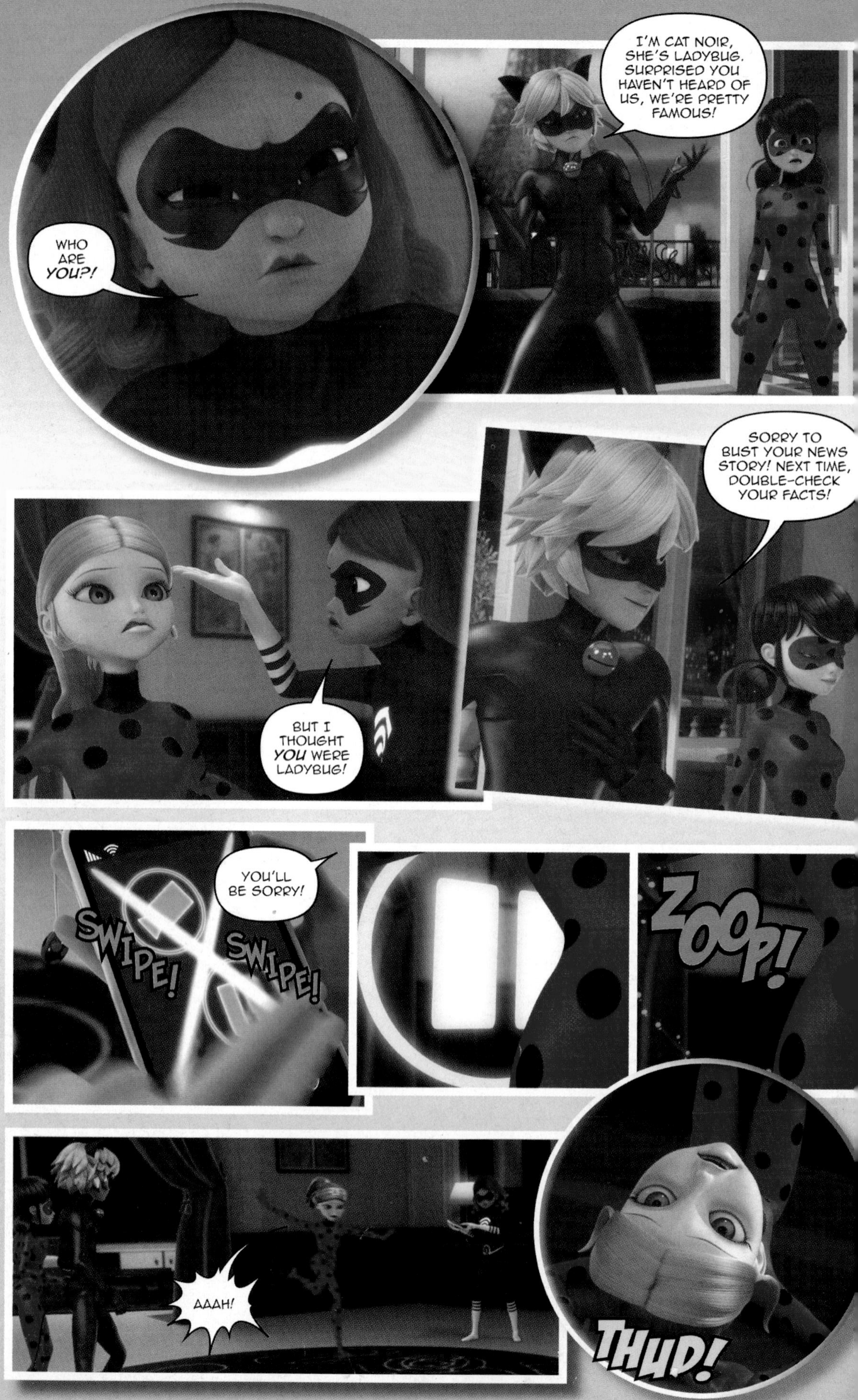
I'M CAT NOIR, SHE'S LADYBUG. SURPRISED YOU HAVEN'T HEARD OF US, WE'RE PRETTY FAMOUS!
WHO ARE *YOU*?!
SORRY TO BUST YOUR NEWS STORY! NEXT TIME, DOUBLE-CHECK YOUR FACTS!
BUT I THOUGHT *YOU* WERE LADYBUG!
YOU'LL BE SORRY!
SWIPE!
SWIPE!
ZOOP!
AAAH!
THUD!

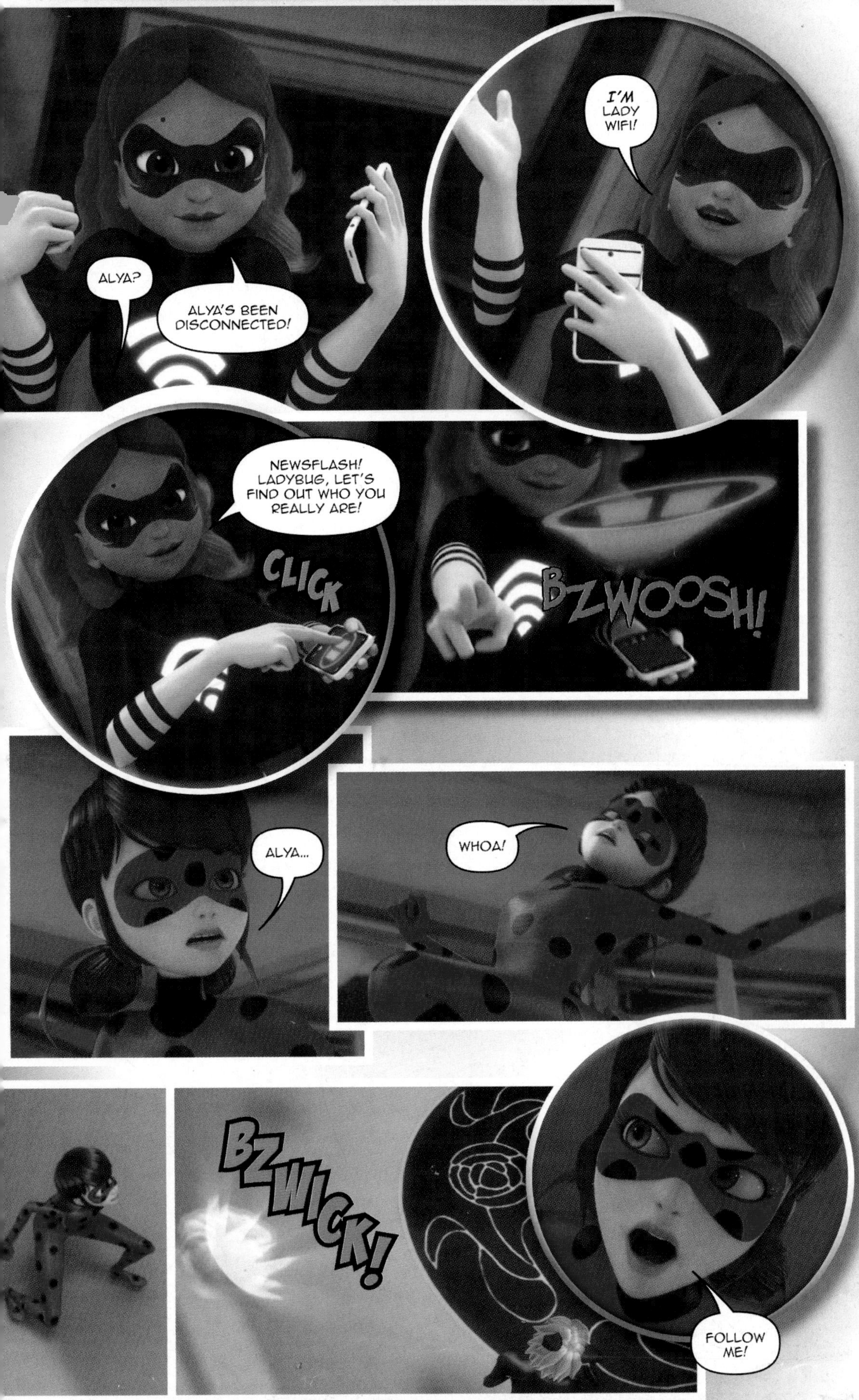
ALYA?
ALYA'S BEEN DISCONNECTED!
I'M LADY WIFI!
NEWSFLASH! LADYBUG, LET'S FIND OUT WHO YOU REALLY ARE!
CLICK
BZWOOSH!
ALYA...
WHOA!
BZWICK!
FOLLOW ME!

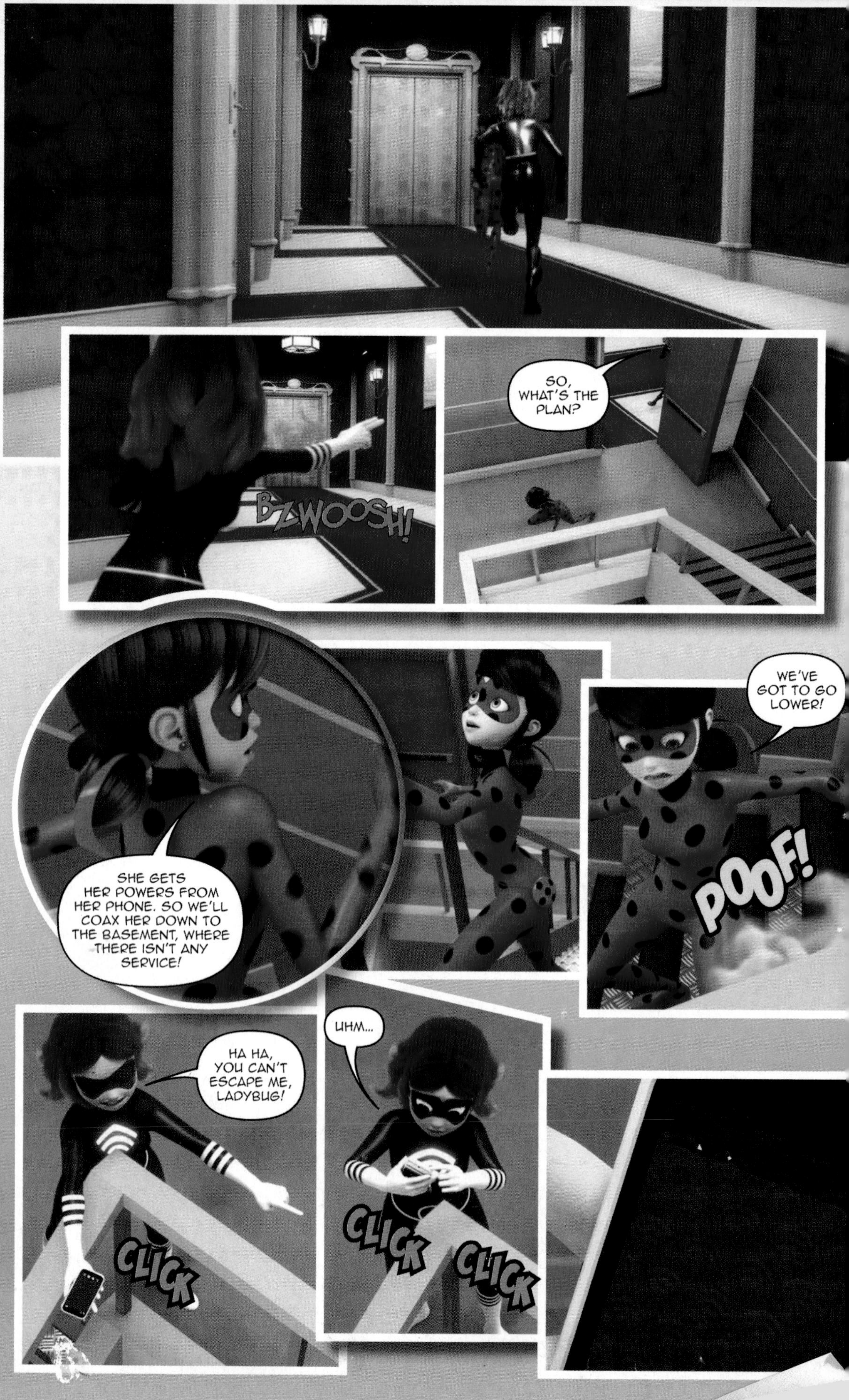
BZWOOSH!
SO, WHAT'S THE PLAN?
SHE GETS HER POWERS FROM HER PHONE. SO WE'LL COAX HER DOWN TO THE BASEMENT, WHERE THERE ISN'T ANY SERVICE!
WE'VE GOT TO GO LOWER!
POOF!
HA HA, YOU CAN'T ESCAPE ME, LADYBUG!
CLICK
UHM...
CLICK
CLICK

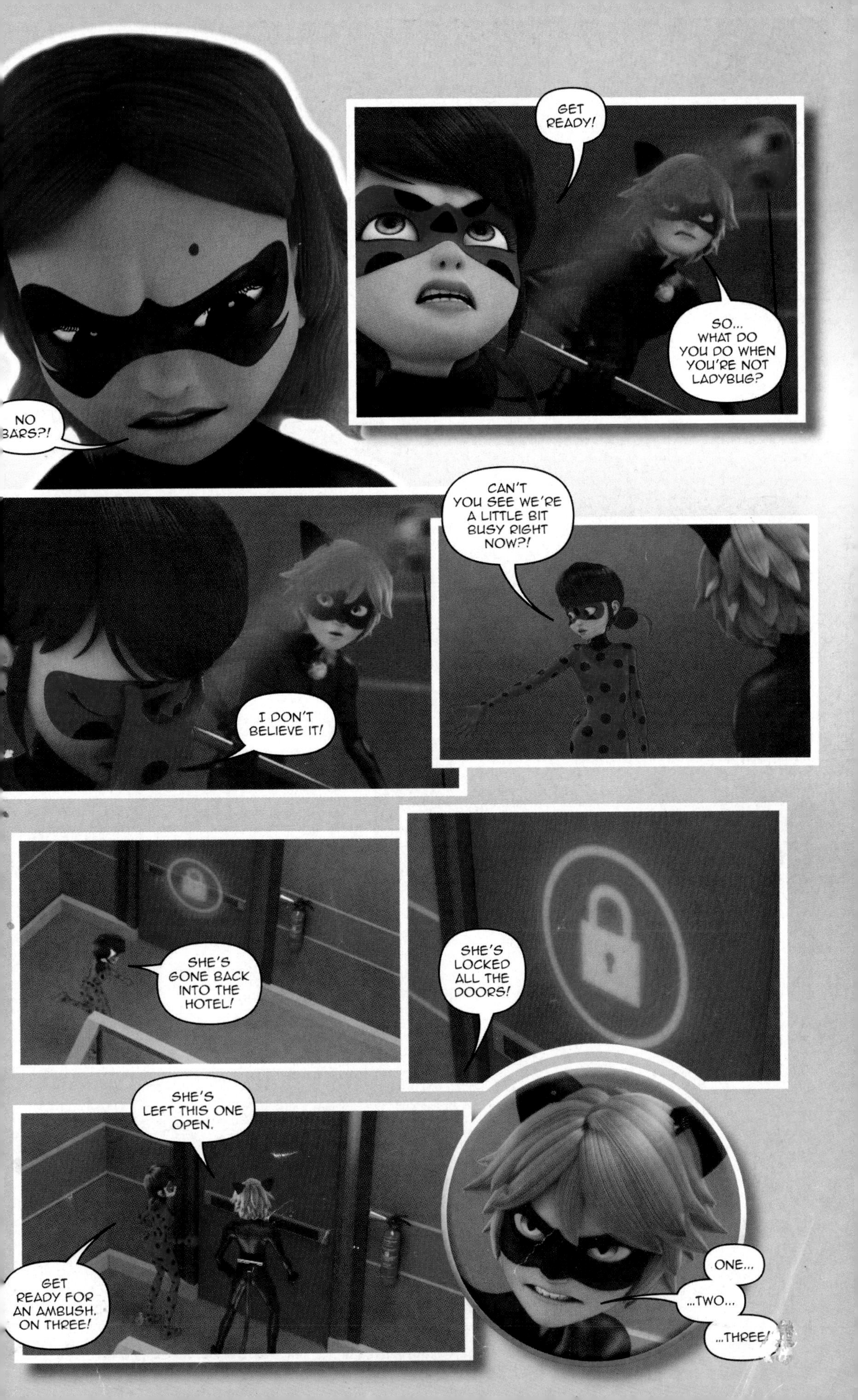
NO BARS?!
GET READY!
SO... WHAT DO YOU DO WHEN YOU'RE NOT LADYBUG?
I DON'T BELIEVE IT!
CAN'T YOU SEE WE'RE A LITTLE BIT BUSY RIGHT NOW?!
SHE'S GONE BACK INTO THE HOTEL!
SHE'S LOCKED ALL THE DOORS!
SHE'S LEFT THIS ONE OPEN.
GET READY FOR AN AMBUSH. ON THREE!
ONE...
...TWO...
...THREE!

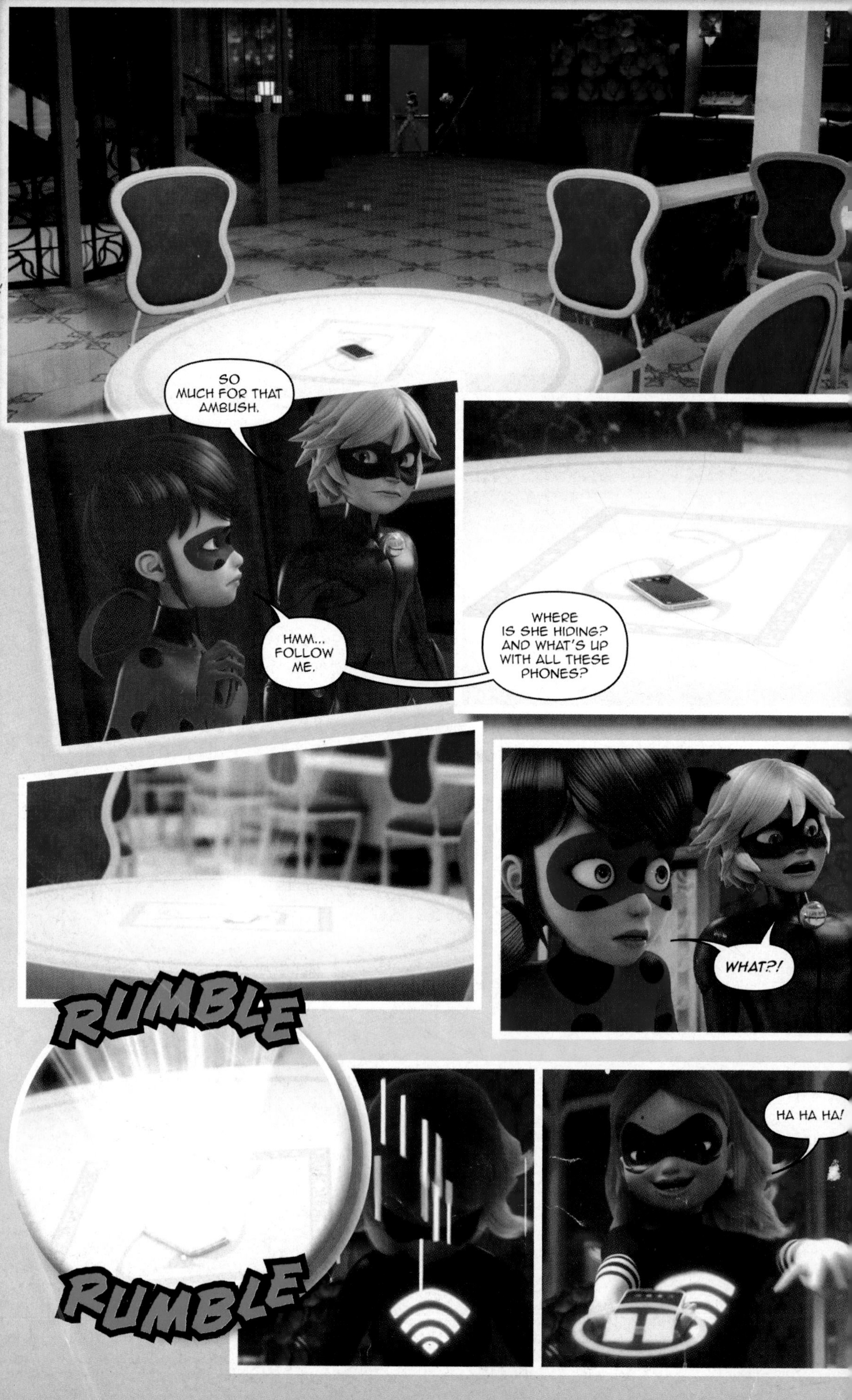
SO MUCH FOR THAT AMBUSH.
HMM... FOLLOW ME.
WHERE IS SHE HIDING? AND WHAT'S UP WITH ALL THESE PHONES?
WHAT?!
RUMBLE
RUMBLE
HA HA HA!

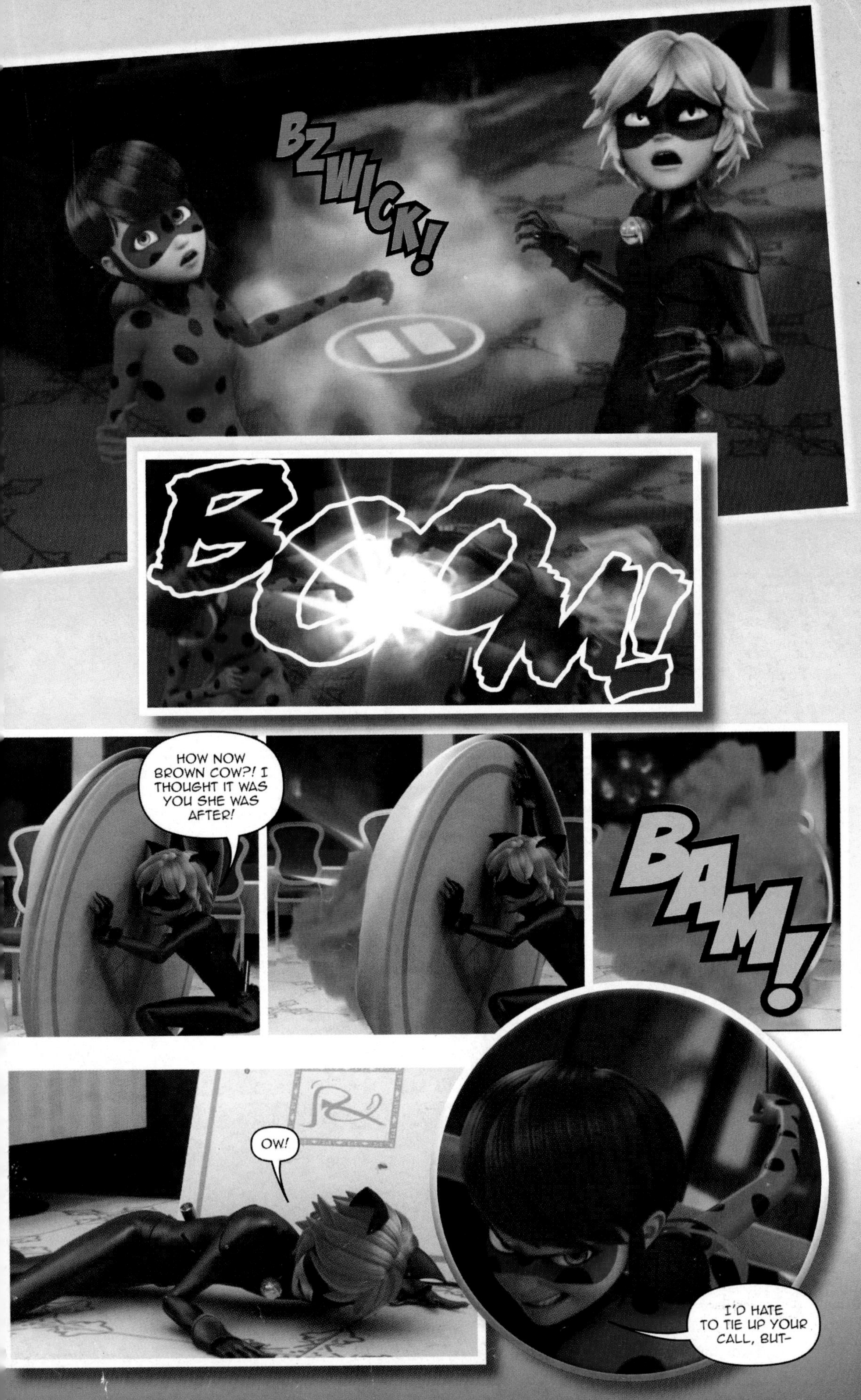
BZWICK!
BOOM!
HOW NOW BROWN COW?! I THOUGHT IT WAS YOU SHE WAS AFTER!
BAM!
OW!
I'D HATE TO TIE UP YOUR CALL, BUT-

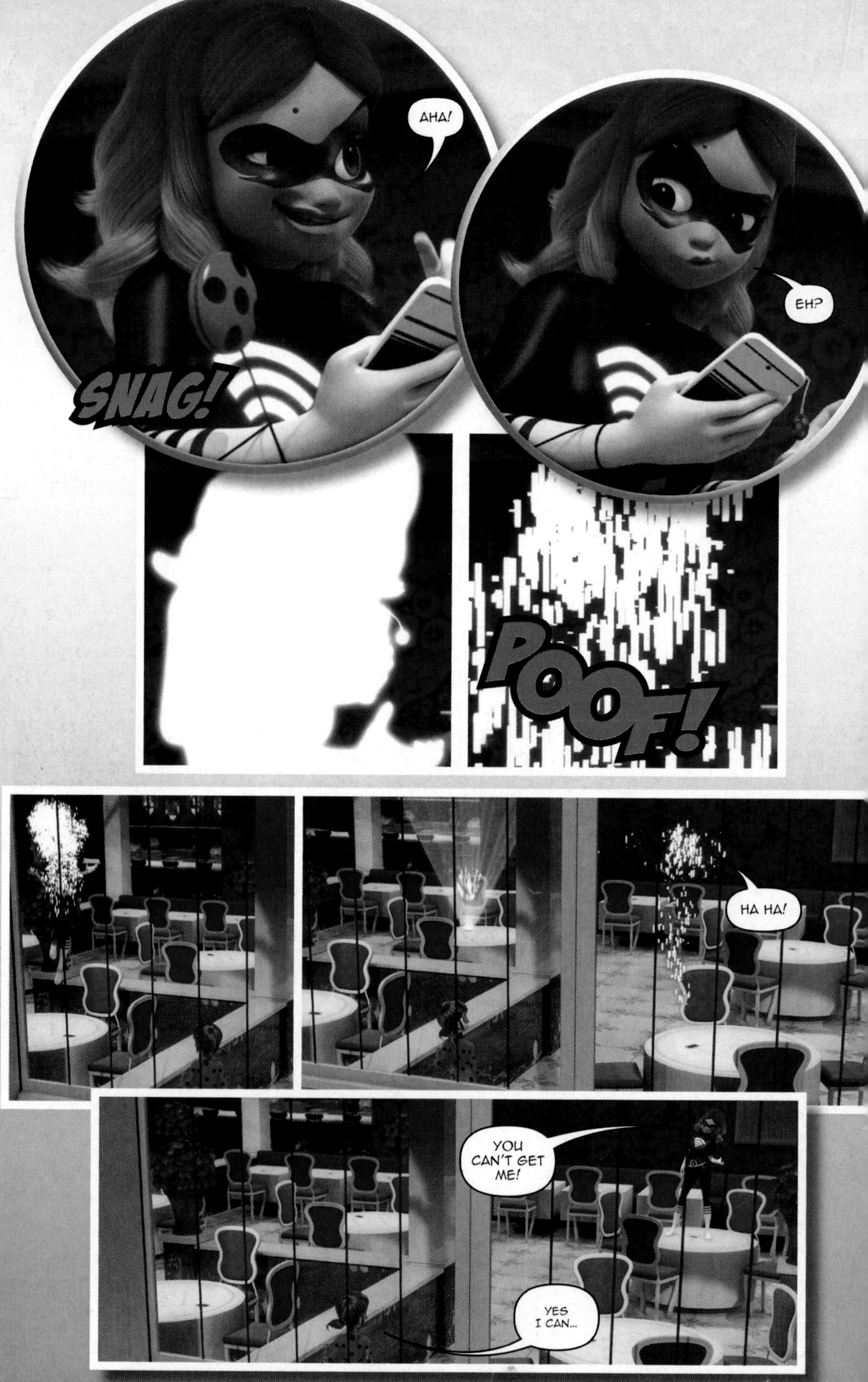
AHA!
SNAG!
EH?
POOF!
HA HA!
YOU CAN'T GET ME!
YES I CAN...

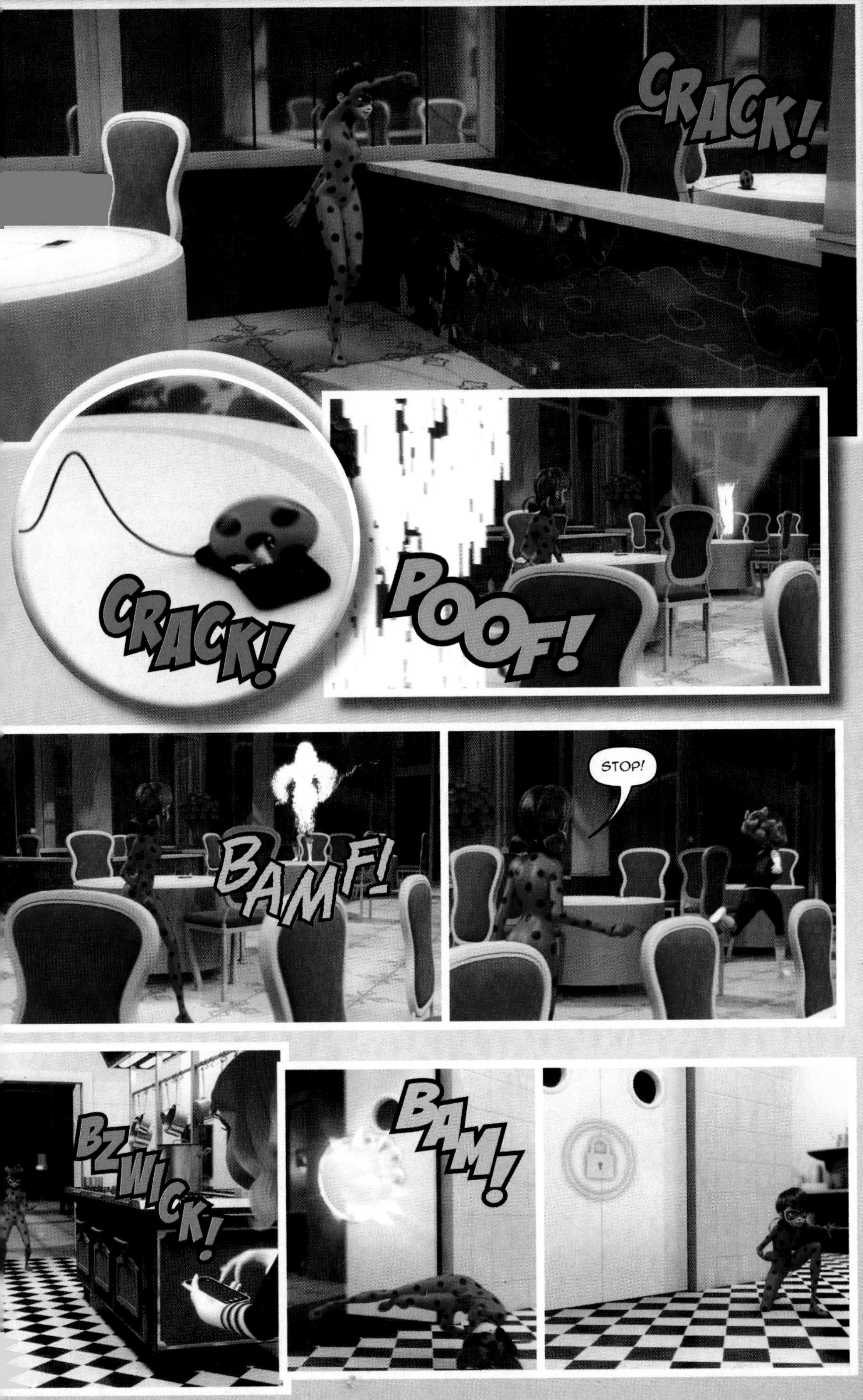
CRACK!
CRACK!
POOF!
BAMF!
STOP!
BZWICK!
BAM!

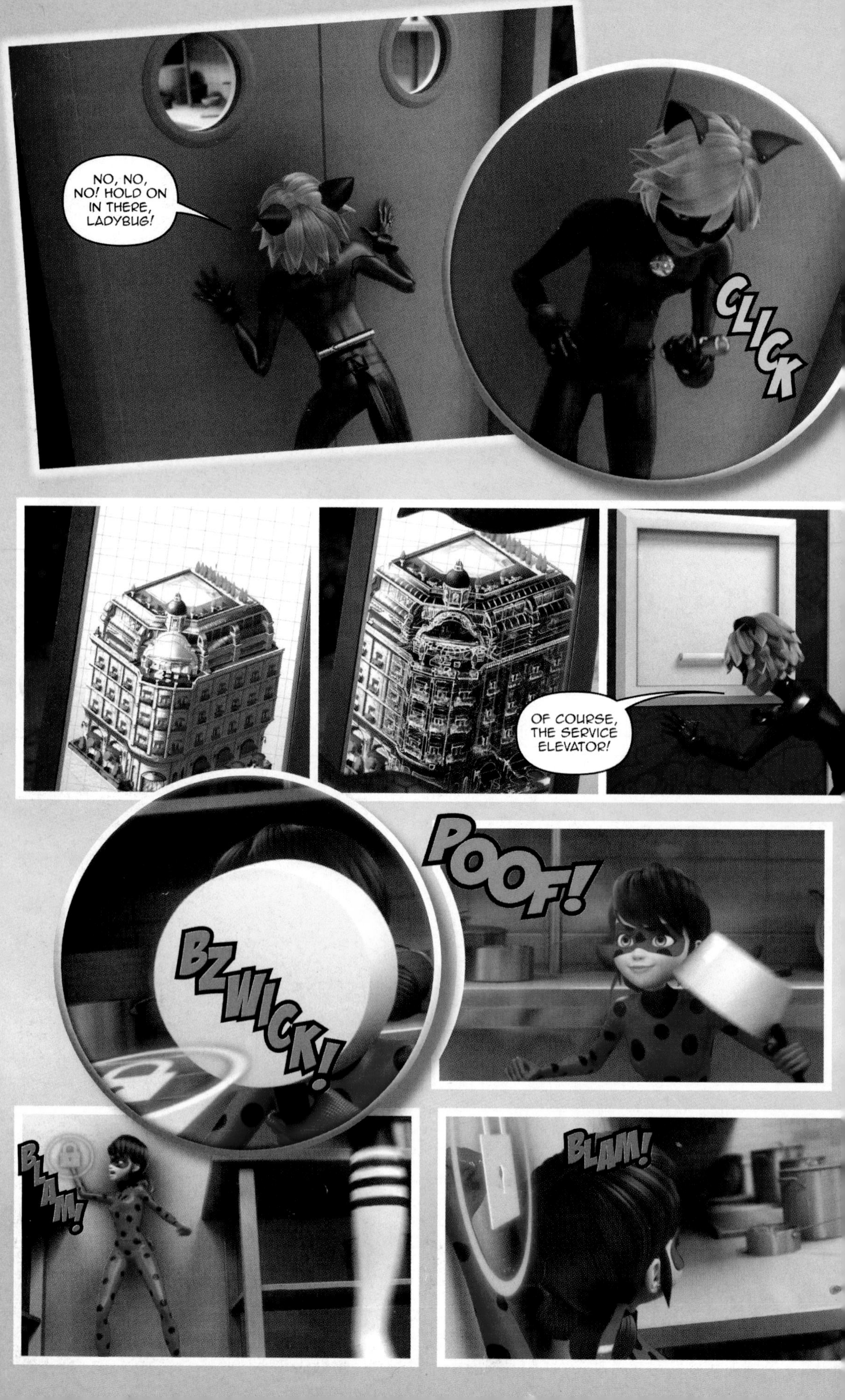
NO, NO, NO! HOLD ON IN THERE, LADYBUG!
CLICK
OF COURSE, THE SERVICE ELEVATOR!
BZWICK!
POOF!
BLAM!
BLAM!

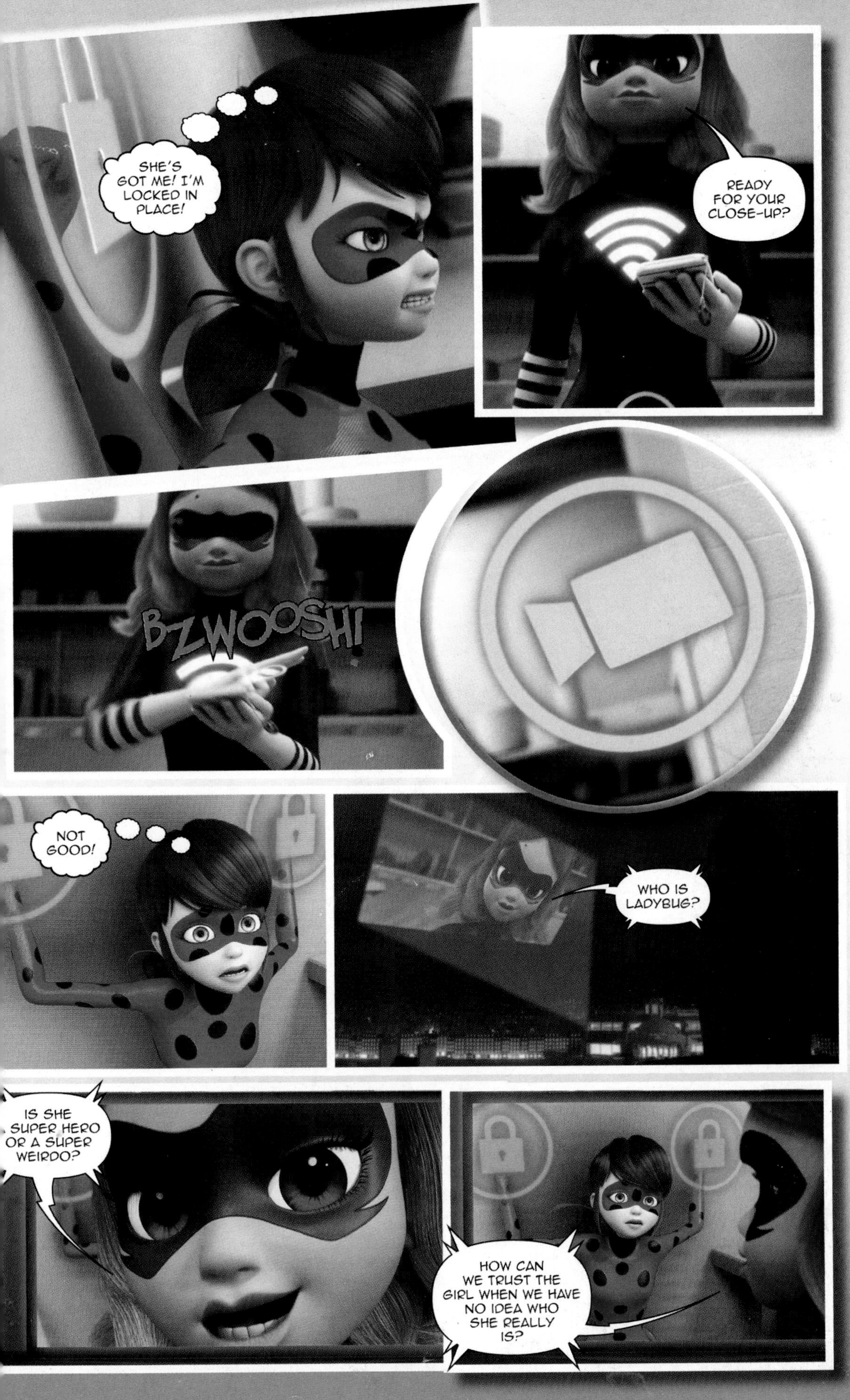
SHE'S GOT ME! I'M LOCKED IN PLACE!
READY FOR YOUR CLOSE-UP?
B-ZWOOSH!
NOT GOOD!
WHO IS LADYBUG?
IS SHE SUPER HERO OR A SUPER WEIRDO?
HOW CAN WE TRUST THE GIRL WHEN WE HAVE NO IDEA WHO SHE REALLY IS?

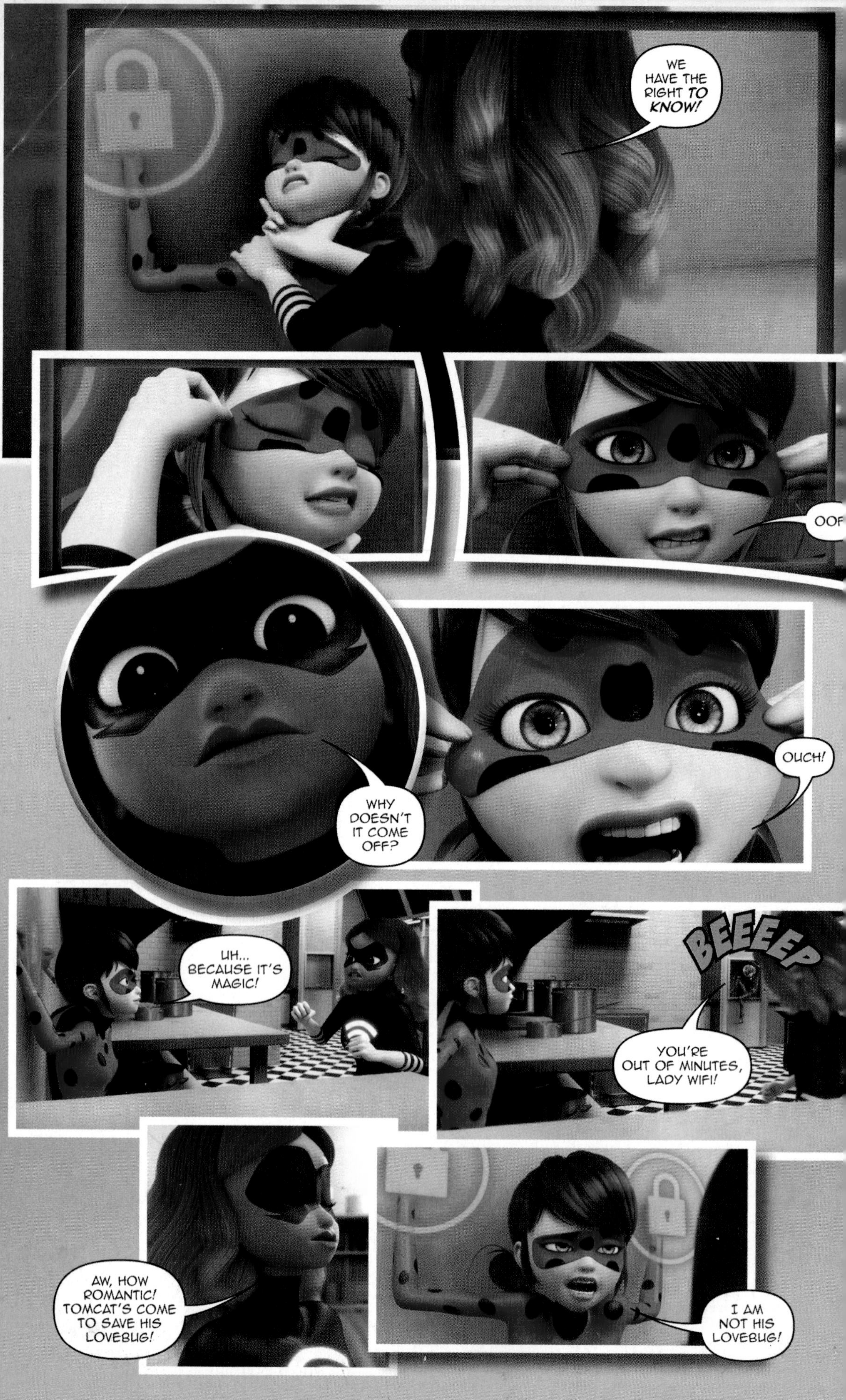
WE HAVE THE RIGHT TO KNOW!
OOF
WHY DOESN'T IT COME OFF?
OUCH!
UH... BECAUSE IT'S MAGIC!
BEEEEP
YOU'RE OUT OF MINUTES, LADY WIFI!
AW, HOW ROMANTIC! TOMCAT'S COME TO SAVE HIS LOVEBUG!
I AM NOT HIS LOVEBUG!

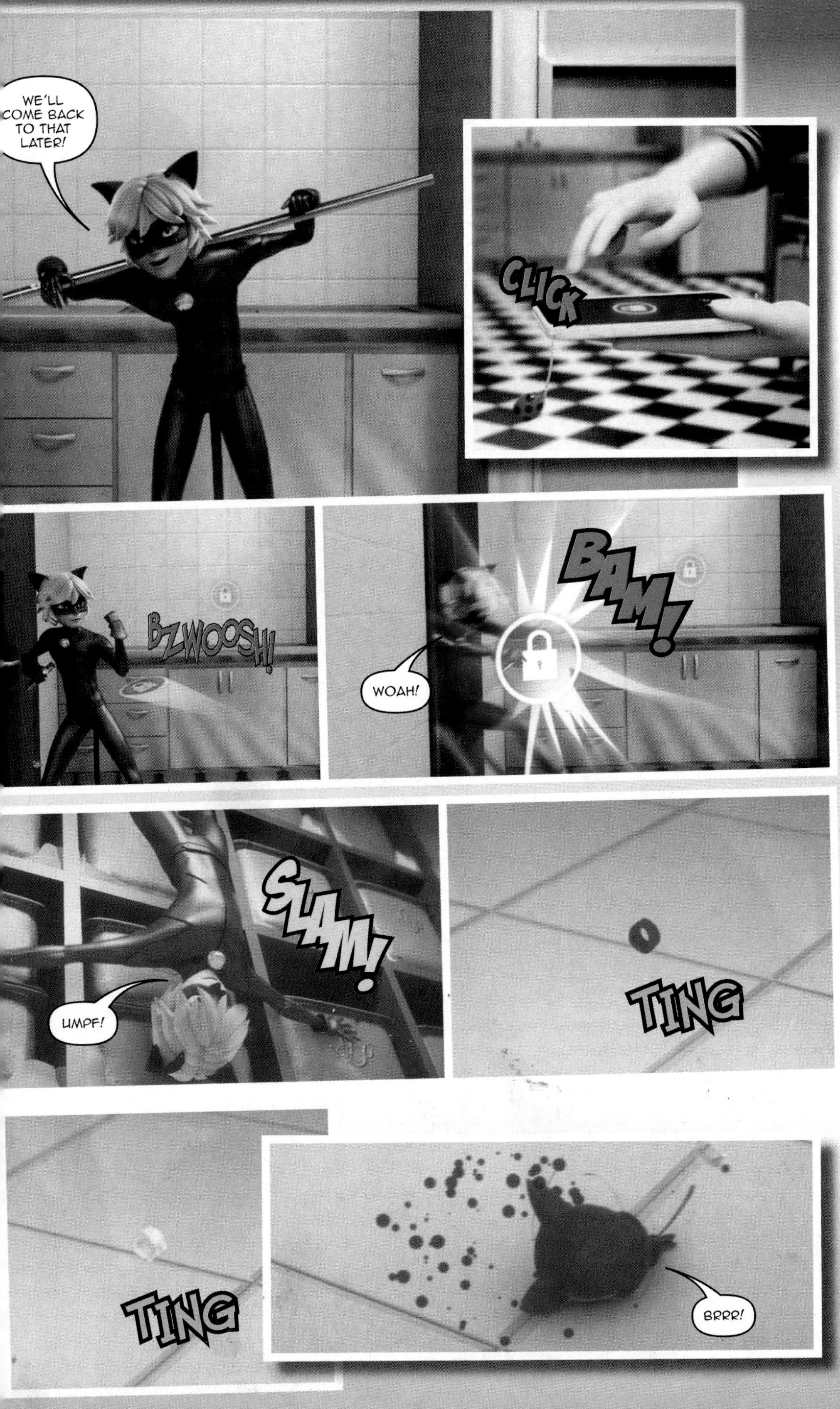
WE'LL COME BACK TO THAT LATER!
CLICK
BZWOOSH!
BAM!
WOAH!
SLAM!
UMPF!
TING
TING
BRRR!

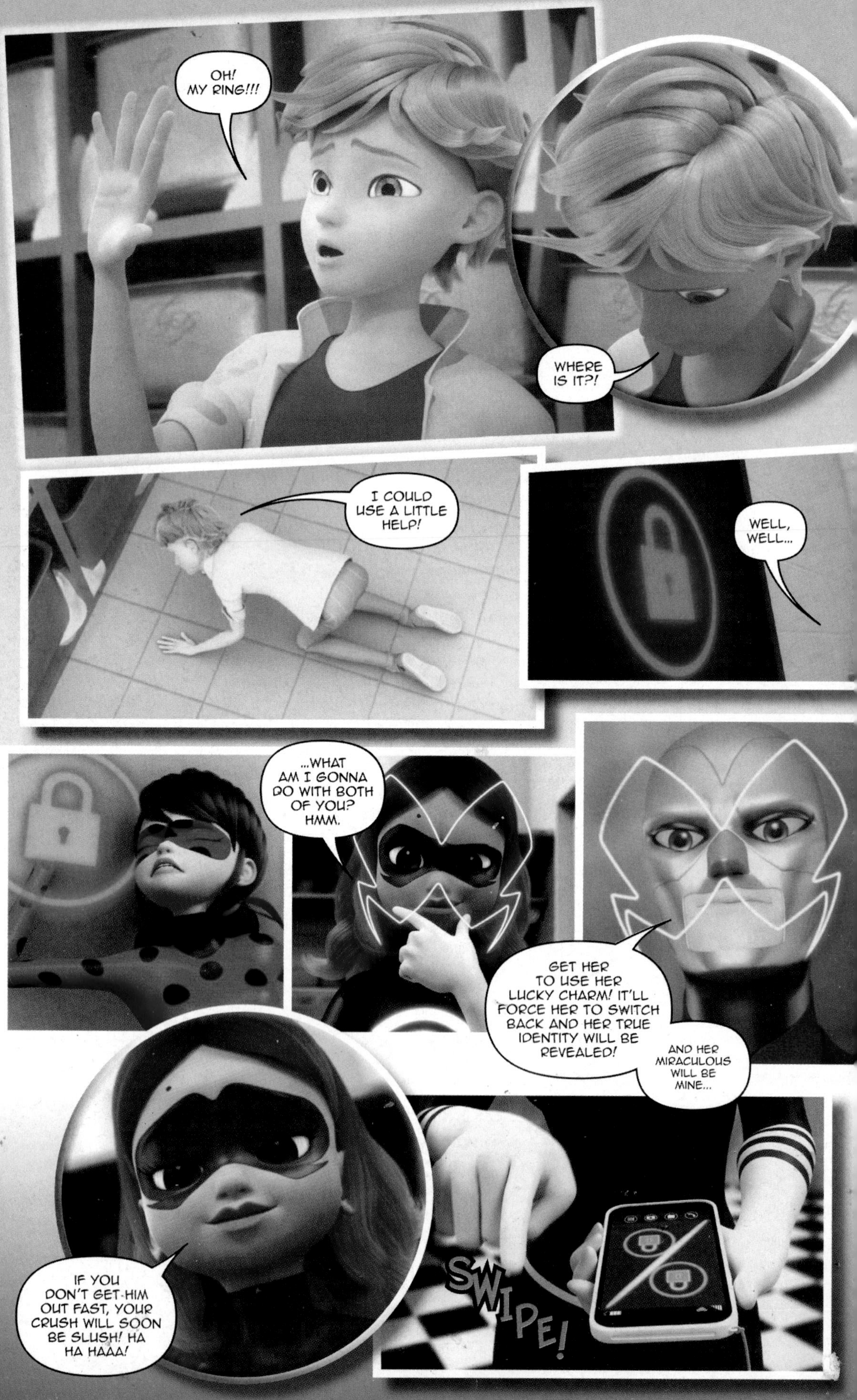
OH! MY RING!!!
WHERE IS IT?!
I COULD USE A LITTLE HELP!
WELL, WELL...
...WHAT AM I GONNA DO WITH BOTH OF YOU? HMM.
GET HER TO USE HER LUCKY CHARM! IT'LL FORCE HER TO SWITCH BACK AND HER TRUE IDENTITY WILL BE REVEALED!
AND HER MIRACULOUS WILL BE MINE...
IF YOU DON'T GET HIM OUT FAST, YOUR CRUSH WILL SOON BE SLUSH! HA HA HAAA!
SWIPE!

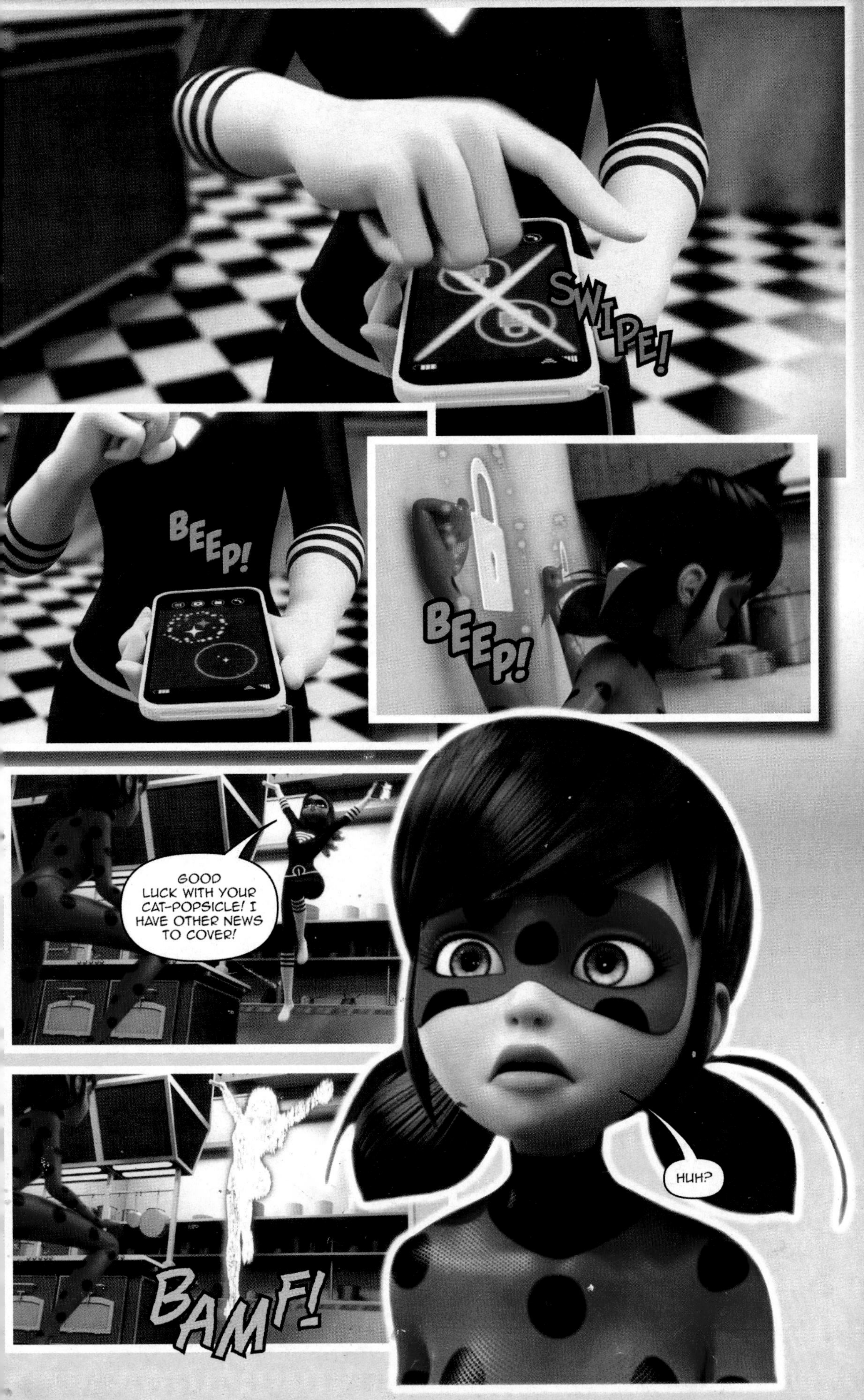
SWIPE!
BEEP!
BEEP!
GOOD LUCK WITH YOUR CAT-POPSICLE! I HAVE OTHER NEWS TO COVER!
BAMF!
HUH?

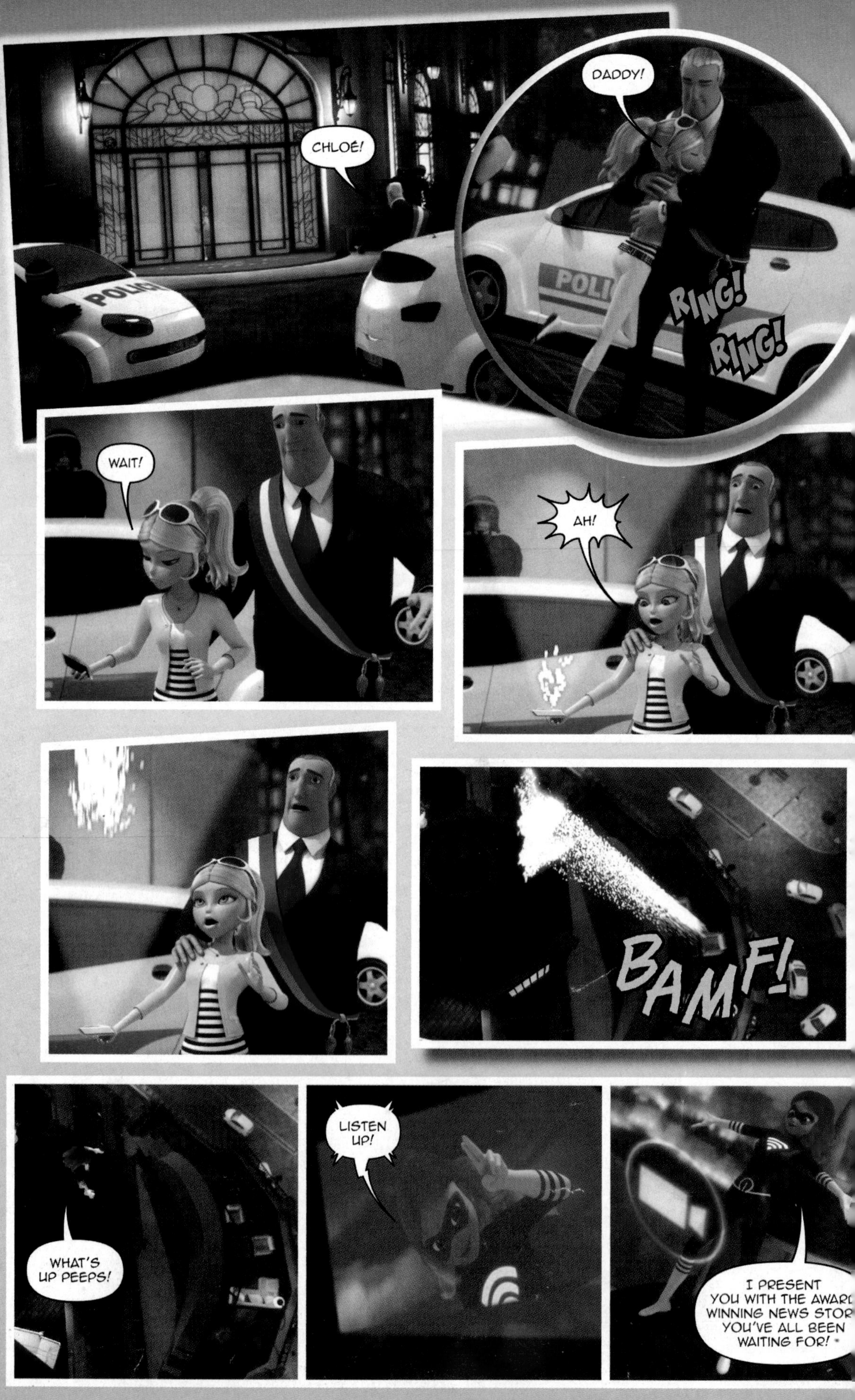
CHLOÉ!
DADDY!
RING!
RING!
WAIT!
AH!
BAMF!
WHAT'S UP PEEPS!
LISTEN UP!
I PRESENT YOU WITH THE AWARD WINNING NEWS STORY YOU'VE ALL BEEN WAITING FOR!

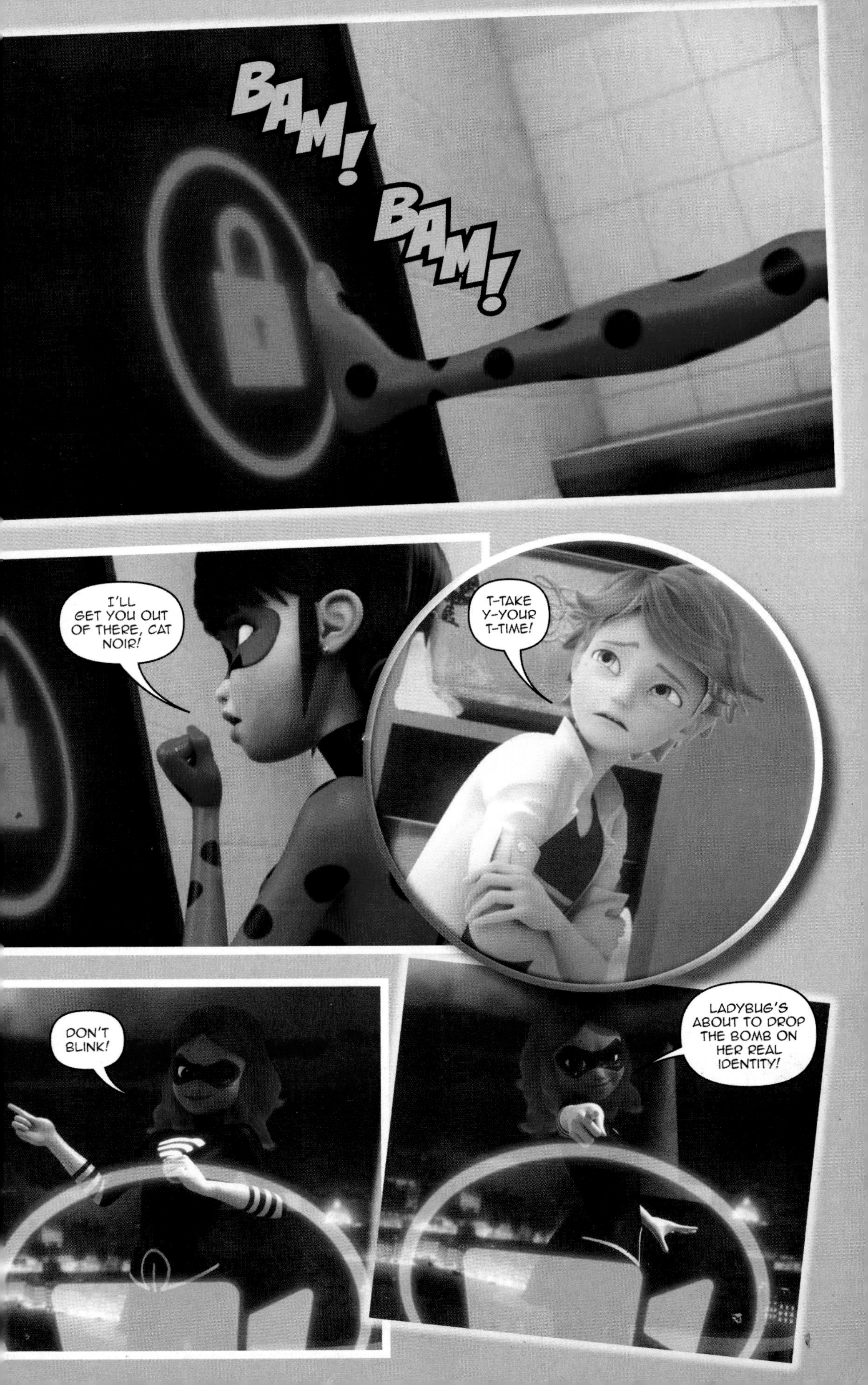
BAM! BAM!
I'LL GET YOU OUT OF THERE, CAT NOIR!
T-TAKE Y-YOUR T-TIME!
DON'T BLINK!
LADYBUG'S ABOUT TO DROP THE BOMB ON HER REAL IDENTITY!

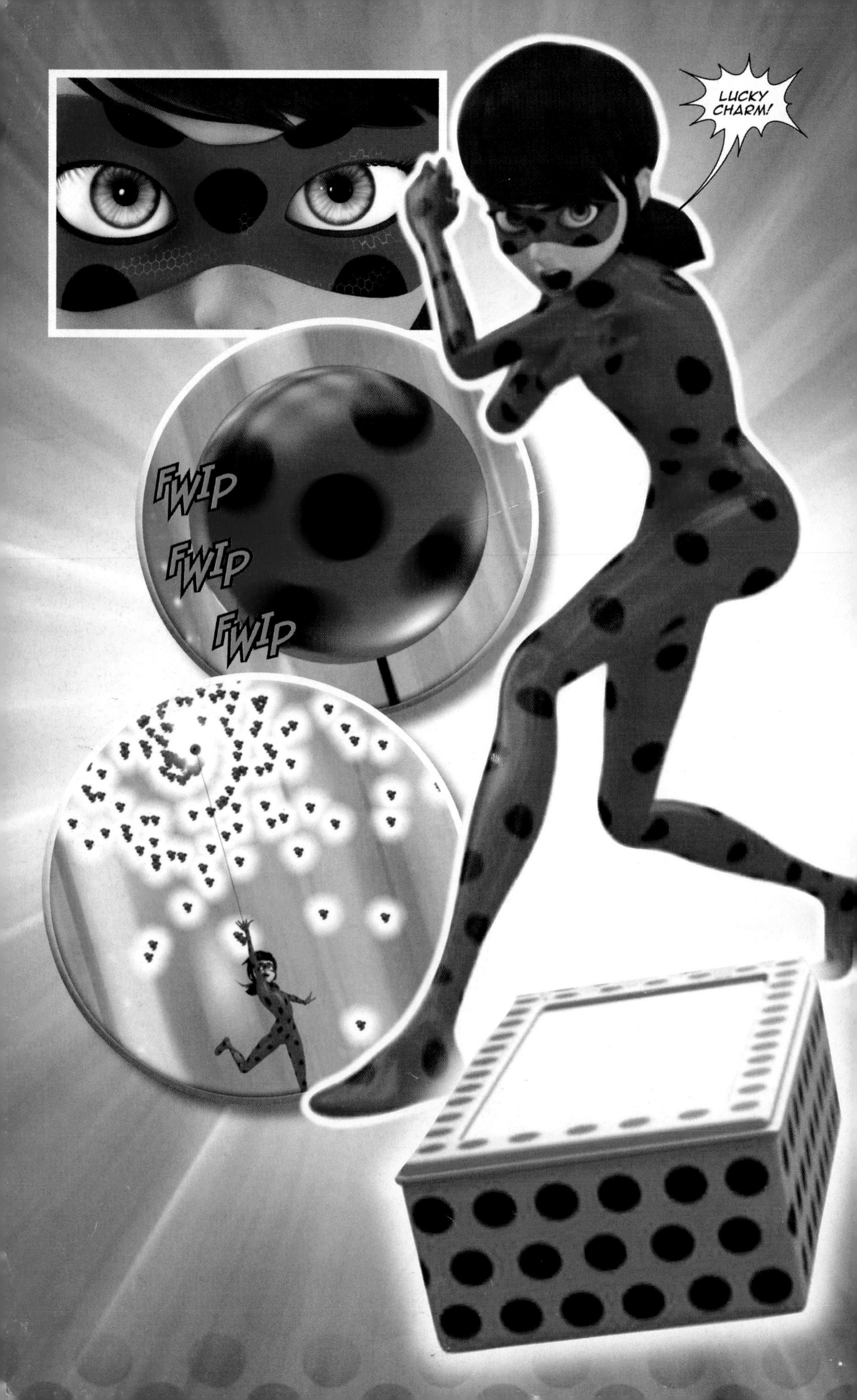
LUCKY CHARM!
FWIP
FWIP
FWIP

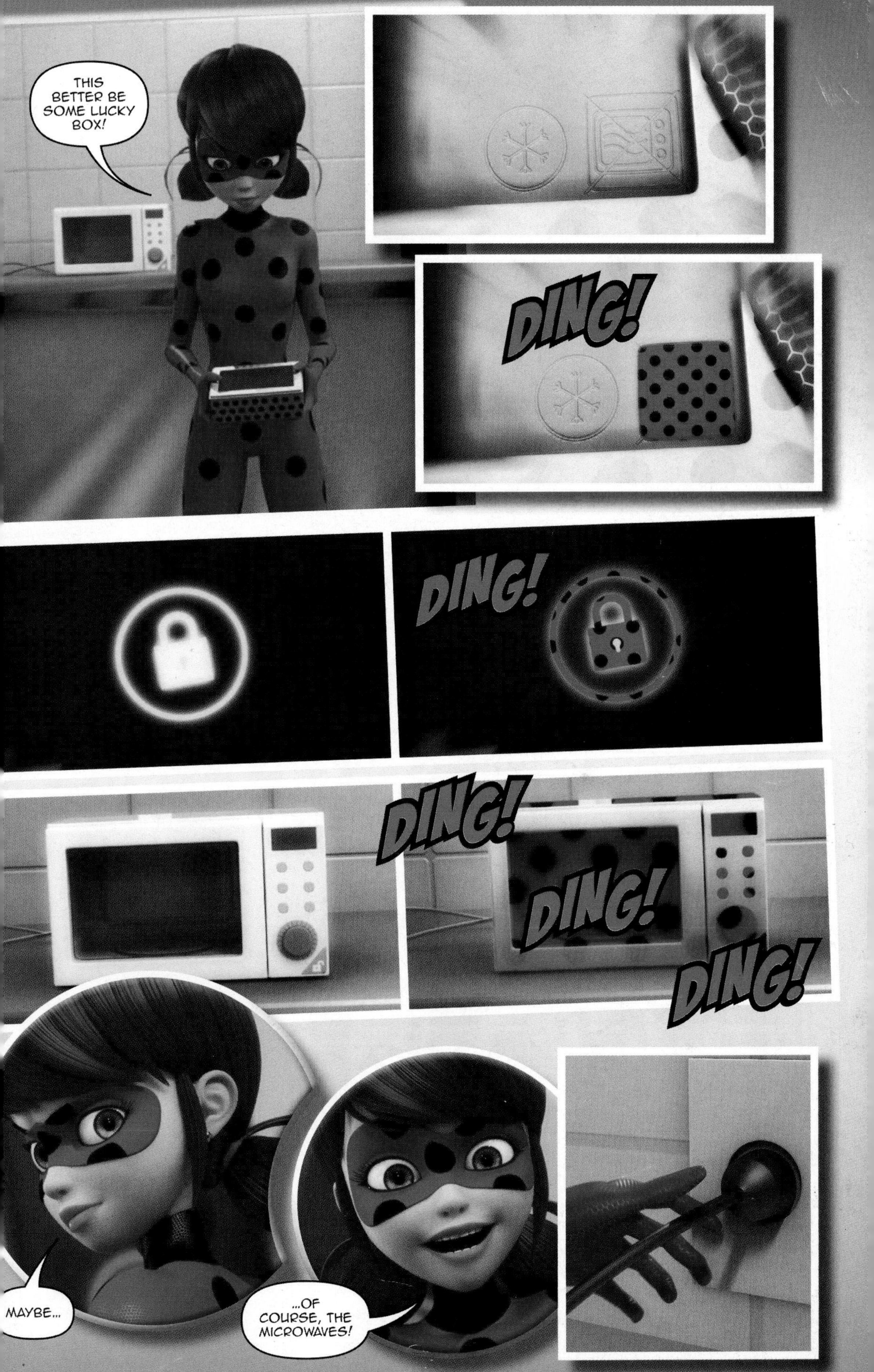
THIS BETTER BE SOME LUCKY BOX!
DING!
DING!
DING!
DING!
DING!
MAYBE...
...OF COURSE, THE MICROWAVES!

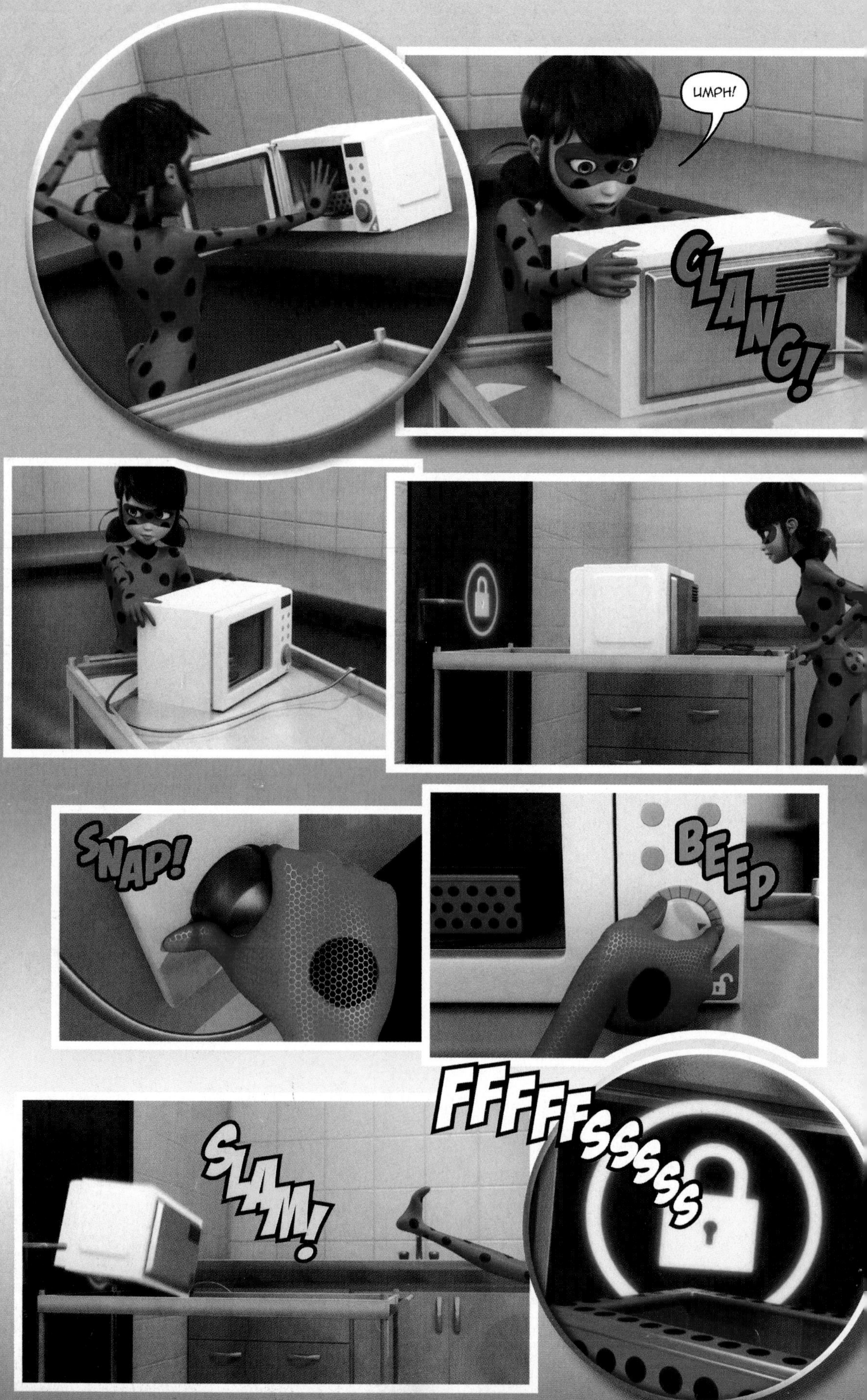
UMPH!
CLANG!
SNAP!
BEEP
FFFFFSSSSSS
SLAM!

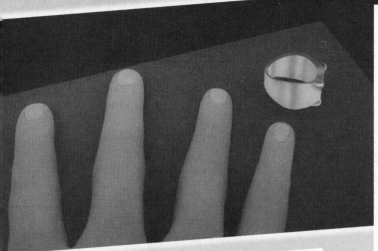

GOTCHA!

FFFFFSSSSS

FFFFFSSSSSHHHHH

COME ON, MICRO-THINGIES! JAM THE SIGNAL!

ZAP!

OOMPH!

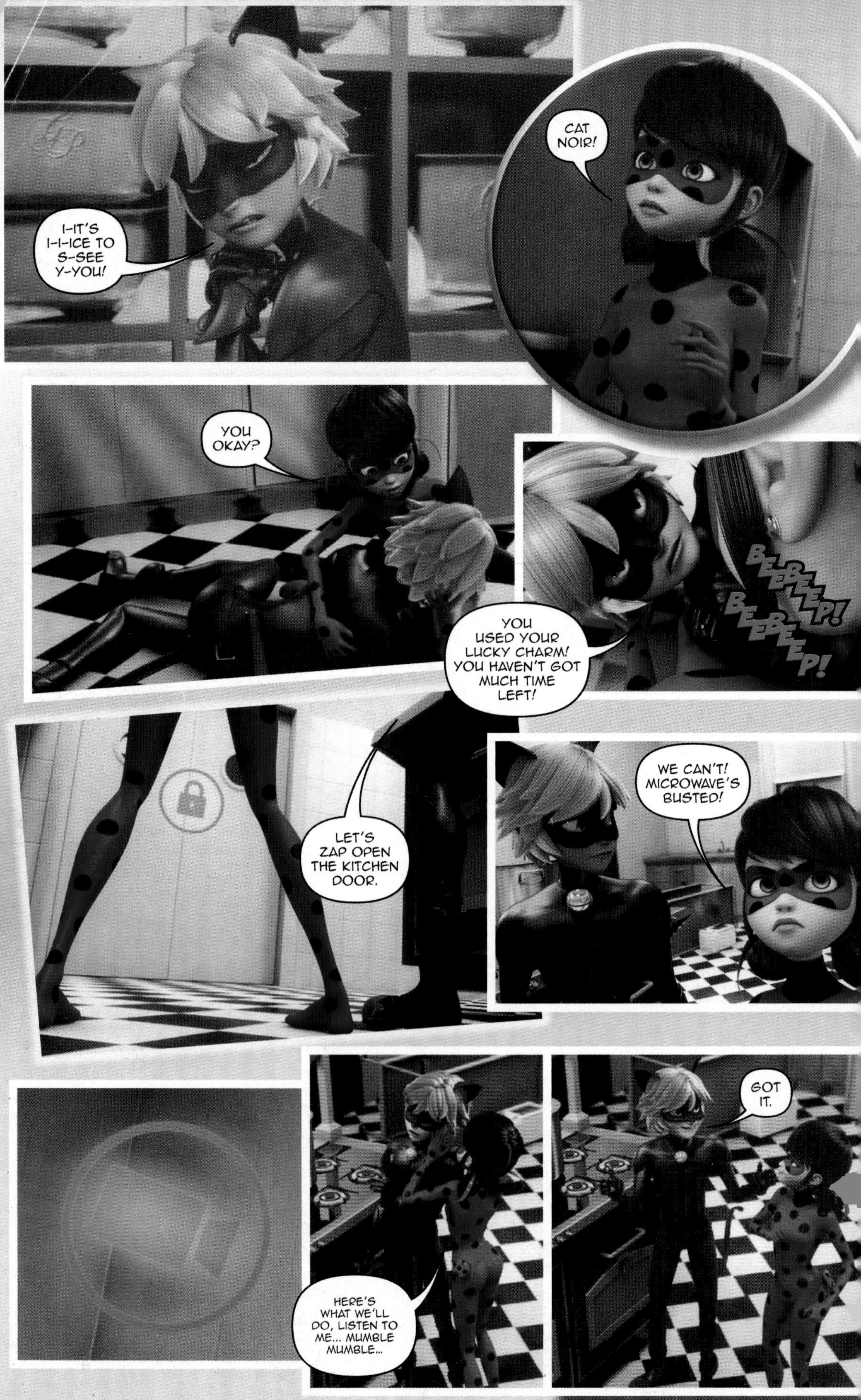
I-IT'S I-I-ICE TO S-SEE Y-YOU!
CAT NOIR!
YOU OKAY?
BEEBEEP! BEEBEEP!
YOU USED YOUR LUCKY CHARM! YOU HAVEN'T GOT MUCH TIME LEFT!
LET'S ZAP OPEN THE KITCHEN DOOR.
WE CAN'T! MICROWAVE'S BUSTED!
HERE'S WHAT WE'LL DO, LISTEN TO ME... MUMBLE MUMBLE...
GOT IT.

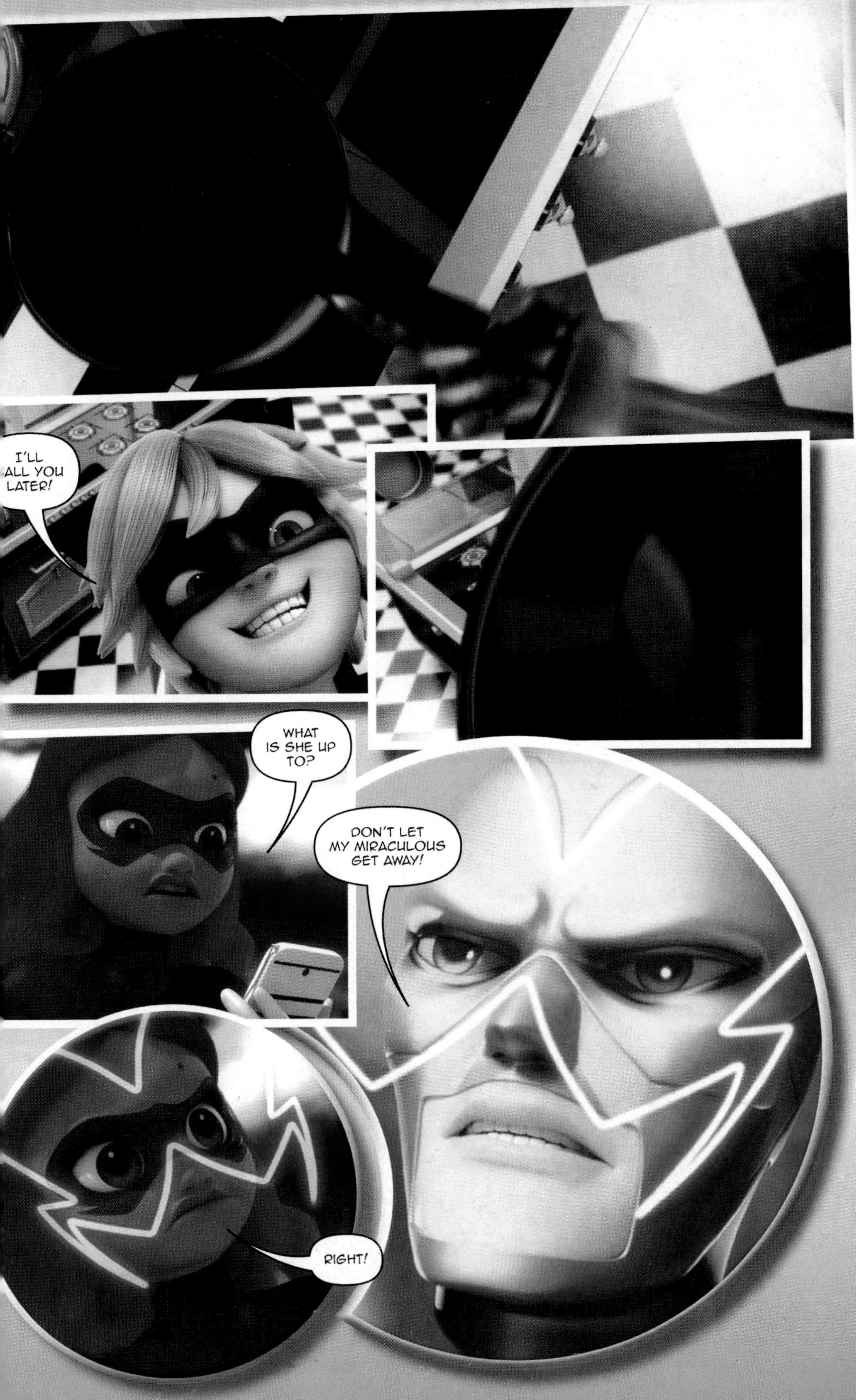
I'LL
ALL YOU LATER!
WHAT IS SHE UP TO?
DON'T LET MY MIRACULOUS GET AWAY!
RIGHT!

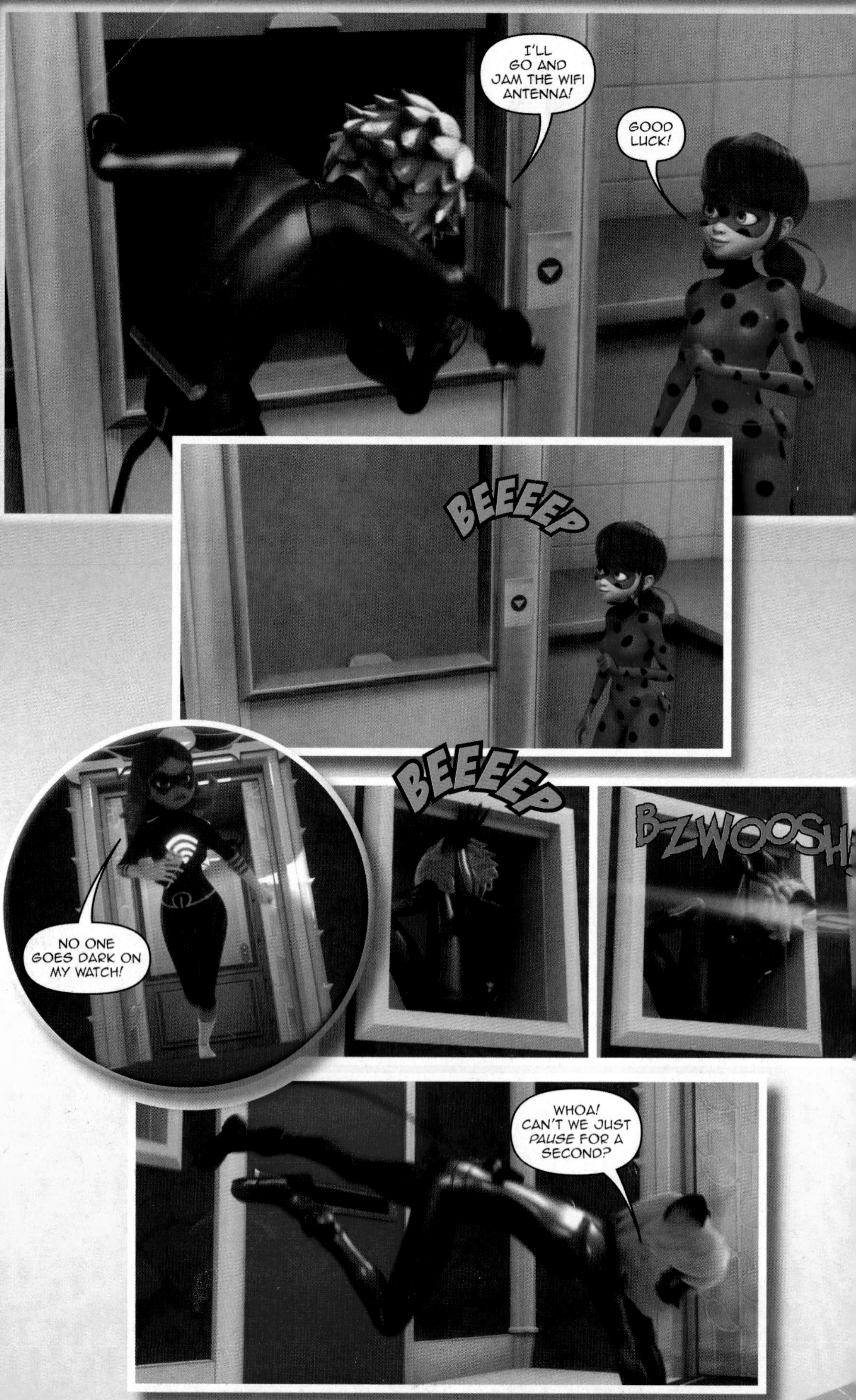
I'LL GO AND JAM THE WIFI ANTENNA!
GOOD LUCK!
BEEEEP
NO ONE GOES DARK ON MY WATCH!
BEEEEP
B-ZWOOSH!
WHOA! CAN'T WE JUST *PAUSE* FOR A SECOND?

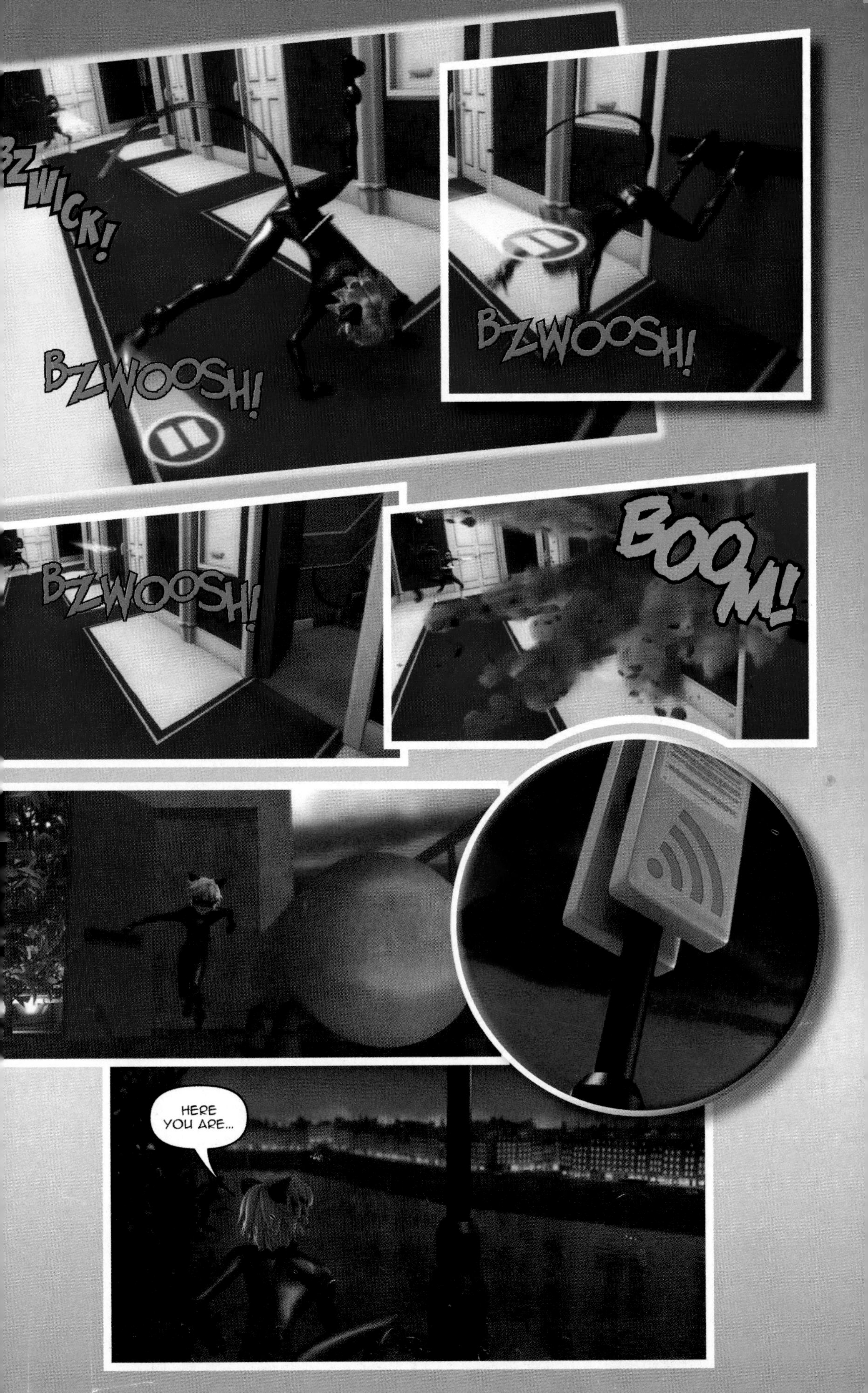
BZWICK!
BZWOOSH!
BZWOOSH!
BZWOOSH!
BOOM!
HERE YOU ARE...

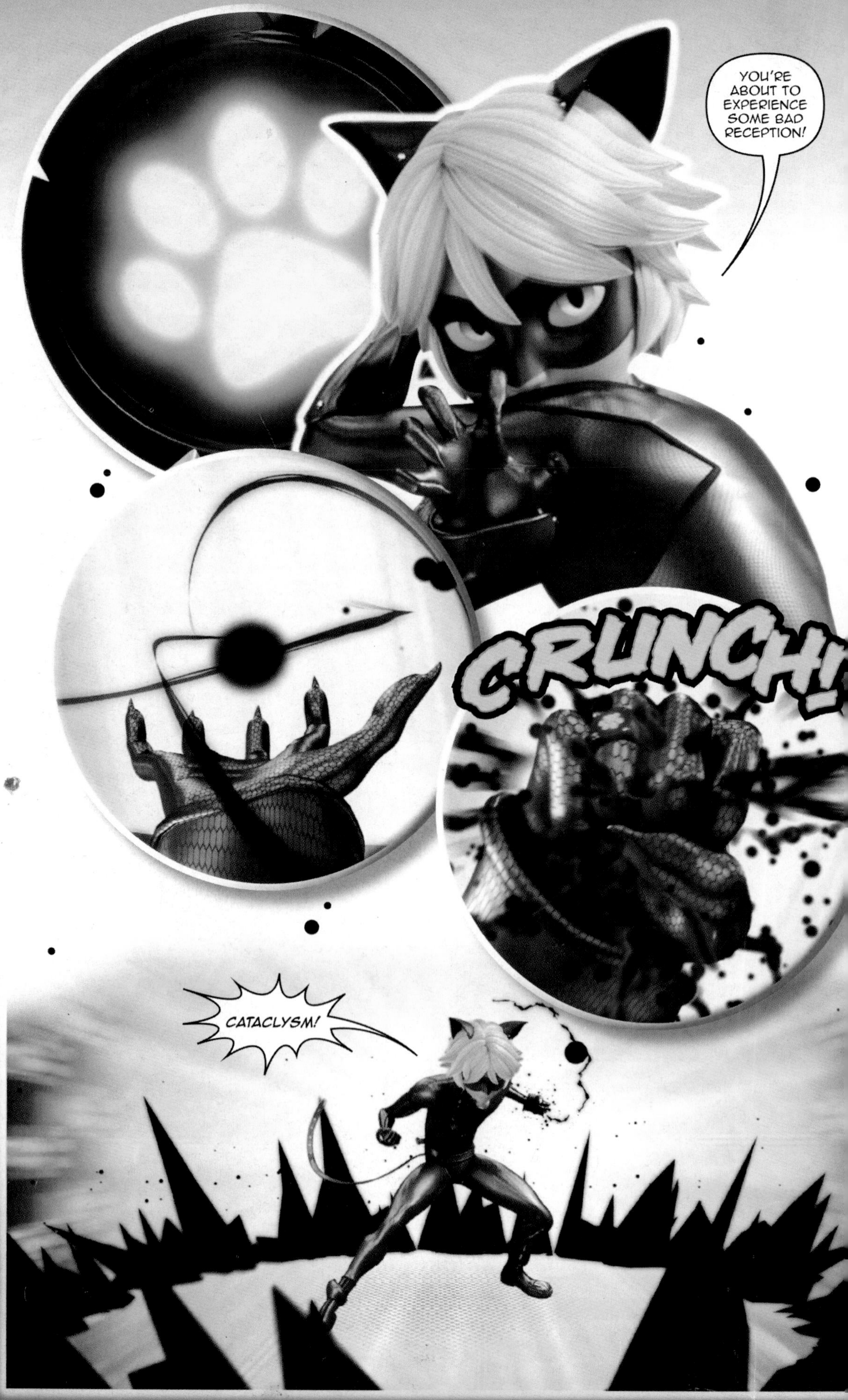
YOU'RE ABOUT TO EXPERIENCE SOME BAD RECEPTION!
CRUNCH!
CATACLYSM!

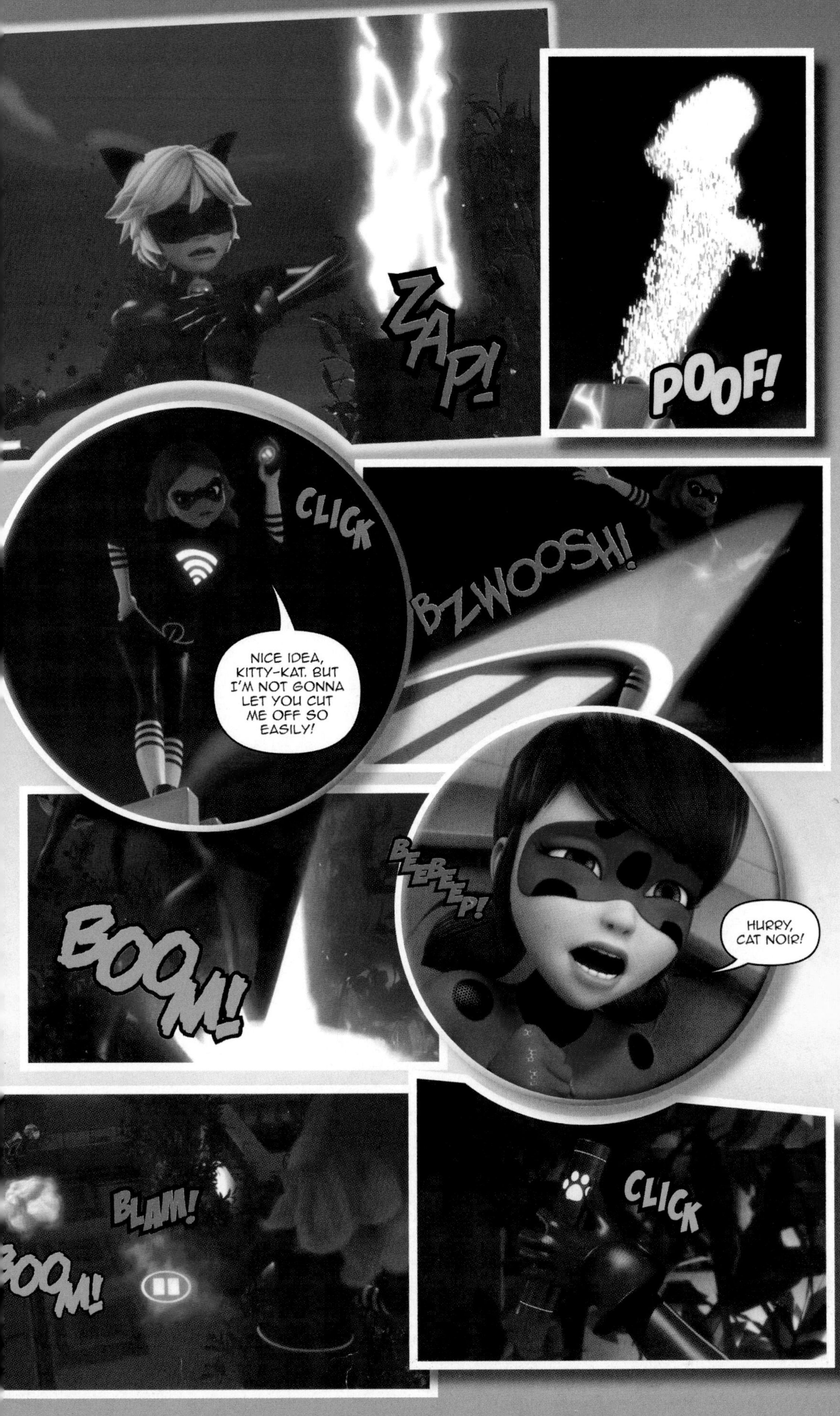
ZAP!
POOF!
CLICK
NICE IDEA, KITTY-KAT. BUT I'M NOT GONNA LET YOU CUT ME OFF SO EASILY!
BZWOOSH!
BOOM!
BEEBEEP!
HURRY, CAT NOIR!
BLAM!
BOOM!
CLICK

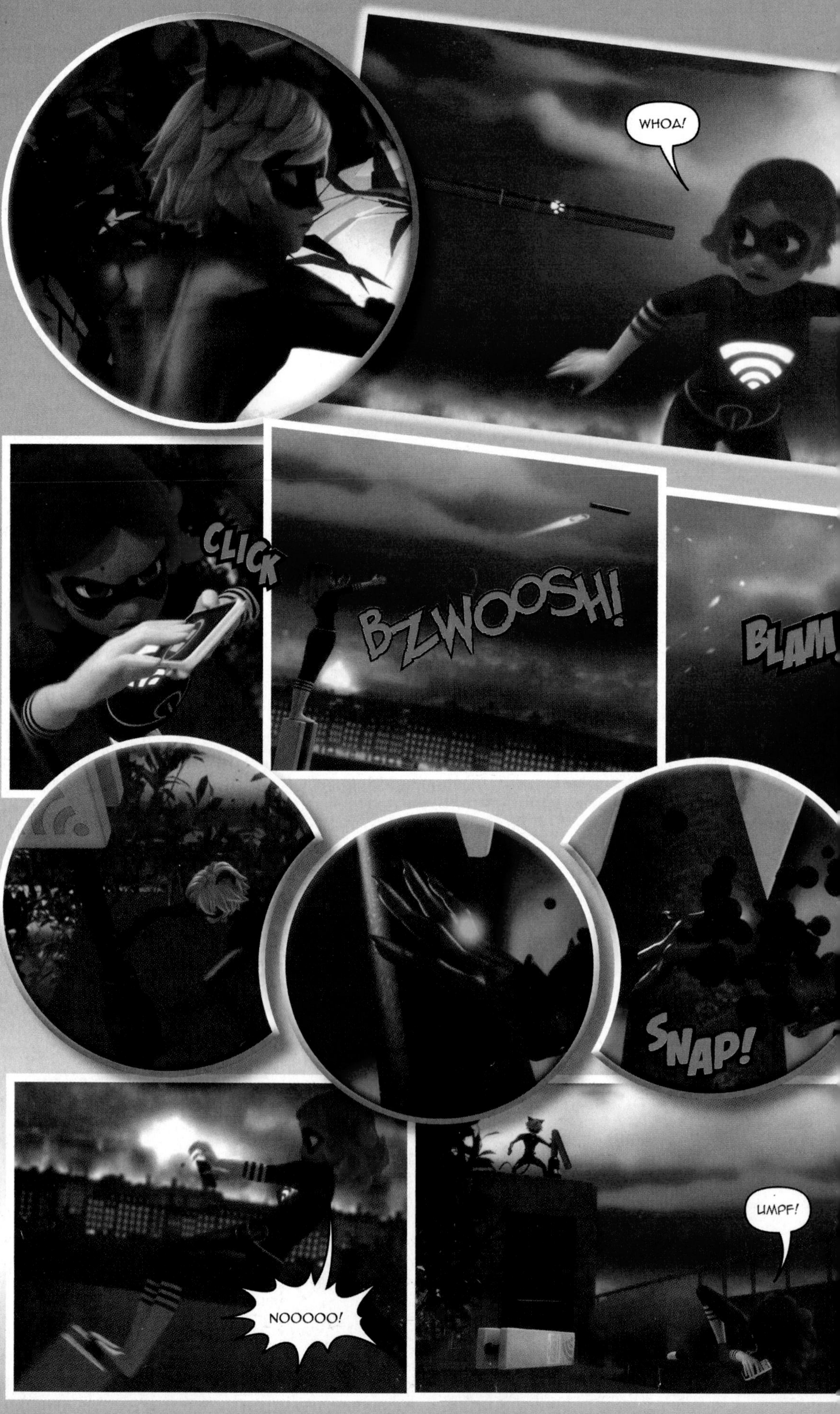
WHOA!
CLICK
B-ZWOOSH!
BLAM!
SNAP!
NOOOOO!
UMPF!

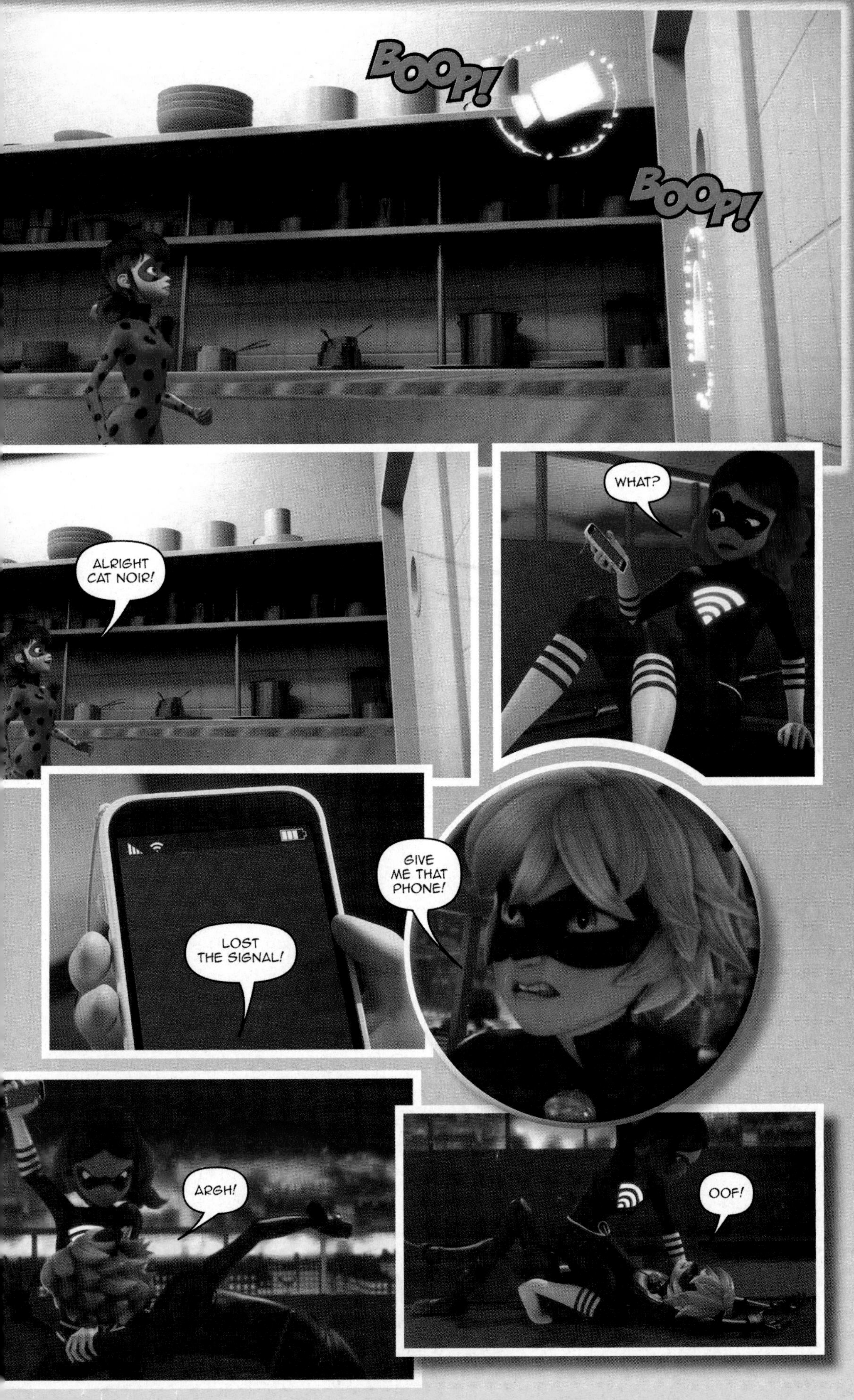

BOOP!
BOOP!
ALRIGHT CAT NOIR!
WHAT?
LOST THE SIGNAL!
GIVE ME THAT PHONE!
ARGH!
OOF!

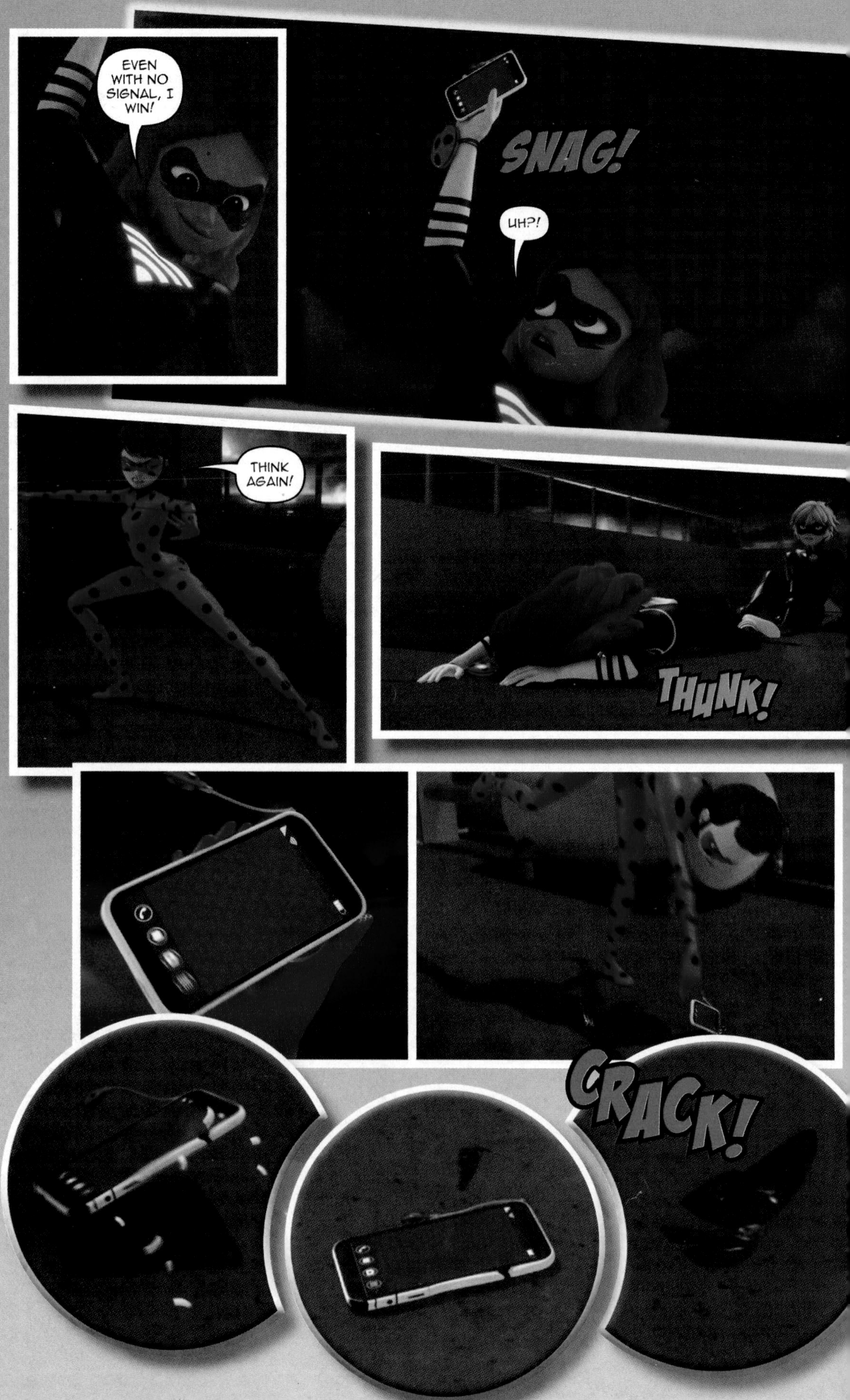
EVEN WITH NO SIGNAL, I WIN!
SNAG!
UH?!
THINK AGAIN!
THUNK!
CRACK!

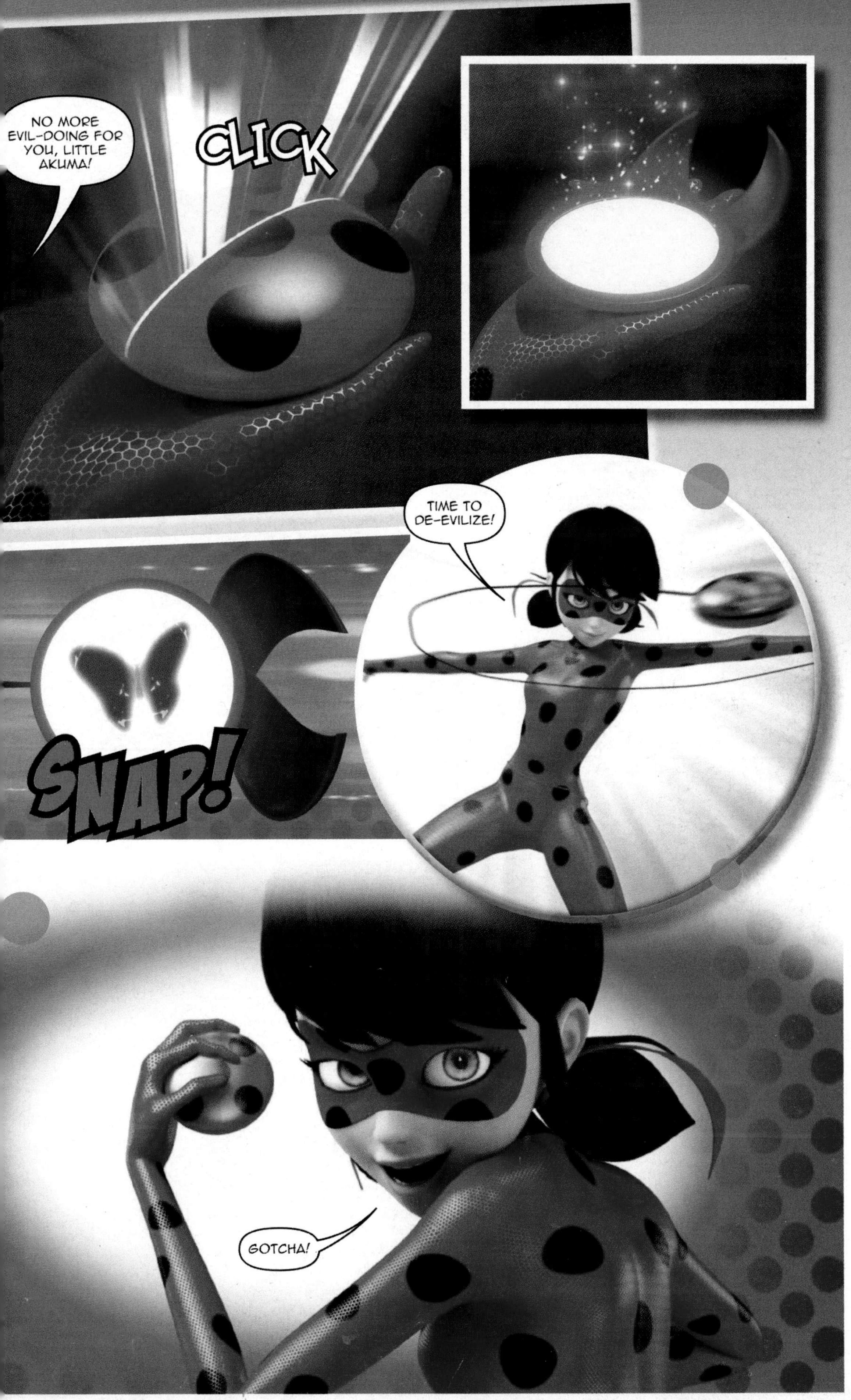
NO MORE EVIL-DOING FOR YOU, LITTLE AKUMA!
CLICK
TIME TO DE-EVILIZE!
SNAP!
GOTCHA!

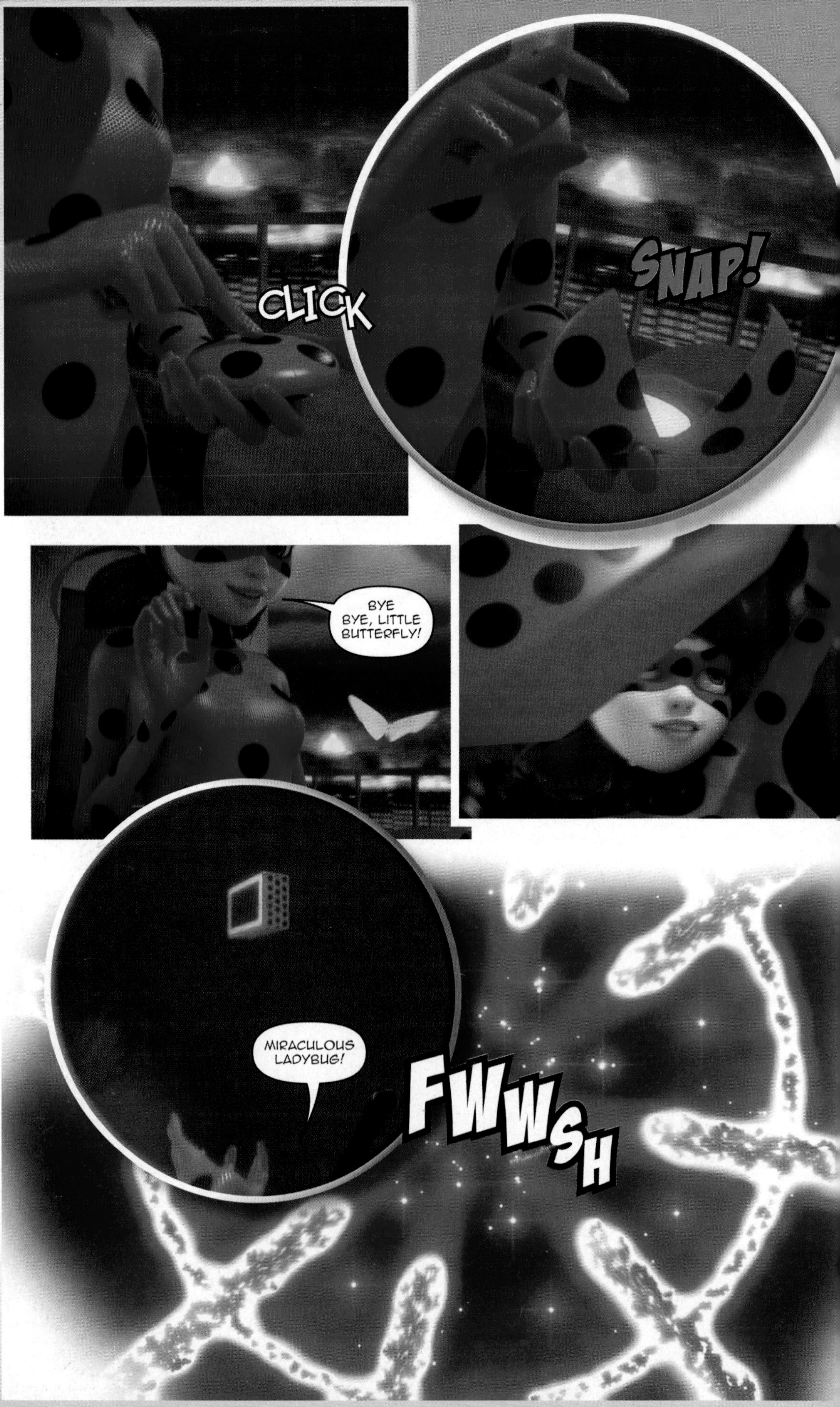
CLICK
SNAP!
BYE BYE, LITTLE BUTTERFLY!
MIRACULOUS LADYBUG!
FWWSH

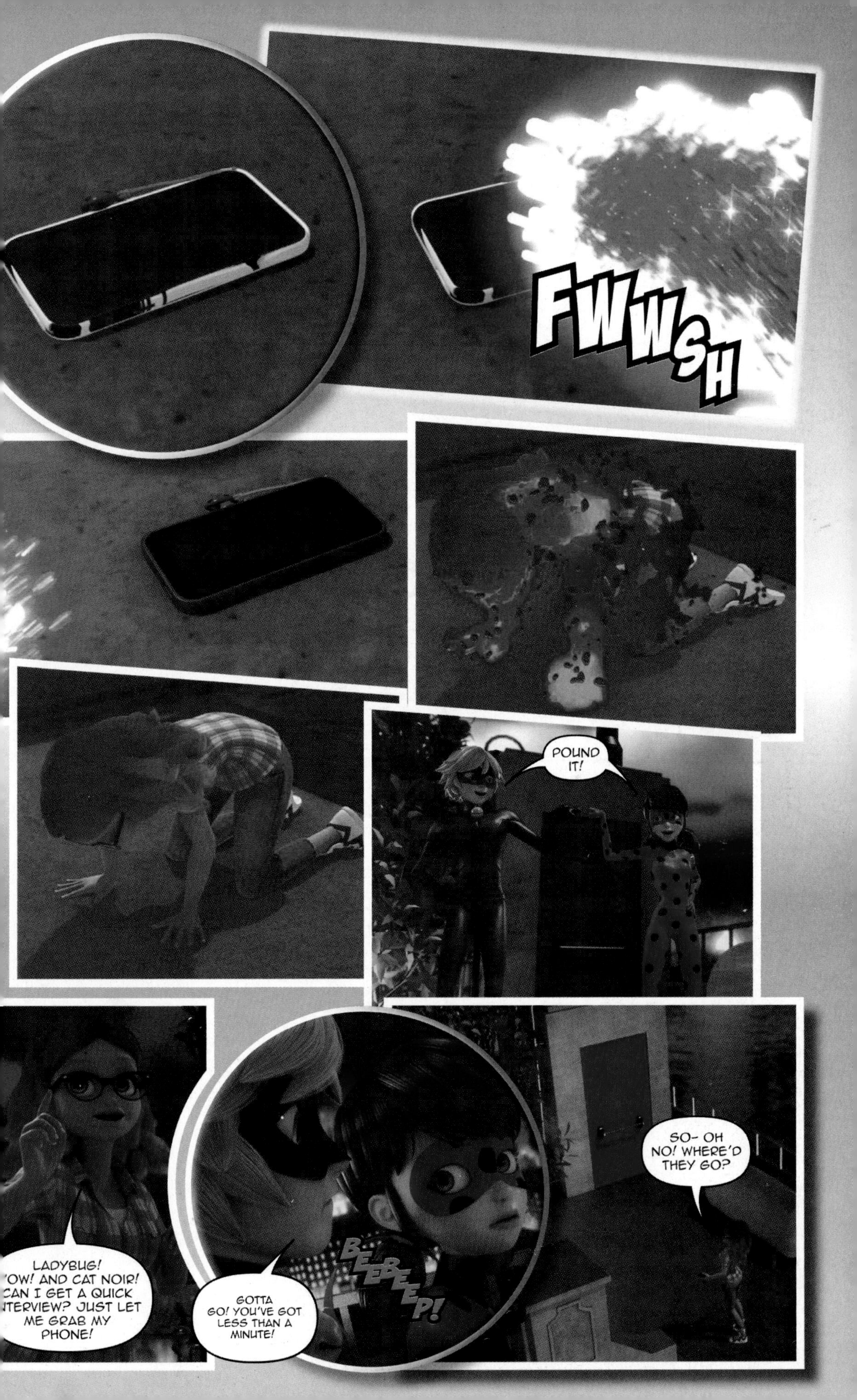
FWWSH
POUND IT!
LADYBUG! 'OW! AND CAT NOIR! CAN I GET A QUICK NTERVIEW? JUST LET ME GRAB MY PHONE!
GOTTA GO! YOU'VE GOT LESS THAN A MINUTE!
BEEBEEP!
SO- OH NO! WHERE'D THEY GO?

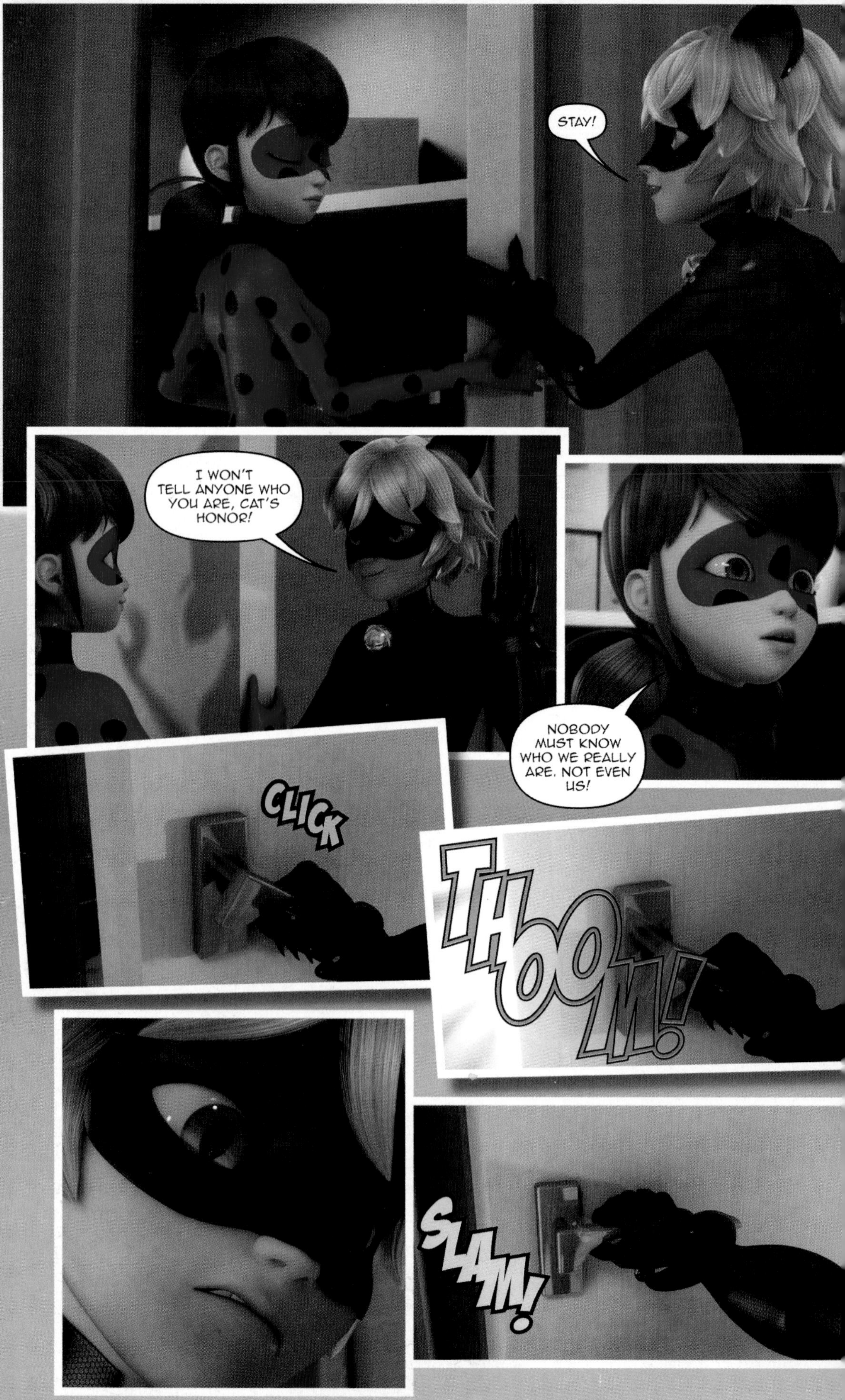
STAY!
I WON'T TELL ANYONE WHO YOU ARE, CAT'S HONOR!
NOBODY MUST KNOW WHO WE REALLY ARE. NOT EVEN US!
CLICK
THOOM!
SLAM!

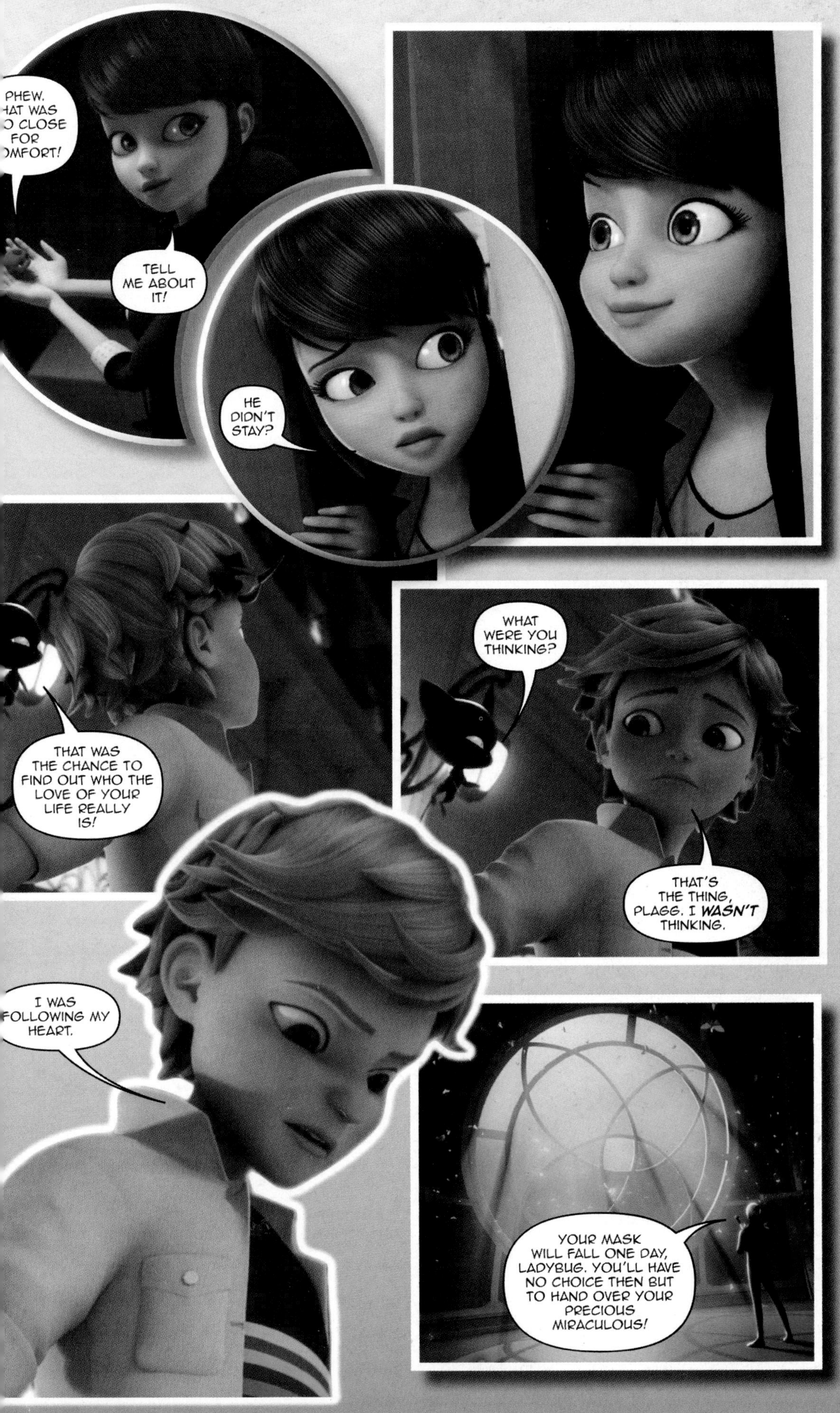
PHEW. HAT WAS O CLOSE FOR OMFORT!
TELL ME ABOUT IT!
HE DIDN'T STAY?
THAT WAS THE CHANCE TO FIND OUT WHO THE LOVE OF YOUR LIFE REALLY IS!
WHAT WERE YOU THINKING?
THAT'S THE THING, PLAGG. I *WASN'T* THINKING.
I WAS FOLLOWING MY HEART.
YOUR MASK WILL FALL ONE DAY, LADYBUG. YOU'LL HAVE NO CHOICE THEN BUT TO HAND OVER YOUR PRECIOUS MIRACULOUS!

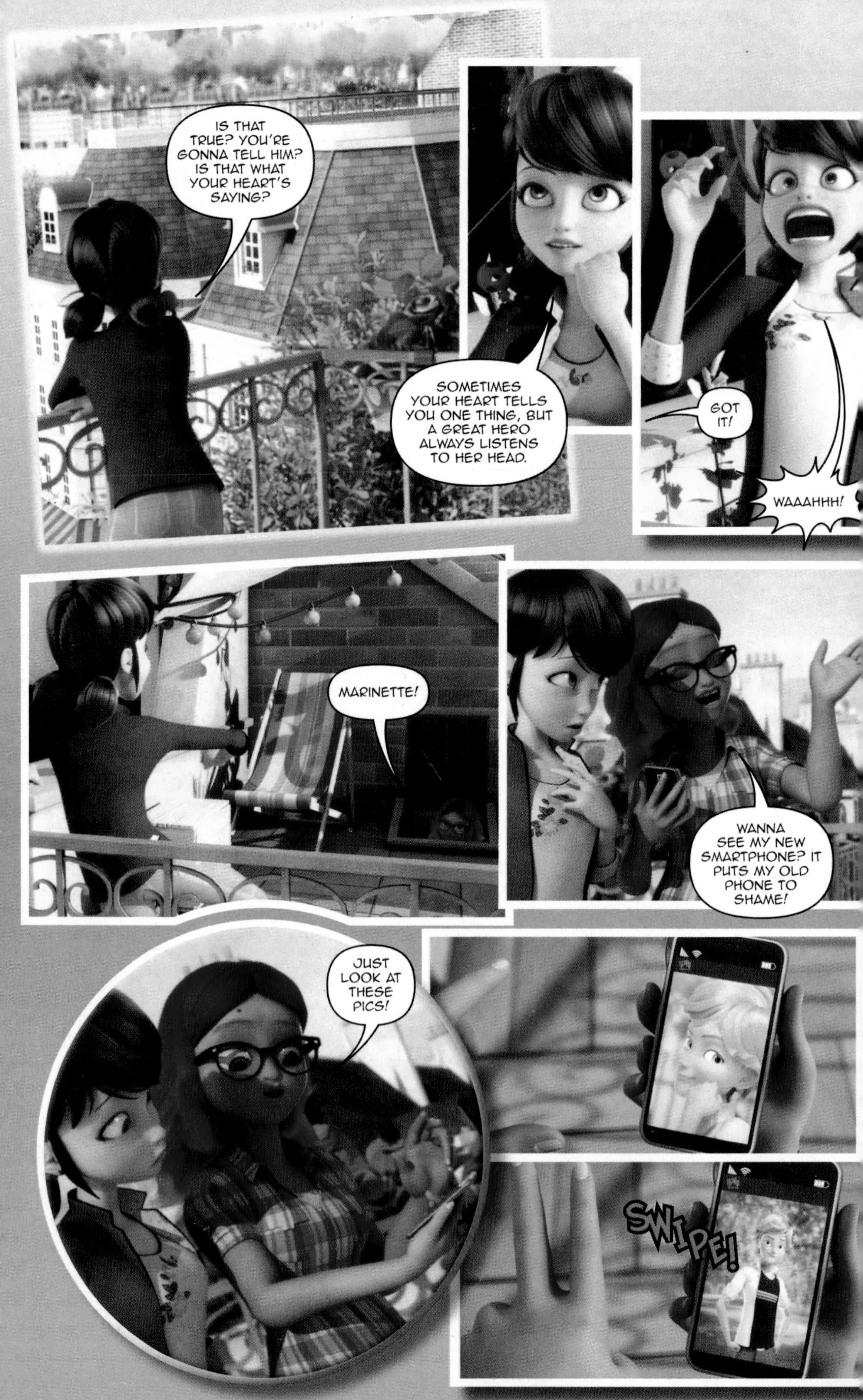
IS THAT TRUE? YOU'RE GONNA TELL HIM? IS THAT WHAT YOUR HEART'S SAYING?
SOMETIMES YOUR HEART TELLS YOU ONE THING, BUT A GREAT HERO ALWAYS LISTENS TO HER HEAD.
GOT IT!
WAAAHHH!
MARINETTE!
WANNA SEE MY NEW SMARTPHONE? IT PUTS MY OLD PHONE TO SHAME!
JUST LOOK AT THESE PICS!
SWIPE!

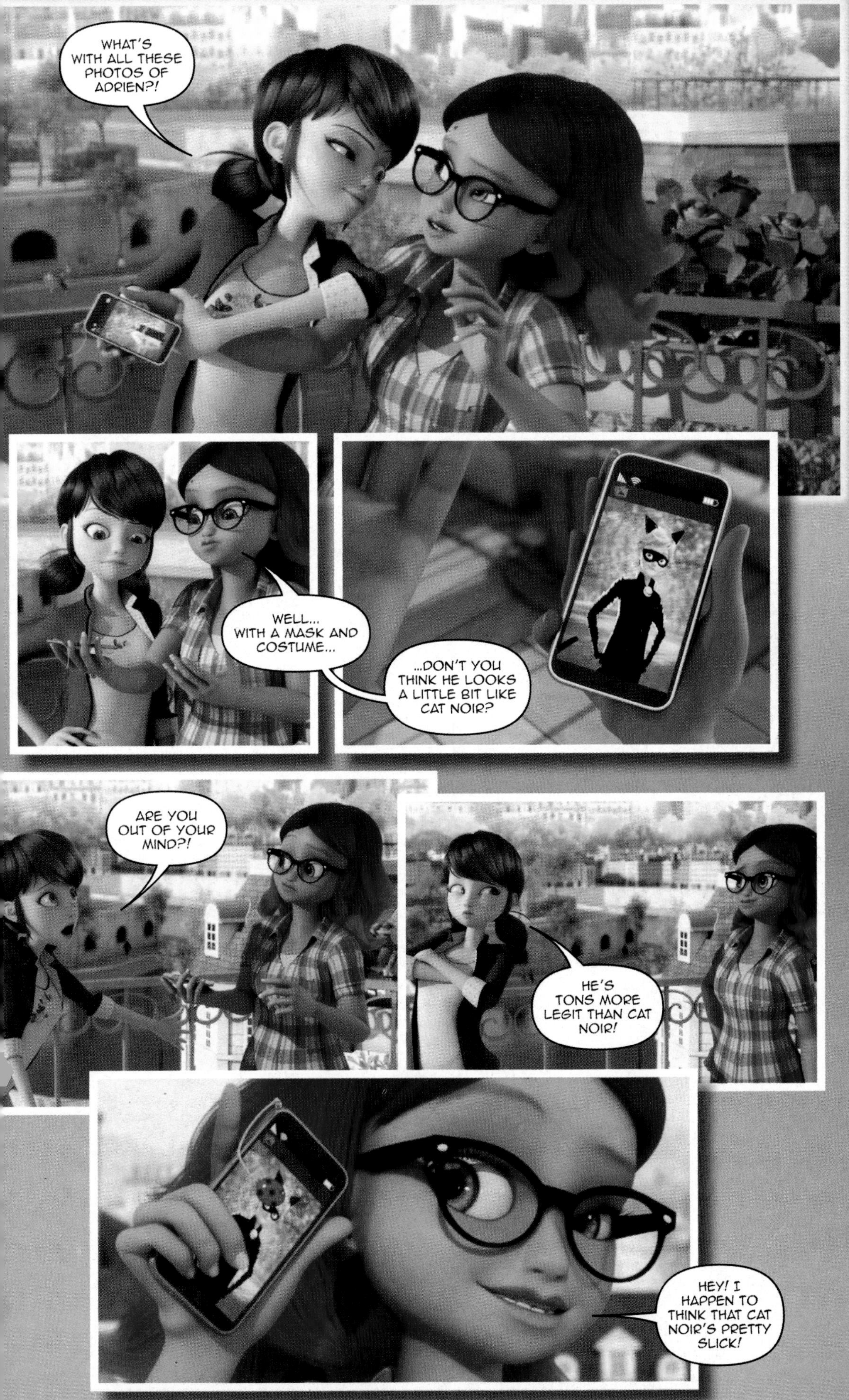
WHAT'S WITH ALL THESE PHOTOS OF ADRIEN?!
WELL... WITH A MASK AND COSTUME...
...DON'T YOU THINK HE LOOKS A LITTLE BIT LIKE CAT NOIR?
ARE YOU OUT OF YOUR MIND?!
HE'S TONS MORE LEGIT THAN CAT NOIR!
HEY! I HAPPEN TO THINK THAT CAT NOIR'S PRETTY SLICK!

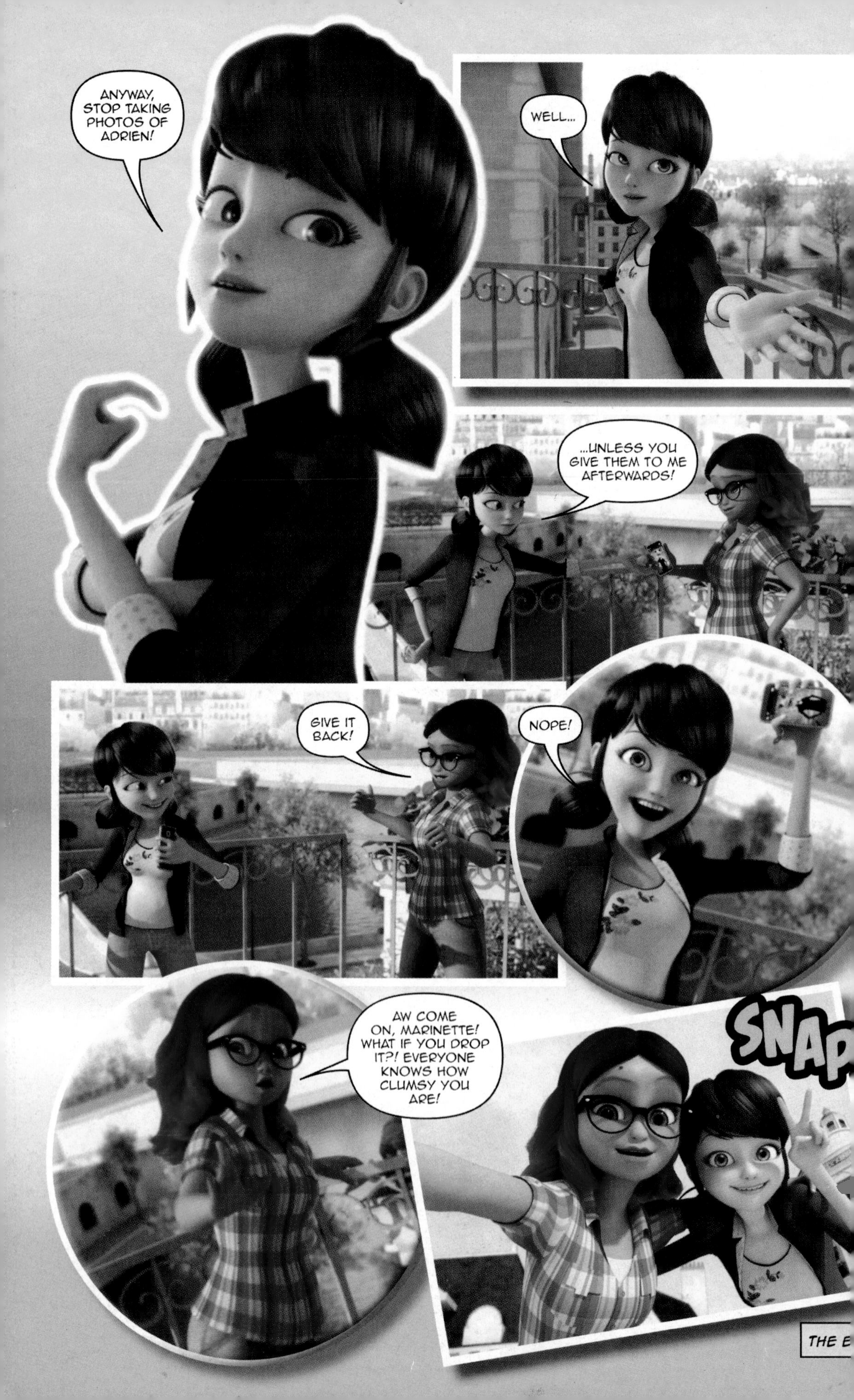
ANYWAY, STOP TAKING PHOTOS OF ADRIEN!
WELL...
...UNLESS YOU GIVE THEM TO ME AFTERWARDS!
GIVE IT BACK!
NOPE!
AW COME ON, MARINETTE! WHAT IF YOU DROP IT?! EVERYONE KNOWS HOW CLUMSY YOU ARE!

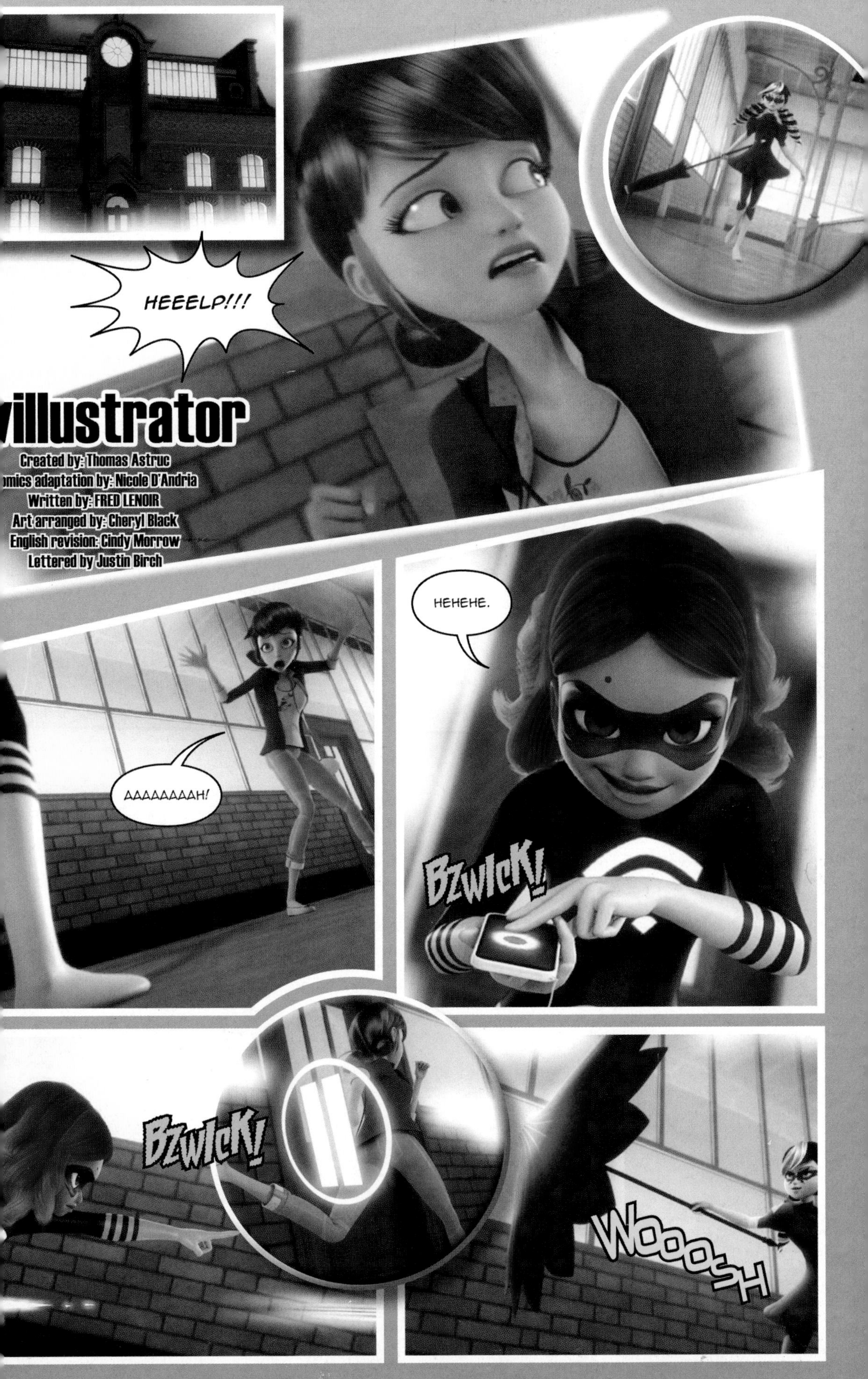
HEEELP!!!
villustrator
Created by: Thomas Astruc
omics adaptation by: Nicole D'Andria
Written by: FRED LENOIR
Art arranged by: Cheryl Black
English revision: Cindy Morrow
Lettered by Justin Birch
AAAAAAAAH!
HEHEHE.
BZWICK!
BZWICK!
WOOOSH

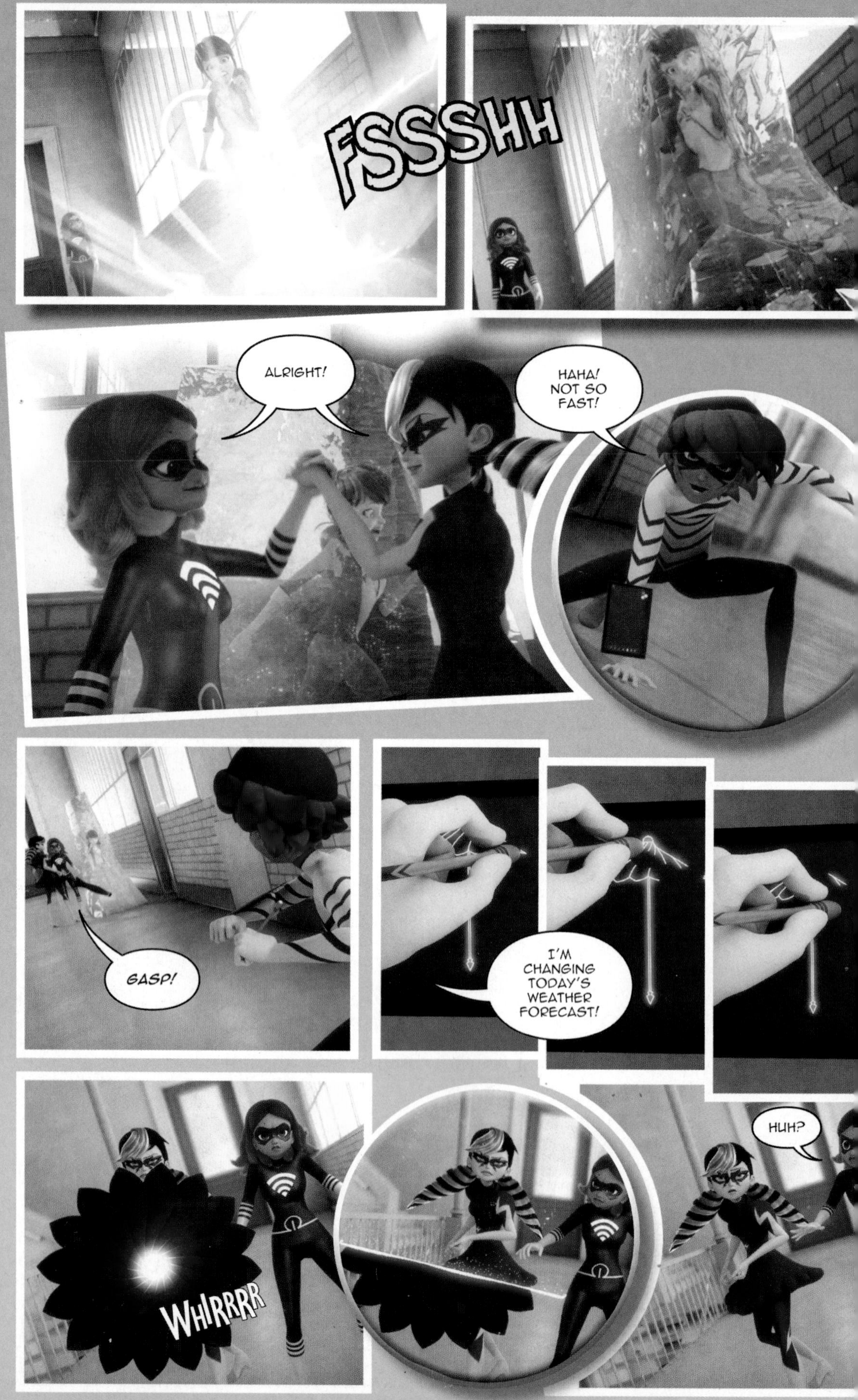
FSSSHH
ALRIGHT!
HAHA! NOT SO FAST!
GASP!
I'M CHANGING TODAY'S WEATHER FORECAST!
WHIRRRR
HUH?

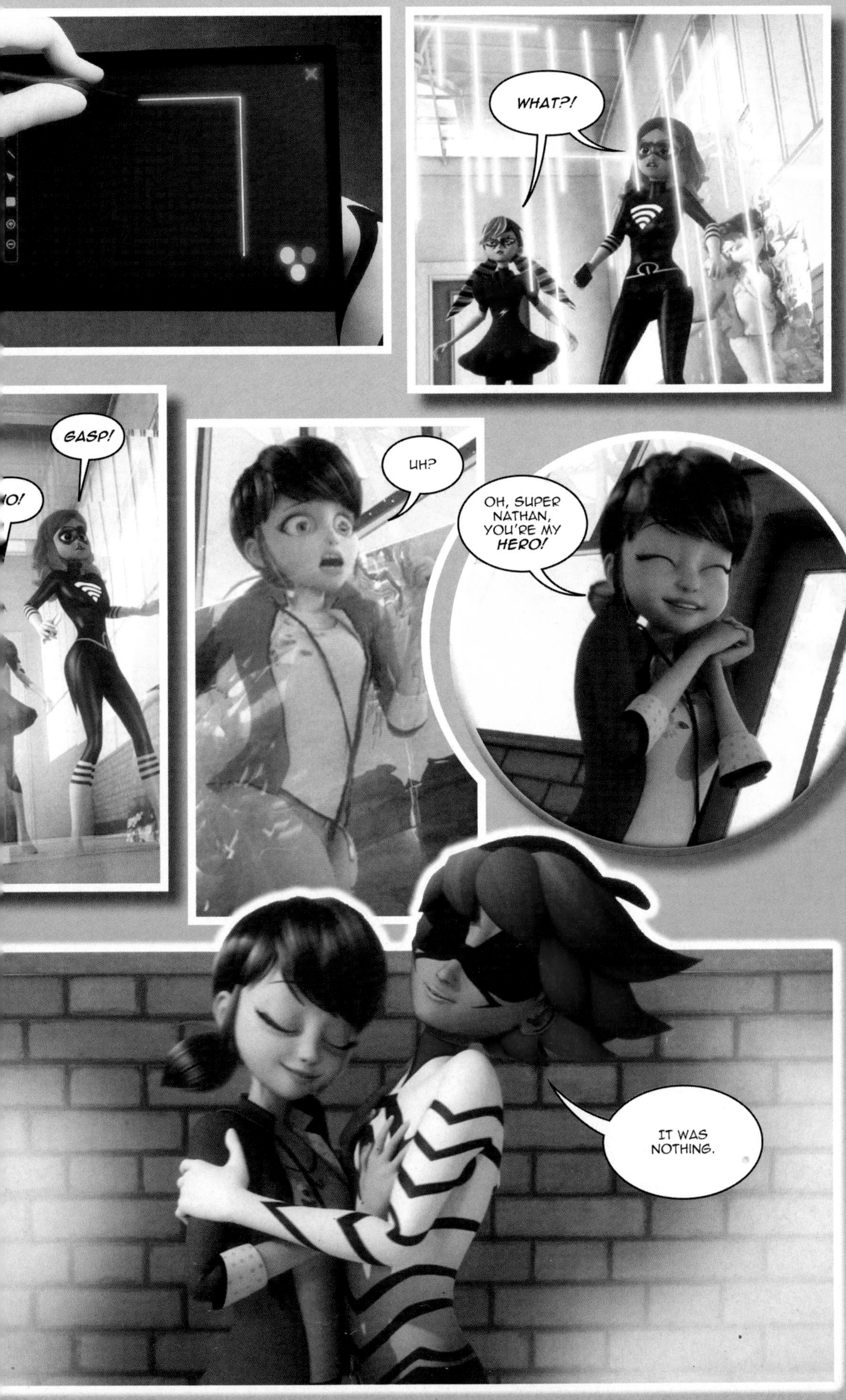
WHAT?!
GASP!
UH?
OH, SUPER NATHAN, YOU'RE MY *HERO!*
IT WAS NOTHING.

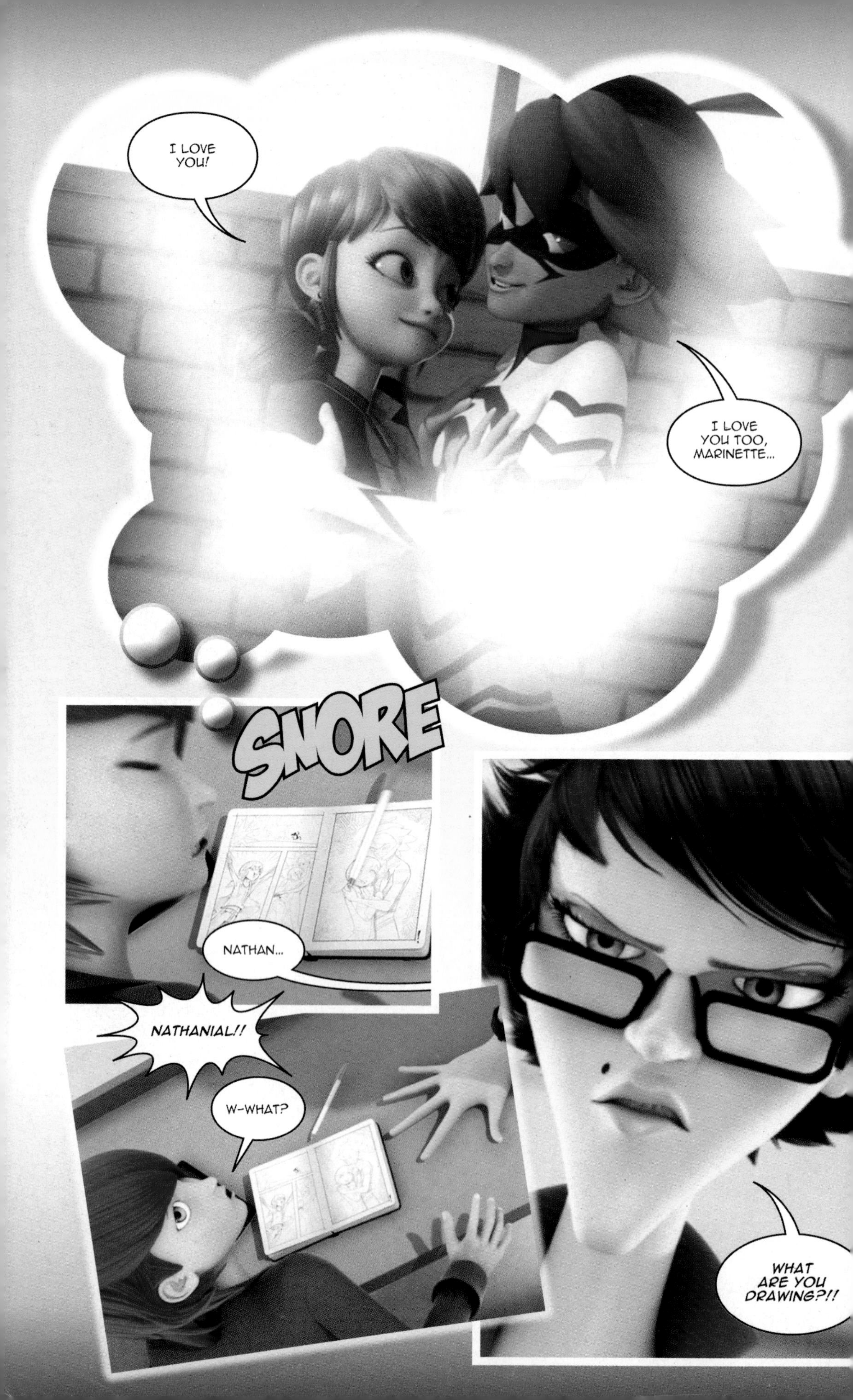
I LOVE YOU!
I LOVE YOU TOO, MARINETTE...
SNORE
NATHAN...
NATHANIAL!!
W-WHAT?
WHAT ARE YOU DRAWING?!!

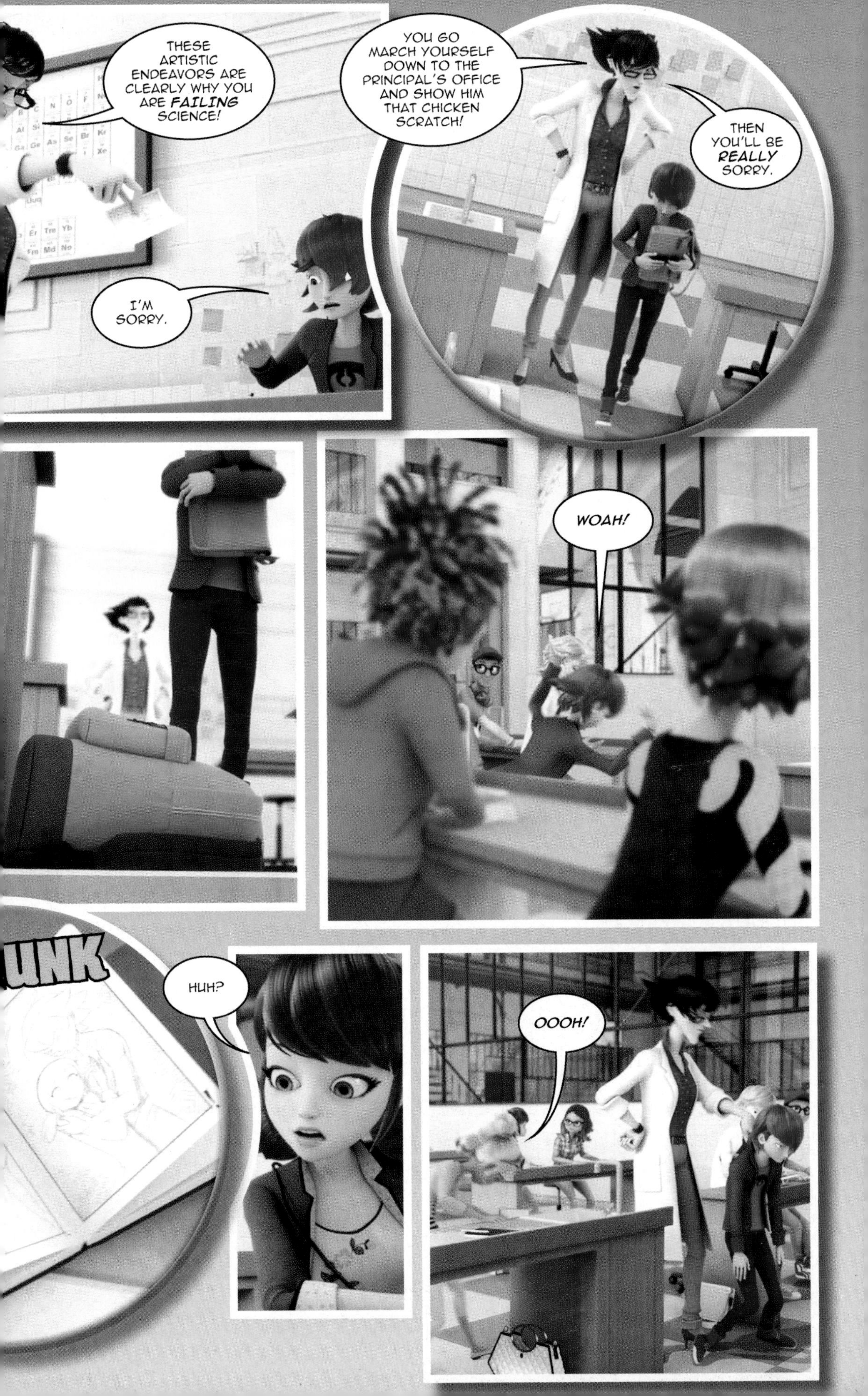
THESE ARTISTIC ENDEAVORS ARE CLEARLY WHY YOU ARE FAILING SCIENCE!
I'M SORRY.
YOU GO MARCH YOURSELF DOWN TO THE PRINCIPAL'S OFFICE AND SHOW HIM THAT CHICKEN SCRATCH!
THEN YOU'LL BE REALLY SORRY.
WOAH!
UNK
HUH?
OOOH!

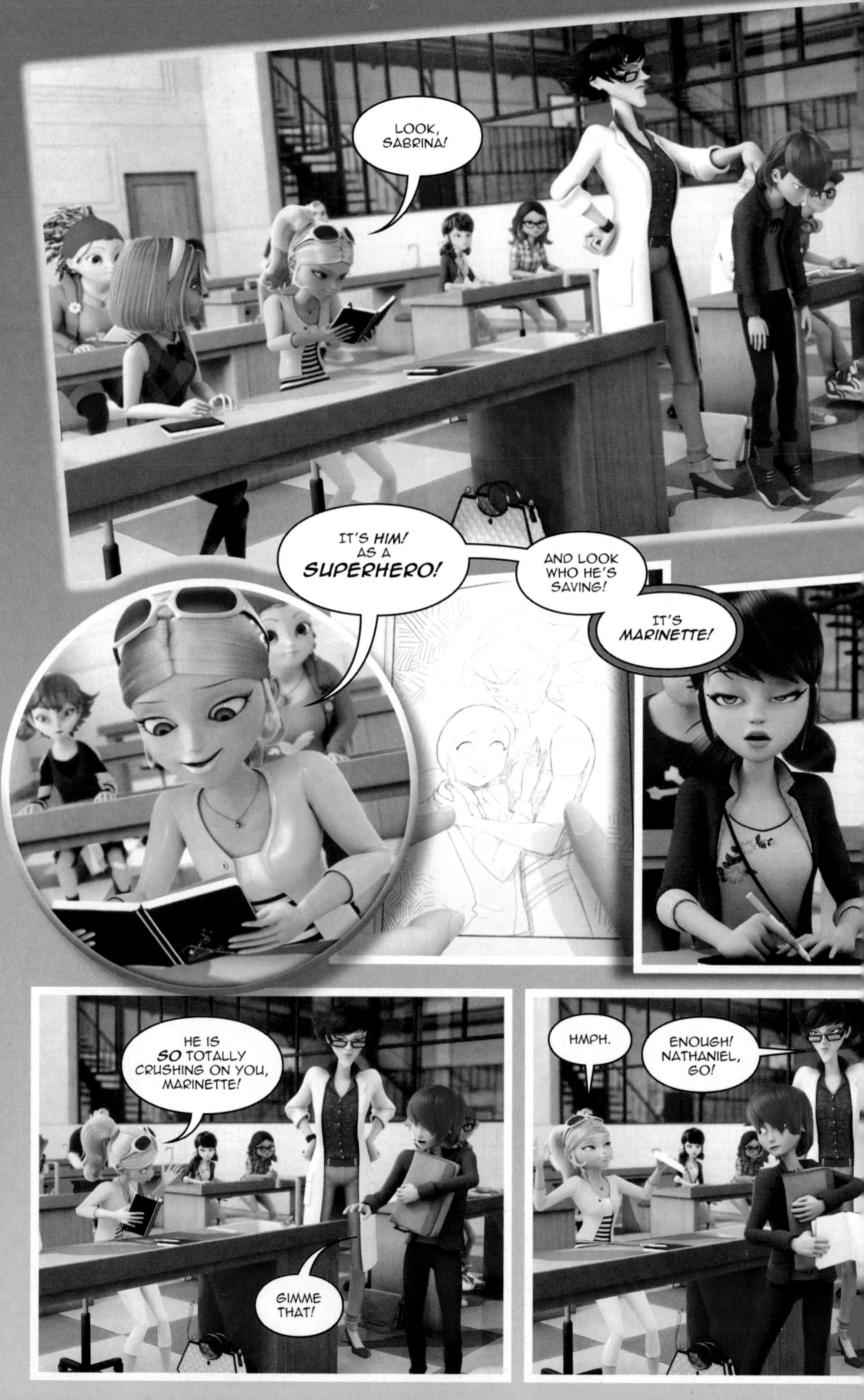
LOOK, SABRINA!
IT'S HIM! AS A SUPERHERO!
AND LOOK WHO HE'S SAVING!
IT'S MARINETTE!
HE IS SO TOTALLY CRUSHING ON YOU, MARINETTE!
GIMME THAT!
HMPH.
ENOUGH! NATHANIEL, GO!

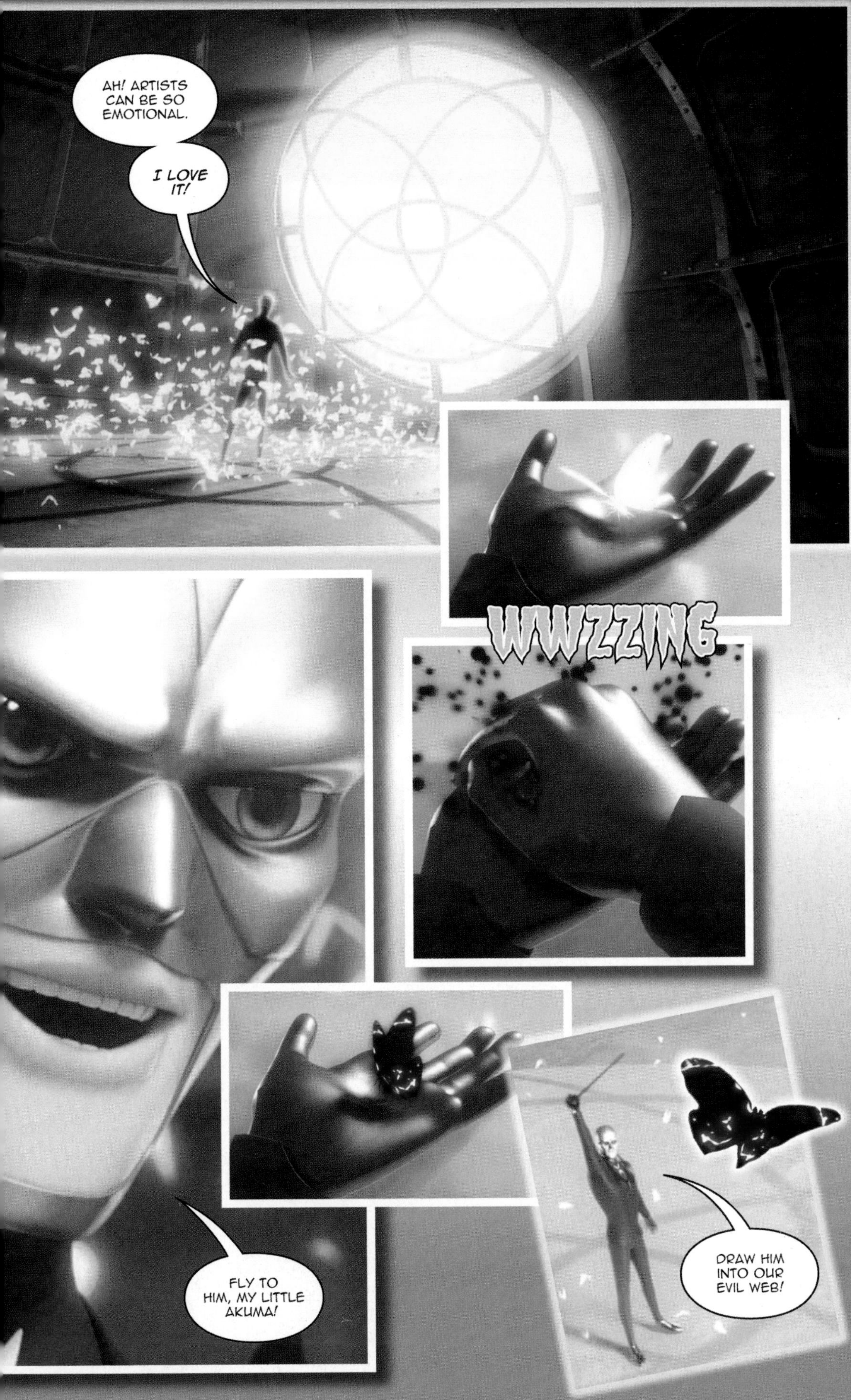
AH! ARTISTS CAN BE SO EMOTIONAL.
I LOVE IT!
WWZZING
FLY TO HIM, MY LITTLE AKUMA!
DRAW HIM INTO OUR EVIL WEB!

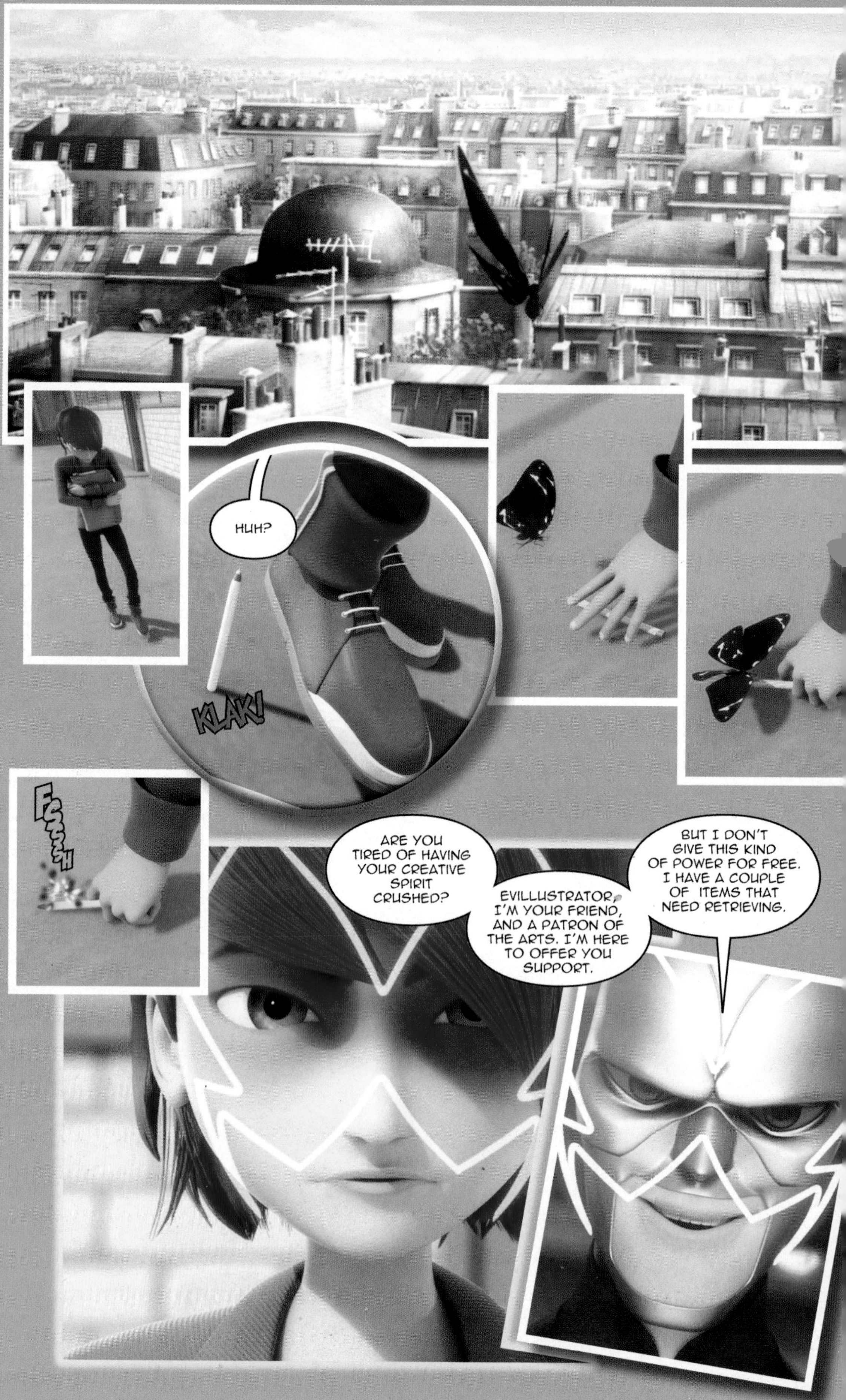
HUH?
KLAK!
FSSSSH
ARE YOU TIRED OF HAVING YOUR CREATIVE SPIRIT CRUSHED?
EVILLUSTRATOR, I'M YOUR FRIEND, AND A PATRON OF THE ARTS. I'M HERE TO OFFER YOU SUPPORT.
BUT I DON'T GIVE THIS KIND OF POWER FOR FREE. I HAVE A COUPLE OF ITEMS THAT NEED RETRIEVING.

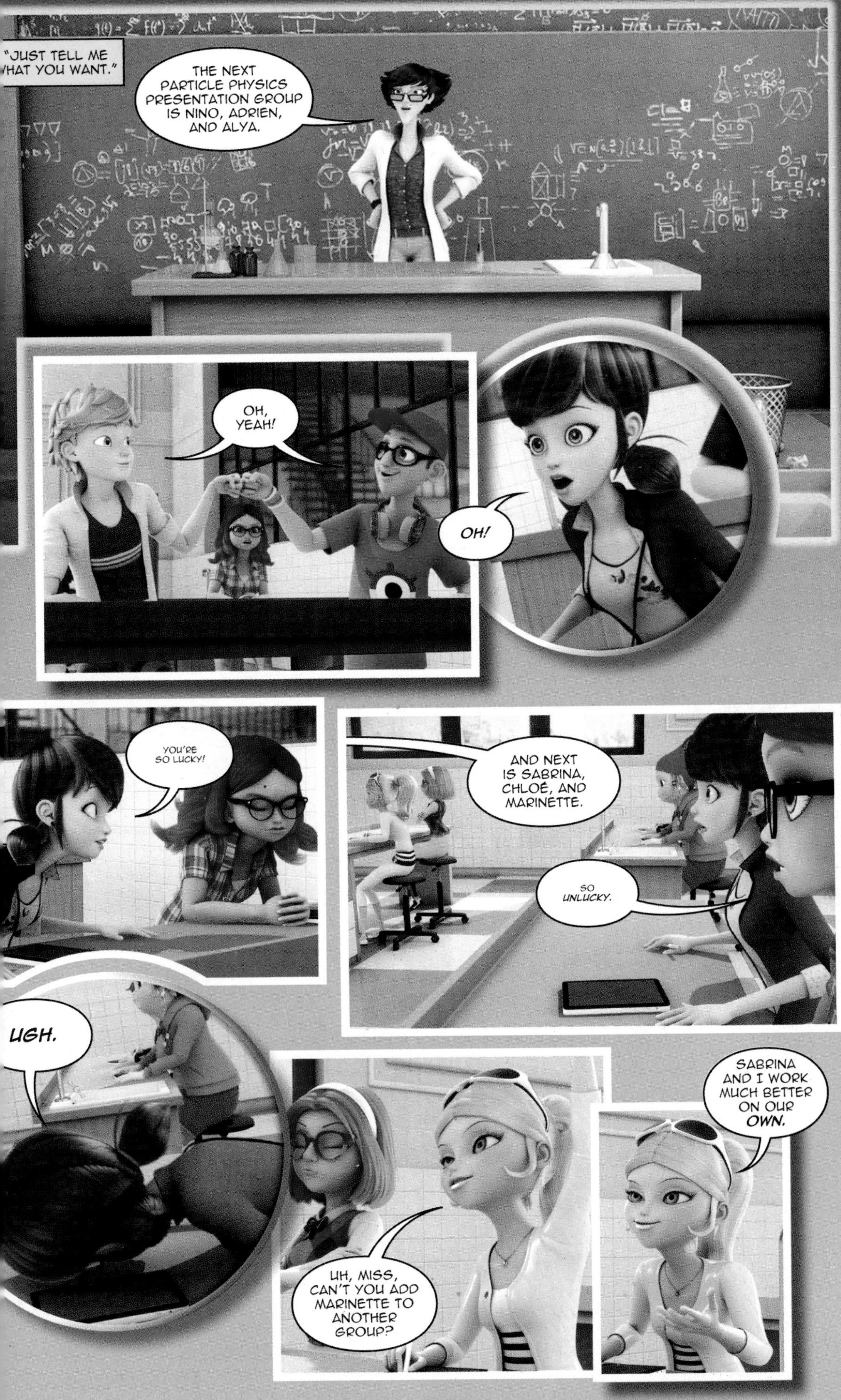
"JUST TELL ME WHAT YOU WANT."
THE NEXT PARTICLE PHYSICS PRESENTATION GROUP IS NINO, ADRIEN, AND ALYA.
OH, YEAH!
OH!
YOU'RE SO LUCKY!
AND NEXT IS SABRINA, CHLOÉ, AND MARINETTE.
SO UNLUCKY.
UGH.
UH, MISS, CAN'T YOU ADD MARINETTE TO ANOTHER GROUP?
SABRINA AND I WORK MUCH BETTER ON OUR OWN.

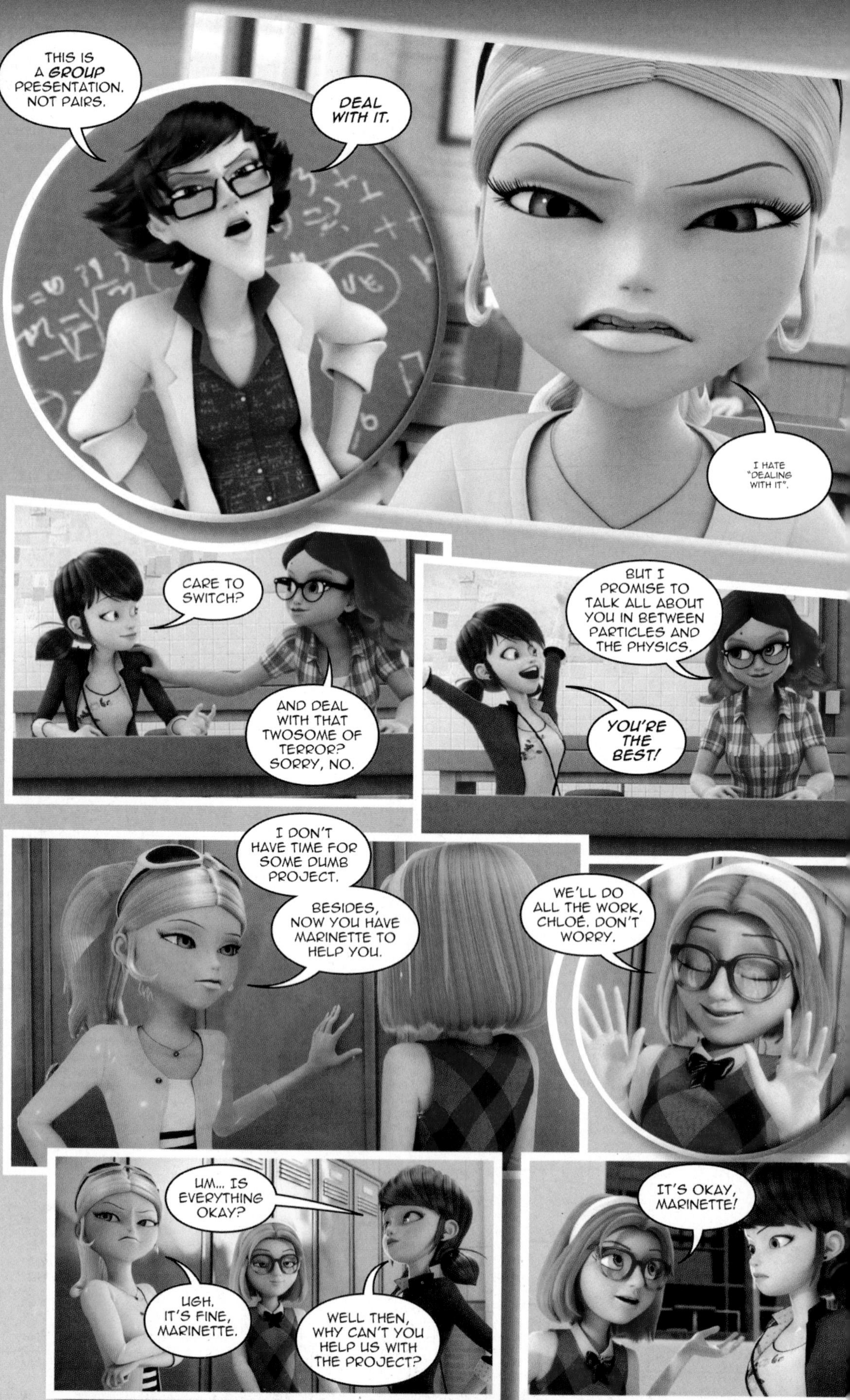
THIS IS A GROUP PRESENTATION. NOT PAIRS.
DEAL WITH IT.
I HATE "DEALING WITH IT".
CARE TO SWITCH?
AND DEAL WITH THAT TWOSOME OF TERROR? SORRY, NO.
BUT I PROMISE TO TALK ALL ABOUT YOU IN BETWEEN PARTICLES AND THE PHYSICS.
YOU'RE THE BEST!
I DON'T HAVE TIME FOR SOME DUMB PROJECT.
BESIDES, NOW YOU HAVE MARINETTE TO HELP YOU.
WE'LL DO ALL THE WORK, CHLOÉ. DON'T WORRY.
UM... IS EVERYTHING OKAY?
UGH. IT'S FINE, MARINETTE.
WELL THEN, WHY CAN'T YOU HELP US WITH THE PROJECT?
IT'S OKAY, MARINETTE!

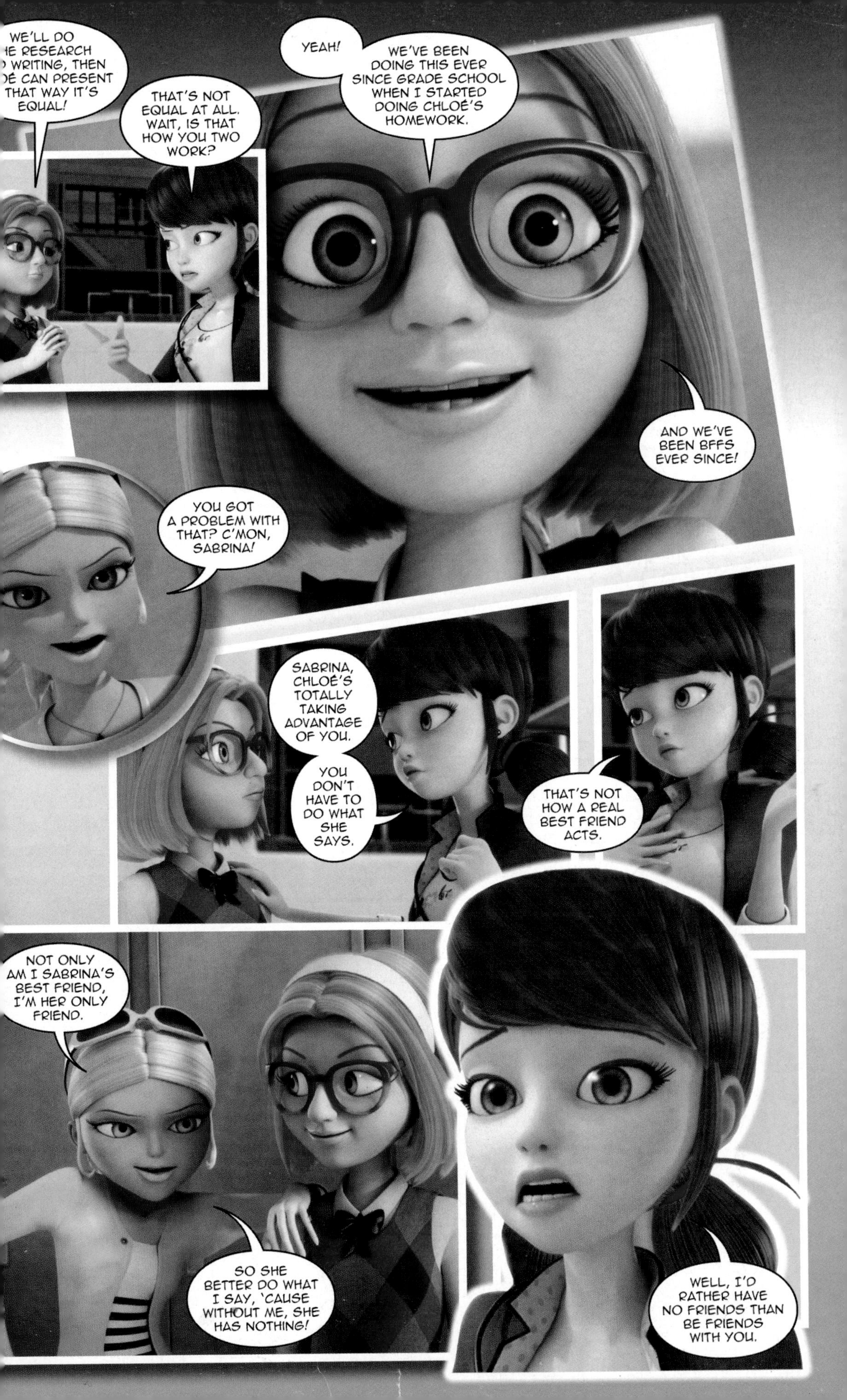
WE'LL DO
HE RESEARCH
WRITING, THEN
OÉ CAN PRESENT
THAT WAY IT'S
EQUAL!
THAT'S NOT EQUAL AT ALL. WAIT, IS THAT HOW YOU TWO WORK?
YEAH!
WE'VE BEEN DOING THIS EVER SINCE GRADE SCHOOL WHEN I STARTED DOING CHLOÉ'S HOMEWORK.
AND WE'VE BEEN BFFS EVER SINCE!
YOU GOT A PROBLEM WITH THAT? C'MON, SABRINA!
SABRINA, CHLOÉ'S TOTALLY TAKING ADVANTAGE OF YOU.
YOU DON'T HAVE TO DO WHAT SHE SAYS.
THAT'S NOT HOW A REAL BEST FRIEND ACTS.
NOT ONLY AM I SABRINA'S BEST FRIEND, I'M HER ONLY FRIEND.
SO SHE BETTER DO WHAT I SAY, 'CAUSE WITHOUT ME, SHE HAS NOTHING!
WELL, I'D RATHER HAVE NO FRIENDS THAN BE FRIENDS WITH YOU.

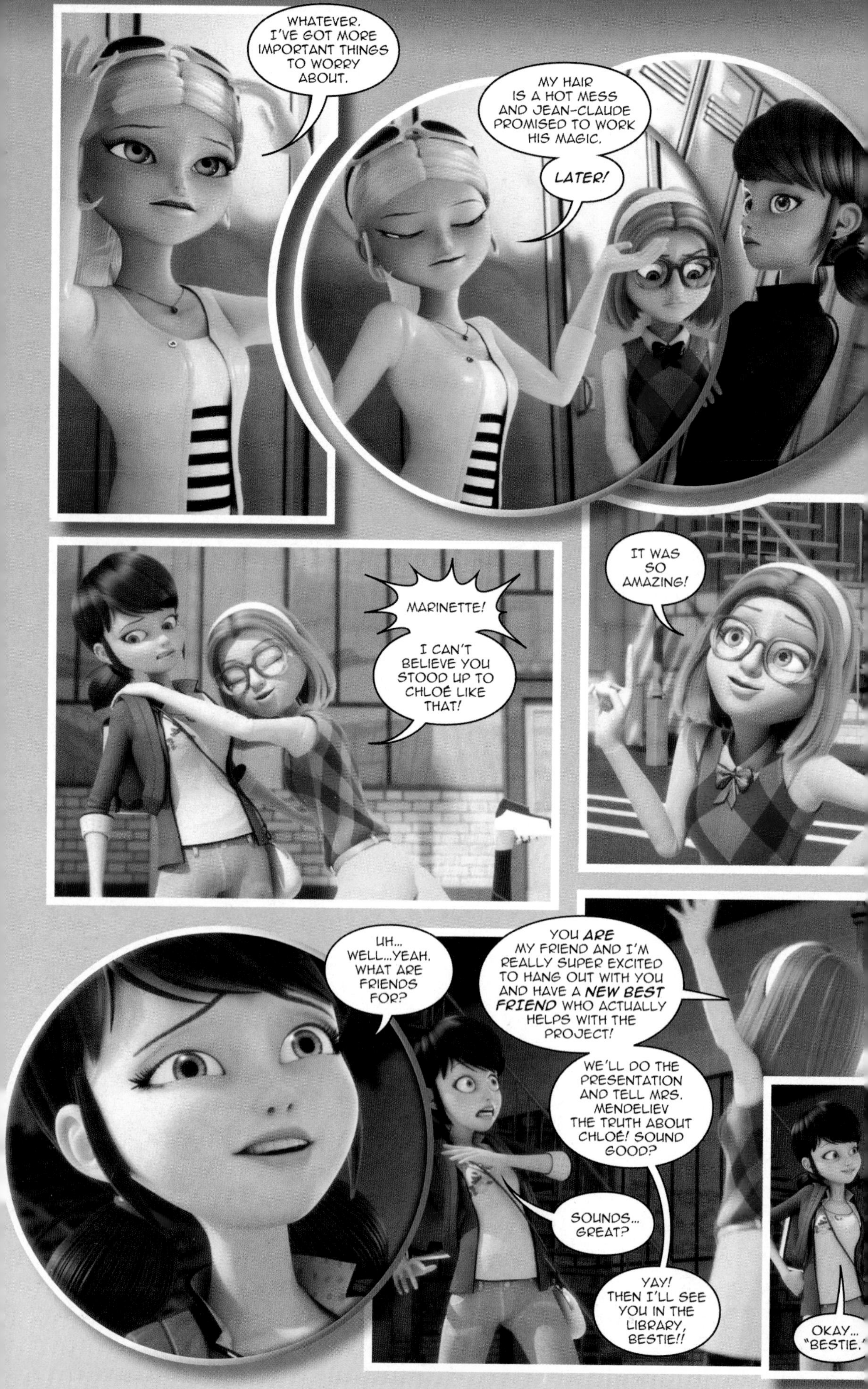
WHATEVER. I'VE GOT MORE IMPORTANT THINGS TO WORRY ABOUT.
MY HAIR IS A HOT MESS AND JEAN-CLAUDE PROMISED TO WORK HIS MAGIC.
LATER!
MARINETTE!
I CAN'T BELIEVE YOU STOOD UP TO CHLOÉ LIKE THAT!
IT WAS SO AMAZING!
UH... WELL...YEAH. WHAT ARE FRIENDS FOR?
YOU *ARE* MY FRIEND AND I'M REALLY SUPER EXCITED TO HANG OUT WITH YOU AND HAVE A ***NEW BEST FRIEND*** WHO ACTUALLY HELPS WITH THE PROJECT!
WE'LL DO THE PRESENTATION AND TELL MRS. MENDELIEV THE TRUTH ABOUT CHLOÉ! SOUND GOOD?
SOUNDS... GREAT?
YAY! THEN I'LL SEE YOU IN THE LIBRARY, BESTIE!!
OKAY... "BESTIE."

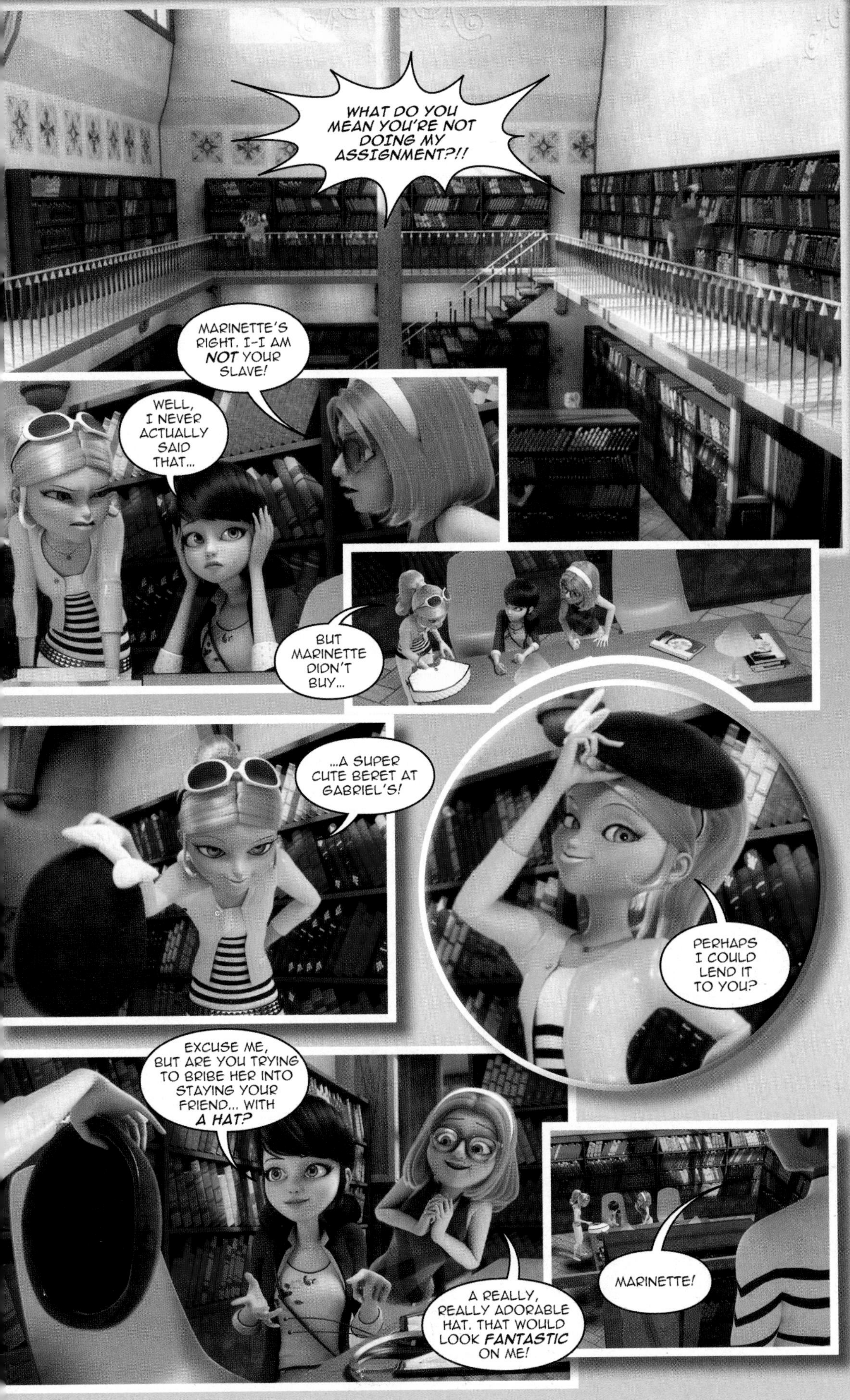
WHAT DO YOU MEAN YOU'RE NOT DOING MY ASSIGNMENT?!!
MARINETTE'S RIGHT. I-I AM NOT YOUR SLAVE!
WELL, I NEVER ACTUALLY SAID THAT...
BUT MARINETTE DIDN'T BUY...
...A SUPER CUTE BERET AT GABRIEL'S!
PERHAPS I COULD LEND IT TO YOU?
EXCUSE ME, BUT ARE YOU TRYING TO BRIBE HER INTO STAYING YOUR FRIEND... WITH A HAT?
A REALLY, REALLY ADORABLE HAT. THAT WOULD LOOK FANTASTIC ON ME!
MARINETTE!

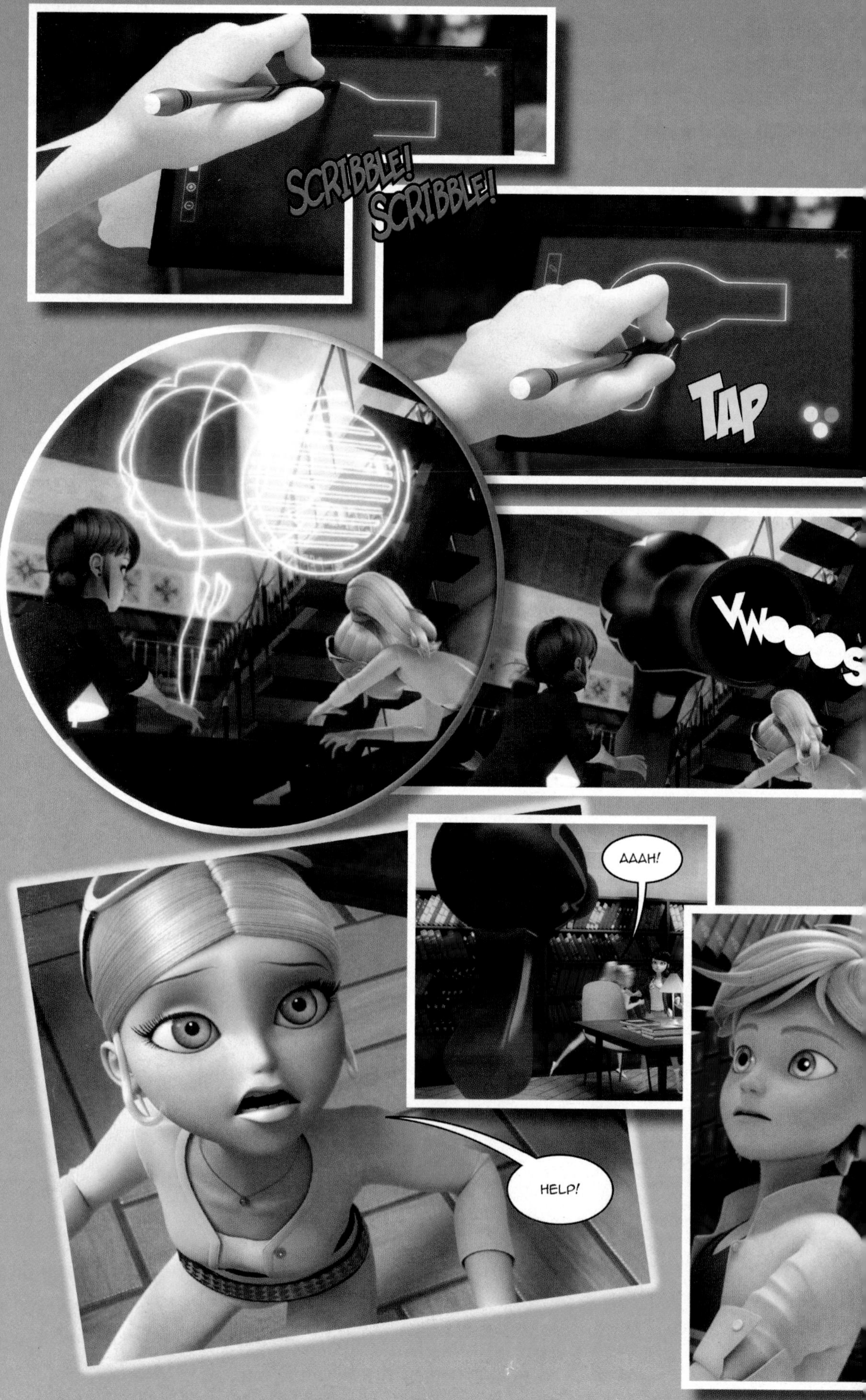
SCRIBBLE! SCRIBBLE!
TAP
VWOOOOS
AAAH!
HELP!

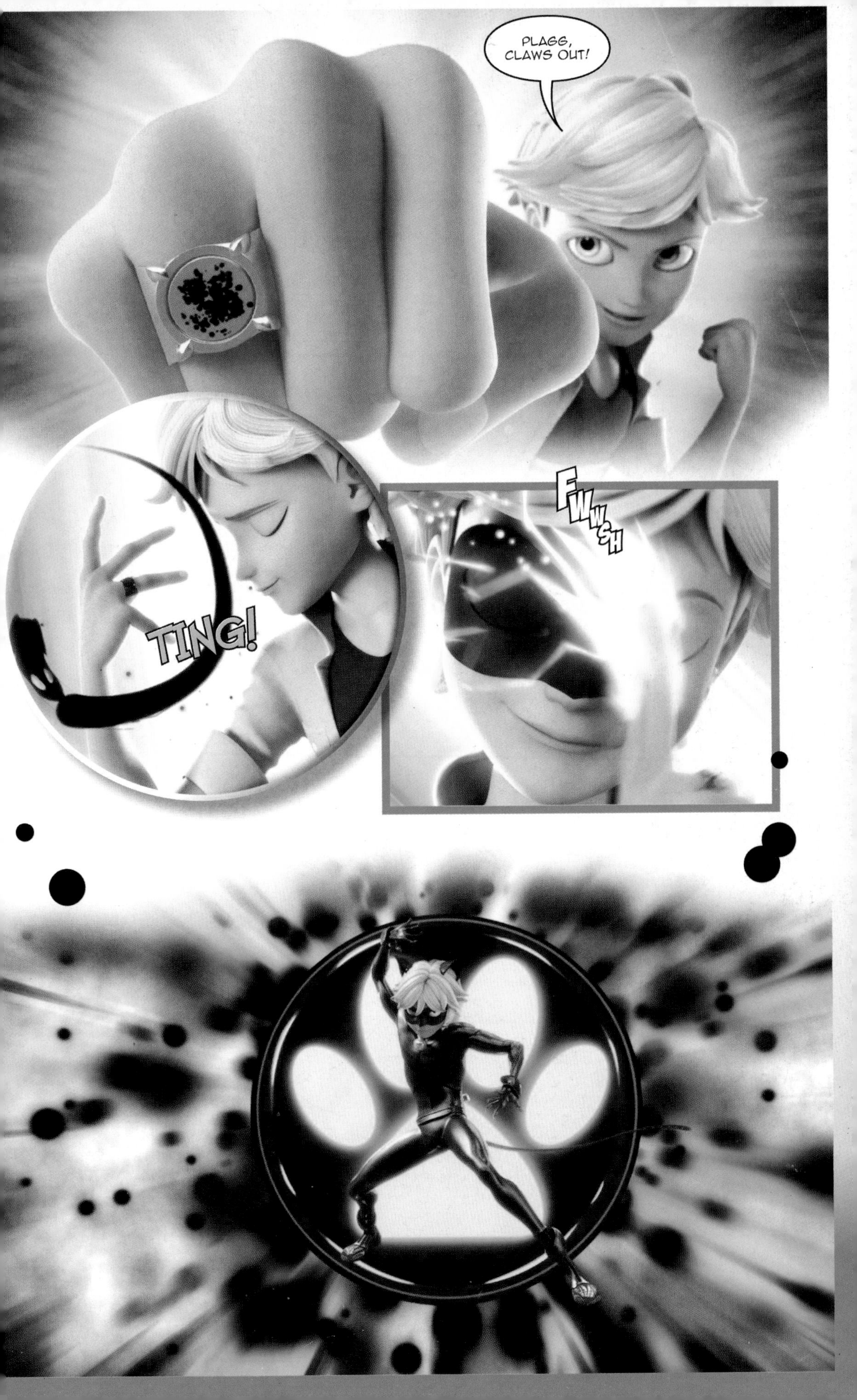
PLAGG, CLAWS OUT!
TING!
FWWSH

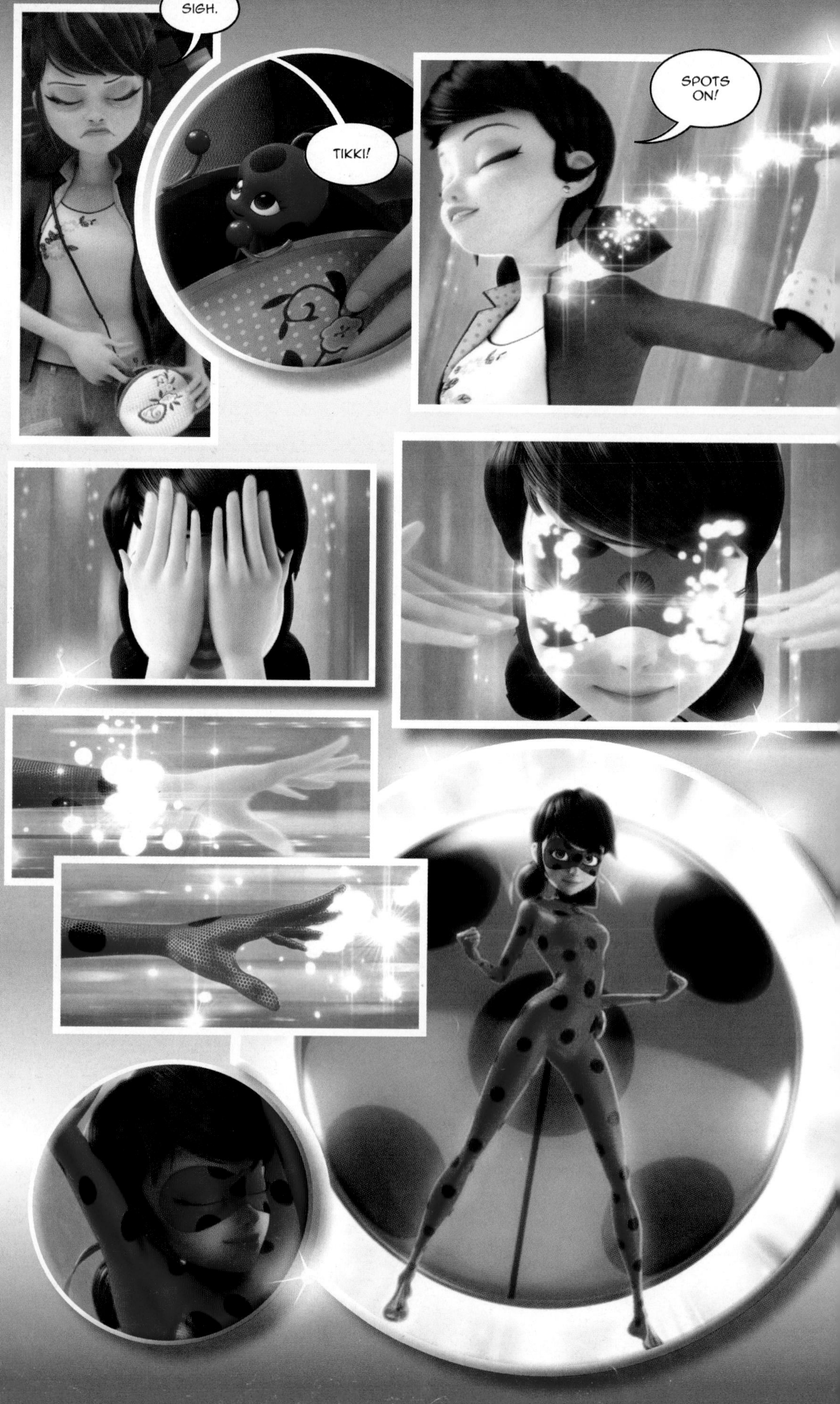
SIGH.
TIKKI!
SPOTS ON!

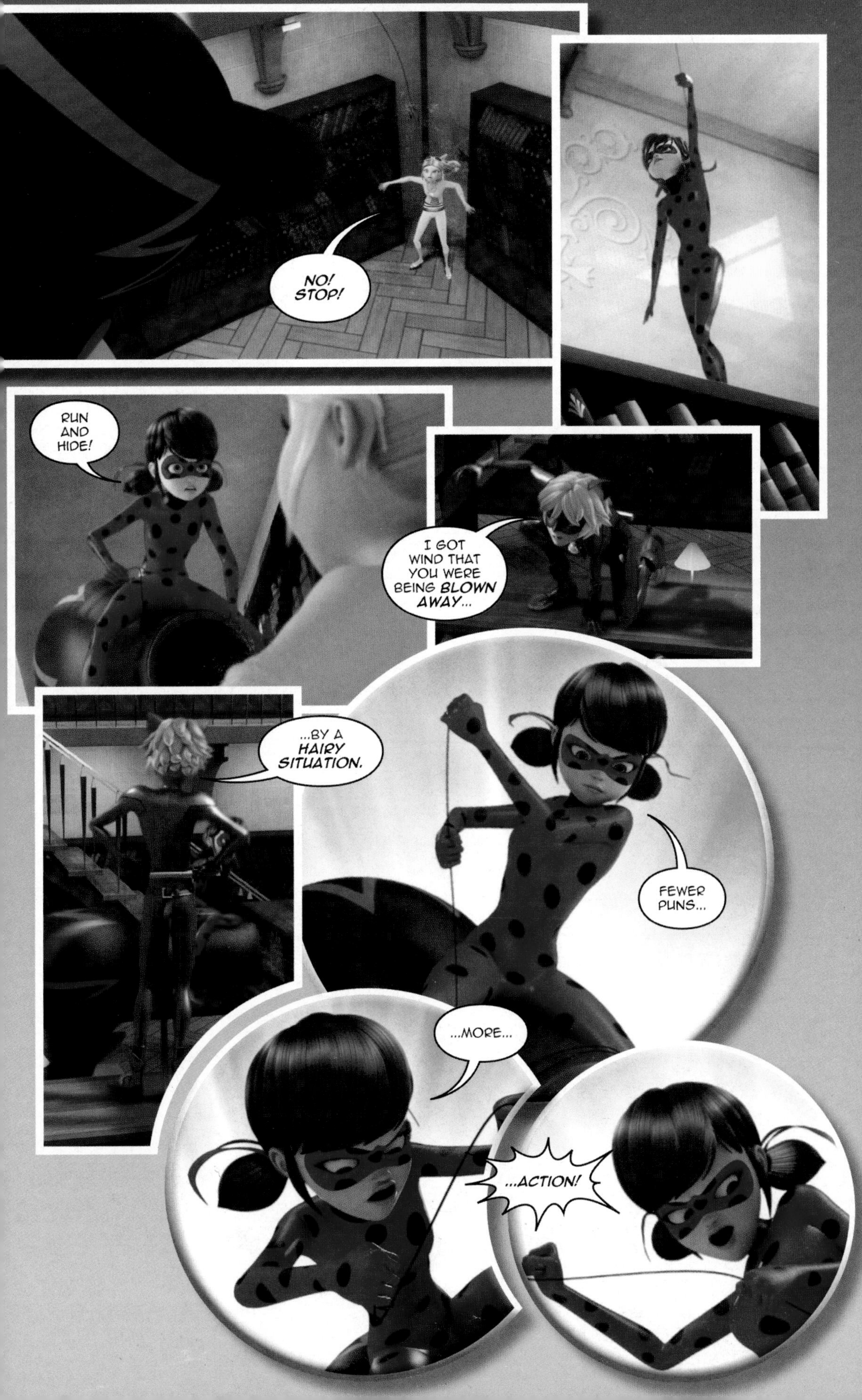
NO! STOP!
RUN AND HIDE!
I GOT WIND THAT YOU WERE BEING BLOWN AWAY...
...BY A HAIRY SITUATION.
FEWER PUNS...
...MORE...
...ACTION!

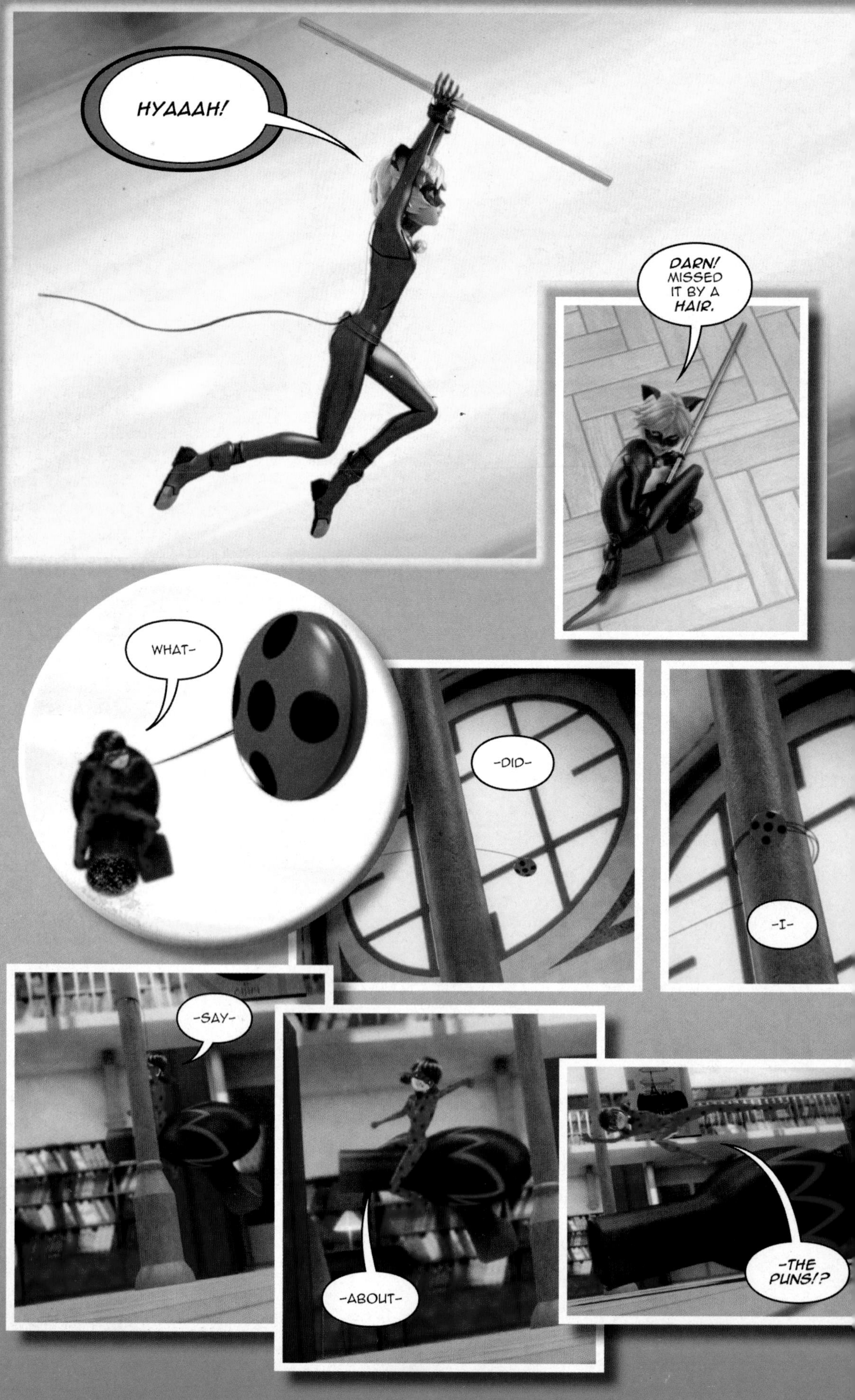
HYAAAH!
DARN! MISSED IT BY A HAIR.
WHAT-
-DID-
-I-
-SAY-
-ABOUT-
-THE PUNS!?

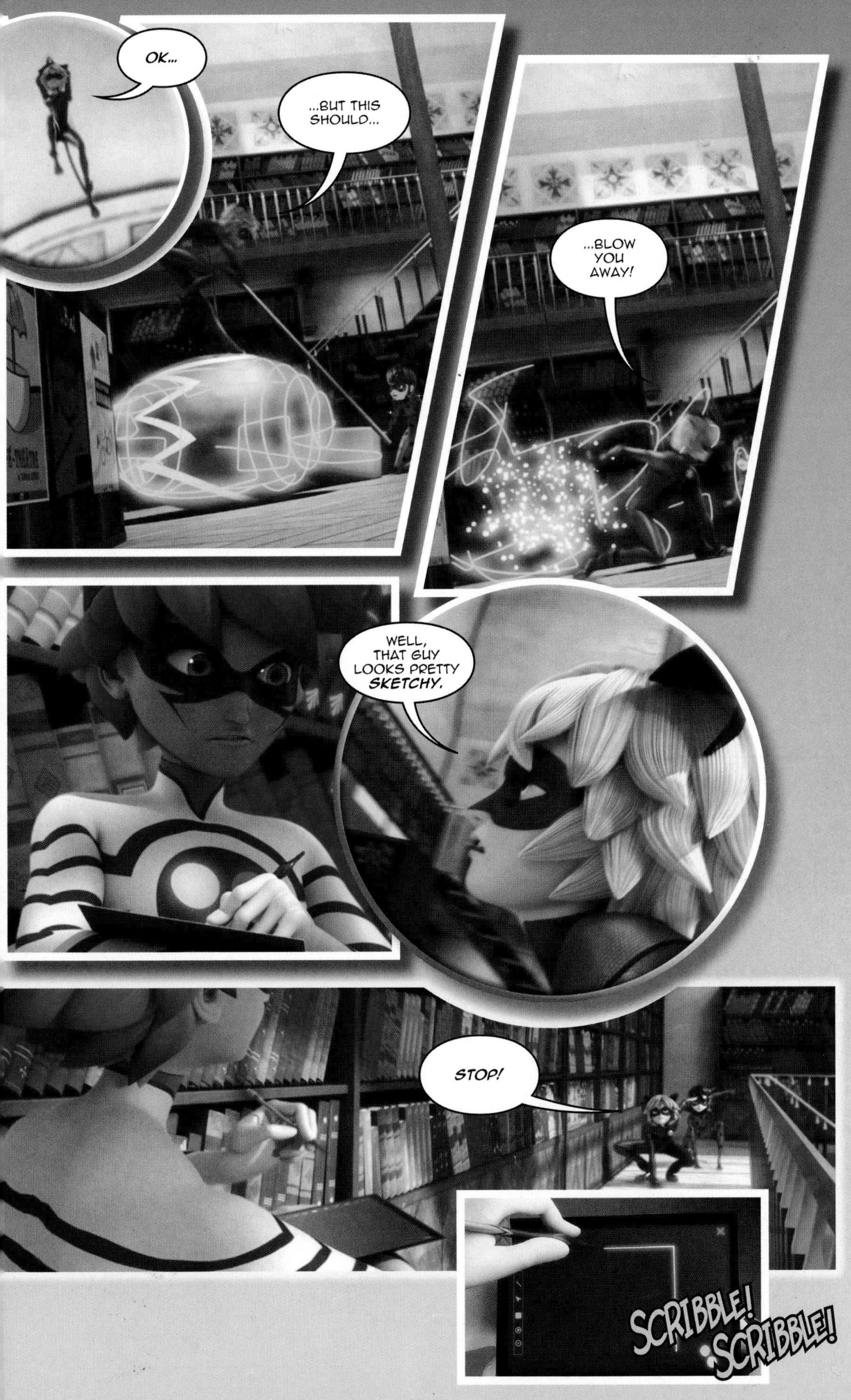
OK...
...BUT THIS SHOULD...
...BLOW YOU AWAY!
WELL, THAT GUY LOOKS PRETTY SKETCHY.
STOP!
SCRIBBLE! SCRIBBLE!

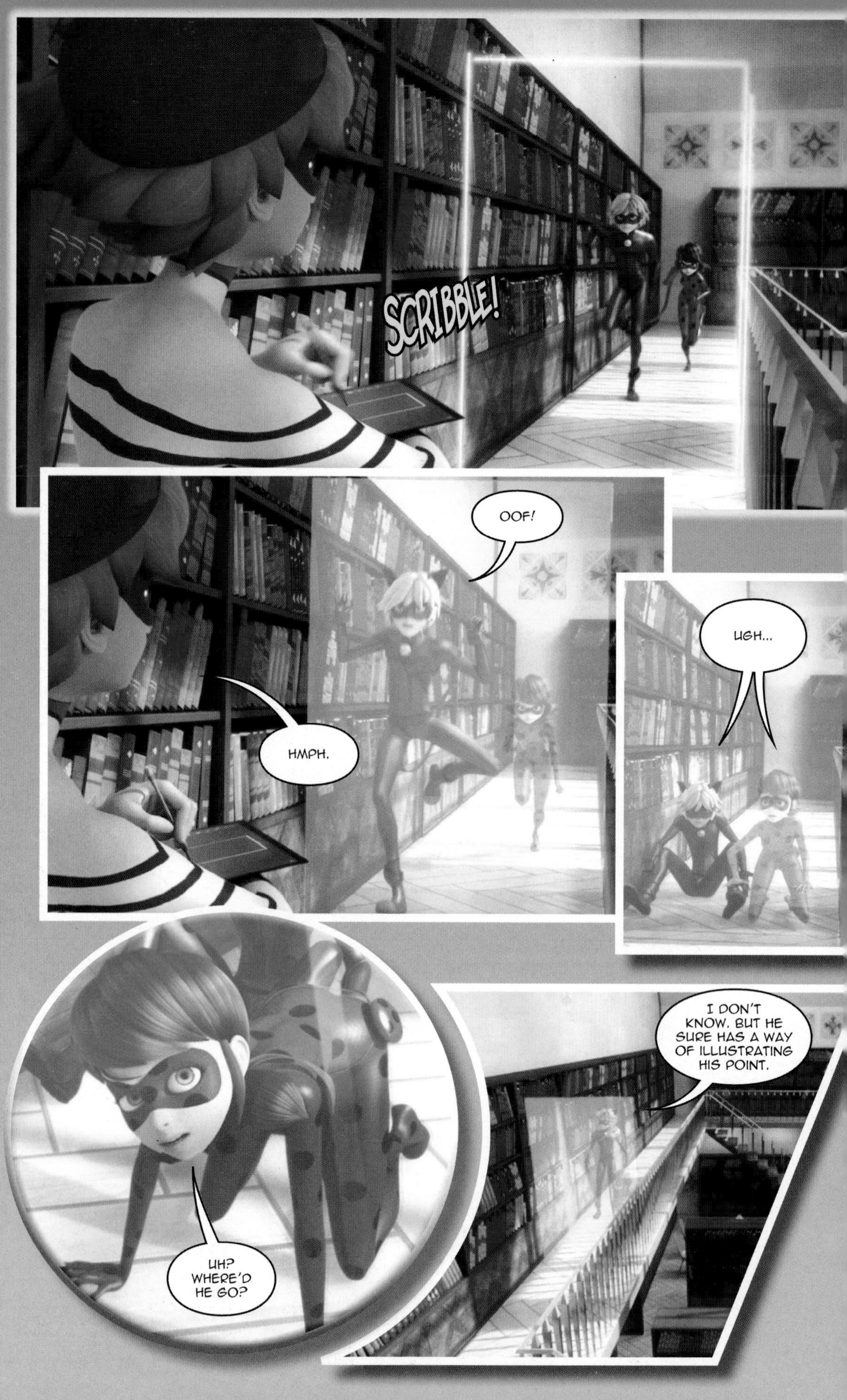
SCRIBBLE!
OOF!
HMPH.
UGH...
UH? WHERE'D HE GO?
I DON'T KNOW. BUT HE SURE HAS A WAY OF ILLUSTRATING HIS POINT.

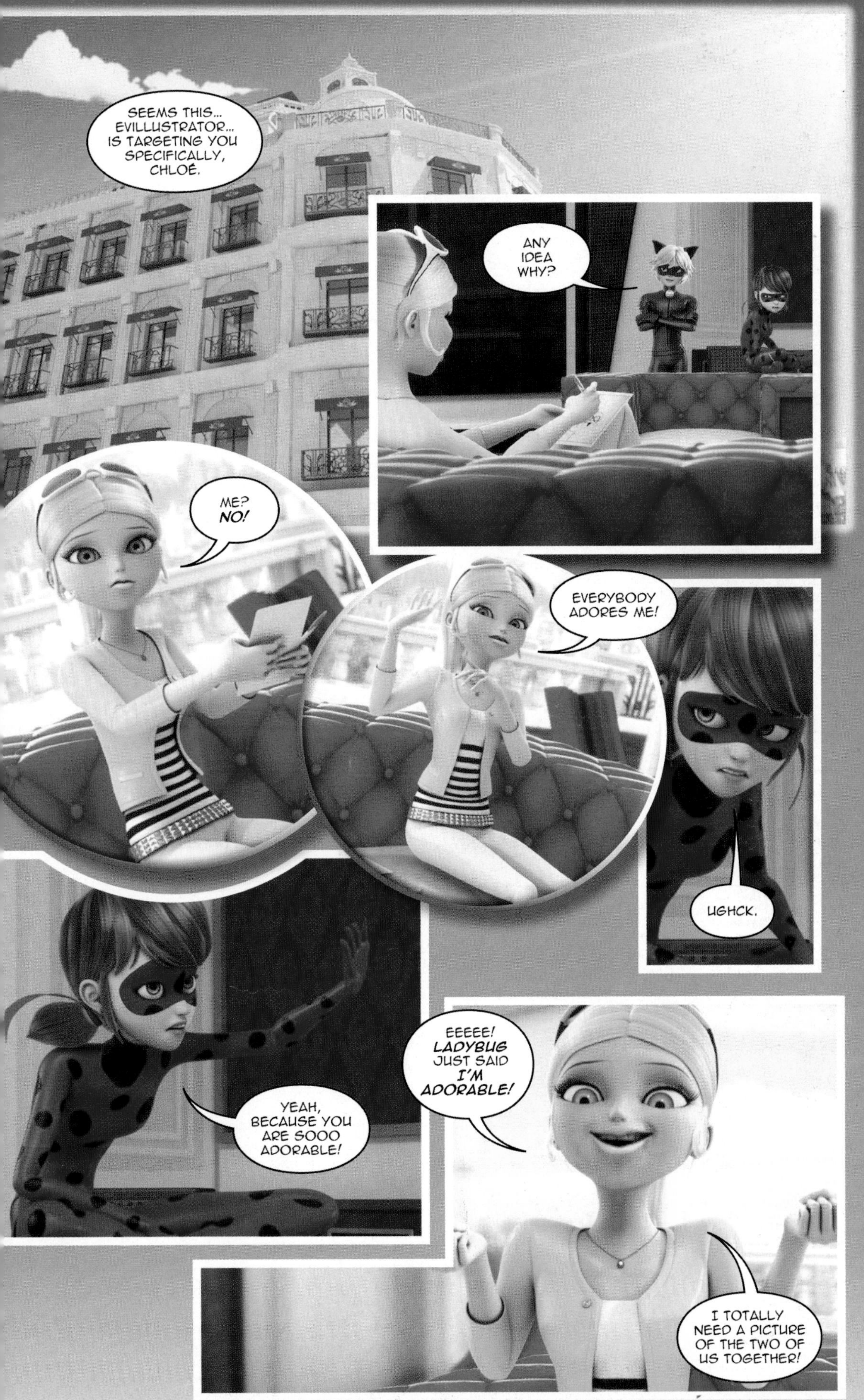
SEEMS THIS... EVILLUSTRATOR... IS TARGETING YOU SPECIFICALLY, CHLOÉ.
ANY IDEA WHY?
ME? NO!
EVERYBODY ADORES ME!
UGHCK.
YEAH, BECAUSE YOU ARE SOOO ADORABLE!
EEEEE! LADYBUG JUST SAID I'M ADORABLE!
I TOTALLY NEED A PICTURE OF THE TWO OF US TOGETHER!

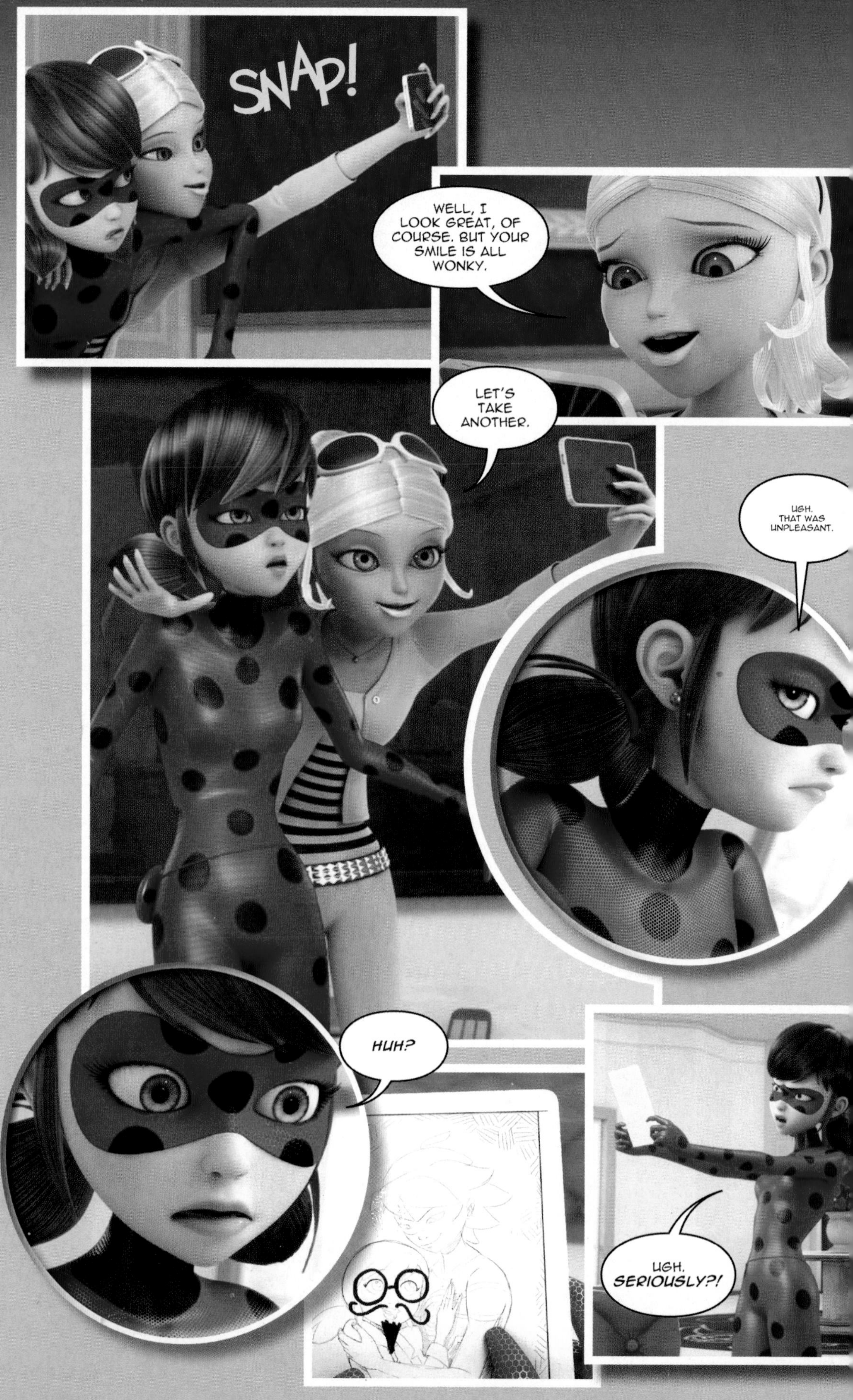
SNAP!
WELL, I LOOK GREAT, OF COURSE. BUT YOUR SMILE IS ALL WONKY.
LET'S TAKE ANOTHER.
UGH. THAT WAS UNPLEASANT.
HUH?
UGH. SERIOUSLY?!

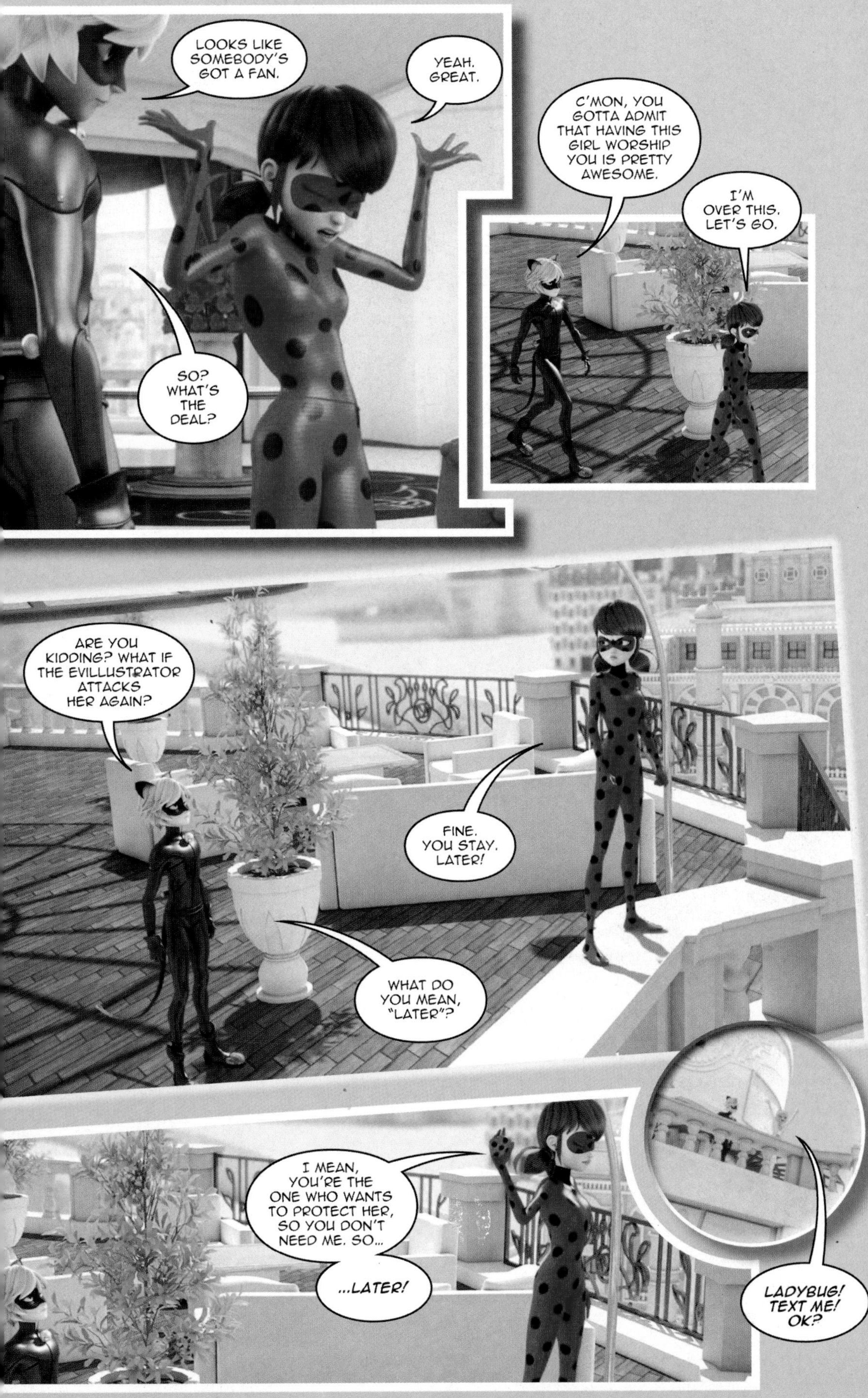
LOOKS LIKE SOMEBODY'S GOT A FAN.
YEAH. GREAT.
SO? WHAT'S THE DEAL?
C'MON, YOU GOTTA ADMIT THAT HAVING THIS GIRL WORSHIP YOU IS PRETTY AWESOME.
I'M OVER THIS. LET'S GO.
ARE YOU KIDDING? WHAT IF THE EVILLUSTRATOR ATTACKS HER AGAIN?
FINE. YOU STAY. LATER!
WHAT DO YOU MEAN, "LATER"?
I MEAN, YOU'RE THE ONE WHO WANTS TO PROTECT HER, SO YOU DON'T NEED ME. SO...
...LATER!
LADYBUG! TEXT ME! OK?

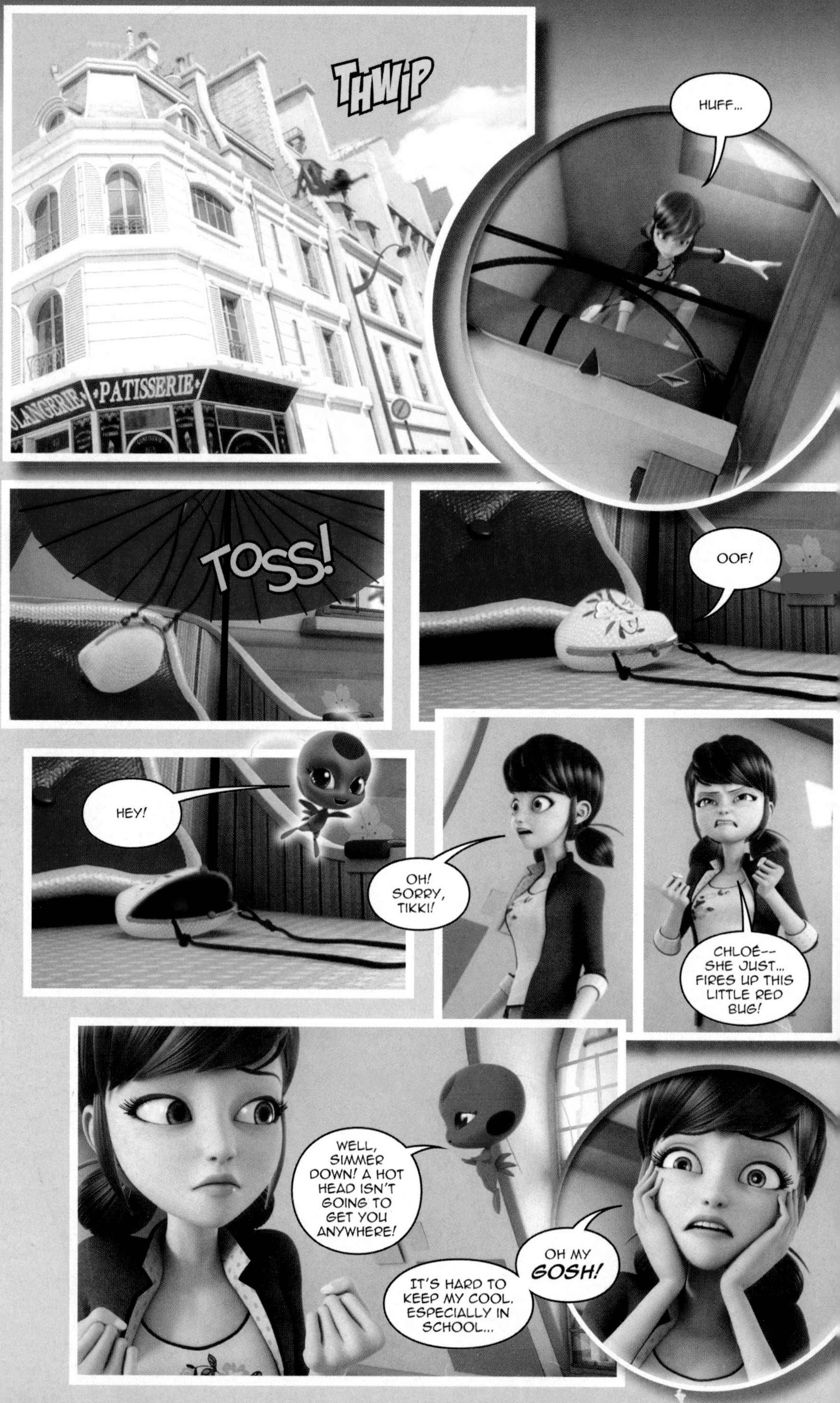
THWIP
PATISSERIE
HUFF...
TOSS!
OOF!
HEY!
OH! SORRY, TIKKI!
CHLOÉ-- SHE JUST... FIRES UP THIS LITTLE RED BUG!
WELL, SIMMER DOWN! A HOT HEAD ISN'T GOING TO GET YOU ANYWHERE!
IT'S HARD TO KEEP MY COOL. ESPECIALLY IN SCHOOL...
OH MY GOSH!

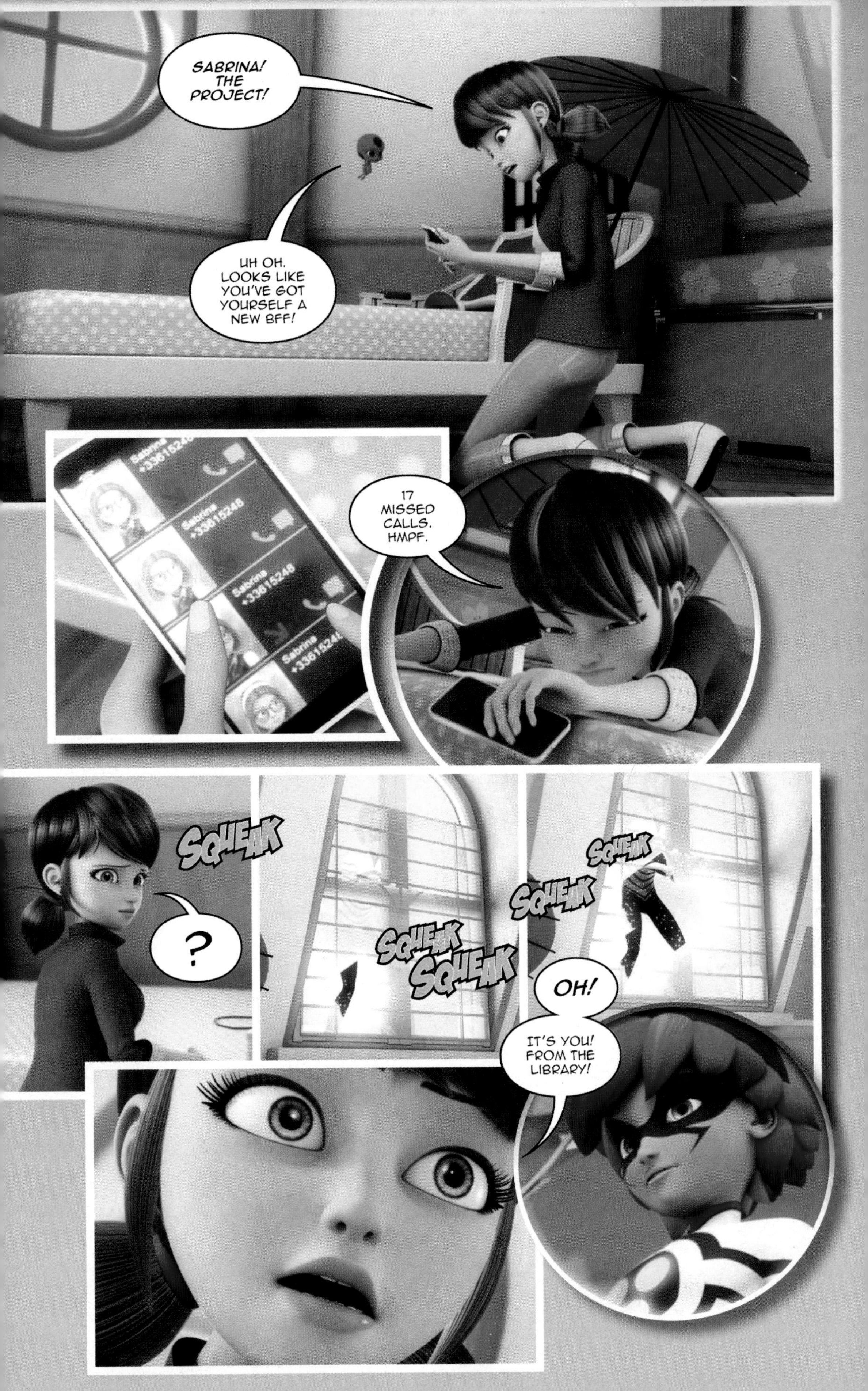
SABRINA! THE PROJECT!
UH OH. LOOKS LIKE YOU'VE GOT YOURSELF A NEW BFF!
17 MISSED CALLS. HMPF.
SQUEAK
?
SQUEAK SQUEAK
SQUEAK
SQUEAK
OH!
IT'S YOU! FROM THE LIBRARY!

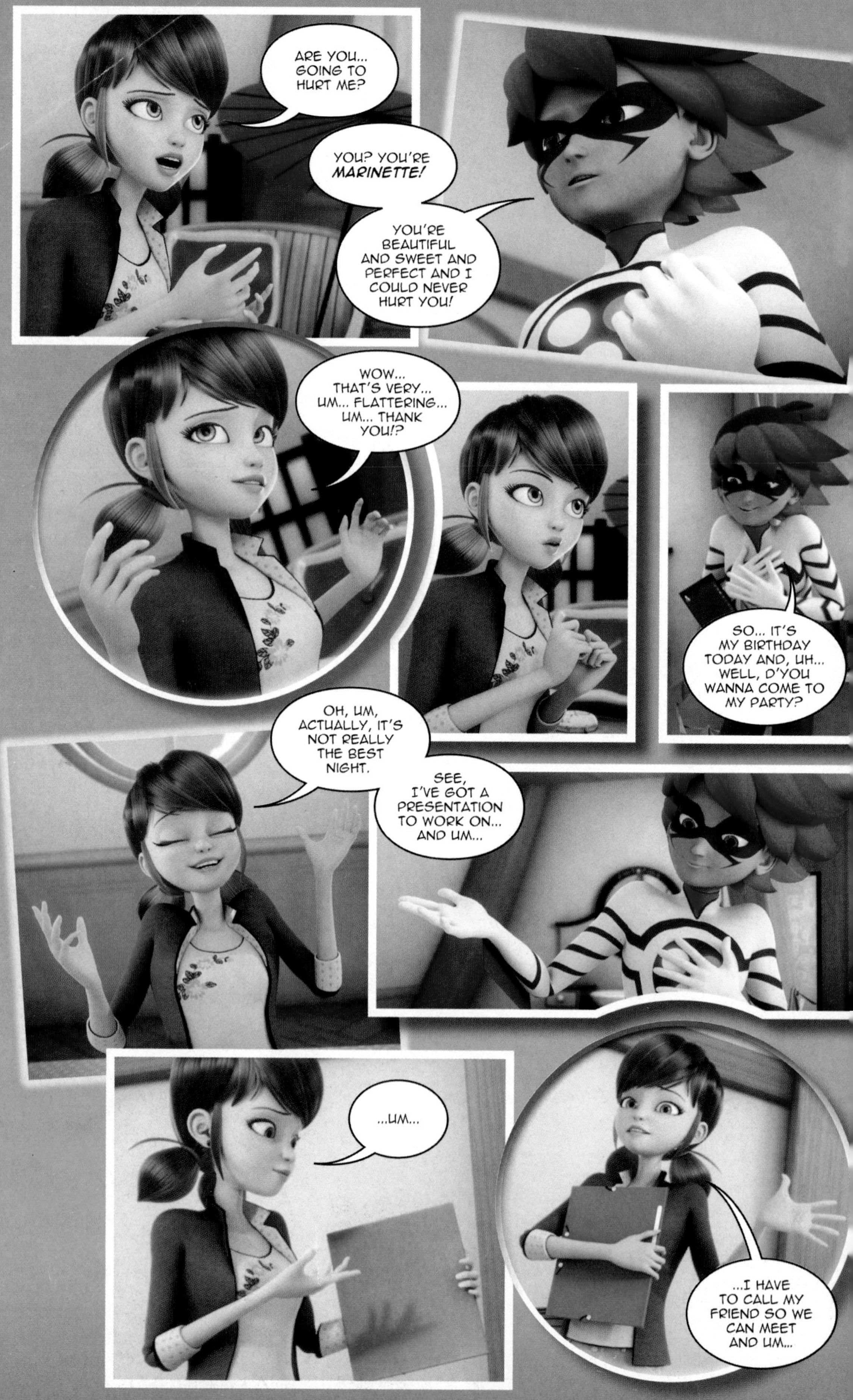

ARE YOU... GOING TO HURT ME?
YOU? YOU'RE *MARINETTE!*
YOU'RE BEAUTIFUL AND SWEET AND PERFECT AND I COULD NEVER HURT YOU!
WOW... THAT'S VERY... UM... FLATTERING... UM... THANK YOU!?
SO... IT'S MY BIRTHDAY TODAY AND, UH... WELL, D'YOU WANNA COME TO MY PARTY?
OH, UM, ACTUALLY, IT'S NOT REALLY THE BEST NIGHT.
SEE, I'VE GOT A PRESENTATION TO WORK ON... AND UM...
...UM...
...I HAVE TO CALL MY FRIEND SO WE CAN MEET AND UM...

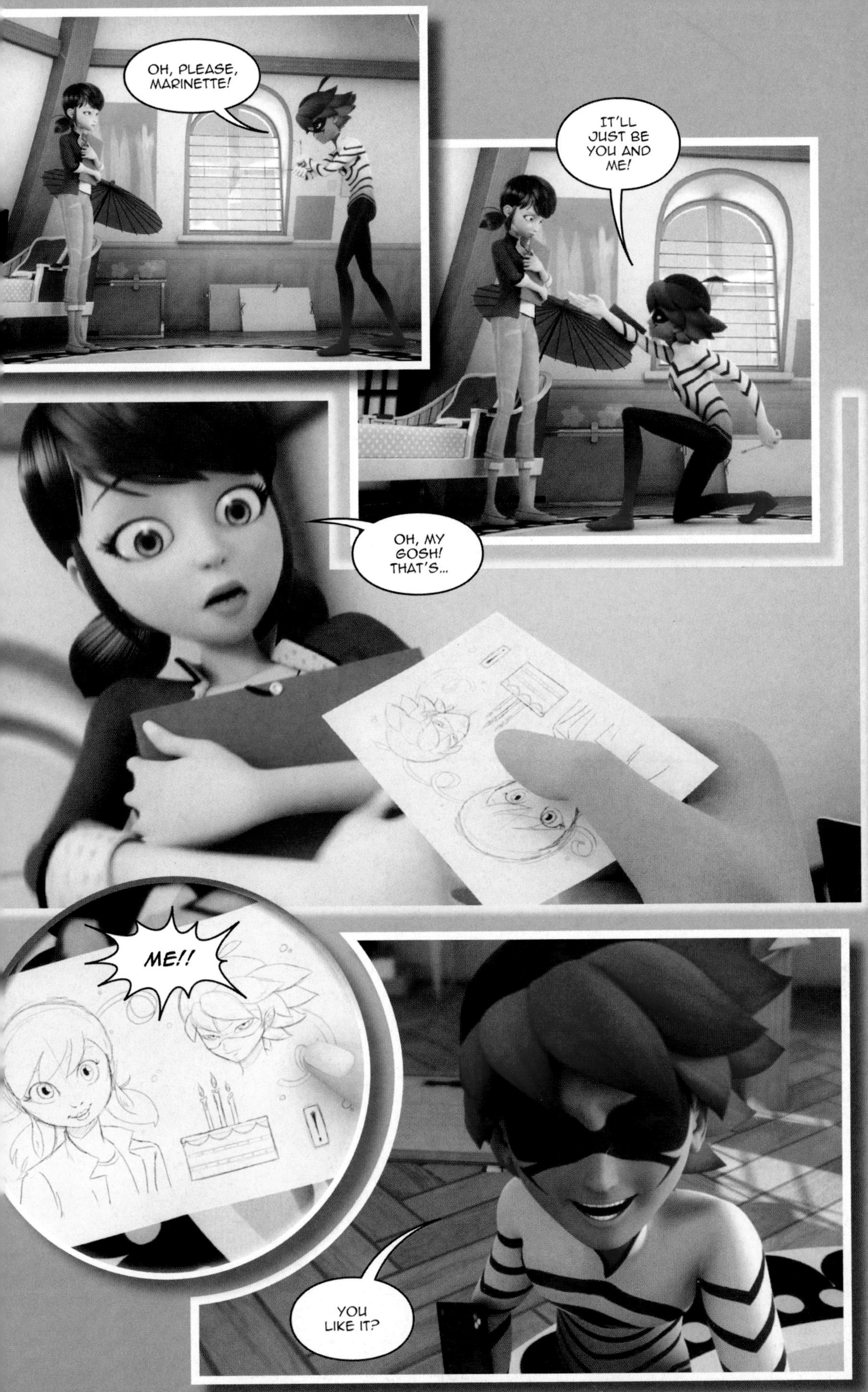
OH, PLEASE, MARINETTE!
IT'LL JUST BE YOU AND ME!
OH, MY GOSH! THAT'S...
ME!!
YOU LIKE IT?

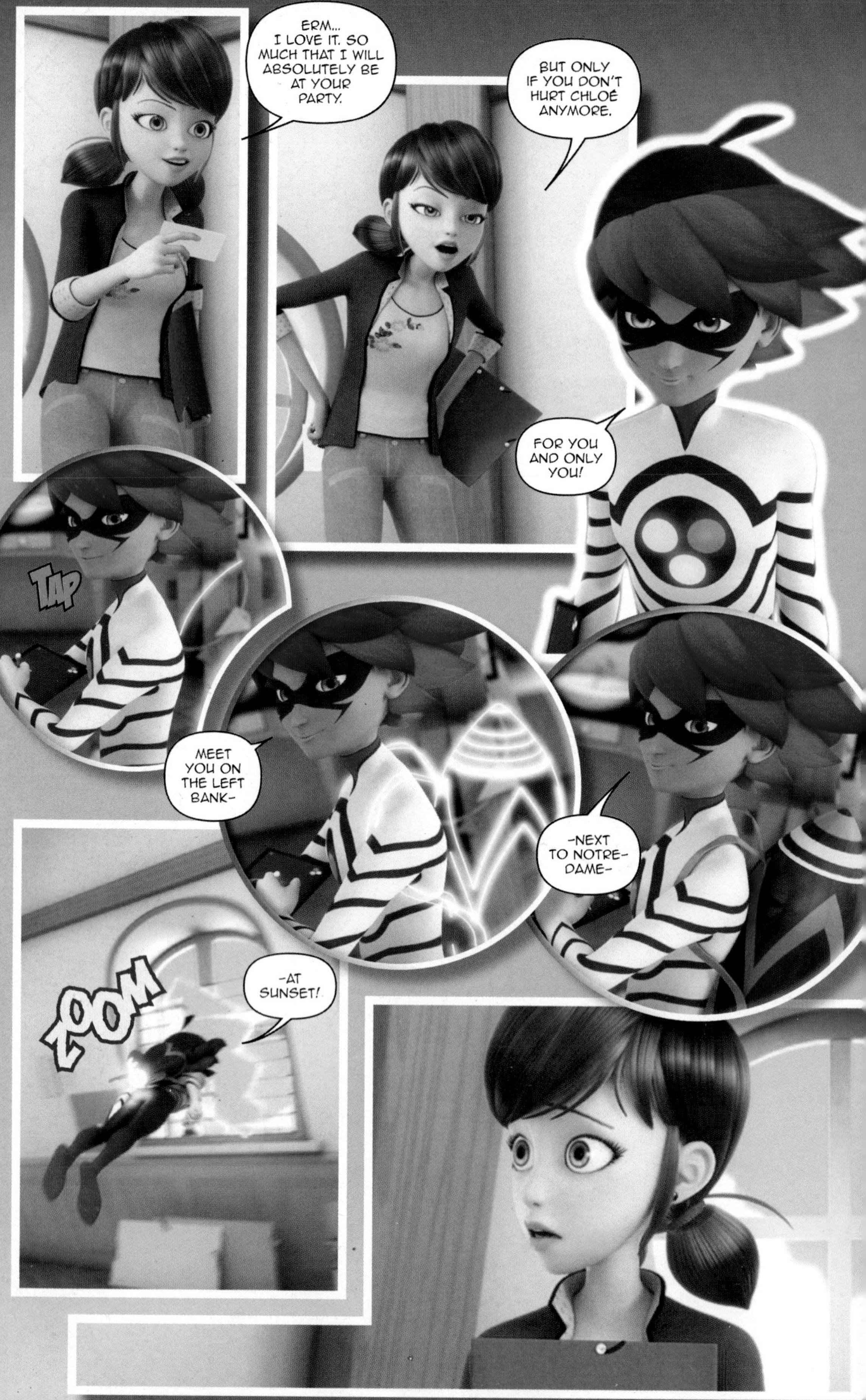
ERM... I LOVE IT. SO MUCH THAT I WILL ABSOLUTELY BE AT YOUR PARTY.
BUT ONLY IF YOU DON'T HURT CHLOÉ ANYMORE.
FOR YOU AND ONLY YOU!
TAP
MEET YOU ON THE LEFT BANK-
-NEXT TO NOTRE-DAME-
ZOOM
-AT SUNSET!

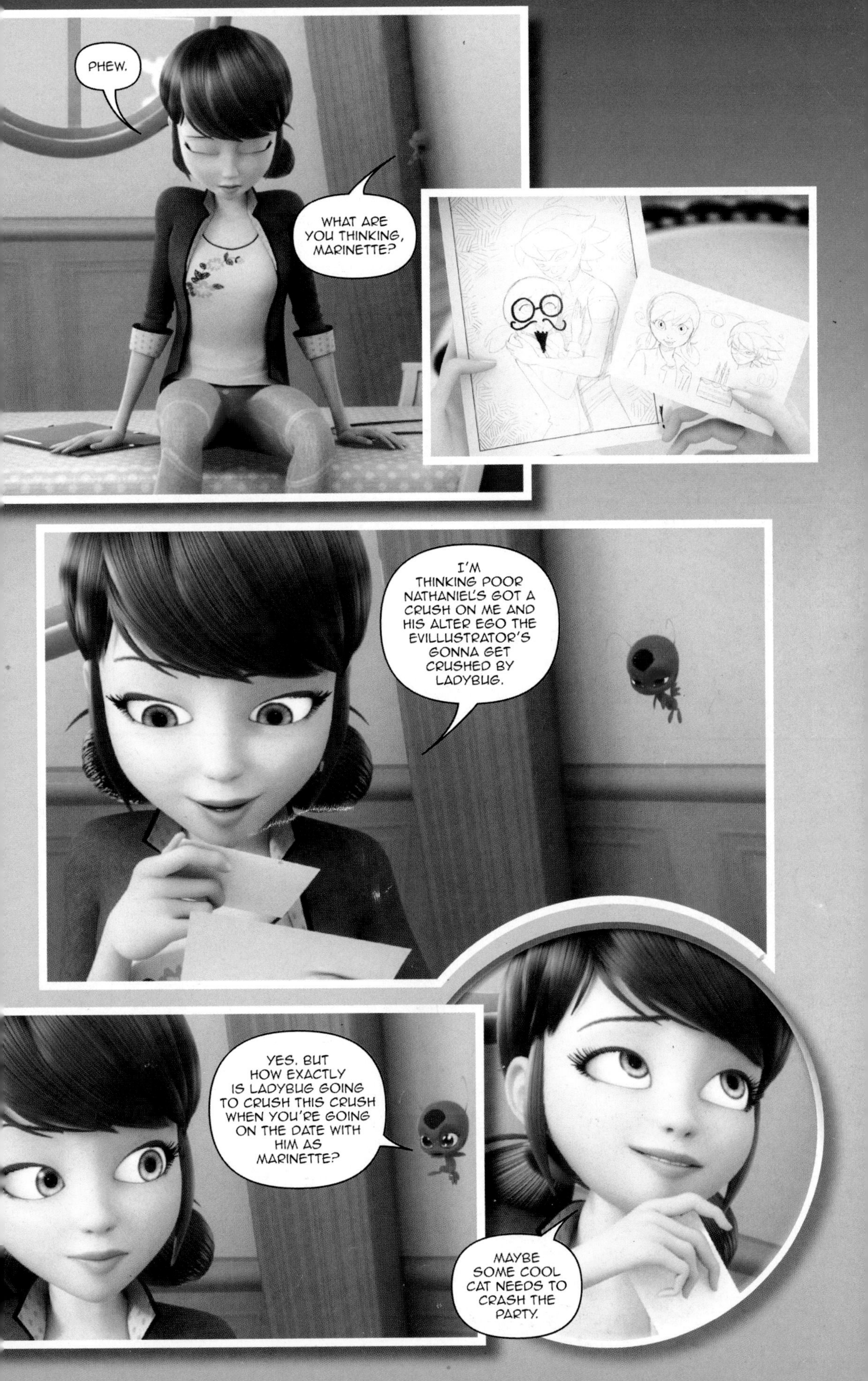
PHEW.
WHAT ARE YOU THINKING, MARINETTE?
I'M THINKING POOR NATHANIEL'S GOT A CRUSH ON ME AND HIS ALTER EGO THE EVILLUSTRATOR'S GONNA GET CRUSHED BY LADYBUG.
YES. BUT HOW EXACTLY IS LADYBUG GOING TO CRUSH THIS CRUSH WHEN YOU'RE GOING ON THE DATE WITH HIM AS MARINETTE?
MAYBE SOME COOL CAT NEEDS TO CRASH THE PARTY.

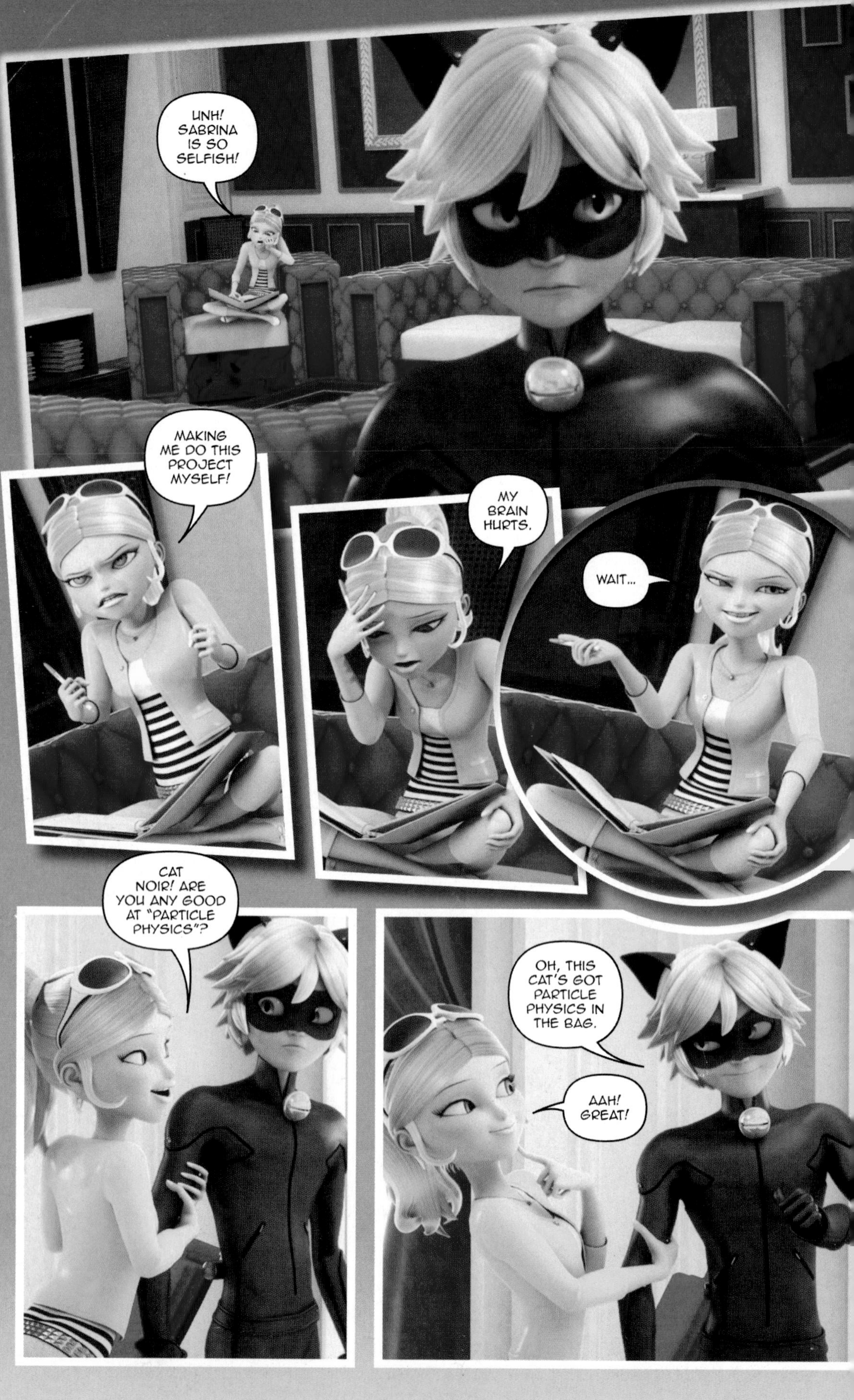
UNH! SABRINA IS SO SELFISH!
MAKING ME DO THIS PROJECT MYSELF!
MY BRAIN HURTS.
WAIT...
CAT NOIR! ARE YOU ANY GOOD AT "PARTICLE PHYSICS"?
OH, THIS CAT'S GOT PARTICLE PHYSICS IN THE BAG.
AAH! GREAT!

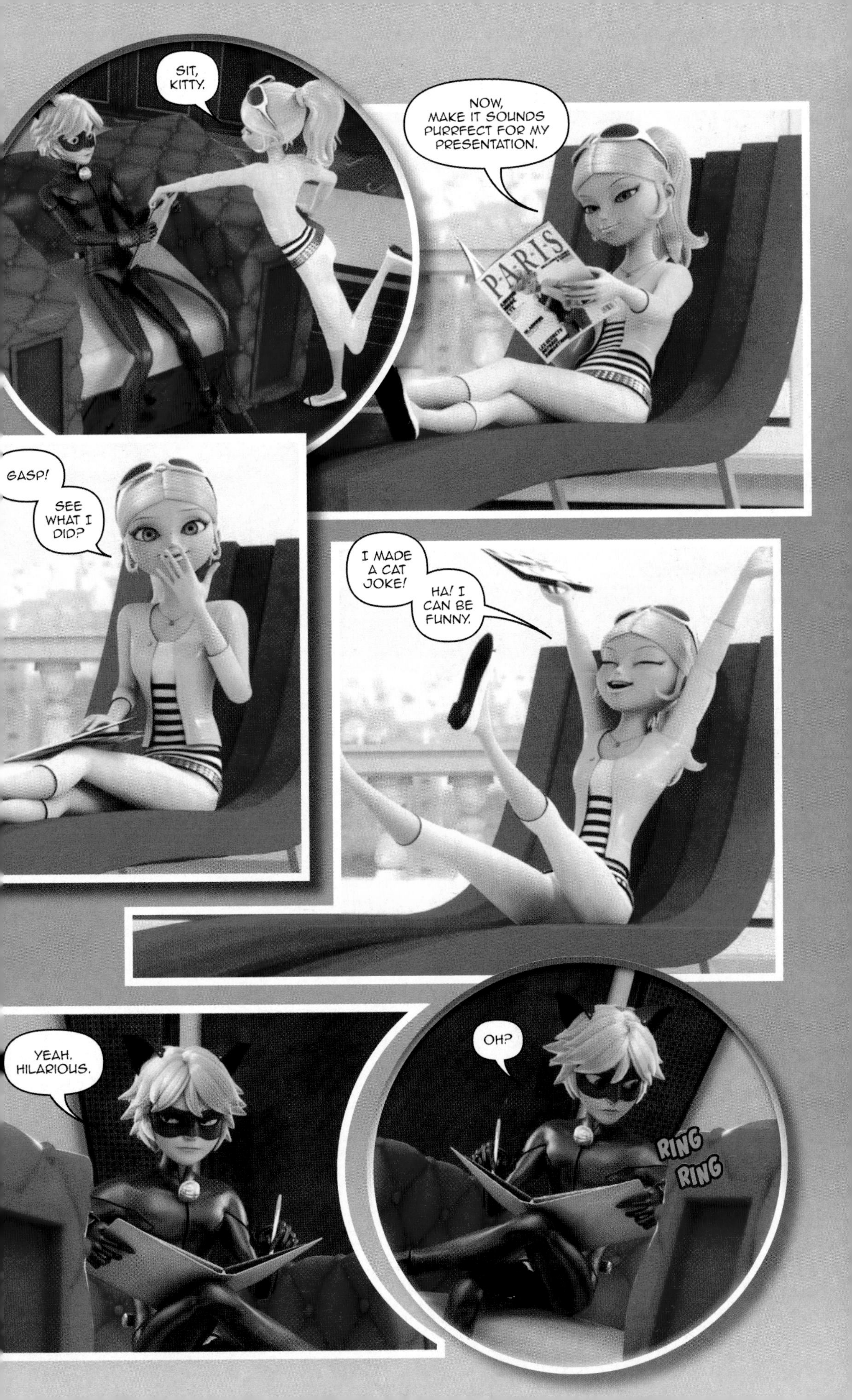
SIT, KITTY.
NOW, MAKE IT SOUNDS PURRFECT FOR MY PRESENTATION.
P·A·R·I·S
GASP!
SEE WHAT I DID?
I MADE A CAT JOKE!
HA! I CAN BE FUNNY.
YEAH. HILARIOUS.
OH?
RING RING

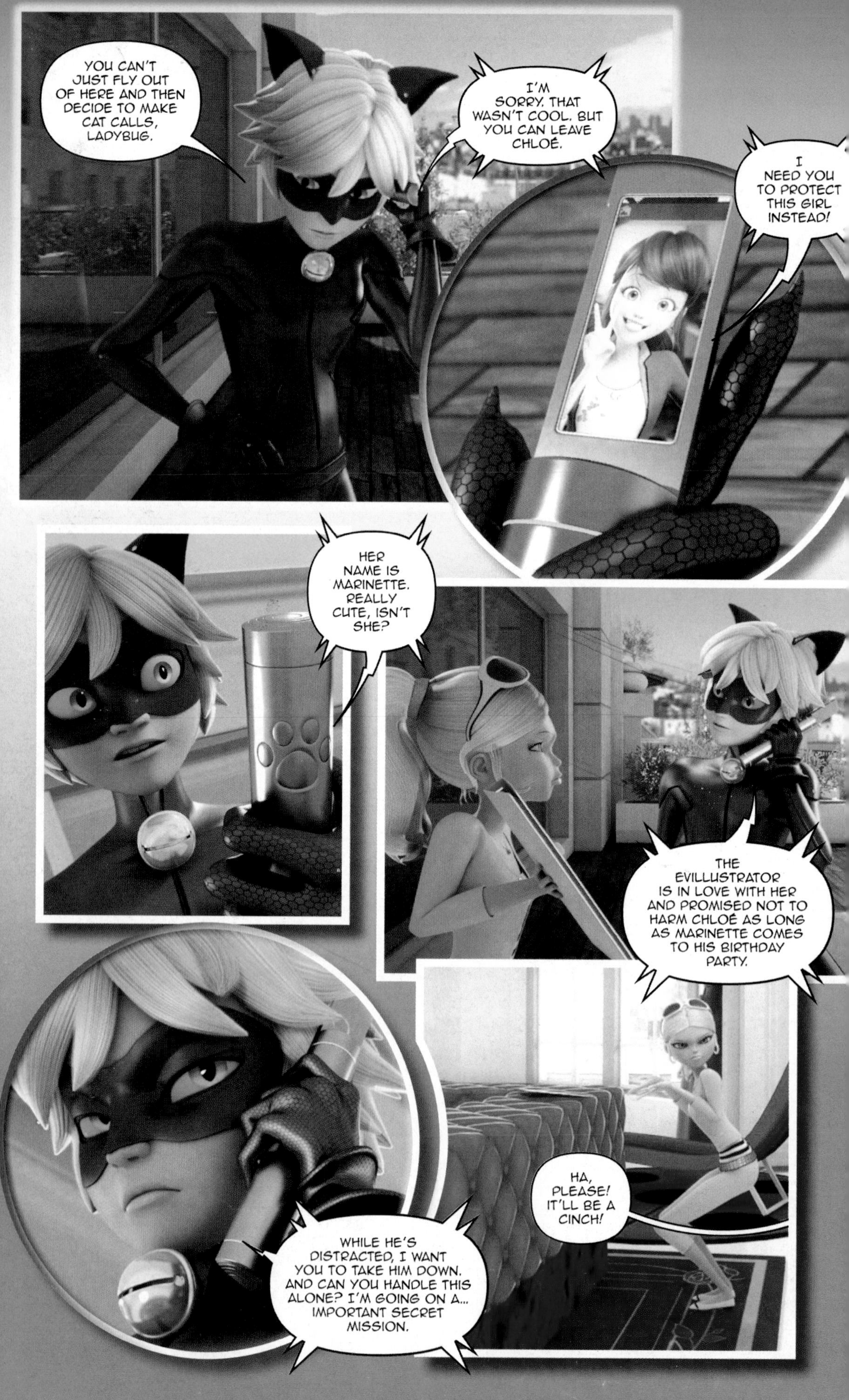
YOU CAN'T JUST FLY OUT OF HERE AND THEN DECIDE TO MAKE CAT CALLS, LADYBUG.
I'M SORRY. THAT WASN'T COOL. BUT YOU CAN LEAVE CHLOÉ.
I NEED YOU TO PROTECT THIS GIRL INSTEAD!
HER NAME IS MARINETTE. REALLY CUTE, ISN'T SHE?
THE EVILLUSTRATOR IS IN LOVE WITH HER AND PROMISED NOT TO HARM CHLOÉ AS LONG AS MARINETTE COMES TO HIS BIRTHDAY PARTY.
WHILE HE'S DISTRACTED, I WANT YOU TO TAKE HIM DOWN. AND CAN YOU HANDLE THIS ALONE? I'M GOING ON A... IMPORTANT SECRET MISSION.
HA, PLEASE! IT'LL BE A CINCH!

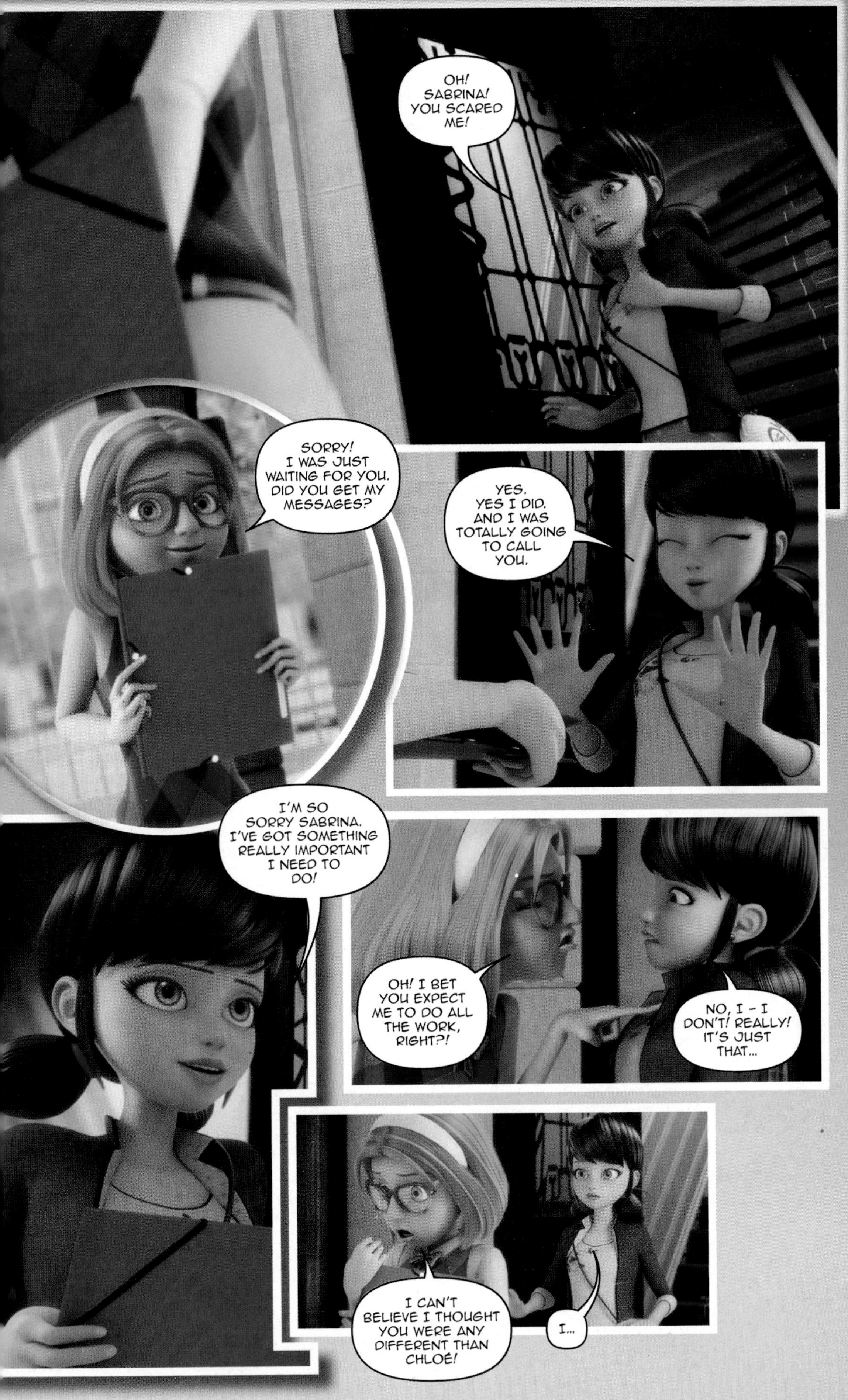
OH! SABRINA! YOU SCARED ME!
SORRY! I WAS JUST WAITING FOR YOU. DID YOU GET MY MESSAGES?
YES. YES I DID. AND I WAS TOTALLY GOING TO CALL YOU.
I'M SO SORRY SABRINA. I'VE GOT SOMETHING REALLY IMPORTANT I NEED TO DO!
OH! I BET YOU EXPECT ME TO DO ALL THE WORK, RIGHT?!
NO, I - I DON'T! REALLY! IT'S JUST THAT...
I CAN'T BELIEVE I THOUGHT YOU WERE ANY DIFFERENT THAN CHLOÉ!
I...

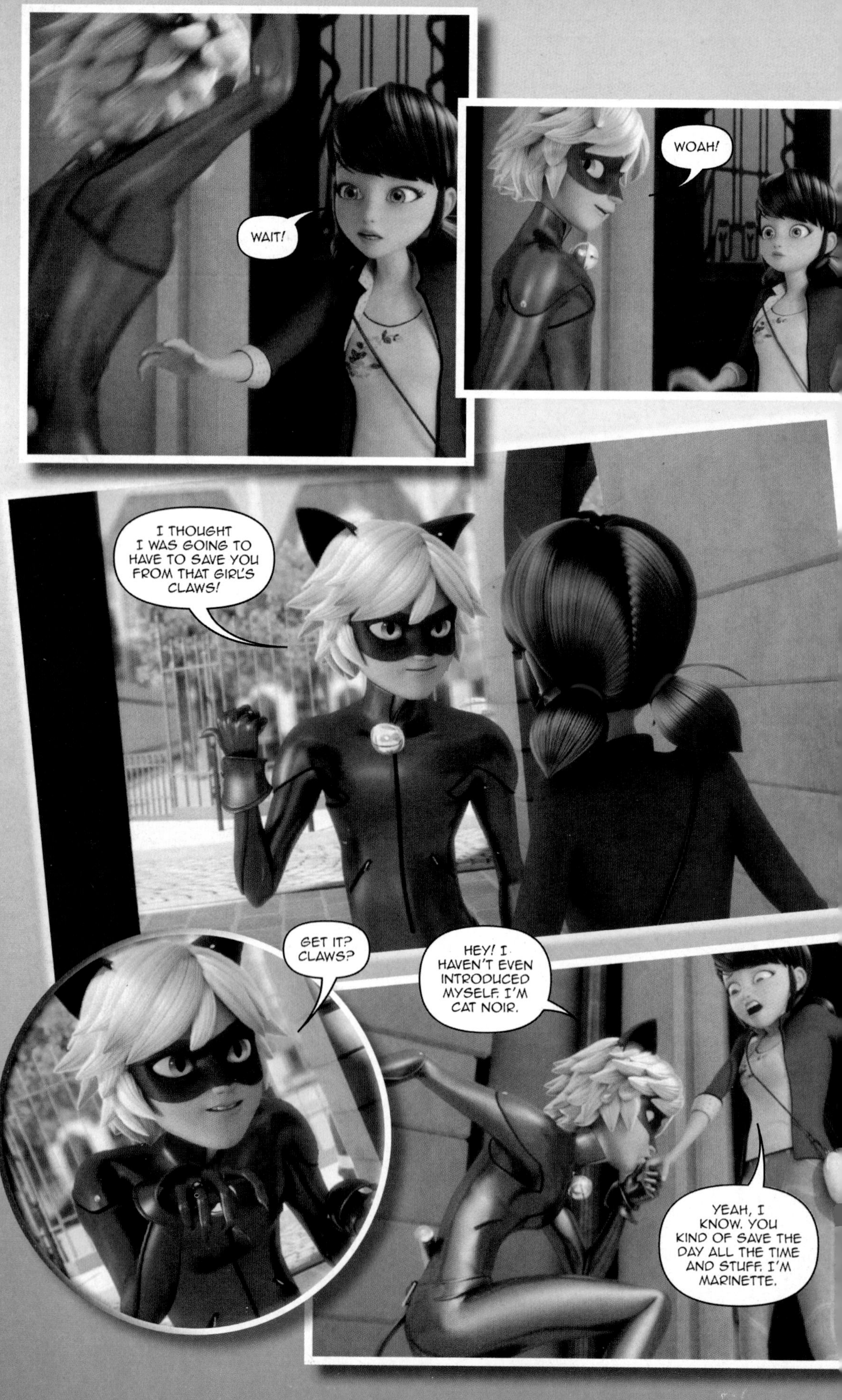
WAIT!
WOAH!
I THOUGHT I WAS GOING TO HAVE TO SAVE YOU FROM THAT GIRL'S CLAWS!
GET IT? CLAWS?
HEY! I HAVEN'T EVEN INTRODUCED MYSELF. I'M CAT NOIR.
YEAH, I KNOW. YOU KIND OF SAVE THE DAY ALL THE TIME AND STUFF. I'M MARINETTE.

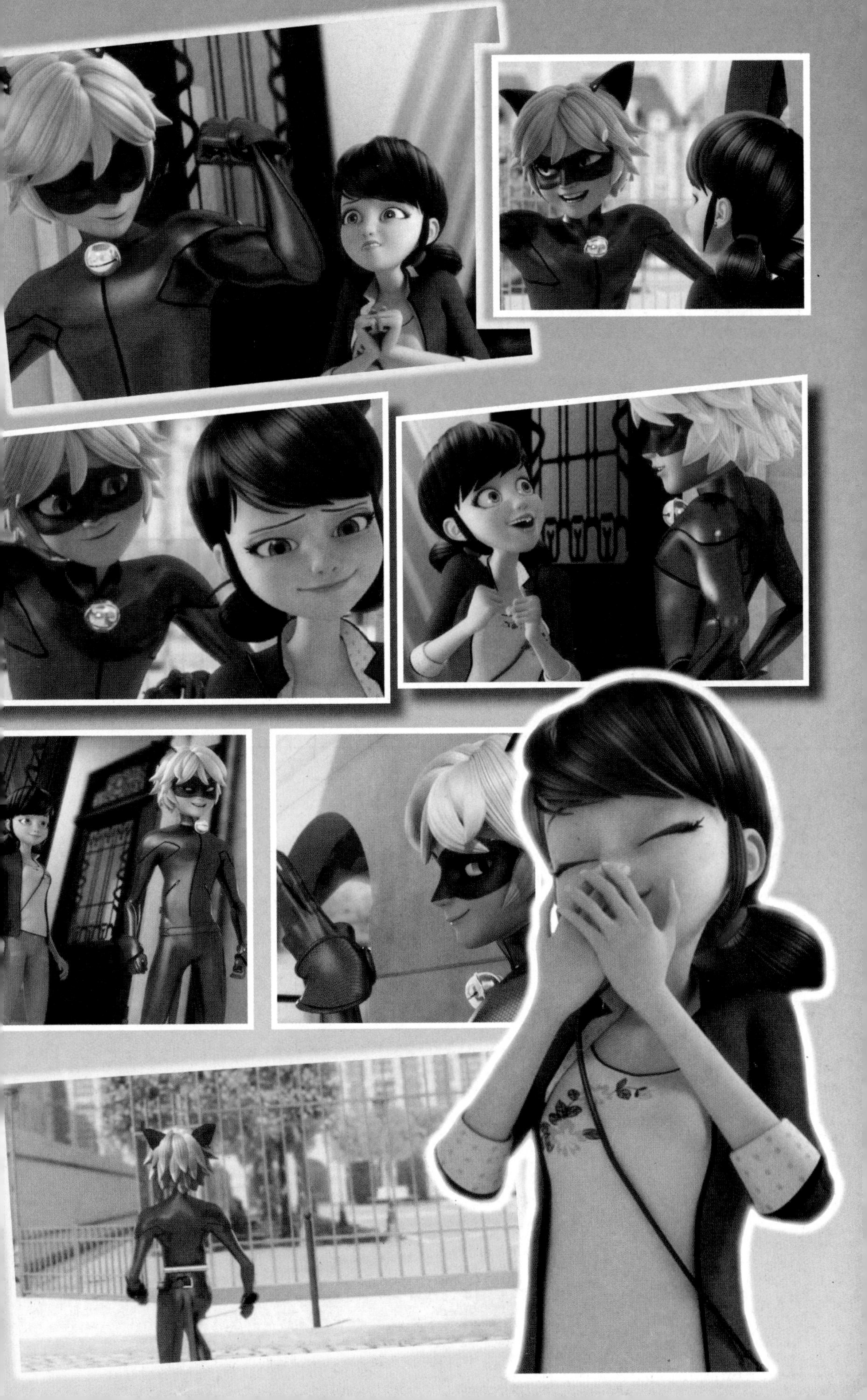

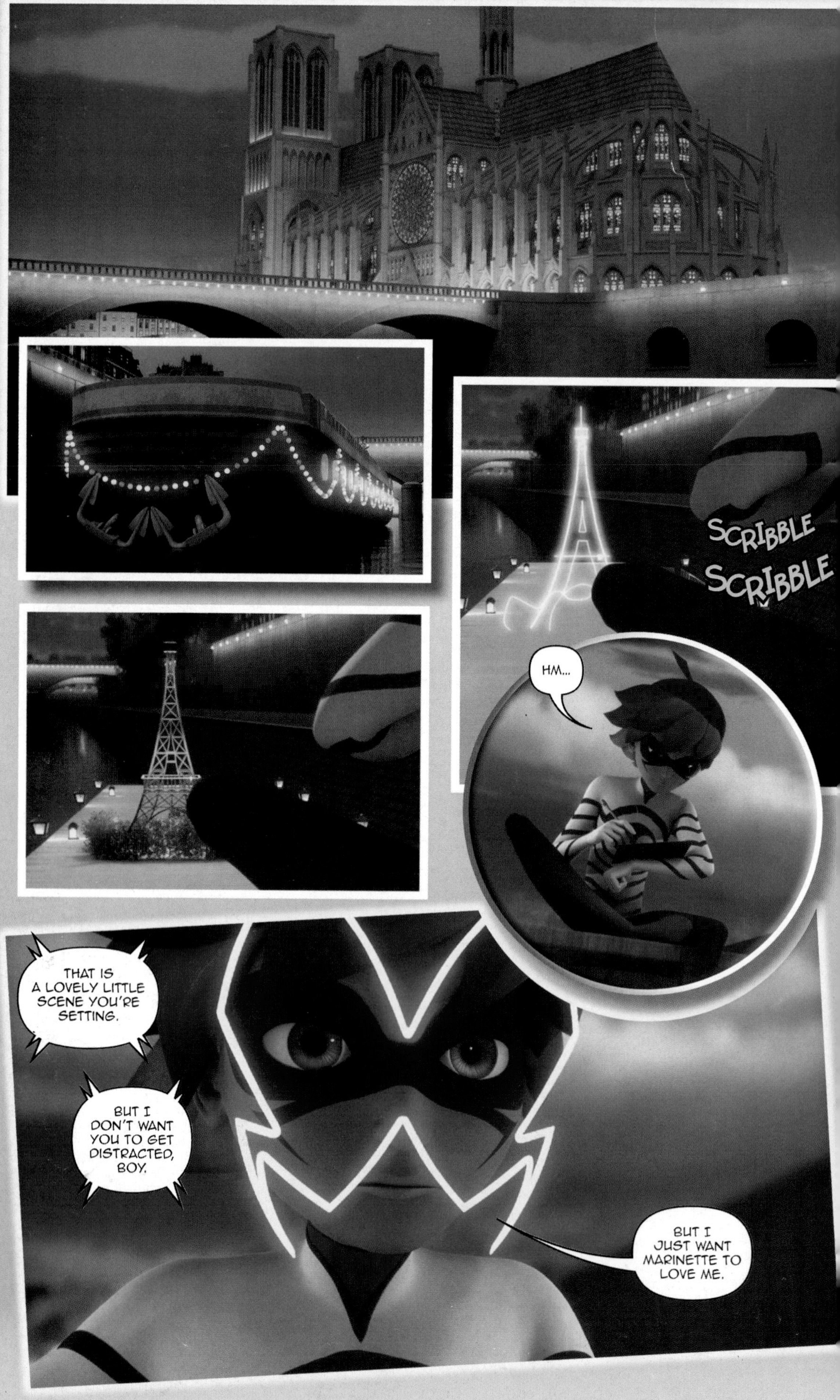
SCRIBBLE
SCRIBBLE
HM...
THAT IS A LOVELY LITTLE SCENE YOU'RE SETTING.
BUT I DON'T WANT YOU TO GET DISTRACTED, BOY.
BUT I JUST WANT MARINETTE TO LOVE ME.

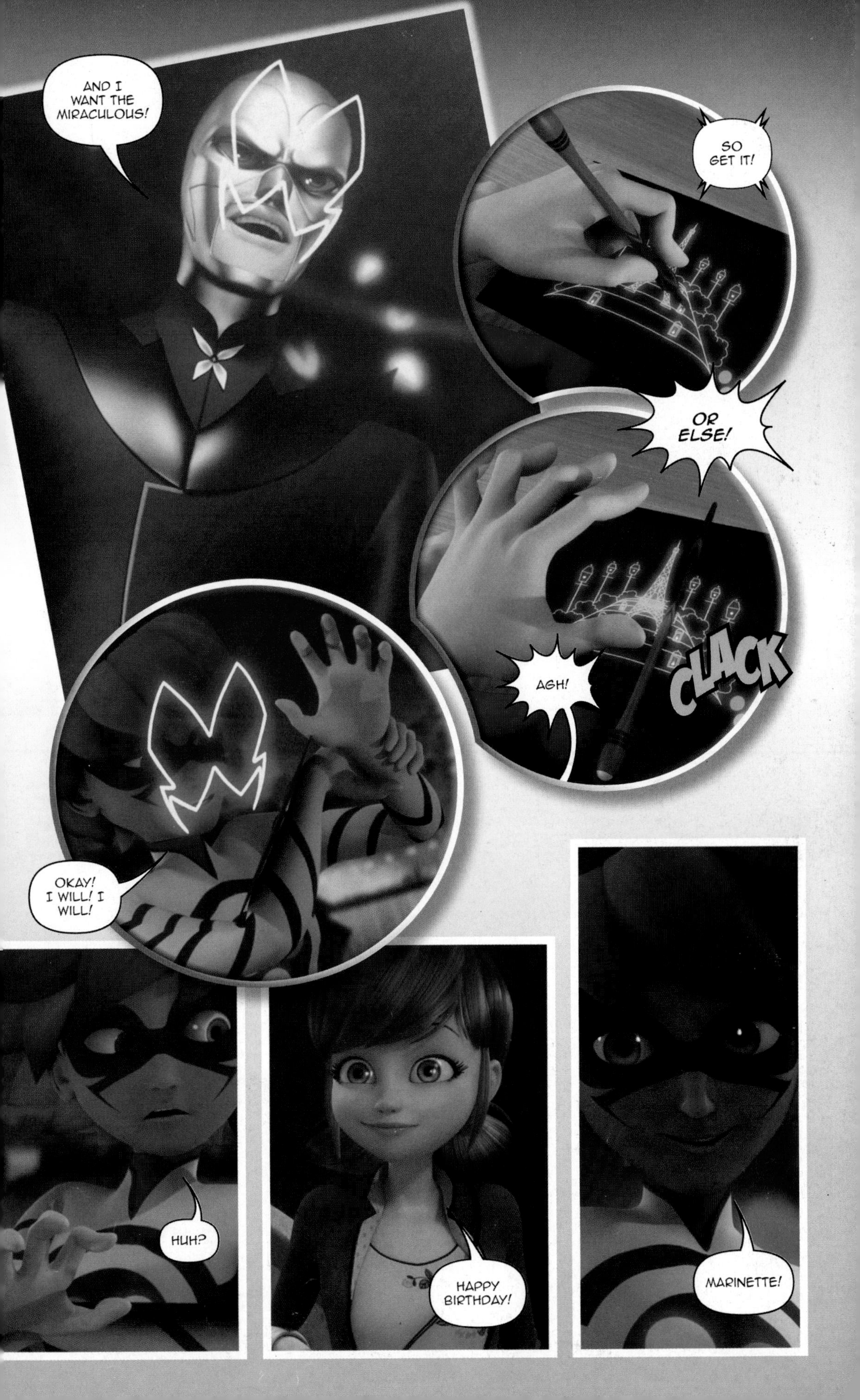
AND I WANT THE MIRACULOUS!
SO GET IT!
OR ELSE!
AGH!
CLACK
OKAY! I WILL! I WILL!
HUH?
HAPPY BIRTHDAY!
MARINETTE!

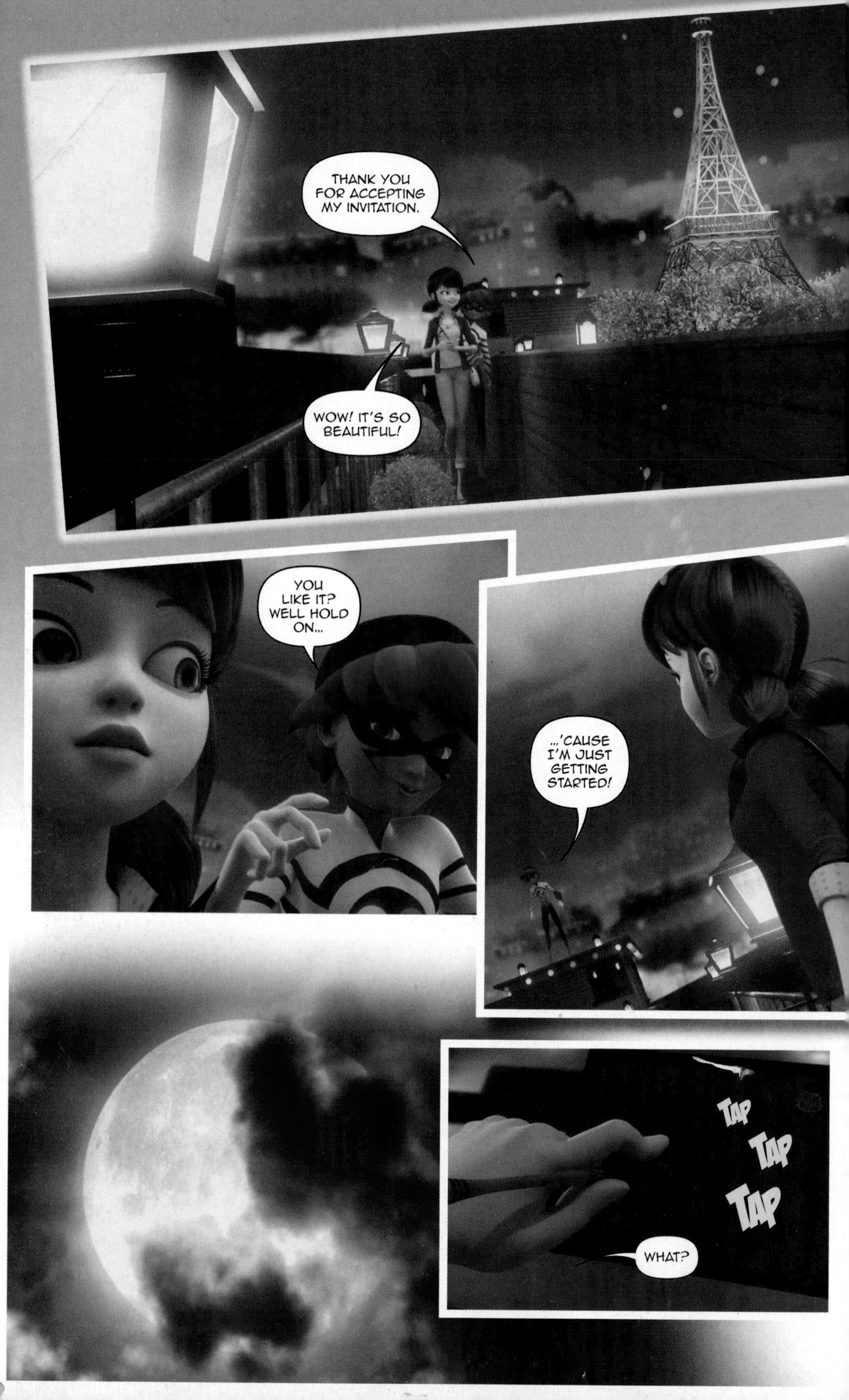
THANK YOU FOR ACCEPTING MY INVITATION.
WOW! IT'S SO BEAUTIFUL!
YOU LIKE IT? WELL HOLD ON...
...'CAUSE I'M JUST GETTING STARTED!
TAP
TAP
TAP
WHAT?

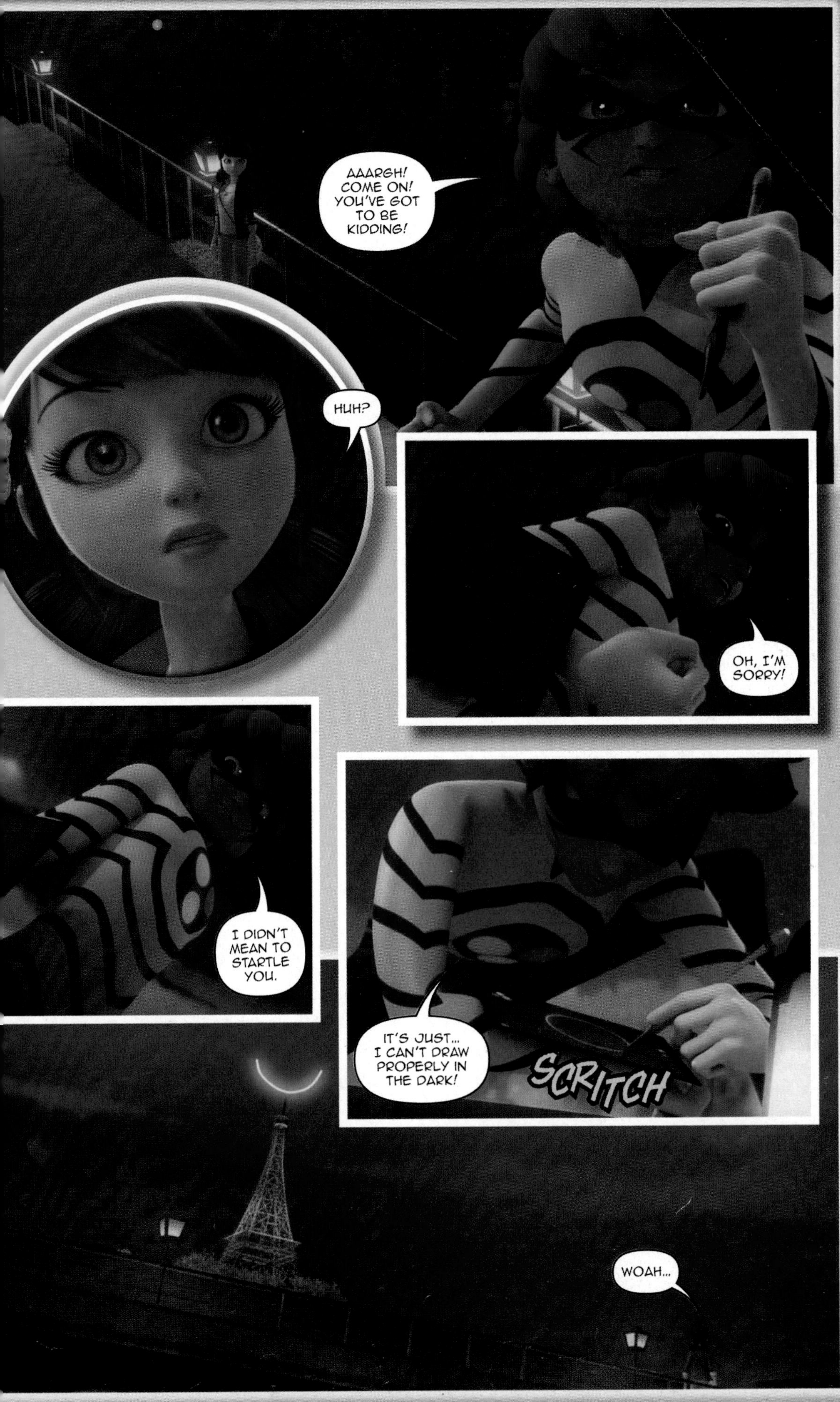
AAARGH! COME ON! YOU'VE GOT TO BE KIDDING!
HUH?
OH, I'M SORRY!
I DIDN'T MEAN TO STARTLE YOU.
IT'S JUST... I CAN'T DRAW PROPERLY IN THE DARK!
SCRITCH
WOAH...

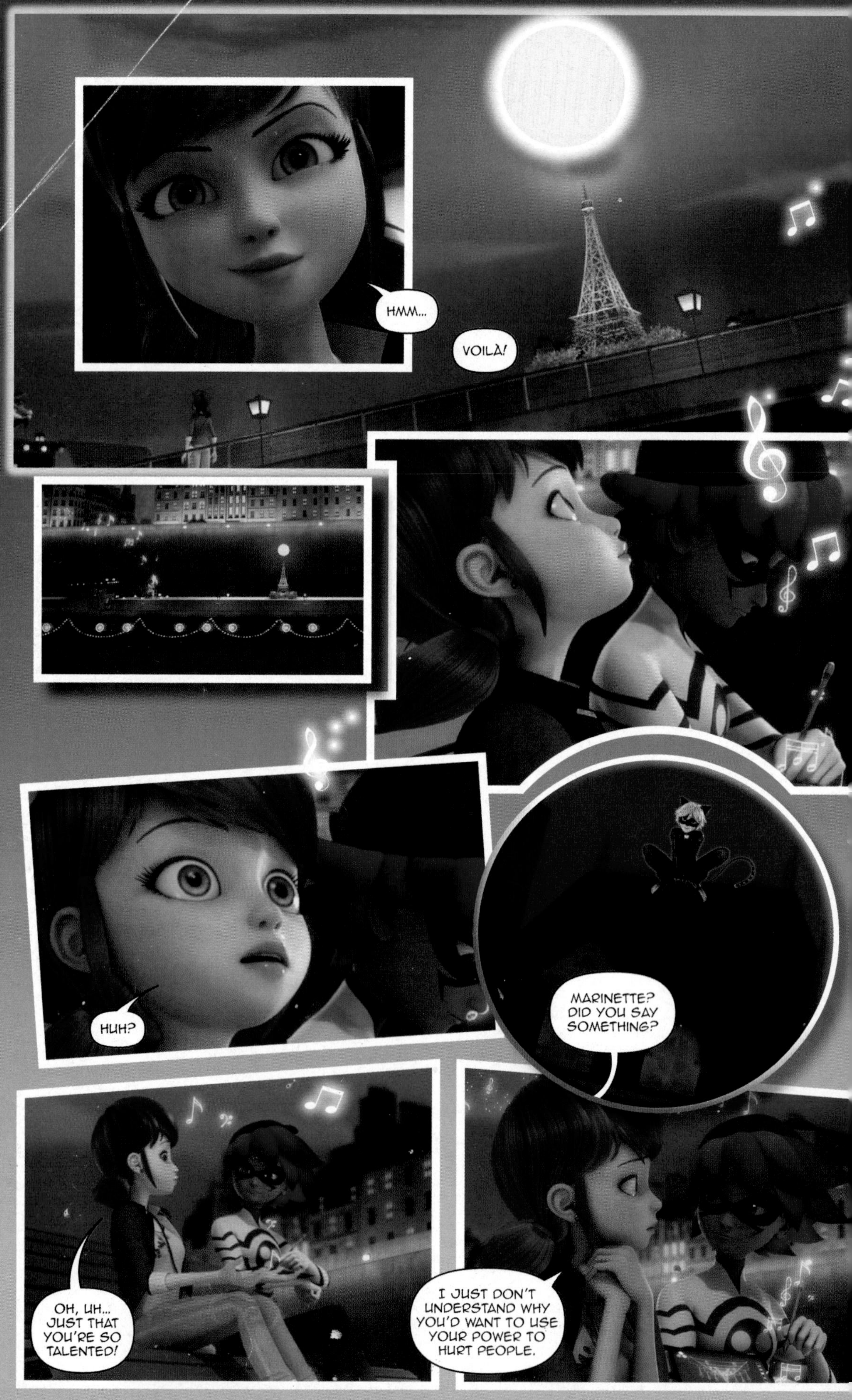
HMM...
VOILÀ!
HUH?
MARINETTE? DID YOU SAY SOMETHING?
OH, UH... JUST THAT YOU'RE SO TALENTED!
I JUST DON'T UNDERSTAND WHY YOU'D WANT TO USE YOUR POWER TO HURT PEOPLE.

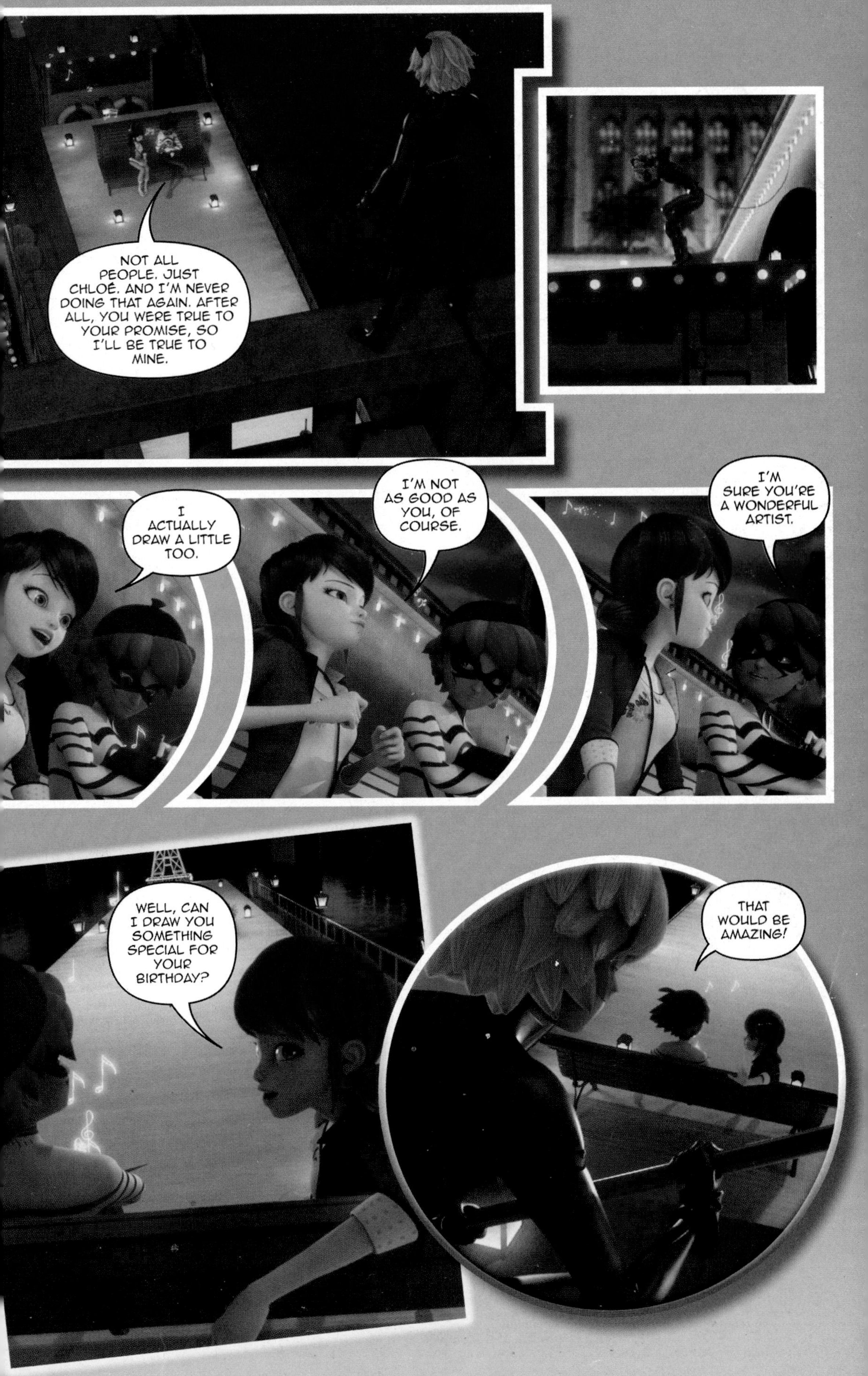
NOT ALL PEOPLE. JUST CHLOÉ. AND I'M NEVER DOING THAT AGAIN. AFTER ALL, YOU WERE TRUE TO YOUR PROMISE, SO I'LL BE TRUE TO MINE.
I ACTUALLY DRAW A LITTLE TOO.
I'M NOT AS GOOD AS YOU, OF COURSE.
I'M SURE YOU'RE A WONDERFUL ARTIST.
WELL, CAN I DRAW YOU SOMETHING SPECIAL FOR YOUR BIRTHDAY?
THAT WOULD BE AMAZING!

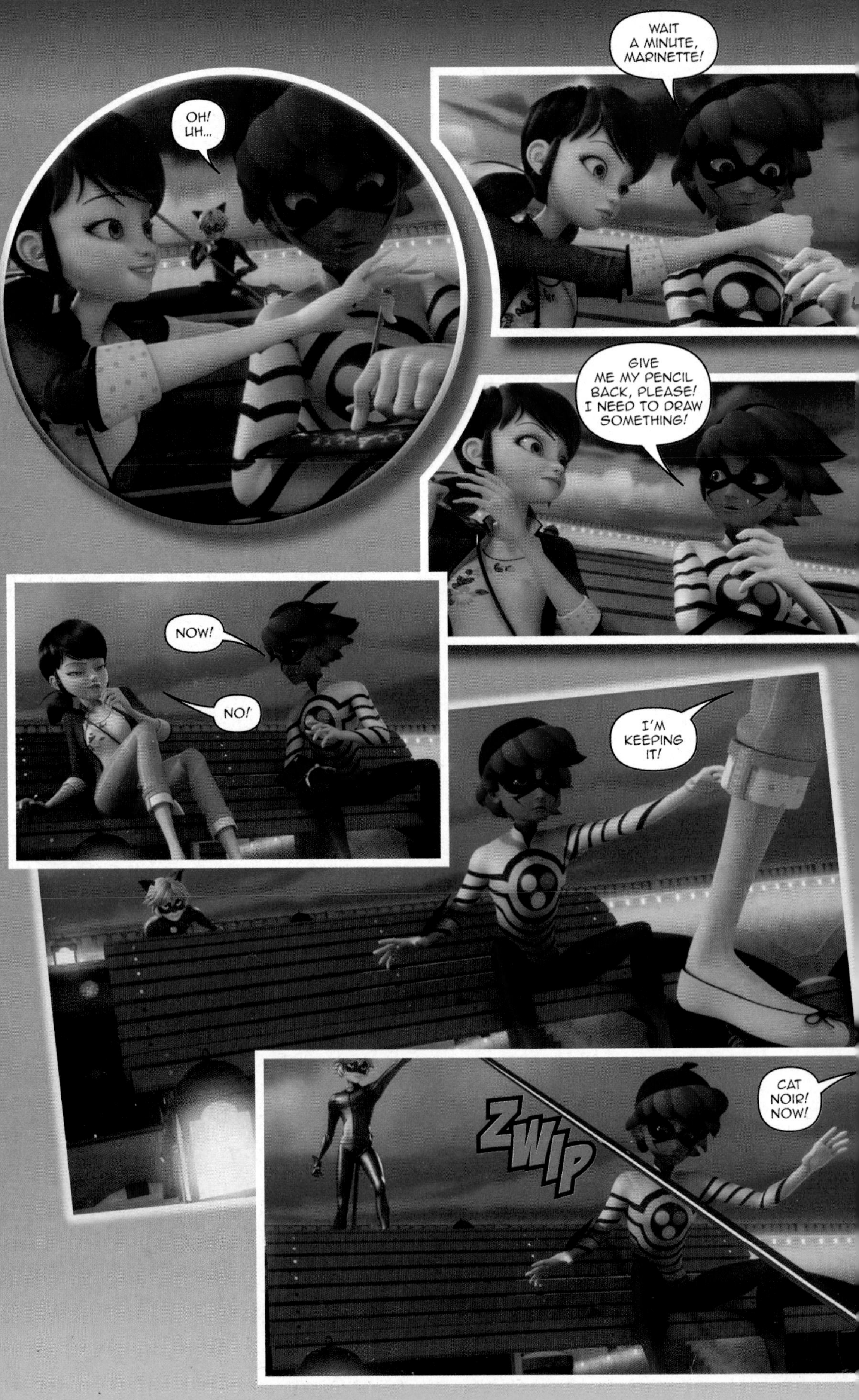

OH! UH...
WAIT A MINUTE, MARINETTE!
GIVE ME MY PENCIL BACK, PLEASE! I NEED TO DRAW SOMETHING!
NOW!
NO!
I'M KEEPING IT!
ZWIP
CAT NOIR! NOW!

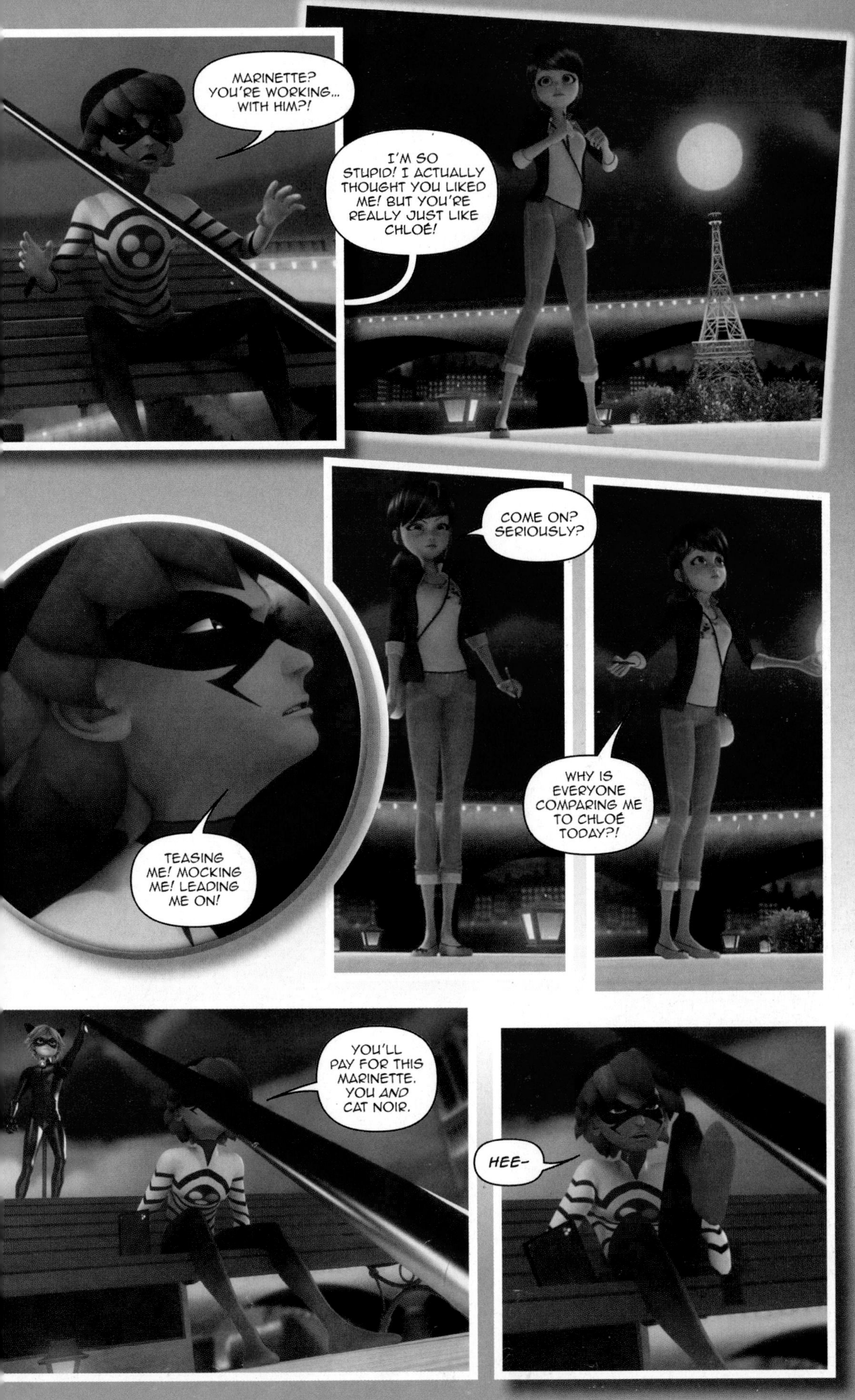
MARINETTE? YOU'RE WORKING... WITH HIM?!
I'M SO STUPID! I ACTUALLY THOUGHT YOU LIKED ME! BUT YOU'RE REALLY JUST LIKE CHLOÉ!
TEASING ME! MOCKING ME! LEADING ME ON!
COME ON? SERIOUSLY?
WHY IS EVERYONE COMPARING ME TO CHLOÉ TODAY?!
YOU'LL PAY FOR THIS MARINETTE. YOU *AND* CAT NOIR.
HEE-

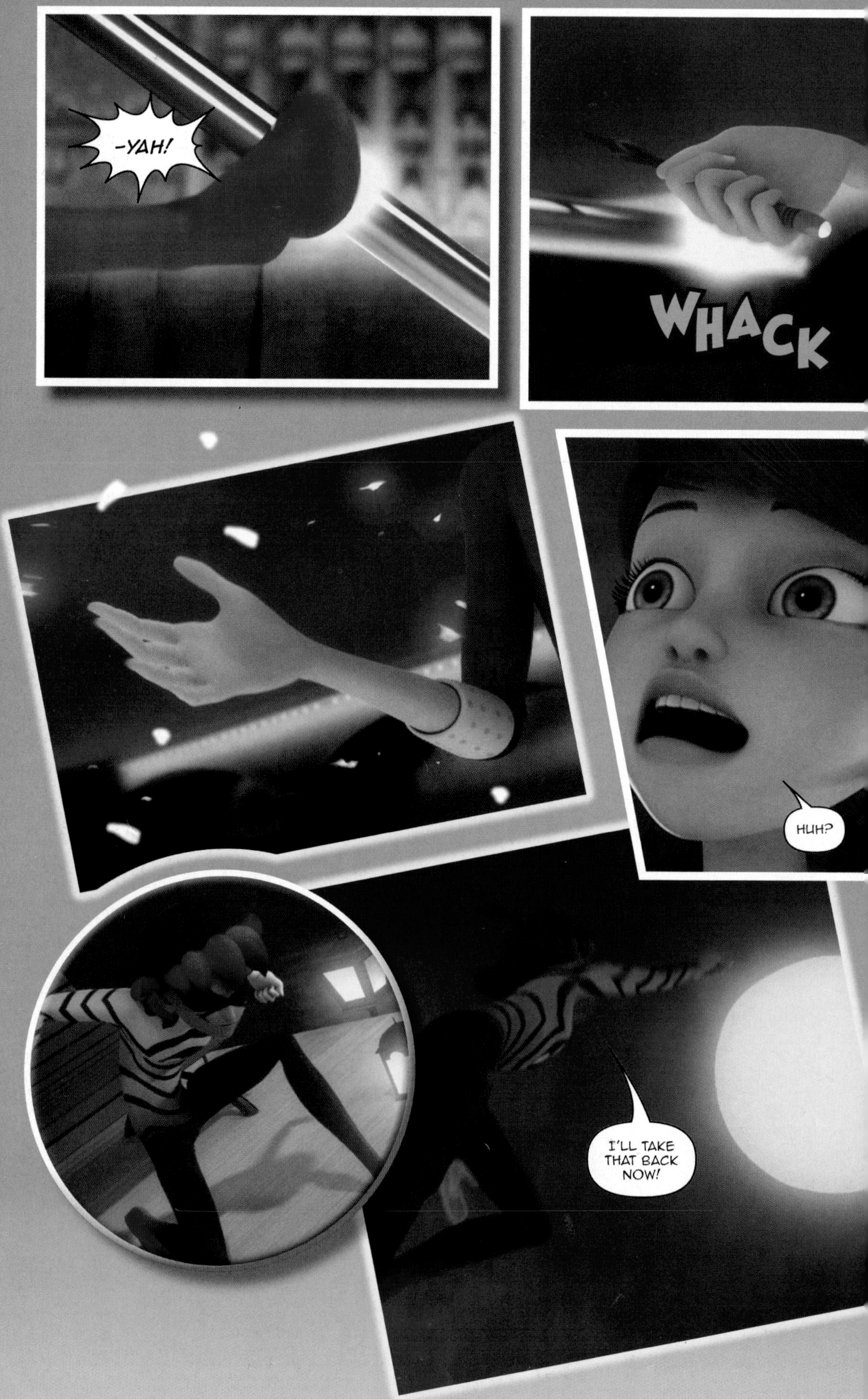
-YAH!
WHACK
HUH?
I'LL TAKE THAT BACK NOW!

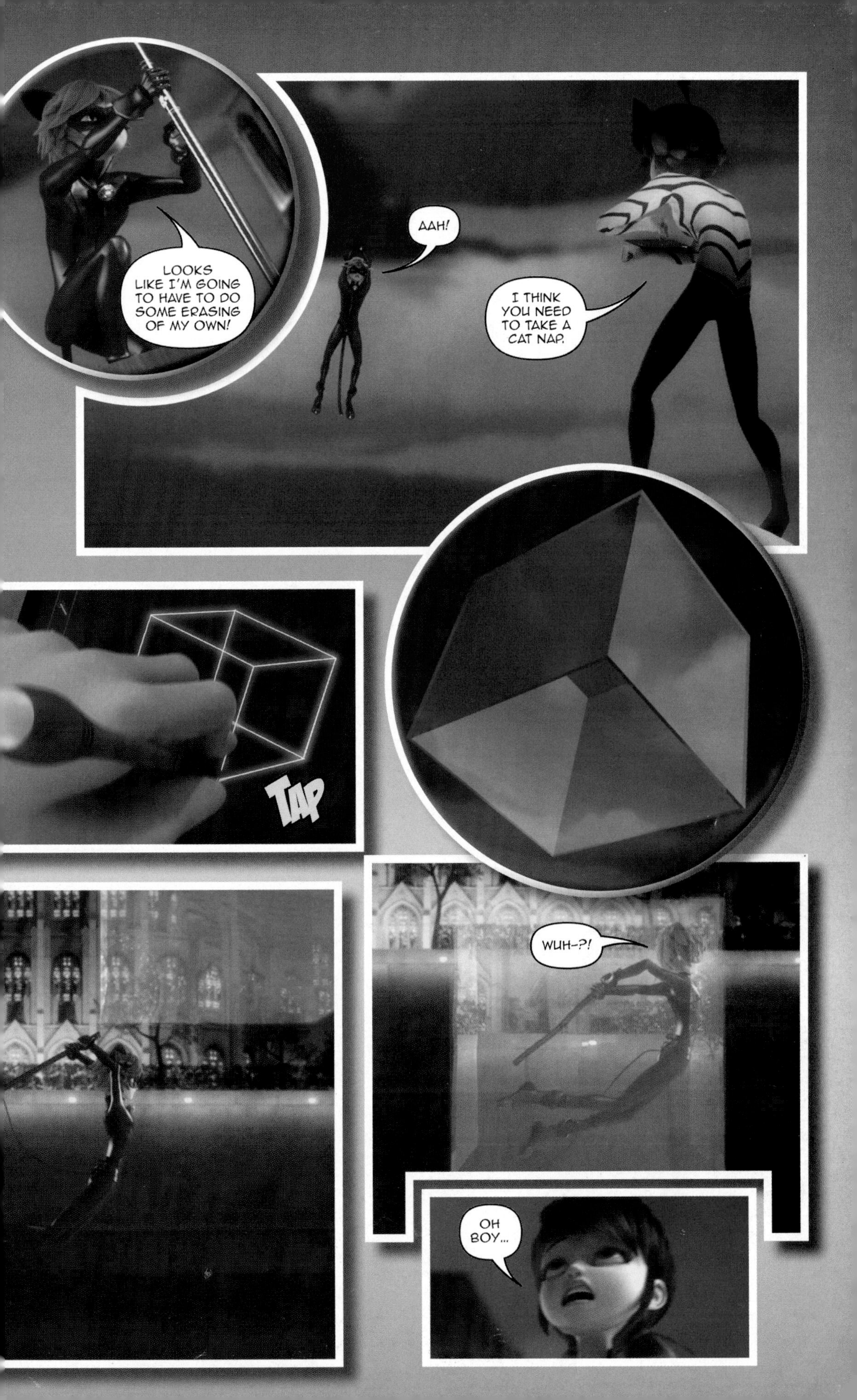
LOOKS LIKE I'M GOING TO HAVE TO DO SOME ERASING OF MY OWN!
AAH!
I THINK YOU NEED TO TAKE A CAT NAP.
TAP
WUH-?!
OH BOY...

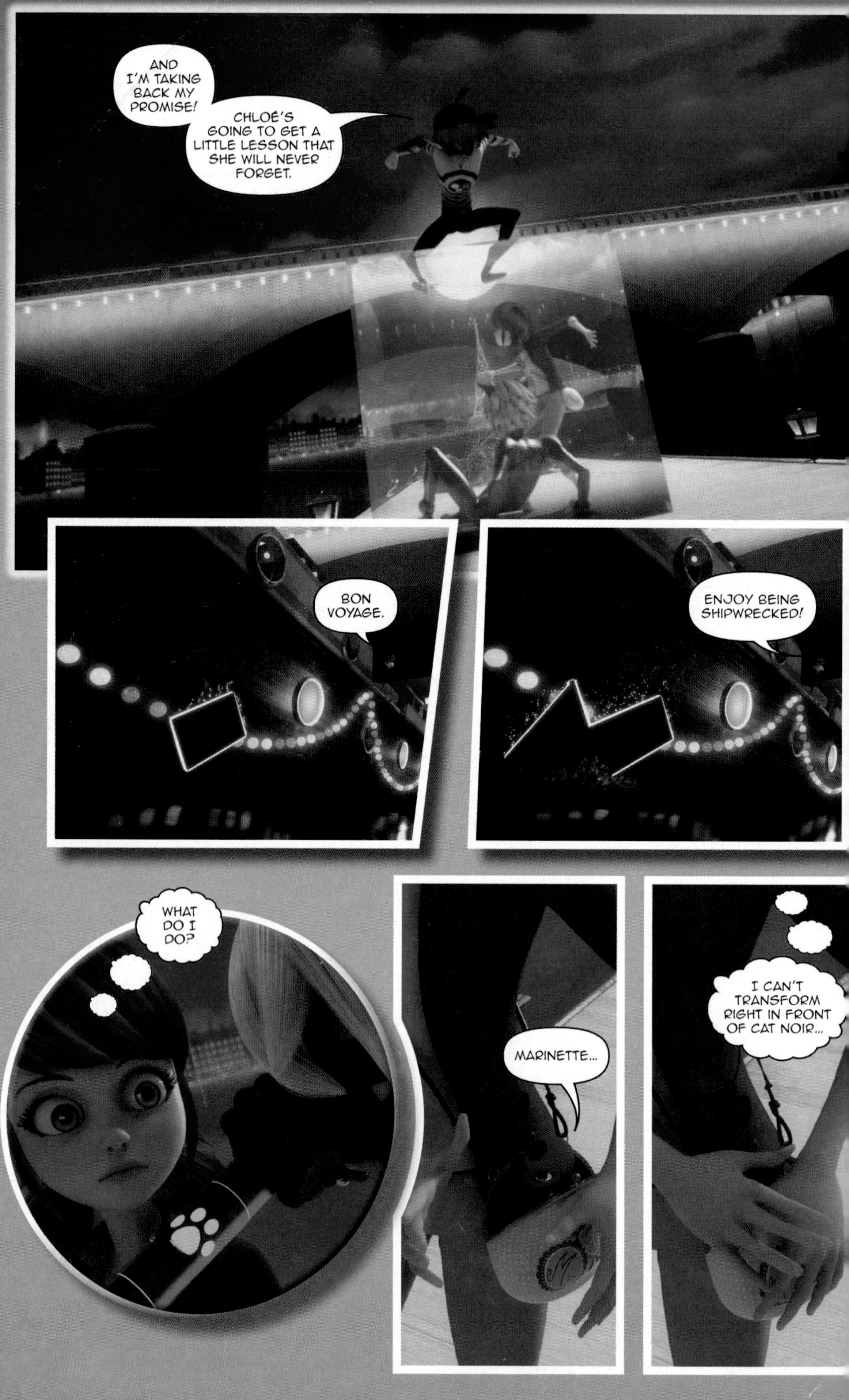
AND I'M TAKING BACK MY PROMISE!
CHLOÉ'S GOING TO GET A LITTLE LESSON THAT SHE WILL NEVER FORGET.
BON VOYAGE.
ENJOY BEING SHIPWRECKED!
WHAT DO I DO?
MARINETTE...
I CAN'T TRANSFORM RIGHT IN FRONT OF CAT NOIR...

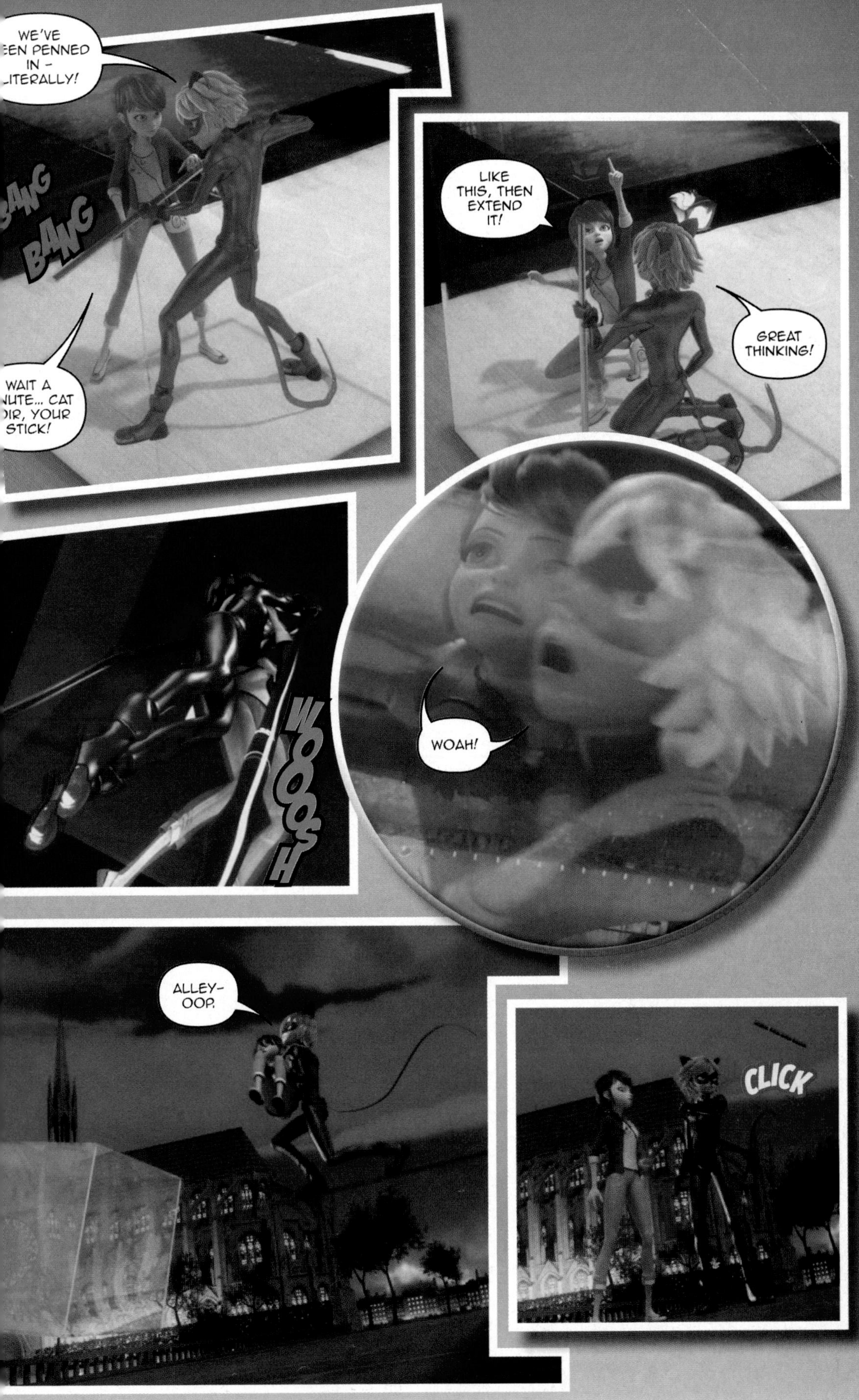
WE'VE EEN PENNED IN – ITERALLY!
BANG
BANG
WAIT A NUTE... CAT OIR, YOUR STICK!
LIKE THIS, THEN EXTEND IT!
GREAT THINKING!
WOOOOSH
WOAH!
ALLEY-OOP.
CLICK

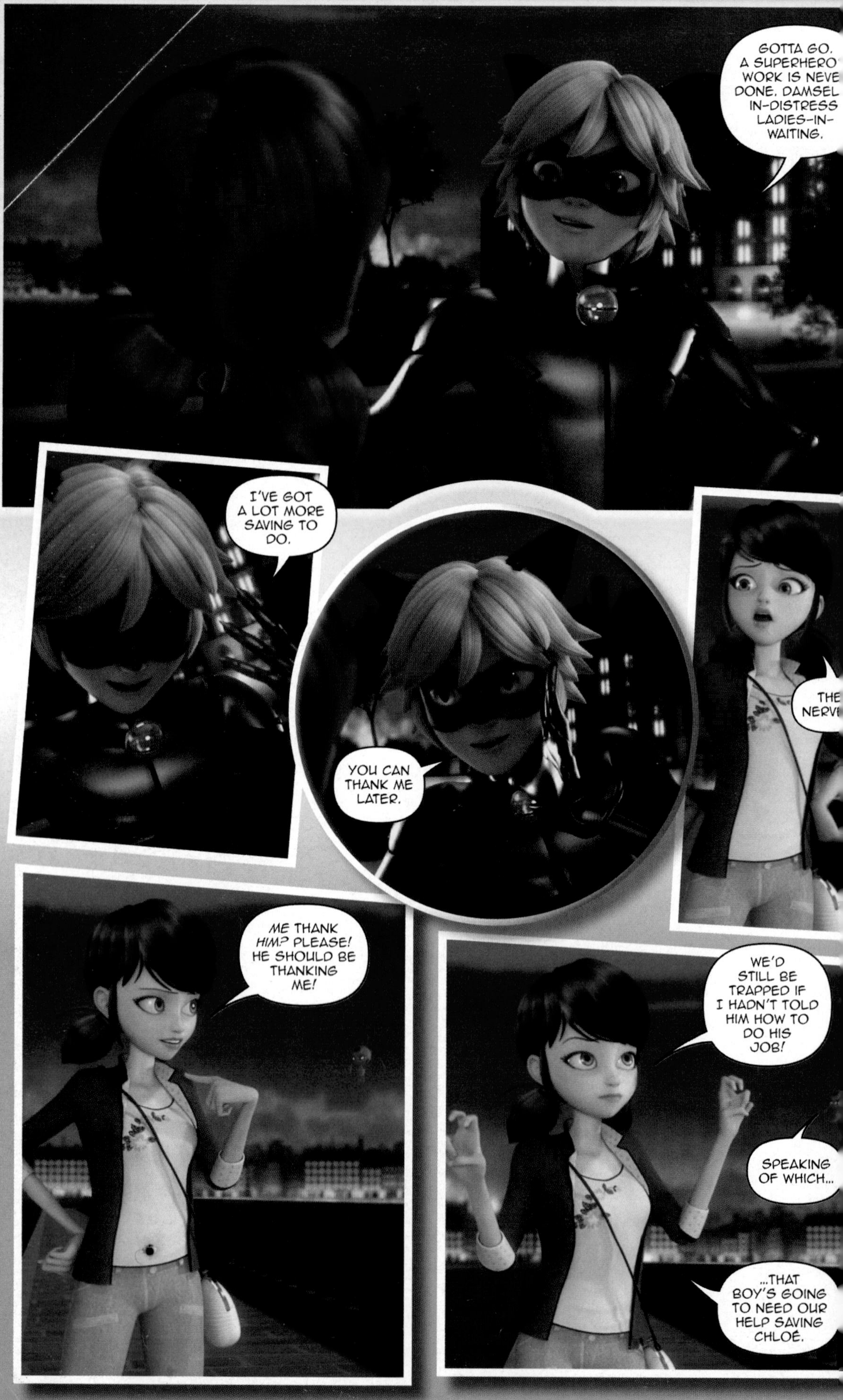
GOTTA GO. A SUPERHERO WORK IS NEVE DONE. DAMSEL IN-DISTRESS LADIES-IN-WAITING.
I'VE GOT A LOT MORE SAVING TO DO.
YOU CAN THANK ME LATER.
THE NERV
ME THANK HIM? PLEASE! HE SHOULD BE THANKING ME!
WE'D STILL BE TRAPPED IF I HADN'T TOLD HIM HOW TO DO HIS JOB!
SPEAKING OF WHICH...
...THAT BOY'S GOING TO NEED OUR HELP SAVING CHLOÉ.

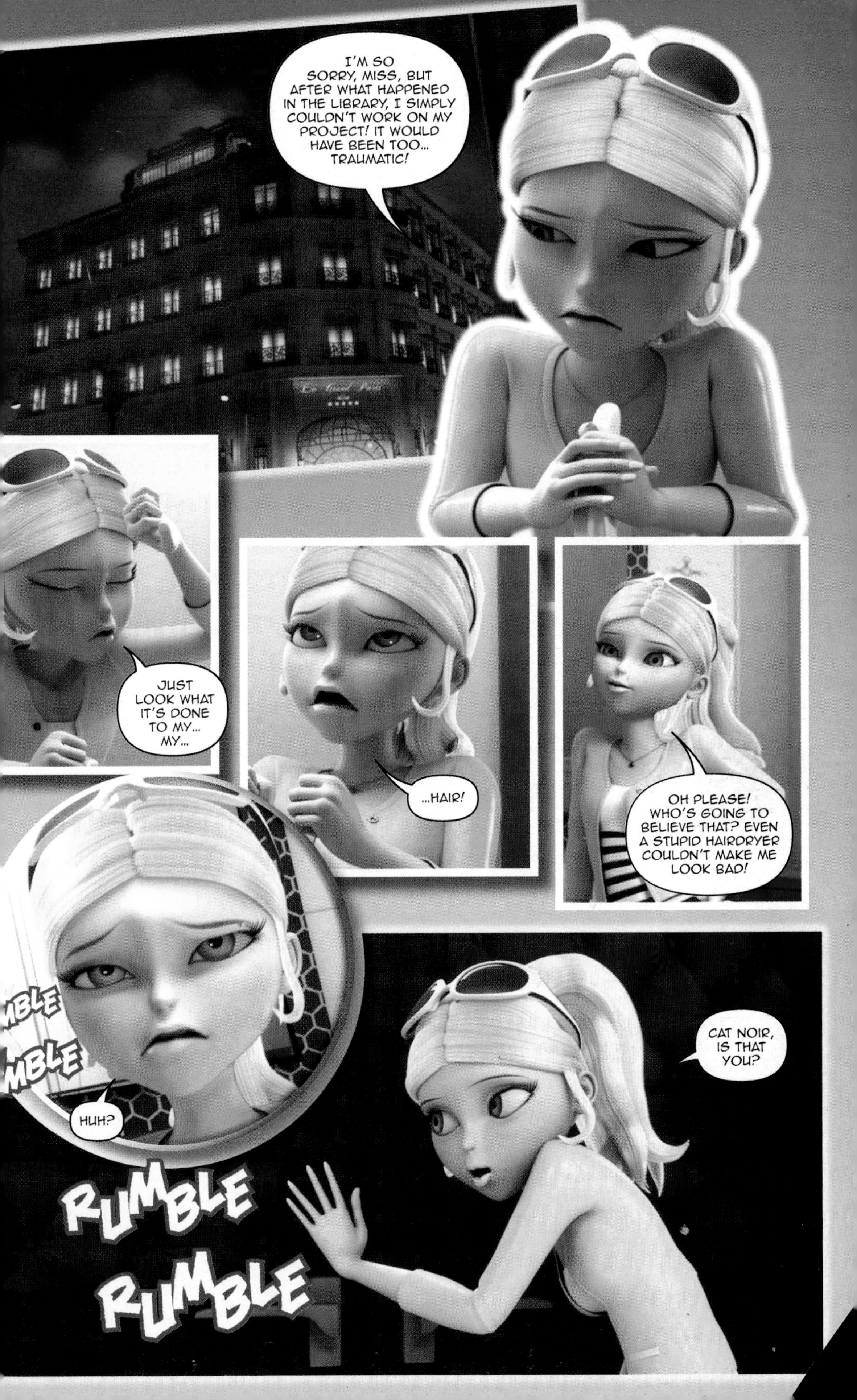

I'M SO SORRY, MISS, BUT AFTER WHAT HAPPENED IN THE LIBRARY, I SIMPLY COULDN'T WORK ON MY PROJECT! IT WOULD HAVE BEEN TOO... TRAUMATIC!
JUST LOOK WHAT IT'S DONE TO MY... MY...
...HAIR!
OH PLEASE! WHO'S GOING TO BELIEVE THAT? EVEN A STUPID HAIRDRYER COULDN'T MAKE ME LOOK BAD!
HUH?
CAT NOIR, IS THAT YOU?
RUMBLE
RUMBLE

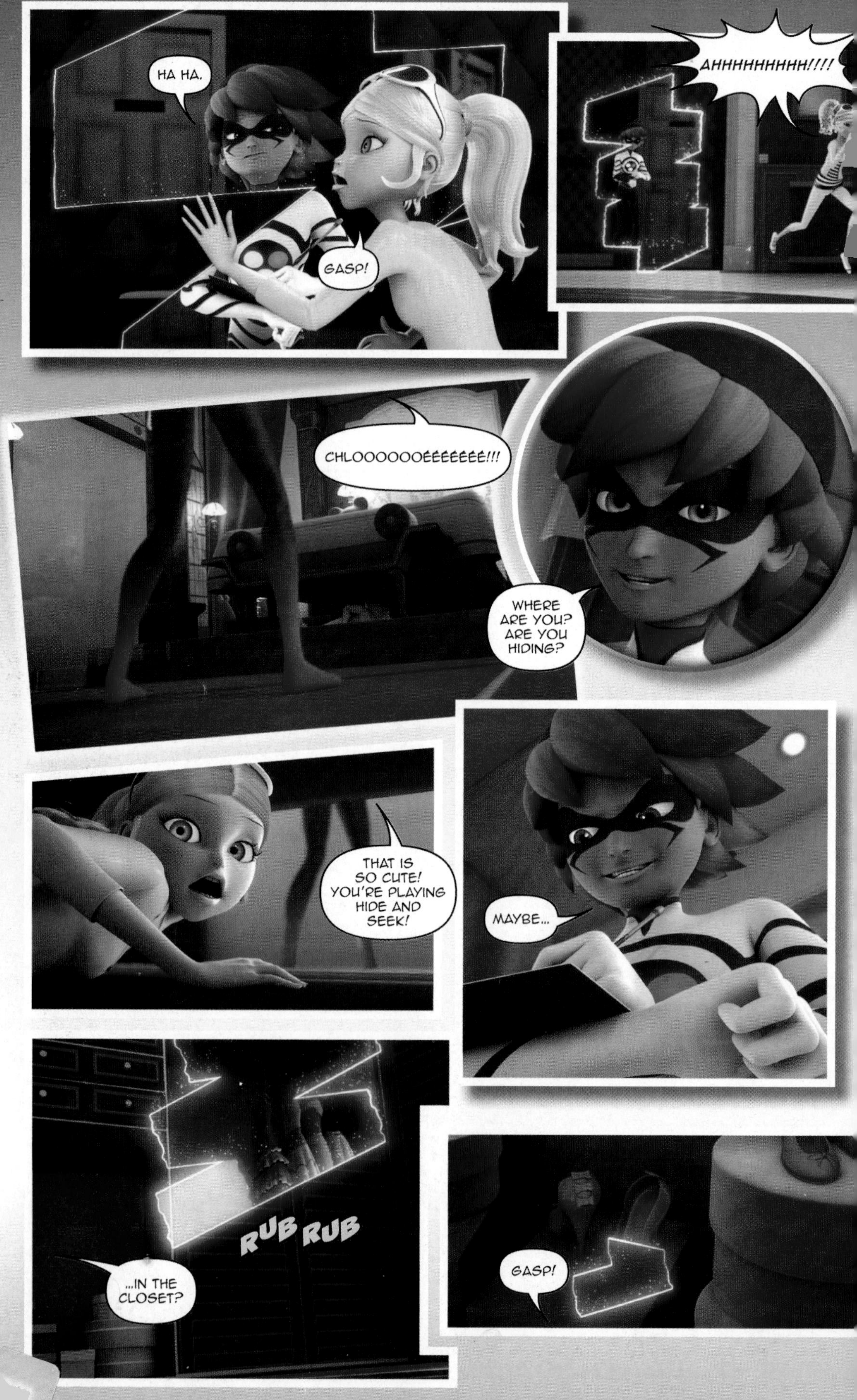
HA HA.
GASP!
AHHHHHHHHHH!!!!
CHLOOOOOOEEEEEEE!!!
WHERE ARE YOU? ARE YOU HIDING?
THAT IS SO CUTE! YOU'RE PLAYING HIDE AND SEEK!
MAYBE...
RUB RUB
...IN THE CLOSET?
GASP!

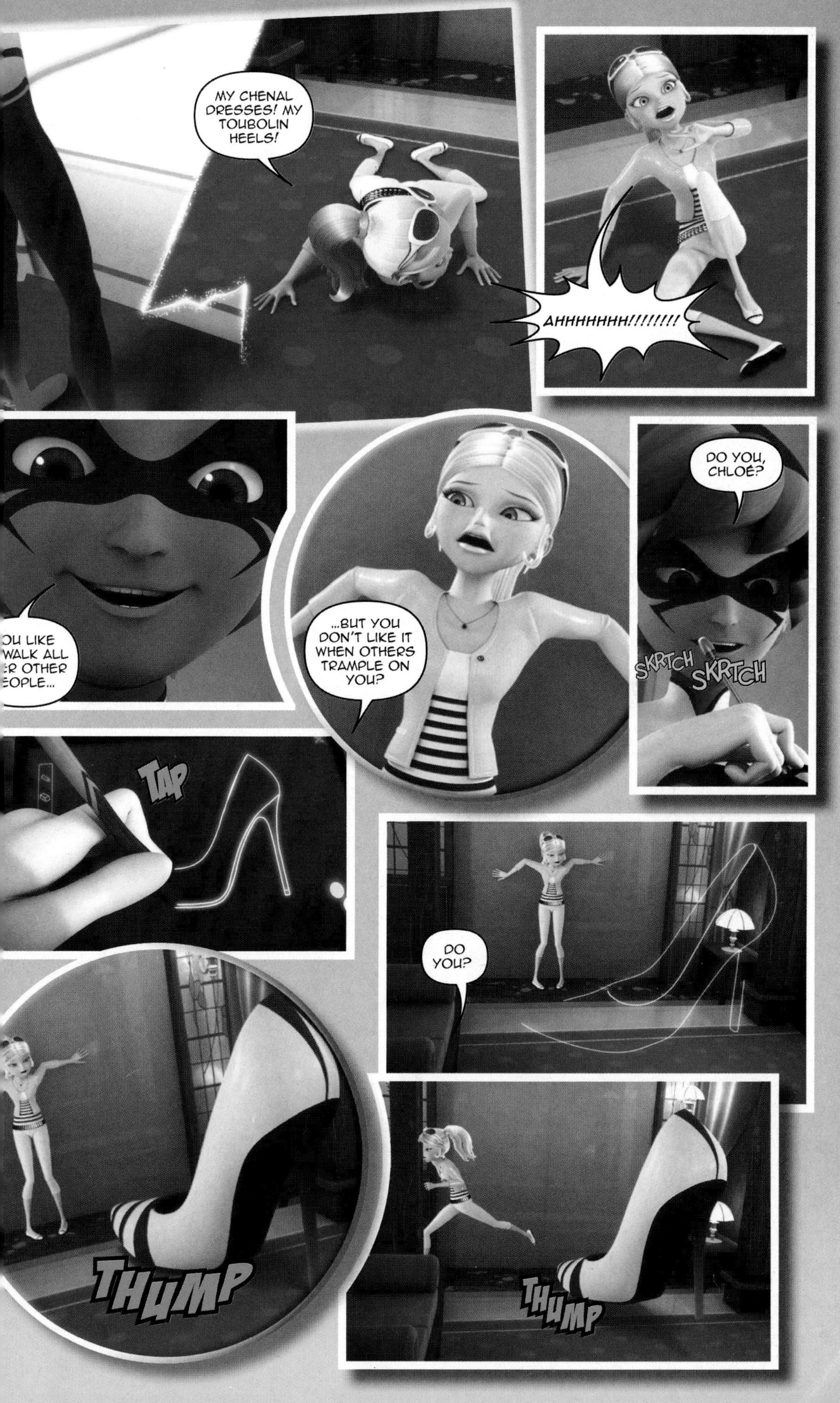

MY CHENAL DRESSES! MY TOUBOLIN HEELS!
AHHHHHHH!!!!!!!!
OU LIKE WALK ALL ER OTHER EOPLE...
...BUT YOU DON'T LIKE IT WHEN OTHERS TRAMPLE ON YOU?
DO YOU, CHLOÉ?
SKRTCH SKRTCH
TAP
DO YOU?
THUMP
THUMP

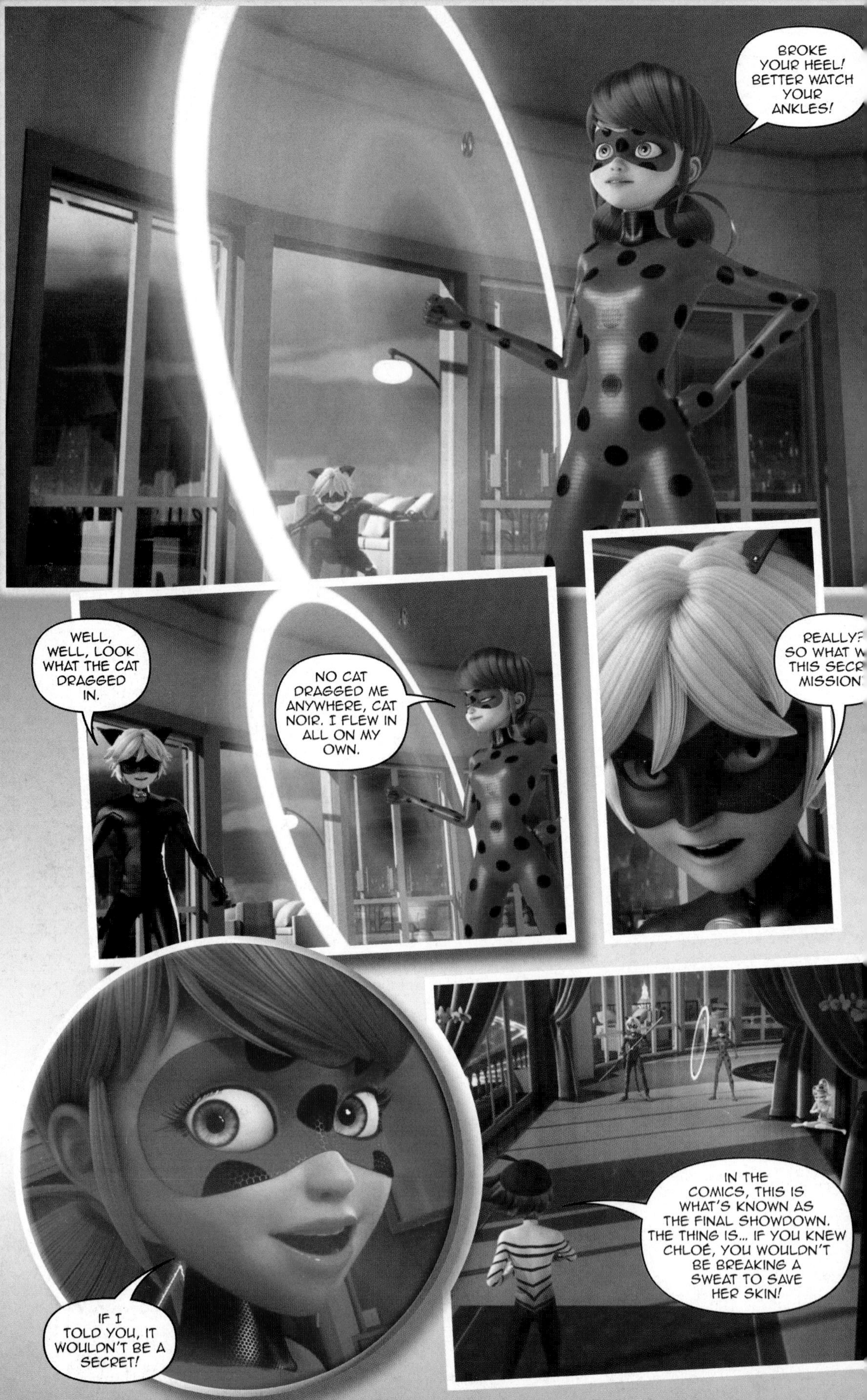
BROKE YOUR HEEL! BETTER WATCH YOUR ANKLES!
WELL, WELL, LOOK WHAT THE CAT DRAGGED IN.
NO CAT DRAGGED ME ANYWHERE, CAT NOIR. I FLEW IN ALL ON MY OWN.
REALLY? SO WHAT W THIS SECR MISSION
IF I TOLD YOU, IT WOULDN'T BE A SECRET!
IN THE COMICS, THIS IS WHAT'S KNOWN AS THE FINAL SHOWDOWN. THE THING IS... IF YOU KNEW CHLOÉ, YOU WOULDN'T BE BREAKING A SWEAT TO SAVE HER SKIN!

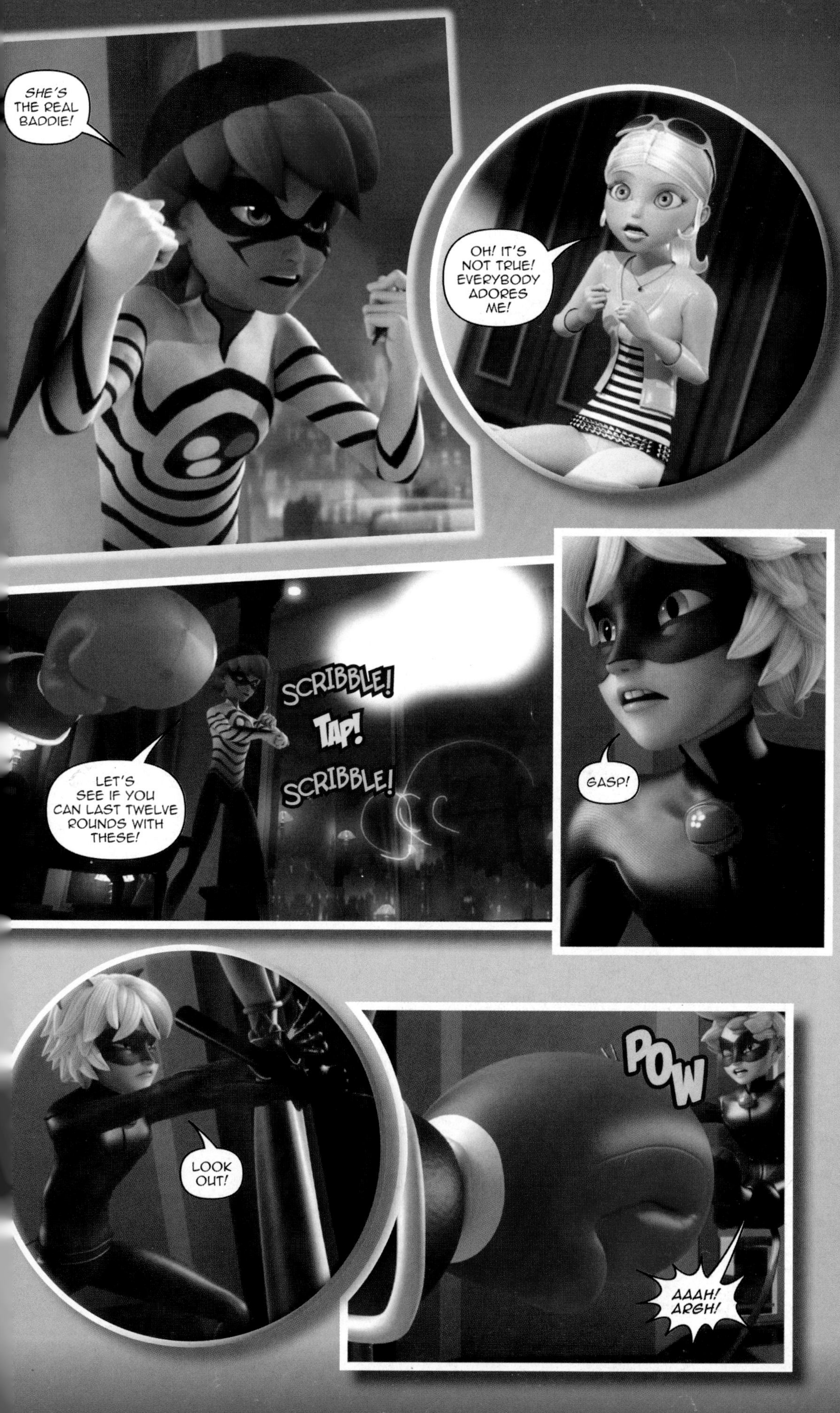
SHE'S THE REAL BADDIE!
OH! IT'S NOT TRUE! EVERYBODY ADORES ME!
SCRIBBLE!
TAP!
SCRIBBLE!
LET'S SEE IF YOU CAN LAST TWELVE ROUNDS WITH THESE!
GASP!
LOOK OUT!
POW
AAAH! ARGH!

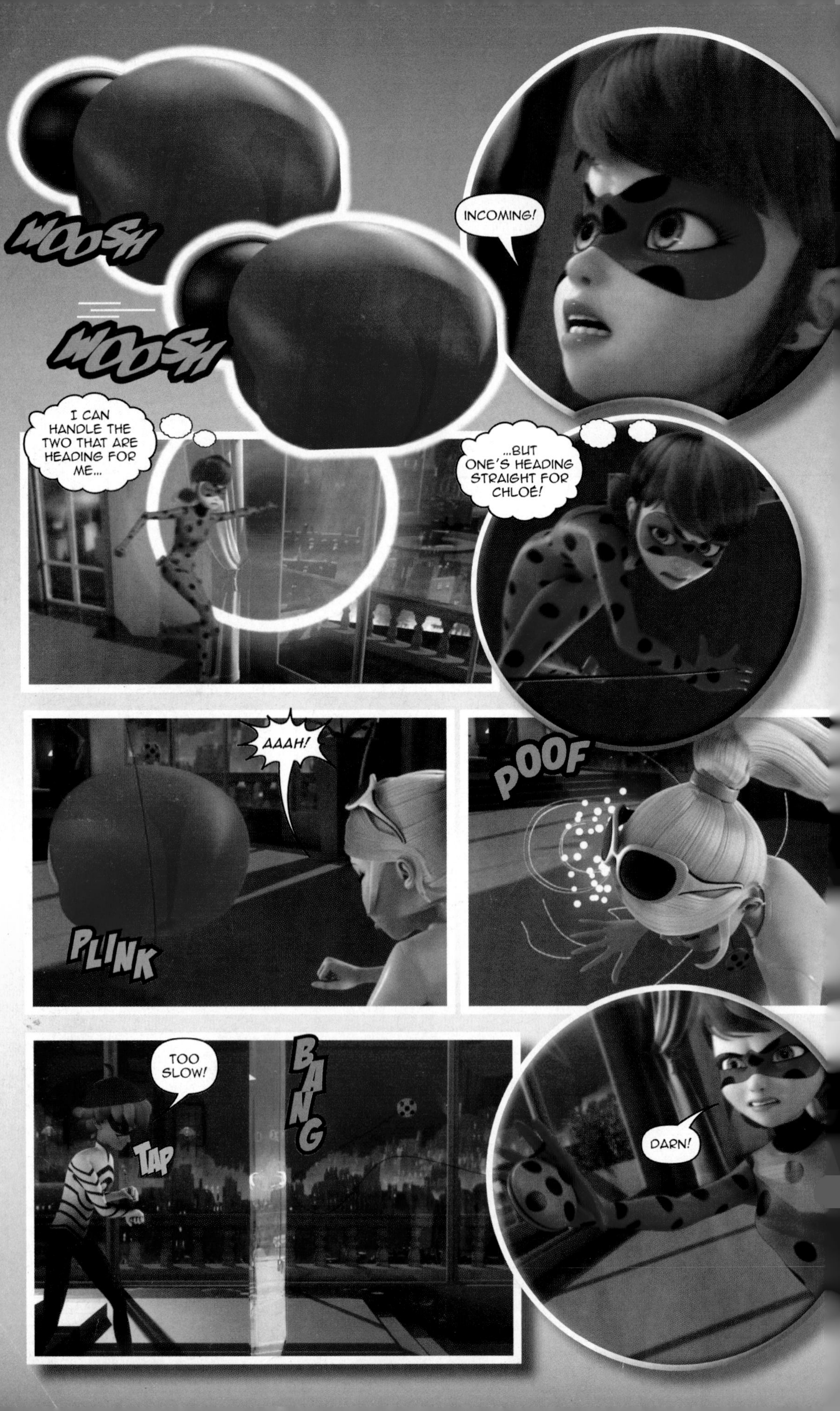
WOOSH
WOOSH
INCOMING!
I CAN HANDLE THE TWO THAT ARE HEADING FOR ME...
...BUT ONE'S HEADING STRAIGHT FOR CHLOÉ!
AAAH!
PLINK
POOF
TOO SLOW!
TAP
BANG
DARN!

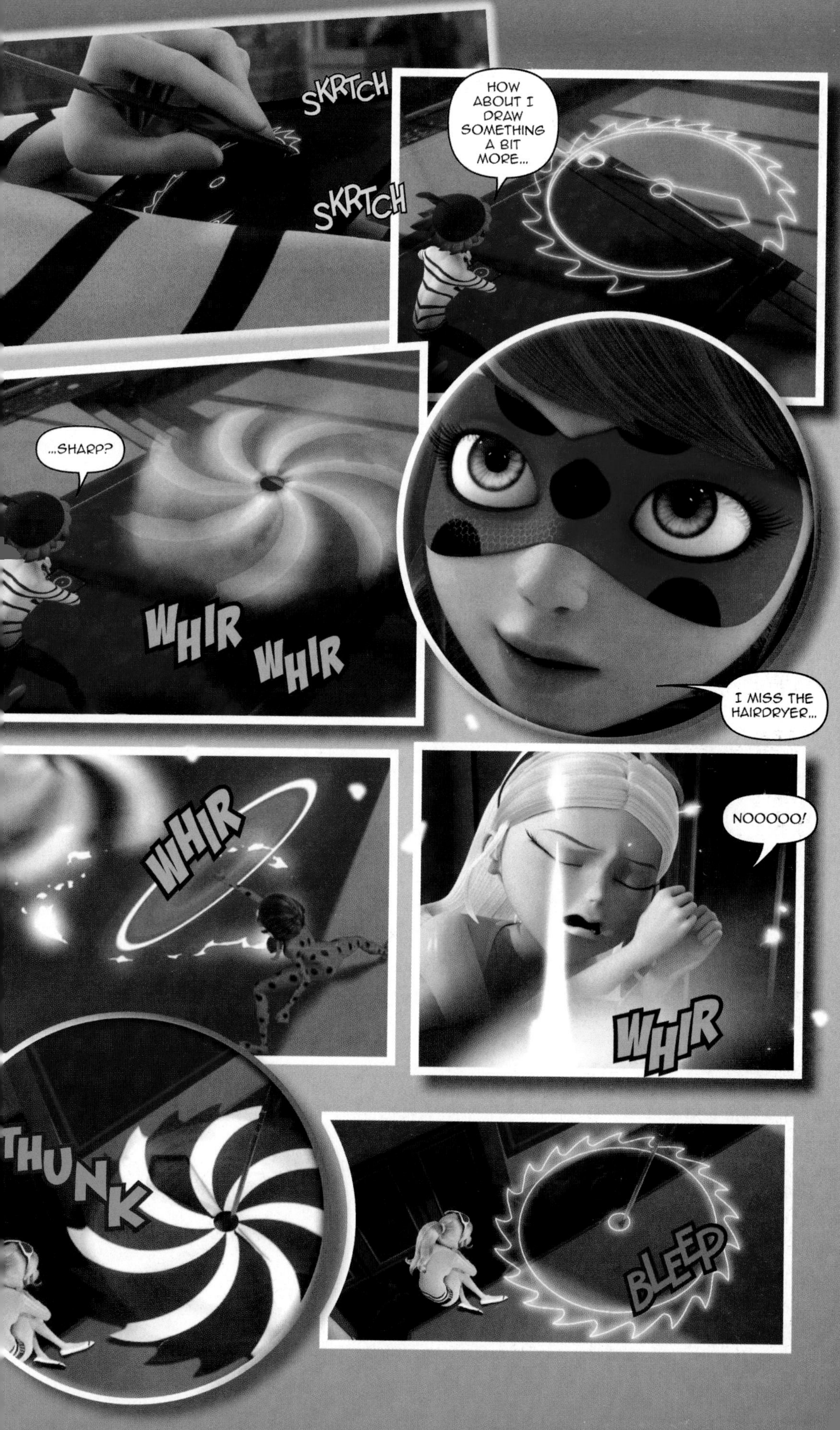
SKRTCH
SKRTCH
HOW ABOUT I DRAW SOMETHING A BIT MORE...
...SHARP?
WHIR
WHIR
I MISS THE HAIRDRYER...
WHIR
NOOOOO!
WHIR
THUNK
BLEEP

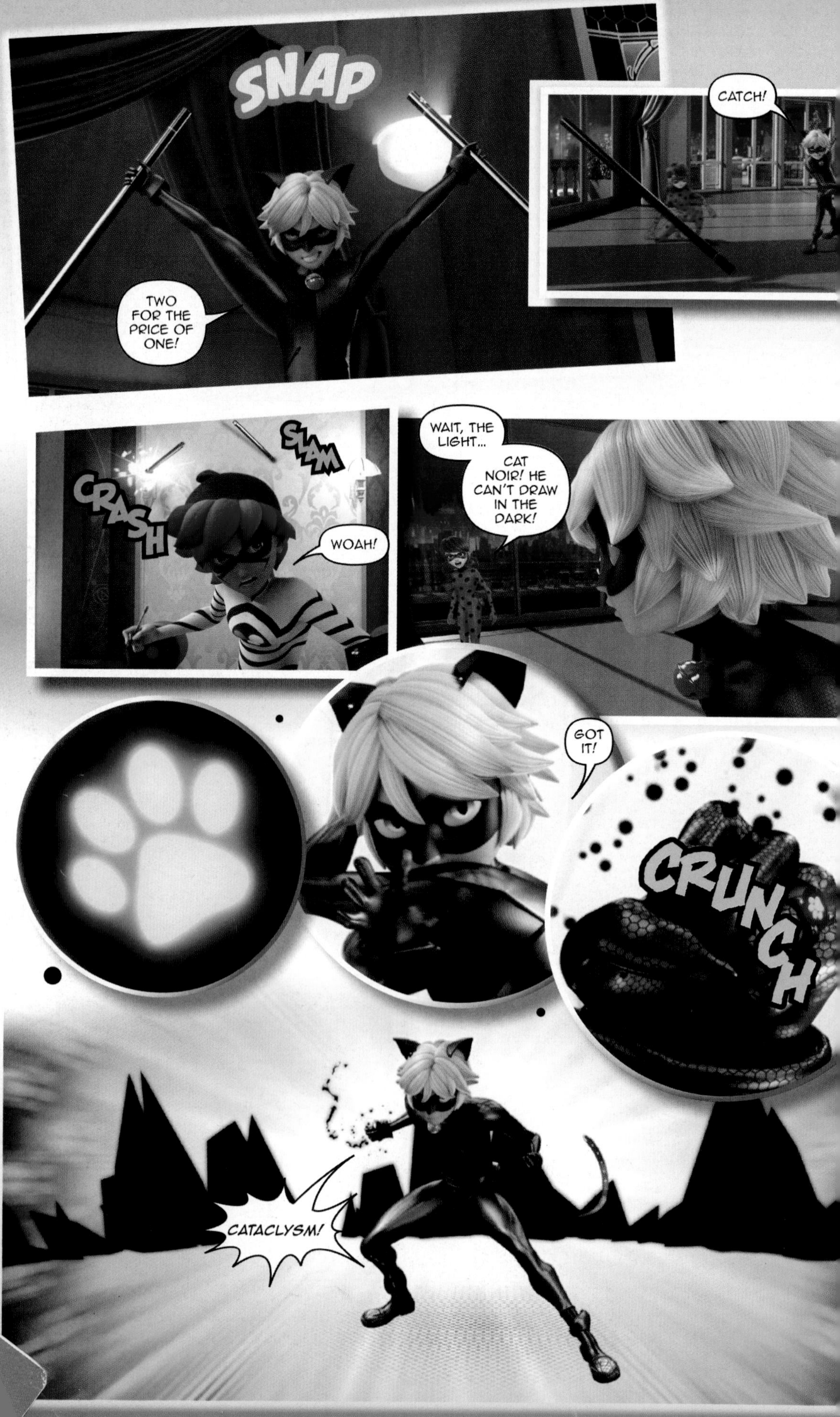
SNAP
TWO FOR THE PRICE OF ONE!
CATCH!
CRASH
SLAM
WOAH!
WAIT, THE LIGHT...
CAT NOIR! HE CAN'T DRAW IN THE DARK!
GOT IT!
CRUNCH
CATACLYSM!

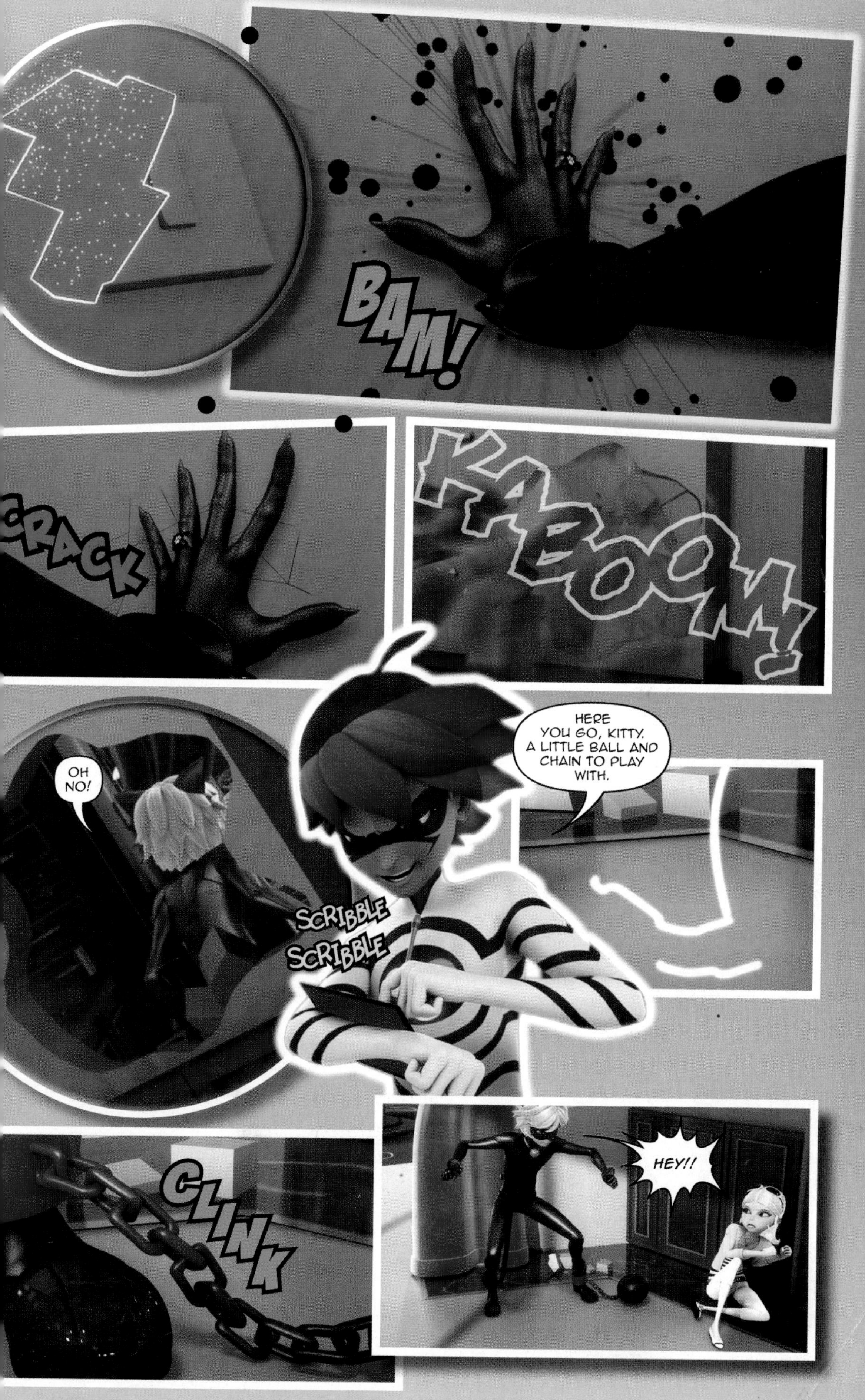
BAM!
CRACK
KABOOM!
OH NO!
HERE YOU GO, KITTY. A LITTLE BALL AND CHAIN TO PLAY WITH.
SCRIBBLE SCRIBBLE
CLINK
HEY!!

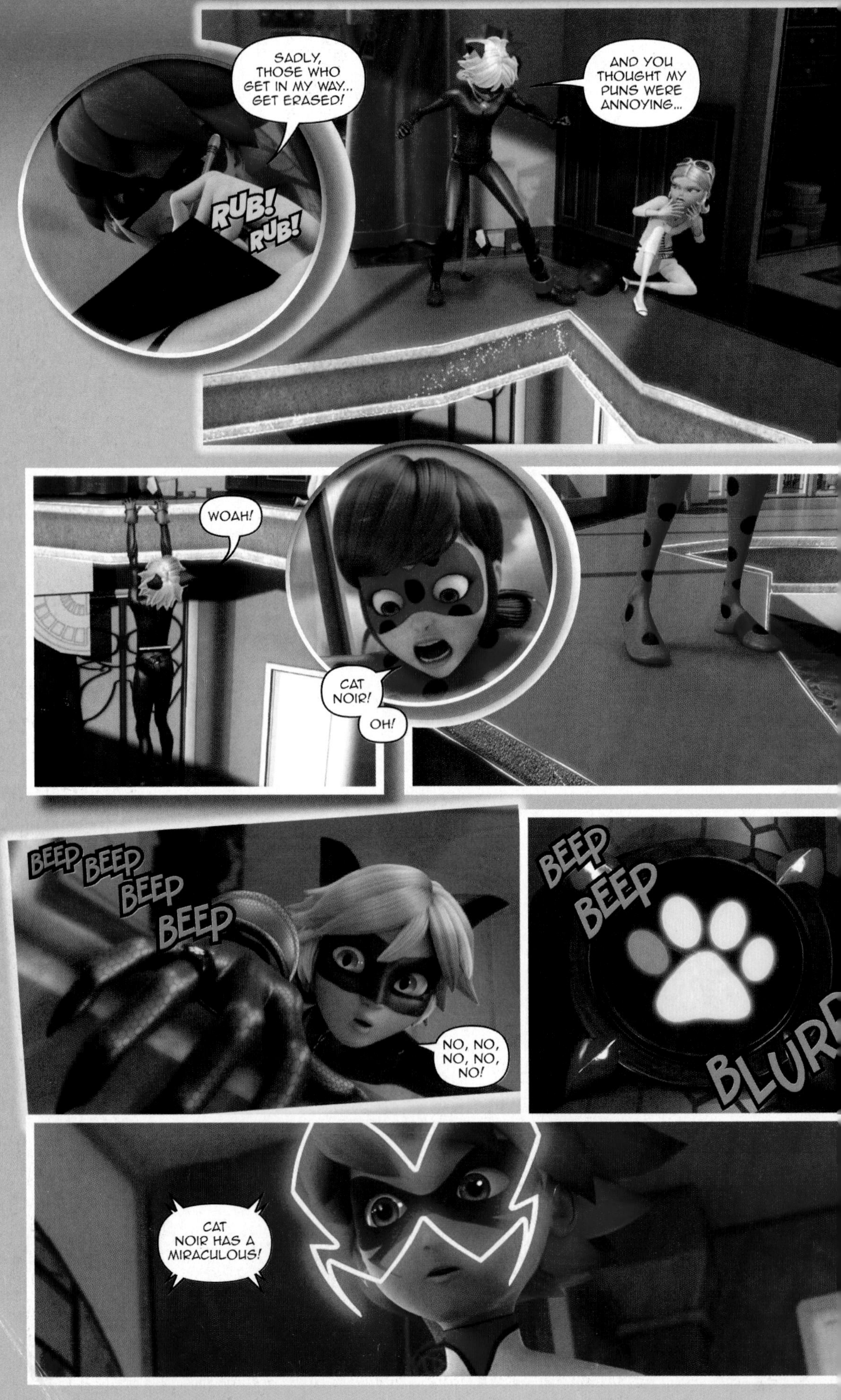
SADLY, THOSE WHO GET IN MY WAY... GET ERASED!
AND YOU THOUGHT MY PUNS WERE ANNOYING...
RUB! RUB!
WOAH!
CAT NOIR!
OH!
BEEP BEEP BEEP BEEP
NO, NO, NO, NO, NO!
BEEP BEEP
BLURR
CAT NOIR HAS A MIRACULOUS!

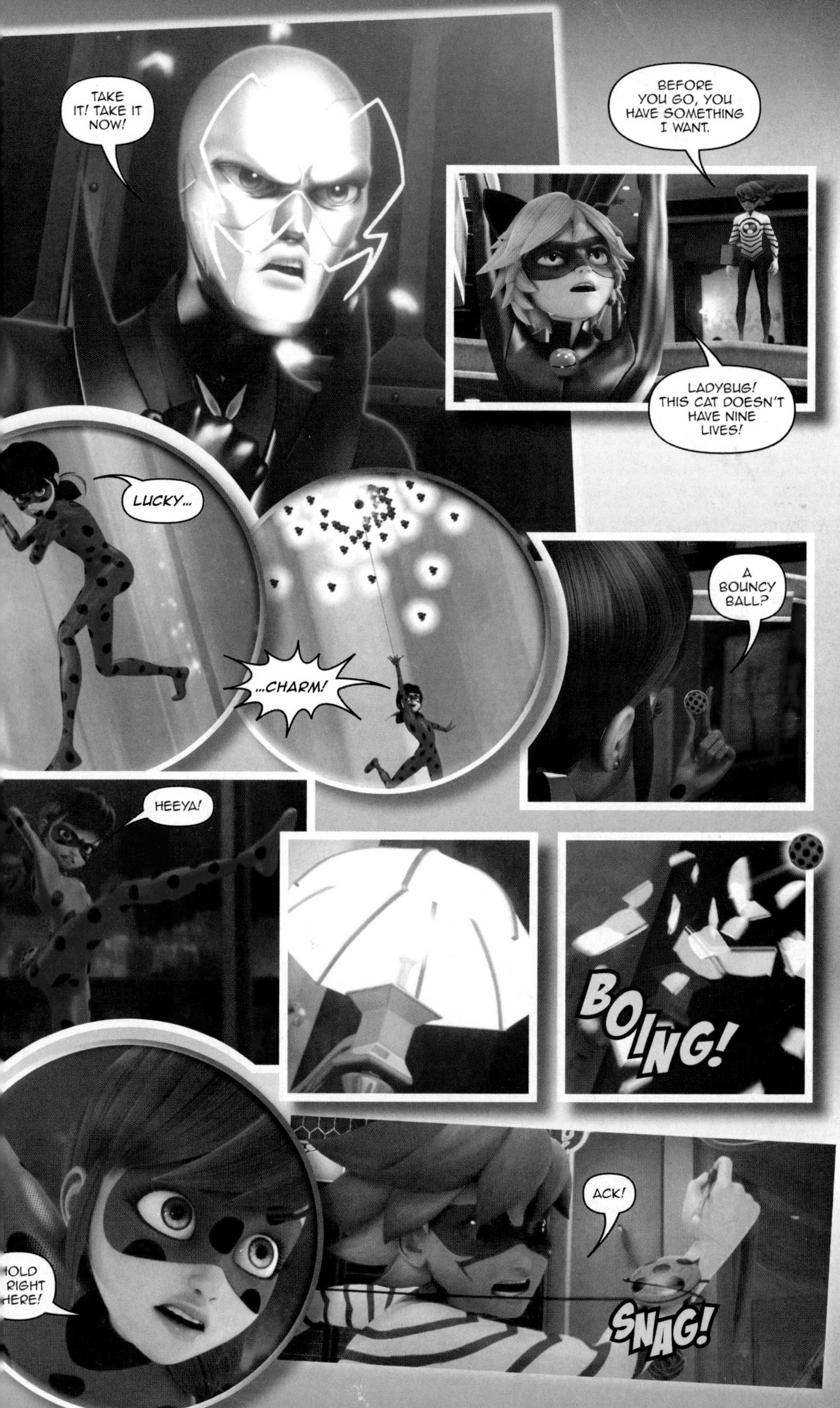
TAKE IT! TAKE IT NOW!
BEFORE YOU GO, YOU HAVE SOMETHING I WANT.
LADYBUG! THIS CAT DOESN'T HAVE NINE LIVES!
LUCKY...
...CHARM!
A BOUNCY BALL?
HEEYA!
BOING!
HOLD RIGHT HERE!
ACK!
SNAG!

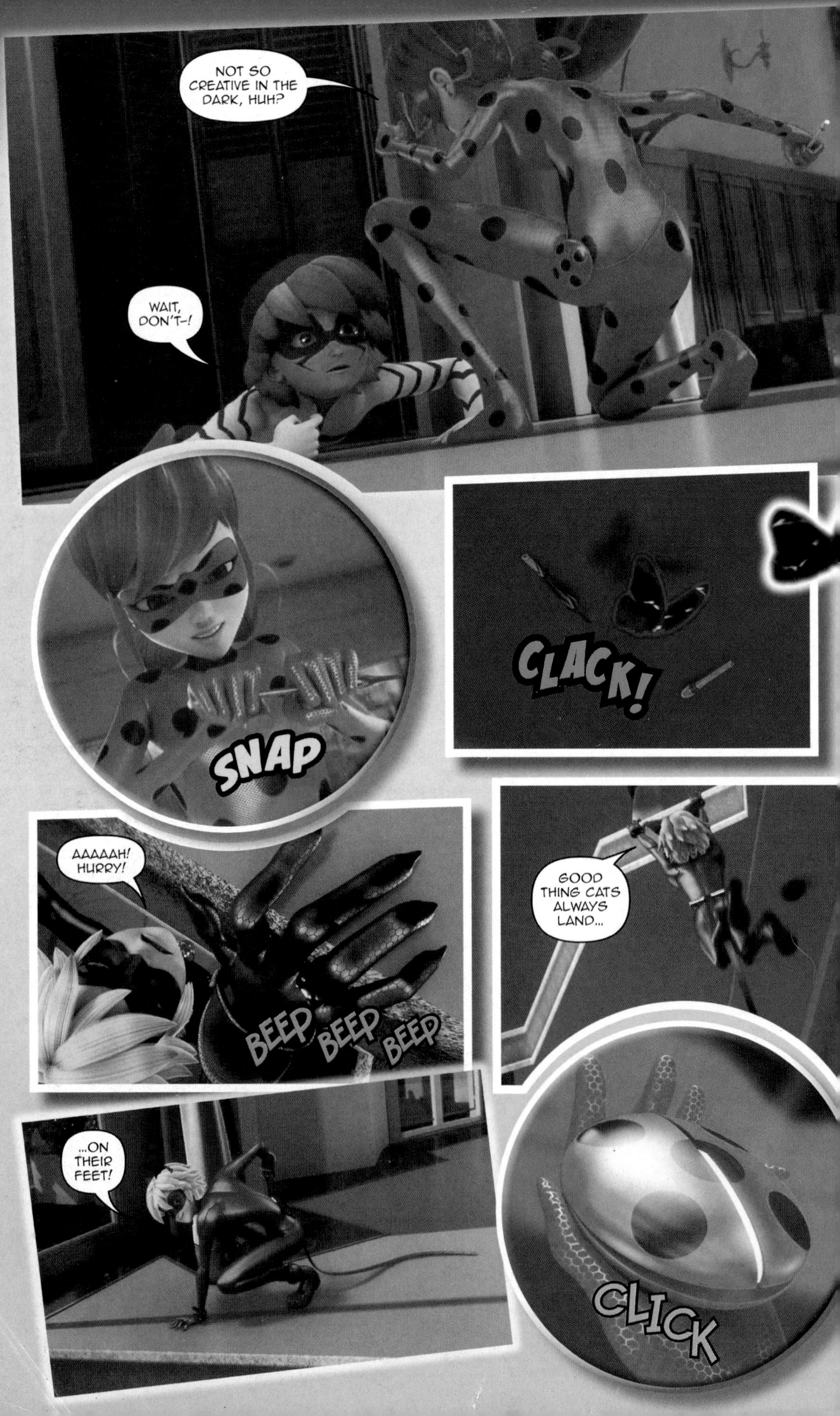
NOT SO CREATIVE IN THE DARK, HUH?
WAIT, DON'T-!
SNAP
CLACK!
AAAAAH! HURRY!
BEEP BEEP BEEP
GOOD THING CATS ALWAYS LAND...
...ON THEIR FEET!
CLICK

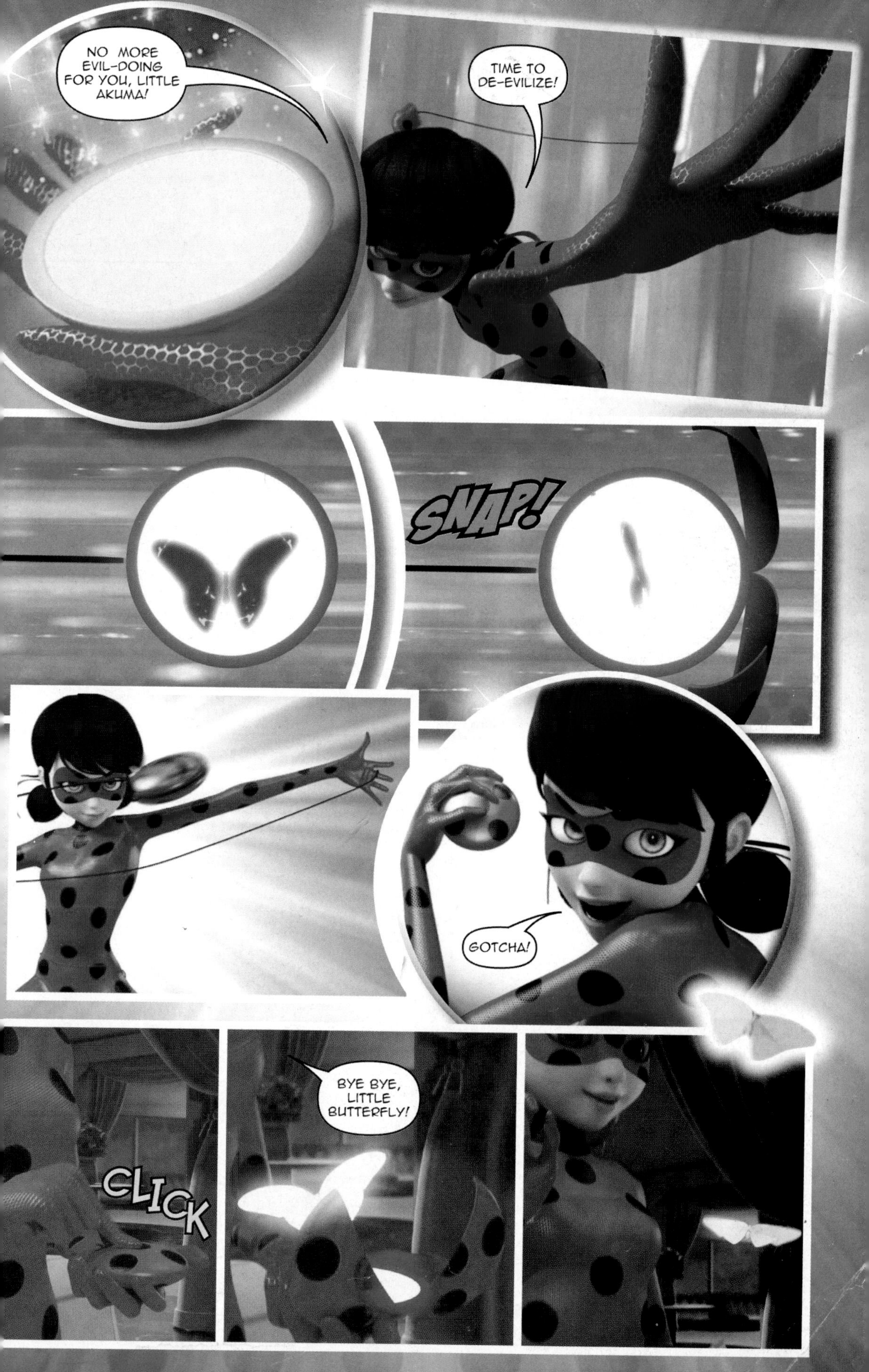
NO MORE EVIL-DOING FOR YOU, LITTLE AKUMA!
TIME TO DE-EVILIZE!
SNAP!
GOTCHA!
CLICK
BYE BYE, LITTLE BUTTERFLY!

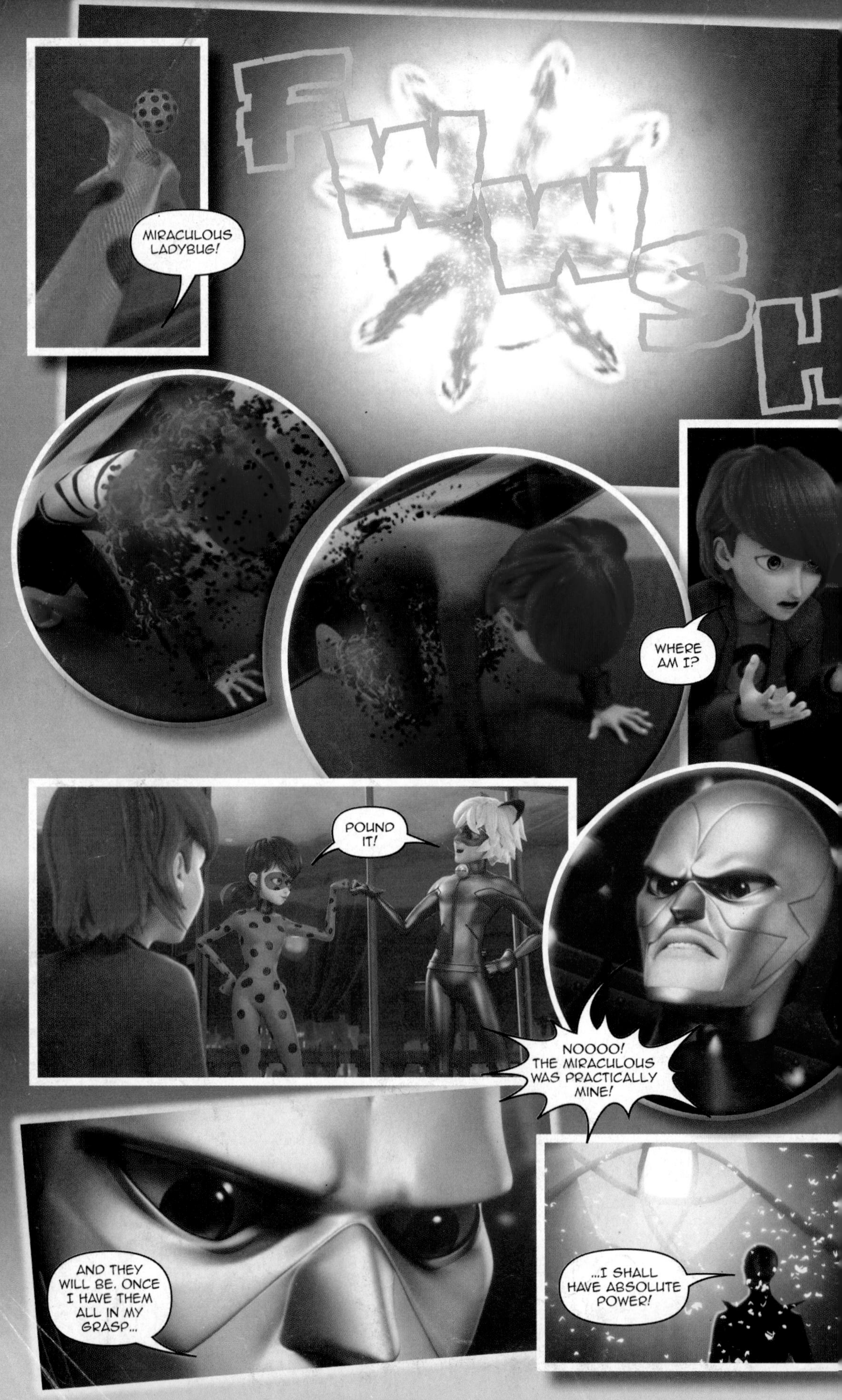
MIRACULOUS LADYBUG!
FWWSH
WHERE AM I?
POUND IT!
NOOOO! THE MIRACULOUS WAS PRACTICALLY MINE!
AND THEY WILL BE. ONCE I HAVE THEM ALL IN MY GRASP...
...I SHALL HAVE ABSOLUTE POWER!

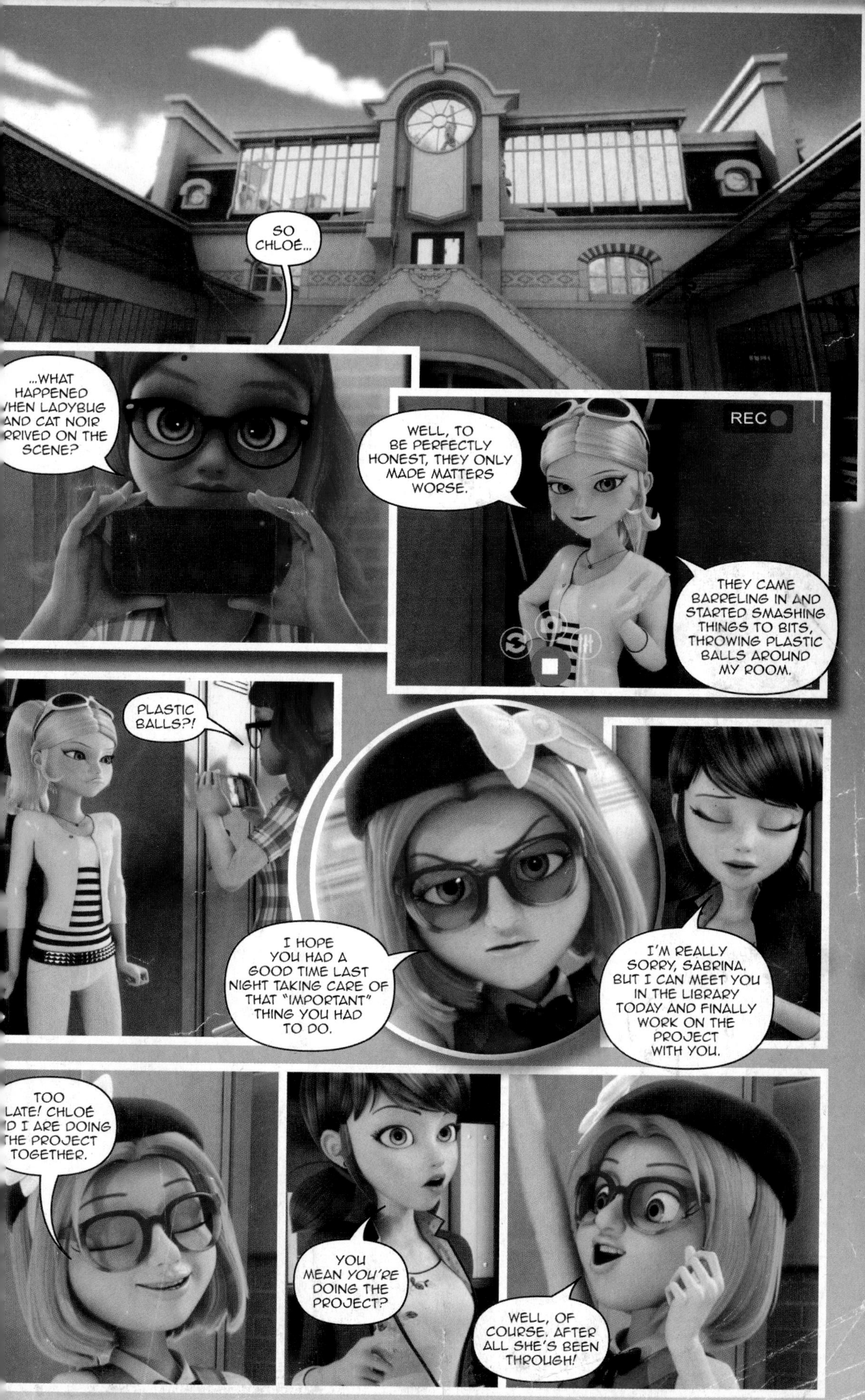
SO CHLOÉ...
...WHAT HAPPENED VHEN LADYBUG AND CAT NOIR RRIVED ON THE SCENE?
REC
WELL, TO BE PERFECTLY HONEST, THEY ONLY MADE MATTERS WORSE.
THEY CAME BARRELING IN AND STARTED SMASHING THINGS TO BITS, THROWING PLASTIC BALLS AROUND MY ROOM.
PLASTIC BALLS?!
I HOPE YOU HAD A GOOD TIME LAST NIGHT TAKING CARE OF THAT "IMPORTANT" THING YOU HAD TO DO.
I'M REALLY SORRY, SABRINA. BUT I CAN MEET YOU IN THE LIBRARY TODAY AND FINALLY WORK ON THE PROJECT WITH YOU.
TOO LATE! CHLOÉ D I ARE DOING THE PROJECT TOGETHER.
YOU MEAN *YOU'RE* DOING THE PROJECT?
WELL, OF COURSE. AFTER ALL SHE'S BEEN THROUGH!

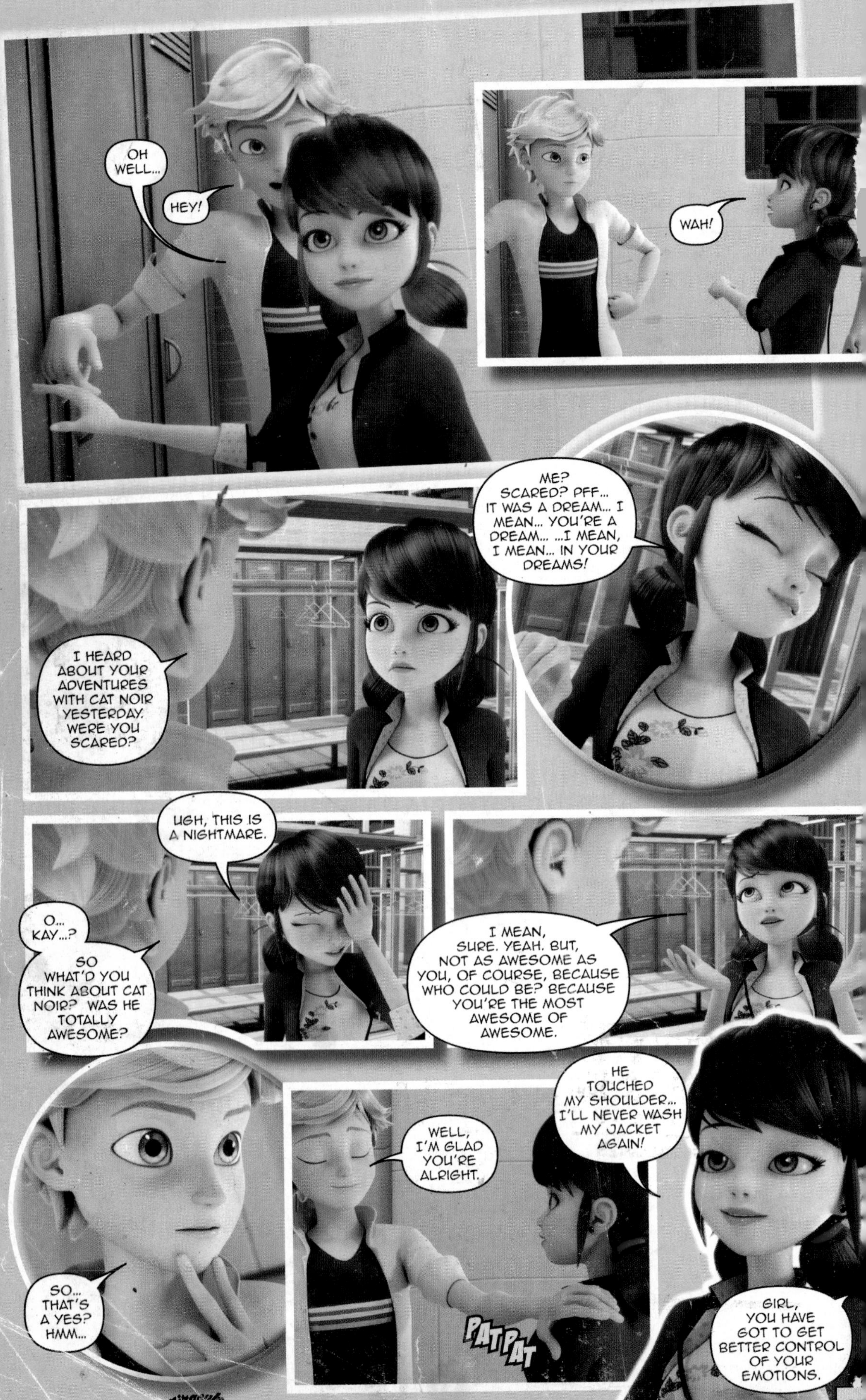
OH WELL...
HEY!
WAH!
I HEARD ABOUT YOUR ADVENTURES WITH CAT NOIR YESTERDAY. WERE YOU SCARED?
ME? SCARED? PFF... IT WAS A DREAM... I MEAN... YOU'RE A DREAM... ...I MEAN, I MEAN... IN YOUR DREAMS!
UGH, THIS IS A NIGHTMARE.
O... KAY...?
SO WHAT'D YOU THINK ABOUT CAT NOIR? WAS HE TOTALLY AWESOME?
I MEAN, SURE. YEAH. BUT, NOT AS AWESOME AS YOU, OF COURSE, BECAUSE WHO COULD BE? BECAUSE YOU'RE THE MOST AWESOME OF AWESOME.
SO... THAT'S A YES? HMM...
WELL, I'M GLAD YOU'RE ALRIGHT.
PAT PAT
HE TOUCHED MY SHOULDER... I'LL NEVER WASH MY JACKET AGAIN!
GIRL, YOU HAVE GOT TO GET BETTER CONTROL OF YOUR EMOTIONS.
TH